VANISHING POINT

MICHAELA ROESSNER

VANISHING
POINT

A TOM DOHERTY ASSOCIATES BOOK
NEW YORK

VANISHING POINT

Copyright © 1993 by Michaela Roessner

A Tor Book
Published by Tom Doherty Associates, Inc.
175 Fifth Avenue
New York, N.Y. 10010

Tor® is a registered trademark of Tom Doherty Associates, Inc.

ISBN 0-312-85213-4

Printed in the United States of America

for Richard
as I promised

Ignorance about people who disappear
Undermines the reality of the world

—Anonymous, 1990

VANISHING POINT

PROLOGUE

Although he'd been preparing for days, in the end he could hardly bring himself to go back inside the home to fire it. From the crude shelter he'd built himself in the backyard of the house next door he peered through the steady spring drizzle at the contaminated building and its surroundings, trying to decide if he'd shorn the new grass close enough and cleared away sufficient brush so that the fire would stay contained.

Perhaps he should check out the adjacent houses, equally untenanted, one last time. Just to be absolutely sure that the disease, the change, whatever it was, had not spread.

He chided himself for stalling. He already knew as much as he needed to of the neighboring houses. When he'd searched through them he found almost thirty years of dust tranquilly blanketing their interiors, as if keeping the furnishings safe and warm for their long-Vanished owners. He'd scraped the dust into ugly piles to investigate what lay beneath. Except for the dust the buildings were clean. They were not infected.

His neck and back ached. His whole body had stiffened from

hunkering down too long. He interlaced his long fingers and cracked his arthritic knuckles, but that didn't ease the pain. Nor did the thriving smell of wet earth and cut new grass. He'd spent hours scything and raking the grass clear, wanting to leave as little fuel as possible for the fire.

Conditions would never be better for a safe burn. The drizzle fell straight down, unwavered by any wind. It had been raining for three days, soaking ground, overgrown vegetation and the roofs of the surrounding tract houses. He stooped to duck out of his shelter, craned his neck to look at the sky. It hung oppressively low overhead; a dense, gray ceiling. Smoke from the fire wouldn't be visible to the communal settlements down-valley. No one would come to investigate.

His equipment was stored in a gardening shed. He pulled a gas mask down and over the thick knit cap he wore, slung it around his neck, and put on industrial gauntlets before hoisting two heavy, sealed canisters. Their wire handles cut painfully into his palms in spite of the heavy gloves.

On the porch of the home he stopped for a moment to push the gas mask into place and seal his coat's high collar up around it before shoving the back door open with his foot. He could no longer smell the cut grass—just the dusty rubber insides of the gas mask.

He walked along a hallway past bookcases filled with bric-a-brac to the front of the home. Before mounting the stairs to the upper level he set down one of the containers.

His itinerary for destruction was blueprinted onto his brain—he didn't have to think. The gas mask cut into his view and insulated him, an automaton guided by remote control. He wanted those limitations to his vision—he didn't want to see again the cans of paint he'd found stored in the laundry room, labeled with names of colors he'd never heard of. He didn't want to see again the strange titles adorning the spines of what should have been familiar books.

In the master bedroom he snipped the seal on the canister's nozzle. With hands made clumsy by the gloves he trailed thin, clear liquid under the drapes and along the baseboards, shoving furniture aside with one foot when he had to. He didn't want to take the slightest chance of stepping into the fluid. He couldn't risk splashing himself. Bright red logos embellished the container's crisply white surface: flames constrained within thick hoops, the traditional slash heralded across them, and slogans that exclaimed in heavy block letters CORROSIVE, FLAMMABLE, TOXIC, DANGER.

As he approached the last bedroom, a pastel-decorated nursery, he began sweating. The home he'd owned thirty years ago had had a similar nursery. He thought of his wife Jennifer lying beside him, rosy and swollen with her pregnancy. The toxic fluid trembled as he poured it.

When he reached the stairs again he focused his attention on trailing the fluid so that it pooled back inward on the surface of each step. He didn't want it to pour over the edge and get ahead of him. At the bottom he put the empty canister behind the stairs, opened the second container and anointed the ground level. Looping in a circle back to the front of the home, he puddled the last of the liquid at the doorsill and set the second emptied container just inside the door.

He stepped outside, pulled the gauntlet off his left hand, and reached into a pocket for a roll of fuse. Reaching back inside the building, he draped the end of the wicking into the fluid. He wedged the front door firmly and began unwinding the roll, stepping backward away from the house, working quickly now, afraid the mild rain might dampen the wick. To his relief, when he touched a match to the end of its length it caught fire immediately. The spark marched slowly but steadily along the twenty feet of fuse to the house, then disappeared under the door.

Eyes trained on the front door, he resumed walking backward till he bumped into a row of bushes separating the property from the sidewalk. He edged around and took cover behind them. Only then did he pull off the gas mask.

As if his will could help guide it, he imagined the flame's route through the home. It would ripple along the fuel's glistening track, encircle the rooms and reconnect with itself like a spiderweb spun out of heat and light. As it grew it would leap higher to catch on brittle, sun-rotted curtains. Those would flare against the windows, whose heat-stressed glass would crack and shatter. More oxygen from outside would rush in to engorge the flames. The flames would use the drapes as a ladder to clamber upward to the ceiling. Ascending and descending fire from the upper floor would meet, disintegrating the flooring, dissolving the roof's support, till the whole house collapsed in an imploding maelstrom.

As he imagined this sequence, he waited for the signal of success he'd become familiar with—that initial flash of light at the windows. He waited long minutes. It was taking too long. The flash didn't come.

Finally he sidled carefully, slowly, back to the home, angling away from the door and the windows as much as he could in case they suddenly exploded. At the spot where he'd lit the fuse he stopped and donned the gas mask again. The door still looked closed, but if any of the toxic fluid had evaporated and leaked out, he wanted every inch of skin possible covered.

Spreading himself flat against the wall, he ducked around for a quick peek through the living room window. It looked gray and peaceful inside; the sofa set mounded high with snowy drifts of dust, the dim light that reached through the dusty windows milkily filming every surface. The most disruptive elements visible were tracks of his footprints crisscrossing the floor from the course of his investigations, and the spots where he'd scraped or plowed aside dust along the baseboards.

He slumped against the side of the house. What had happened? The other four fires he'd set had burned like cauterizing miracles. Maybe the door had crimped the wick too much, starving the flame. Or the chemicals were old, a bad batch. Or the canister had been breached or weakened long ago.

Even though it was obvious the fire hadn't caught he exercised caution before reentering the building. Near the door he exposed the smallest patch of skin on one wrist, waited for any caustic stinging. Then he pulled off a glove and laid his palm against the door. Feeling no sensation of heat he donned the glove again and opened the door in small increments. With that release of tension, the blackened wick slumped to the floor. It hadn't been pinched too tightly—a burn trail ran from a scorched section just inside the door to halfway up the stairs, then disappeared.

There was no trace of fluid leading away to the rooms on either side. If the fuel had evaporated, why hadn't this level caught, instead of part of the stairs?

Puddling . . . the puddling on the steps. With its greater fluid mass, it had taken longer to evaporate and the fire had caught at least on that little bit. Either that, or the chemicals in the first canister had retained at least some potency, but the second hadn't.

To hike to his hidden storage space and haul back more canisters would take a full day, even with the crude pull-cart he'd jerry-rigged. Considering that some of the fuel might have reached a chemical turning point, he'd have to drag back extra canisters to be safe, slowing him even further. He sighed and reluctantly reentered the home. He'd need to find out exactly what went wrong.

Just to the right lay the dining room. Everything there looked the same. Even in this room's shuttered light and through the blinkered, limiting vision of the gas mask he could see no sign of the liquid left on the floor, other than a mild pitting. He'd expected more from the fluid's supposedly corrosive qualities.

He went back and crossed the front entrance hall and stairs to the living room.

It was as he knelt beside the baseboards there that he began to hear the sounds. *Ziiiing-plop, ziiiing-plop,* like some sort of mutant rain pattering on the roof. He straightened back onto his heels and tried to look out at the rain through the double barrier of dust-smudged windows and the scratched plastic goggles of the gas mask. Sleet? Unusual but not impossible, this early in the spring. Would sleet make that kind of a sound?

Then he realized that he'd never be able to hear rain, sleet, or even violent hail on the roof that clearly from here—through both the mass of the second floor of the home and the muffling effect of his cap and gas mask. Whatever was falling was falling onto the second floor itself.

He looked up, then flattened to the ground. The underside of the ceiling was moving, twitching like the coat of some enormous, flea-plagued beast. An ashy mist of disintegrated plaster began to waft down.

He'd been so wrong. The second batch of chemicals had been completely volatile, its flammable elements evaporating before he'd even lit the fuse. The fumes had floated straight upward and begun to corrode the ceiling. He looked up again. The vapors formed a roiling, upside-down sea above his head that he could see even through the gas mask. How long before the ceiling disintegrated and collapsed downward? The noises he heard upstairs must be larger chunks of the interior of the roof pelting down onto the second floor.

Then there came a sharp, clattering report from overhead. He started, confused. The noise was followed by a huge whooshing that compressed the whole house. A golden glow streamed down from the stairwell; suffusing, then replacing the dull gray light. With horror he recognized that first sound; it was the one he'd been waiting for earlier, outside by the hedge—the noise of fire-stressed glass shattering outward.

He'd overlooked the fire on the stairway. It hadn't died halfway up the steps after all; it must have hitchhiked—jumped along the trail of evaporating fuel and flashed back into the bedrooms of the second

level, where the fuel he'd laid down earlier would have already per-
meated the upper ceilings.

The fire followed it, chewing its way deeply into the roofline,
dripping blazing detritus onto the second floor like some ravenous
animal dribbling excess food from its jaws in its haste. Then it had all
coalesced in a great rush of flame. Now the entire upper floor was
ablaze. If only he'd waited outside a few minutes more, he would have
seen smoke beginning to ooze out from under the eaves.

Getting down on all fours, he started to scuttle back toward the
open door, cursing himself for his stupidity. When he'd come back in
the house he hadn't even looked up at the ceiling of the stairwell. He'd
looked no further than where he believed the flame had died mid-
stairway. Had there been scorch marks he'd failed to see? Why hadn't
the ceiling caught on fire in the stairwell, instead of racing on to the
back rooms? He couldn't fathom the chemicals acting like that.

A thought struck him, halted him in mid-crawl. If books could
change, if the names of colors and maybe even the *color* of colors could
change, why not something much more basic—the very nature of
chemicals?

His shock saved him. As he crouched, paralyzed with revelation,
flames reached the head of the stairwell and rippled back along its
ceiling, then exploded downward, annihilating the hallway in a mon-
strous gout of flame.

Before he could react a fiery backwash lapped into the living
room, sparking the suspended vapors there. They ignited with a roar.
The heat and force of the blast threw him onto his stomach.

He felt a searing sensation on his back. His coat must be scorch-
ing, catching on fire. He rolled over and over to smother it. As he rolled
he could see the ceiling floating arrested above him like an unearthly
molten ocean. Heat convection drew clumps of dust upward. When
they wafted close enough to the conflagration they caught fire—sparkling and crackling in a miniature fireworks display before they were
engulfed.

He rolled up against a glass-topped end table, reached up to yank
down a heavy earthenware vase, almost dropped it as its heat singed
through his glove. Panting, he looked out the living room windows at
the cool greens and grays of trees, rain and sky. If he could break
through the window, could he survive scrambling through the broken
glass? Was his clothing thick enough to withstand the lowering fire?
Propping himself up on an elbow, he took aim to throw the vase.

The fire beat him to the task. Glass sprayed outward, a wash of flame following it, filling the window.

Inside the gas mask he swore and scrambled frantically away. The arms of his coat were steaming. He rolled out the back doorway of the living room. Fragments of the ceiling, transformed into small sizzling fléchettes, pattered down around him. Smoke filled the rooms. He fled, crawling, lost, blindly smashing into furniture, aware only of the heat, his panic, the horrible effort of his lungs sucking for air but only drawing in the taste of hot rubber and plastic from the gas mask.

Suddenly he fell forward, banging his chin as he first slid and then rolled downward. He landed in a metallic clutter, stunned and exhausted. His jaw was numb from the fall. He dazedly wondered if he'd broken it. Bending his head to the right his vision filled with paint cans. Latex House Paint, the label of one read. Color: Abelard.

He was in the laundry room, half a level below the rest of the house. He didn't want to move or struggle any more. What sort of a color was Abelard? If he had the strength to pry the lid off, would it be some wondrous and unrecognizable hue? Or would it just be white, nondescript, its true shade inaccessible to the human eye? When he'd first found the cans he'd been too frightened to look. Other cans caught his eye—Magandá, Hearn, Strangury, Croze, they told him. He turned his face to the ceiling. The flames there burned only lightly, flickering as delicately as foxfire—most of the fumes must have escaped to the higher levels of the house.

He couldn't fight anymore. What would be the point, in a world now so contaminated that even molecules, atoms, had betrayed the laws that bound them? And he didn't want to fight anymore—not for the world, not for his life, either. When the smoke started to filter down here he'd pull off the gas mask and be gone before the flames reached his body. No more mornings of waking and reaching for Jennifer, the shock of patting his hand into the empty space next to him.

He'd leave his loneliness behind at last. He'd tried to escape it before, years ago, when he could no longer bear living in his own empty house. He'd abandoned it and tried, unsuccessfully, to barricade his heart and thoughts against his longed-for past.

Now he'd finally be free—free of the unasked-for vigilantism, the grief and loneliness. He felt himself emptying, becoming as empty as his home had been—as empty as his home would be forever.

He shivered. Or would it? What if against all odds there was a Great Return? What if the changes had contaminated *his* home? What would happen to those who Returned if their homes had been infected?

He thought of the changes in the children born since the Vanishing—their shimmering metallic-hued hair; how strange they were. He thought of transmuted paint colors and books. What would happen to Jennifer if she Returned? If she recorporated in their bed and their home was diseased? He drew his knees up underneath him and began to search for a way out.

CHAPTER ONE

Renzie opened sleep-gummed eyes to the dark simple shapes of her room. Blackness surrounded her, as if it were still middle-night. But she could feel the sun's huge presence rolling toward the House just beyond the horizon, toasting the range of grassy eastern hills to their dry, bristly summer pelt of gold.

If she rushed straight up through the House, she could beat the sun to the fourth-floor tower. If she lingered in bed just a little longer the sun would arrive first and be waiting for her, welcoming her home. She chose to linger.

Renzie stretched, luxuriating in the sensation of clean sheets against clean skin, and in being back in her own quarters, on her own time. The House spiraled and expanded about her, room after room, floor after floor. Renzie felt as safe as if she nested in the heart of a nautilus shell.

She dug work-callused fingers into streaked, bronze-colored hair, dragging the fingernails across her scalp. The hard work of three weeks on a road-repair crew had left her tendons and joints tight, her muscles sore. Not thirty years old yet, she thought, but I don't bounce back as quickly as I used to.

She ducked under the low ceiling of her sleeping area, skirting around piles of half-read books. This section, her section, was one of the last vestiges of the property's original barn, a fragment of the hayloft eaves. The House had grown up around the barn and engulfed it long before the Vanishing or Renzie's birth.

Limbs still sleep-stiffened, Renzie stumped across the adjoining area, a big open space originally intended as a storeroom. Cupboards lined its far wall. Renzie pulled open a drawer full of clothing and groped around till she felt the nubby texture of a pair of drawstring pants. She fished them out and pulled them on. She stood for a moment, deciding which route to take up to the tower. She considered going downward first.

That would entail traversing the switchback stairs, the glass warehouse room, then around and up the steep climb starting at the firearms museum. But the stained-glass storeroom temporarily housed a minicolony of newcomers sleeping in the throughway. Renzie didn't want to have to pick her way among them.

She opened another drawer in the cupboard, yanked out a pullover, started to put it on, then changed her mind. It would be hot as blazes by mid-morning. She liked the thin layer of chill now gilding her bare skin—it felt like swimming; those first minutes after plunging into a lake or pond, before her body temperature adjusted to the water. She tied the pullover around her waist by its arms.

A doorway marked the boundary of her territory. Renzie slipped through it and chose an upward route to the tower.

The air of the House at this quiet hour weighed heavy, its movements as discernible as currents of water. Only a few noises reached her, muffled as if she moved through the green silence at the bottom of a pond. From some far wing of the House came the dim echo of pounding as Carpenter or one of his crew worked, as they always did, night and day. Rising up the tubelike length of an enclosed skylight the vibrations of first morning stirrings in one of the kitchens reached her.

It wasn't just the quiet that was special at this hour. The usual smells of people and activities were dormant, too. The odor of the House itself came forth—a not-smell, a smell like trying to breathe underwater. Renzie had always imagined that just as there existed sounds too high and low for humans to hear, so too there were smells that people lacked the ability to sense, smells too obscure for even the fine noses of cats and dogs, and that the House embodied these smells.

Renzie slipped up twisted hallways, gliding past curtained-off rooms with their sleeping inhabitants. Even without light she knew where windows were set in the floors and where gingerbread trim hung like stalactites from the ceiling.

By way of a narrow passageway she detoured around the original owner's séance room and the denuded room after it, stripped long ago to its bare lathing. Hammer, the House dispatcher, lived there now. The first room was his radio center and the second his sleeping quarters. It seemed symbolic to Renzie that the voices of what was left of the world came to the House through the séance room. For it was there that the voices of the spirit world had supposedly come to instruct the elderly woman who'd built the House. She'd constructed it to their ghostly specifications.

But in actual fact, Hammer lived in those two rooms because they led to the Northern Conservatory. Years ago Carpenter and his crew had revamped the elevator there to better accommodate Hammer's wheelchair.

Renzie guessed that if she burst into the room she'd find her brother Tuck curled up on a cot. He often spelled Hammer off and on during the airwave night shifts.

She journeyed onward to her rendezvous with the sun. Past the multiple fireplaces of the Hall of Fires, the linen rooms, a converted sewing room. She'd lived in many of these rooms at one point or another during her life.

She climbed up to the "earthquake" wing, a section once badly damaged by the great tremor of 1906, an excitingly petty catastrophe compared to the Vanishing. Her own family, when it still pretended to be that—a family—had lived there, just prior to the single interruption in Renzie's lifelong affiliation with the House: In one of his panics about Vanishing, her father had moved them briefly into the Watchers' Domes across from the House.

Renzie ascended to the servants' call room with its light yellow walls, then up the final set of easy risers. With a sensation that she'd been swimming underwater the whole way, lost in the exploration of a deep, dim riverbed till she could no longer hold her breath, she burst from the dark quiet of the House into a sky so bright and blue it was noisy.

CHAPTER TWO

The fourth-floor tower stood mostly open—a lacework of balconies extending from the fortresslike core of the House. This series of porches looked out onto the central flower gardens and across the breadth of that side of the House. In the distance the huddled stretch of San Jose's empty and decaying homes crawled outward to the horizon. Half naked, Renzie leaned out over the railing as she'd done when she was a young girl, into a sun as new and soft and warm as rabbit's fur.

She basked for long moments, her body at rest, her mind humming and expanding under the sun's warmth, filling with thoughts and questions.

She wanted to know everything that had happened in her absence. Had Hammer heard any interesting news from the rest of the world? What had the House children been up to? What newest additions had Carpenter and his crew grafted onto the House? What was the latest gossip? Who was sleeping with whom?

Silicon Valley lay to the north, out of her view. What was happening with the Hackers there and all their research projects? When she'd left the Hackers had been in a tizzy about some physicist coming clear across the country from Carnegie-Mellon to work with them.

Renzie wondered what it would be like to make a journey like that. Parts of the country were still risky. The new physicist had probably arrived by now. Renzie wondered what sort of an addition to the community the newcomer would make. New people didn't always fit in.

Thinking of that, a tinge of unease crept in and clouded her thoughts. She stole a glance at a "room" to her left, then pulled her eyes away.

Enclosed in part from the elements by windows on two sides and a wall on its far side, open to the porches, the space formed an illusion of a room. It had no floor. A catwalk hemmed by a low rail crept nervously around its sides and down the middle. This divided the area into two giant square holes like cubistic skull eyes. The holes dropped twenty feet.

When she'd been little Renzie had liked it, as she liked all the asymmetrical aspects of the House. But the summer after she'd turned eleven, the Krit had moved into the House and picked this "room" as his space.

Years later Renzie realized that he was just another sad, strange, wounded victim of the Vanishing. But at the time of his arrival she found him sinister and terrifying. Thin, gray-skinned, sunken-faced, he wedged himself like an awful waiting insect into those narrow spaces no one else would have thought to live in.

Early this last spring the Krit had walked off, knapsack on his back, without a word or note to anyone. Under those circumstances, according to the custom of the House, he forfeited his room to anyone who wished it.

But no one wanted that nonspace, so narrow and uncomfortable, cold and damp in the winter. His belongings should have been dumped and distributed. Instead they still lay piled together in the far corner of the catwalk as if holding his place for him.

A nursery rhyme her mother had taught her long ago came to mind.

> I do not love thee, Dr. Fell.
> The reason why I cannot tell.
> But this I know, and know it well.
> I do not love thee, Dr. Fell.

Renzie mentally crooned the words as a sort of cheerful, sarcastic melody to the sun, an exorcism of the Krit's memory. But it didn't work entirely. When a sudden movement caught her eye she jumped, half expecting that her thoughts had conjured the Krit back.

"Ha! Gotcha!" Her brother Tuck stepped out of the stairway, grabbed one sleeve of her pullover and yanked it from her waist. "En garde," he cried, expertly snapping the other sleeve at her bare midriff.

"Blast you!" As she jumped toward him Tuck tossed the sweater onto her head, momentarily blinding her. She threw it back at him. He ducked. The pullover flew over his head and down the stairway. He retrieved it, laughing, and handed it to her. "Put this back on so I can give you a hug."

He joined her in leaning against the railing, closing his eyes and smiling his pleasure at the sun's touch on his face. "I missed you," he said. The strands of his dark hair caught the light and broke it into a prismatic shimmer that haloed his head.

"I missed you too," she said. His long thin mouth curved into a happy crescent expressing all of his good-natured impishness. The distance between his mouth and small nose was considerable, making his lower face, with its rounded chin, look muzzlelike. His large dark eyes were canopied by thick eyebrows. Not a handsome face, but an attractive one, in the sense that everyone was attracted to Tuck. He reminded Renzie of the little feral monkeys she sometimes saw in the overgrown underbrush around the Homes. Squirrel monkeys, their mother had called them.

"You get in last night?" he asked, eyes still shut to the sun.

"Yeah, late. No one seemed to be around. Was there a party going on somewhere?"

The sudden color in his cheeks came from within, not from the sun. "Maybe," he said.

Renzie was intrigued.

"What about you?" he asked. "How was the road crew? Did you do your bossy older sister bit on them?"

He was switching the subject. Renzie let him. Anything she needed to find out about him she would, eventually, and without pushing.

"Just boredom and hard work, pretty much. No feuds between any of the groups." Her crew had been patching up sections of Highway 880, which formed a link with the trading enclaves that had grown up around the industrial warehouses in Union City and lower Hayward. "We biked up to coordinate with the Union City repair crew one day and had a hell of a party, but that was it as far as actual excitement."

"Actual excitement? Yeah, right." He nudged her. "What else was going on?"

Renzie shifted restlessly. There were only a few things that hiked the old nagging, festering fears straight up into her chest. Things like the Vanishing, or fires. It had been such a dry summer . . . now she wished that *she* could change the subject.

"Nothing. Just something odd I ran across. No big deal."

"If it's no big deal then you can tell me."

She saw that she'd worried him with her unexplained concern. All through their childhood they'd had the fear of the unknown held over their heads by their father. They made a point of trying not to do that to each other.

"It's probably nothing. We passed some burned-out places, fairly new burns."

"Big burns?"

The Richmond refineries had blown shortly after the Vanishing, before either of them were born. Storytellers had woven epics about the firestorms that had obliterated most of the northern part of the East Bay. They said down here in the South Bay that day was like night from the smoke, the nights like hellish days from the firelight, and the air had been as hard to breathe as charred mud.

Renzie and Tuck *had* been alive and just old enough to remember when raiders torched the college center of Ohlone in nearby Fremont. The fire had swept down from the foothills out of control, driving refugees before it. Renzie would never forget the panic as grown-ups had rushed out to divert the flames from the lowlands, trying at the same time to avoid being trapped by the marauders. The House had become a belltower clanging constantly with the frantic litany, over and over again, "Water, oh my god, there's not enough water to stop it, not enough water." She shuddered.

"No, not big burns; controlled burns."

Tuck looked relieved. "So what were they—collapsed Homes, that even the Homers gave up on?"

Renzie shook her head. "No, I don't think so. That's what bothers me. The burned spots I saw had been torched and left just as they were, not cleaned up or flattened."

Tuck turned from the railing, giving her his full attention. "Did it look like precautions had been taken to control the burnings?"

"Some. Not nearly enough. They were set during the spring rains, though. New greenery'd already taken over. So it wasn't arson, or whoever did it would have waited for the dry season and let the whole thing blaze away."

"It can't just be left at that, Renzie."

"Of course not. I'm going to report it to Eric. He can send someone to check it out more thoroughly."

Tuck's smile was half grimace. "That's *if* you can find Eric, *if* he can give you some time, and *if* there's anyone he can spare right now."

"Why can't he spare me some time? What's going on?" She grasped her brother's arm and shoved one shirtsleeve up slightly, exposing a red plastic band around his forearm. "What *has* been going on since I left?"

Tuck's smile tried to turn into a mischievous smirk, but a look of concern still shaded his eyes. "Bad news, good news, bad news," he offered her.

Renzie chose. "All right. I'm a coward. Good news first."

"Orinda township is coming down for a big trade fair. When lots were drawn for the site, the House and company won." His arm swung wide, encompassing the House and its property, what little could be seen of the Office Buildings across Winchester Boulevard, and behind him, to where the Watchers' Domes were hidden by the bulk of the House.

Renzie whooped with glee. "Did anybody grumble?"

Tuck shrugged. "Not to mention. It's been years since we played host." He rotated his arm, exposing the red band. "You'd better get labbed pretty quick. *No* fun for you for a while. All of us have already passed our tests."

Renzie groaned.

Tuck held up a finger, hushing her. "Don't grouse. It'll be worth it. Lots of old friends from Orinda are coming down—like Sepulveda, Bolivar, and the rest."

Renzie grinned. "That's worth getting stuck like a pincushion and not getting laid for a while. All right, I'm sufficiently fortified. You can give me the bad news now."

The concern in Tuck's eyes reemerged. "These meetings draw folks from all over," he stalled. "People that haven't been seen in years, like Sepulveda and the rest."

Renzie tensed. "Tuck, stop it. Just tell me."

Tuck sighed. "Old George is coming. He sent word yesterday by way of the Salinas airwaves."

At hearing their father's name, Renzie hunched her shoulders angrily.

"There's more." Tuck pushed on. "He's bringing the whole crew with him, a regular family outing—Ginny and the children, and Brad and his brood."

Renzie's forearms, braced on the railing, clenched into ropes of muscle.

Tuck slid over and put an arm around Renzie. She leaned into him. It seemed strange but good, him comforting her. All during their childhood she'd protected and comforted him. She felt the difference in their ages as far greater than two years, as a dimension unrelated to the accrual of days and months. An image leapt to her mind: a night picture of a very young Tuck, standing frightened in the dark. Frightened by . . . Renzie squeezed her eyes tight, shutting the vision from her mind's eye.

Tuck hugged her against him. "Come on, Renzie. You're tough. Don't let them spoil the fair for you."

She shook her head. "I'll try not to. I won't."

Having discharged his duty, Tuck looked relieved. "Let's get some breakfast. I'm starved."

"You're on." Renzie headed for the doorway.

"Not that way." Tuck ducked into an adjoining tower room that opened onto another porch. He swung over the railing, perched on the roofing on the other side. "C'mon. This way. Like we used to."

Renzie clambered after him. On this side of the tower small descending cupolas interrupted the pitch of the roof. Layers of asphalt shakes fashioned into fish-scale shingling, studded with silicon cells and intersected by vane-shaped solar panels, stretched down and away like a giant reptile's pelt. Narrow catwalks twined between the cupolas.

How long had it been since she'd clambered about the passageways of the House's outer skin? Years, surely, though this had once been one of her normal routes. With it one didn't have to traverse through the adult living areas. All you ran into were other youngsters and the House cats.

But as she wedged herself through a narrow space between a lower tower and the main wall of the House, she saw why she'd abandoned the outside routes. Like Alice in Wonderland, she'd grown too large. She swung herself down a half-level onto a thick plumbing pipe where Tuck waited to steady her. They balance-walked along it, hunching over to grasp the projecting gingerbread struts which had been just the right handhold height when they were children.

Scat from the House felines mounded in most of the accessible crannies, dried by the summer heat to an inoffensive chalkiness. Grappling around a corner, Tuck gave a yelp and pulled his legs back. A blur of fur swept under him, ricocheted off a casement at an angle, and stretched into a great leap for a gable, resolving itself into a cat. It glared down at them.

Renzie laughed.

They shimmied down a large drainpipe to the courtyard that faced the old tourist gift shop. As they entered the closest doorway into the House proper the scent of slow-cooking onions lured them toward one of the kitchens.

Children scampered past with muffins and scones clutched in sticky hands. Renzie dodged them with bullfighter flourishes. Tuck stood in their path, hunched over, arms forming a giant scoop. The children squealed like piglets as they tried to evade him. Those he caught he swept up and gently tossed behind him. The children regrouped and charged in a pack. Tuck and Renzie linked arms and countercharged. The youngsters' laughter screeched into the upper decibels. They turned as deftly as a school of little fishes and streamed away from Renzie and Tuck down the hallway. Turning a corner, hot on their heels, Renzie came to an abrupt stop. The children had disappeared. No sounds reached her of running, fading footsteps down any of the corridors. She looked at Tuck. He put his finger to his lips. Together they tiptoed to the next corner and peered around it, expecting to find the children clustered there in an ambushing pack, stifling themselves into unnatural silence. No children. Renzie smiled uneasily.

Tuck shrugged.

Peals of youthful laughter chimed dimly from somewhere deep in the House.

"Kids! Who can figure them?" Tuck said, and offered Renzie his arm. Out of breath, they walked slowly the rest of the way back to the kitchen.

CHAPTER THREE

Warm smells of fresh bread and muffins baking filled the kitchen like plumped pillows. The air above the grill shimmered from the sizzling heat of eggs and meat cooking. Dishes clattered as cooks brought them down from shelves.

The kitchen crew filled plates with scrambled eggs, scones, and fresh fruit for Renzie and Tuck. They seated themselves in the stark unadorned room that served as the dining commons.

The first friend to welcome Renzie back into the fold was Chloe. Chloe was incredibly tall, but had the proportions and structure of someone much smaller. If you didn't know Chloe and saw a photo of her, Renzie thought, and there was nothing in the picture that hinted at scale, you'd think she was probably average sized. Chloe's mid-neck-length hair was unusual too. It shone in shades of gleaming silver gray, although she was only a year older than Renzie.

"It's good to have you safely back, Renzie," Chloe said as she slid her plate next to Tuck's, her voice the same silk and satin texture as her hair. "When did you get in?"

"Days ago," Tuck told her with a straight face.

Renzie elbowed Tuck. "Don't listen to him, Chloe. I got in last night."

"Any interesting adventures?"

Renzie shook her head. "No fights, no banditos, no fun at all. Just hard, sweaty work. What about here?"

"Tuck's already told you about the trade fair with Orinda?"

Renzie nodded.

"There's a shift in the work schedule and step-up in the work load because of it, of course," Chloe said. "You're due a break after all that roading you just finished, but I doubt that you'll get it."

Renzie moaned.

Tuck cleared his throat as if to add something, but Chloe had already continued. "Not much else other than that," she said. Some House children ran through the dining area into the kitchen. "Except the kids. They've got some weird new notions."

"Like what?"

"Like . . . aagh!" Chloe had started to talk around a mouthful of scrambled eggs, and was frantically fanning her mouth. Tuck handed her a ceramic tumbler of milk. Taking a big gulp, Chloe drowned the eggs and muttered thanks at Tuck.

"That's better. Where were we? Oh yeah, the kids. They're going through a new slang phase. And they've got some weird stories they're concocting among themselves about the Homers."

She was interrupted by the arrival of two more breakfasters.

"Renzie! So the wandering metal-flake baby returns."

"Hi, Hot Rod. It's good to see you." Renzie scraped back her chair and got up to give the man a hug. Hot Rod was in his early sixties; lean, pale, clean-shaven, his slate-gray hair slicked straight back from his forehead to trail off into a long ducktail at the nape of his neck. Hugging him was like hugging a skinny old coyote—all ribs.

"Me too," his companion said, putting a full plate down on the table, waiting his turn.

"You too, Hake," Renzie agreed.

Hake was a honey-colored black man with a square face, distinguished features, and a tidily trimmed beard. Renzie had always guessed him to be about Hot Rod's age, although with his almost unlined face and hair just beginning to salt and pepper, he looked younger. He was about Tuck's height, five nine or five ten, neither fat nor thin, and solid to the touch.

Homecoming embraces over, the two men drew up chairs to the table.

"You've heard about the trading fair, I assume?" Hake asked.

Renzie nodded through a bite of buttery, crumbling scone.

Hake rolled up his shirt sleeve to expose a red plastic bracelet, which he tapped. "Right after breakfast, first things first. Meet me at the lab for testing. You've barely got time for the results before the fair starts."

Renzie nodded again, glad that her mouth was full. Otherwise she might have burst out that she didn't need to test, that she hadn't slept with anyone in all the time she'd been gone. It would have just leapt straight out of her mouth before she could have stopped it, left her open for teasing for weeks. And for no good reason—she still would have to test. No one got by on just their word.

She sipped some tea to clear her throat. "What about other news? Hake, you're tight with the Hackers. What's going on with their new physicist?"

"Nothing. Easterman hasn't arrived yet, hasn't been heard of for weeks on any of the communication circuits. Dr. Yorheim and Pax Willster are worried. Traveling alone across the country is no joke. There's huge unpopulated stretches, and other places have come up with pretty weird solutions for surviving the Vanishing. And from some areas"—he drew the tines of his fork through the scrambled eggs, harrowing their bumpy surface—"we still get rumors of marauders and raiders."

That drew a pall over the table. Renzie, Tuck, and Chloe knew that in the silence the two older men were remembering compatriots who survived the Vanishing only to be lost in the violence that followed.

"Why the hell *would* anyone want to come clear out here from Pennsylvania?" Tuck asked.

Hake shrugged. "We've got bigger and better facilities. No blizzards, no hurricanes and electrical storms—just earthquakes. And Easterman apparently felt more in touch with the research being done out here. Really excited about it, I heard. It can get frustrating correlating data through satellite bounce and the radio network. Let's pray for Easterman and hope we hear good news soon." He cheered up. "Which is likely with the fair scheduled. Fairs attract as much news and gossip as they do trade."

"May I join?" Hammer rolled up, a tray slung across the front of his wheelchair. They cleared away space at the end of the table for him.

"Exactly the person we need," Hake said. "What have you heard over the airwaves? Anything about the physicist?"

"All of the local radio operators have been helping the Hackers look," Hammer mumbled around mouthfuls of cottage-fried potato. "Last item I heard placed Easterman in Warm Springs, Nevada, over a month ago. After that, nothing. What's making the Hackers jumpy is that a big pack of Heaven Bounders are camped just westward of that, near Tonopah Summit, in a straight line to us. To my mind, that's more important: keeping track of any wasps and flies the fair will draw in along with the bees."

"Any of the other cults been heard from?" asked Renzie.

Hammer's mouth was still full of food. Tuck fielded the question. "Nobody malignant like the 'Bounders. The Neo-Christians, Redemptionists, Rosies, and the Apocalyptics straightforwarded us—they all just want to come in and trade and have agreed to ideological truces. We're waiting to hear from Los Milagros and the rest, but expect the same from them."

"I'm sort of sorry to hear that," Hot Rod said. "There's no more high-octane amusement than seeing those folks set up their soapboxes across from each other and go at it."

Hammer ran one hand through gleaming blond hair curlier and stiffer than Hake's. He favored Hot Rod with a tolerant look. "But that's just a few contacts. The bulk of the calls coming in have been from traveling peddlers, out-of-valley settlements, and former friends and fam— Residents of the House and associates." He looked cautiously at Renzie.

Renzie's comforted feeling of being back with the House clan evaporated. Depression settled on her like sodden clothing at the reminder of Old George and *his* clan's impending visit.

Tuck nudged her. She jumped and glared at him.

"Be ready for more homecoming hellos," he said. "I think I hear Kip."

Noisy as a half-grown puppy, lanky, taller even than Chloe, a young man wearing a flour-dusted apron spun out of the kitchen. "All right, that's it! I'm off shift. Where is she?" Renzie didn't have time to get out of her chair before he descended on her like a tornado and whirled her up in a flurry of powder. "Jorda had me in the back and didn't tell me you were home till two minutes ago, just as our shift was up." He swung her around.

Renzie pulled her knees in and feet up to avoid kicking the backs of other diners. Over Kip's shoulder she could see a heavyset woman in her early fifties, Jorda, emerge from the kitchen bearing two plates with stately grace, her fine-boned and unlined face serene.

"Welcome home, Renzie," she said. She deposited the plates, one for her and one for Kip, and drew up two more chairs. The table bristled with breakfasting revelers.

"It's nice to see you back, Renzie." Renzie turned toward a new voice. A young man of about Tuck's age stood there, well muscled and lean, deeply tanned skin almost matching his mahogany-colored hair. He looked like an unsmiling tin woodsman who'd been built of wood rather than tin.

"Uh, thanks, Sun," she said.

"We'll squeeze you in a space," Tuck said. Renzie kicked him under the table.

"No, thanks," Sun said stiffly. "Too crowded. I just wanted to say hi, and that I look forward to working with you." He made his way across the room to seat himself alone at a counter space.

"What does he mean, working with me?" Renzie asked.

"He's being polite," Kip said. "You'll actually be working *under* him, like the rest of us. He's been designated acting foreman for a couple of weeks while Eric commutes down-valley to help with distilling at the wineries."

"No!" said Renzie, scandalized. Then she lowered her voice. "You're putting me on. Sun *can't* be acting foreman. He can't."

"C'mon, Renzie," said Hot Rod. "Everybody has to be acting foreman at some point. Sun's been a Houser for seven years. It was more than time. How old were you the first time you were acting foreman?"

She'd been sixteen, as everyone there well knew. "But now? Right before a big trade fair?"

Hot Rod shook his head. "No big deal. Eric will be back in the saddle long before then. Sun doesn't have anything to do with the fair planning. He just has to implement some of the work."

"But he doesn't fit in," Renzie whispered. She looked around. Sun sat with his back to them, far enough away to be out of earshot. "I don't know why he ended up at the House. He always acts as though he hates it. He'd be happier over at the Office Buildings or up-valley."

"Yes, he does lack social graces and isn't always pleasant to be around," said Hake.

"*Never* pleasant," muttered Renzie.

Hake raised a finger to silence her. "But that's true of a lot of people. Nobody knows what he went through before he came here. He doesn't talk about it, which is his right. The point is that he's trying hard, especially hard since he got this assignment. Don't make things more difficult for him."

Renzie glared at Tuck. "Why didn't you warn me?"

Tuck looked sheepish. "Bad news, good news, bad news," he reminded her. "I didn't get around to telling you the second bad news. And it's not all that bad. Sun really is trying. For example, he knew you'd be overdue for a break, so he went out of his way to find you an easy job you'd like."

"Such as?" Renzie wasn't mollified.

"Overseeing curing the tomato and mushroom crops in time for the fair. He handpicked a crew of the kids for you. He's even been helping them get set up."

A new wave of youngsters stormed through the room. A little girl, Minda, split away from the pack and shot straight for their table.

"I hear you're going to be our boss, Renzie. That'll be real stance. What are you going to teach us while we work?" Minda clambered all over Kip as she shotgunned her questions at Renzie, tickling the tall man.

"Stance?" Renzie looked at Tuck.

He raised his eyebrows and shrugged. "I told you they've got new slang," he said.

Kip was trying to fend Minda off with questions. "What have you been learning lately that you particularly like?" he asked as he tried to pin her hands behind her back. "Maybe Renzie will do a follow-up."

"Where nursery rhymes come from." Minda laughed breathlessly, as if she were the one being tickled. "Did you know that 'Ring Around the Rosy' is about the *plague,* the Black Death? Eee-yuck! Most unslide."

Renzie grinned. She liked all the children, but Minda was one of her favorites. She glanced around at Sun, eating his breakfast alone. Perhaps Tuck was right, and Sun's constipated personality was loosening up.

Minda's voice, droning a familiar tune, distracted her.

> I do not love thee, Dr. Kip.
> The reason why, I think I'll skip.
> But this I know, though you're a pip,
> I do not love thee, Dr. Kip.

Renzie snapped her head around to stare at the little girl. All of the fine hairs on Renzie's back stood on end. Why would Minda recite a cockeyed version of the Dr. Fell rhyme now?

The child squeezed herself between Kip and Tuck. She rolled her eyes at Kip, mocking him.

Kip made a long face of feigned hurt. "Aw, really? That's how you feel about me?"

Minda nudged him. "Naah, not really, but that's my own nursery rhyme. I made it up myself. I bet I could make one up about everybody here." She shot a sly glance at Renzie.

"I'm so glad you didn't mean it." Kip pursed his lips in a grotesque parody of a kiss and planted it slobberingly on her cheek.

"Ick!" exclaimed Minda, rubbing her face dry. "Now I know why I made up the poem."

"You didn't make up that poem. You just changed an old one. I bet you don't know the original one," Tuck challenged her.

"Yes I do. Listen:

> *Non amo te sabide*
> *Nec poseum deciere quore*
> *Hoc tantom pusum deciere*
> *Non amo te sabide.*"

"Great. Now you're delirious," Kip said.

"No I'm not. That was the *most* original poem. Dr. Fell at Oxford, a long time ago, was going to kick out a student if the student couldn't extempor . . . aneously"—she stumbled over the word—"translate that. It means something like 'I do not love you, wise man, nor can I say why, et cetera, et cetera, I do not love you, wise man.' So the student said the Dr. Fell poem, just like that." She snapped her fingers. "Off the top of his head."

"Who taught you all that? And why?" Kip asked.

"Chloe did. Poetry-origins lesson."

"I did not," Chloe protested.

"Slide, slide, slip, slide. Did too." Minda stuck her tongue out at Chloe.

"Did *not.*" Chloe stuck out her tongue back and crossed her eyes.

Renzie thought frantically. Could Minda have been up near the fourth-floor tower that morning and spotted her? Had she overheard Renzie reciting the Dr. Fell poem? That had to be it. But Renzie could

have sworn that she hadn't said the verse out loud, that she'd sung it
only in the privacy of her thoughts.

As if reading her mind Minda said, "Sometimes I go up to the
seventh-floor tower to get inspiraaaation." She rolled the last word out.

"There is no seventh-floor tower," scoffed Kip. "For that matter,
there is no seventh floor; or sixth or fifth, either. You know that."

But there had been once, before the 1906 earthquake brought it
all down. Minda knew that. All the children had been raised in the
history of the House. Renzie felt even more unsettled.

"Really?" said Minda, all innocence. Then, dismissing the subject
by changing it, "So what are you going to teach us, Renzie?"

"I haven't decided. I just found out I'll be supervising you. Maybe
stuff about hunting; tracking and skinning. Sort of early preparation
for the camp outing I'll lead this fall."

Minda's face brightened.

Renzie picked at the last of her breakfast. "But in light of the
circumstances, I'll probably gear lessons to the trade fair, tell you guys
about economics, barter systems, and so on. Stuff you could use at the
fair."

Minda's face fell.

"What's the matter, Minda? Aren't you looking forward to the
trade fair?" Renzie teased, though she was surprised. Children usually
loved the excitement.

"I guess so." Minda had gone from manic to sullen.

"You don't sound terrifically enthusiastic," Tuck observed.
"Why? Don't you like the people who'll be coming?"

"I don't know. That depends." She spoke the words so low they
barely heard her.

"Depends on what?" Renzie asked.

"Depends on . . . are the ghosts coming?"

"Ghosts? What ghosts?"

"That's what the kids are calling the Homers," said Tuck.

"Why do you call them ghosts, Minda?"

Minda wouldn't answer, but instead repeated her question. "Are
they coming to the fair?"

"They may not like us much . . ." Renzie said, thinking, just like
we don't like them, "but yes, a few of them will still come to do the
trading they need. I guess you kids don't favor them much, either."

Minda still didn't respond.

"Are you afraid of them?"

"No."

"Then what is it?"

Minda looked at her and shrugged. "I don't know. They're too slipping with no slide. They can't shift at all." Another pack of children swung by their table. Minda ran off and joined them.

"Hey, wait! Come back," Renzie yelled, half getting up. "I'm sorry. What did I say?"

Tuck pulled her back. "It's okay," he said. "Let it go. Minda isn't mad at you. All the kids have gotten weird about the Homers the last couple of weeks."

"That's what I'd begun to tell you earlier," Chloe said. "No one knows what's going on, but the change to calling the Homers ghosts gives you some idea. It's as if the kids believe the Homers are on the way out, and don't want to have anything more to do with them than they would with a corpse."

"They *are* on the way out," Tuck said. "Most of the Homers are ancient. They know once they're all dead and gone that no one else will keep their precious Homes ready for the 'Great Return.' They know we'll flatten them and reclaim the land."

Kip cleared his throat noisily, gathering their attention. "Speak of devils and they will appear." He nodded his chin over his shoulder. They all turned in unison. The entire room quieted.

Three people stood at the main entrance to the dining area; a man, woman, and young girl, clinging together, staring back at the diners defiantly. Renzie didn't recognize them, but everything about them—stance, attitude, dress—shouted Homers. Renzie scanned the room. Not a single House child remained to be seen.

None of the dozens of breakfasters said a word. The Homers had come here for a reason. Let them speak first.

The Homer cleared his throat. "Is Eric here? Eric Lindquist?"

"Eric's not here," someone called out from the other end of the dining room.

"Somebody go fetch him, then," the Homer said, his voice tinged with anger.

And nervousness, Renzie thought. The little group had entered unfamiliar territory. The dining room wasn't far into the House, a space deliberately accessible to visitors. But even penetrating this far could make outsiders dancey as cats.

"I'm the foreman." Sun spoke up from his solitary seat.

Hake picked up his plate and slid away from the table, the only person to leave the room.

"You're not Eric," the Homer said, sounding unsure.

Everyone knew Eric by sight. That meant the man must be a Drift-back Homer. Considering his youth, probably a returned child investment.

"I'm the acting foreman." Sun uncoiled himself and stalked toward them. Renzie was impressed in spite of herself. Sun normally moved like a wooden mannequin. Now, under pressure, it was as if someone had oiled his stiff, inhibited joints. Only his face maintained its customary rigidity.

"What do you want?" he asked the Homers.

"We need help shoring up a Home."

"Is it yours? The Home?" Sun said.

The man's eyes flickered away from Sun for an instant, then returned. "Yes."

The whole room knew he'd lied.

"All right," Sun began reasonably. "This is how it is. We're backed up with work on account of the trade fair, but I'll tell you what we'll do. Right now, just for you"—his tone turned sarcastic—"this very moment, I'll put together a short crew and we'll march over to this Home of yours and we'll see just how lived in it looks."

The Homer flushed vermilion, caught out. His woman stared at the floor. The girl, maybe eight or nine, glared around the room through tears of angry humiliation.

"All right, so it's not mine," the man admitted. "But it's only one Home down from me."

Sun looked at him with eyes dead as stones. "You know the rules. If it's not an occupied Home, it gets salvaged and demolished."

"If you won't help us, fine! Just lend us the machinery," the man said. The beleaguered trio hung on to each other tightly.

The ties that bind, Renzie thought. Like what they tell us real families used to be like.

"No way," Sun said, sure of his ground. "You don't even know how to run it. Your precious Homes are yours, and welcome to them. The machinery is ours."

Next to Renzie, Tuck shifted in his seat. He looked embarrassed. Renzie knew how he felt. Sun had begun to enjoy himself too much. And he himself was still considered an outsider. The mood of the diners was shifting toward the Homer.

The Homer, oblivious to the swing, ruined his own chances. "You son of a bitch," he snarled. He spun around, knocking the woman and child off balance. "You're all sons of bitches," he said, grabbing and steadying his family. "Keep your blasted machinery while you can. Someday they'll be back from wherever they've gone. Millions, billions of people. They'll take back their Homes. And for every flattened Home, they'll look for the bastards that did it, and make you pay."

All the collective hackles in the room raised.

"You'll be out on the streets. You'll be rounded up into holding camps like cattle," he snarled.

Sun stood not more than two feet in front of the man, rocking up and down on his toes in delight, his usually blanked-out eyes glowing.

"Enough." One word from one voice, enough to break the spell. Eric walked into the room. Hake lingered in the doorway behind him.

Sun's eyes dulled like dying coals.

"Let's start all over again, shall we?" Eric said.

"I came to ask for help with a Home," the man muttered. "It needs to be jacked up, foundation work."

Eric shook his head. "If it could be easily fixed, the Homers' Council would throw together a crew for you. By the time you come to us it means demolition."

Sun stalked off. "Come back here. You could learn something," Eric called after him. Sun kept walking.

Renzie groaned. "Great. He'll be barrels of fun to work with later."

Eric didn't dwell on Sun. He'd already turned back to the Homer. "It takes one or two days to demolish a place and get it ready for planting over. But it takes weeks to repair a Home whose foundation and roof are shot. Even if we did nothing but work on the Homes, neglected our own survival, we still couldn't stop the Homes from going under."

The Homer started to protest.

"Until the Return, of course," Eric soothed. "But isn't it better that people rematerialize on safe, level, unobstructed ground, rather than in the middle of collapsed walls and floors?" Eric pulled out chairs for them at a nearby table. He gestured to Jorda. She went back into the kitchen.

"I don't recognize you," Eric told the man.

"I'm a Returnee. I was snatched away as a child by raiders after my parents Vanished."

Another sad case who'd finally found his way back to a deserted and decayed Home.

———

Even though her father had chosen to settle in the House, Old George had kept up his original Home, right through his liaison with Renzie's mother and up to his marriage to Ginny and departure.

When she'd been very little, Renzie hadn't known what he was doing, but she sensed differences in her father's absences. Sometimes he'd leave on work details and become irascible beforehand. But before his other absences he'd be quiet days in advance, as if he were fading away from all of them. And then he'd be gone for only a little while—an afternoon or a day.

She couldn't have been more than six the first time she followed him. Her heart had beat large in her too-small chest. She ducked behind bushes and Homes more than necessary to avoid detection by her father.

By then the Valley was relatively secure from raiders, but they still gathered in the hills. The fire attack on Fremont was a year in the future. Adults kept children from straying by frightening them with cautionary tales of kids grabbed for investment. As she'd slunk along Renzie had felt the presence of hordes of large, shadowy people searching for her. When the House receded behind a horizon full of Homes she realized she no longer had a choice. She had to keep up with her father. If she lost track of him she'd be completely lost. She decided she'd scream if any raiders snuck up on her. Run fast and scream. Her father would be mad, but he'd rescue her.

After a long time Old George had stopped in front of a well-maintained Home with a flower-bordered front yard.

Renzie sidled along the wall of the Home next to it until she could peer around the corner at him.

He pulled some keys out of his pocket and stuck one in the front door, but he didn't go in at first. He put his head against the door and just leaned there. At last he turned the key in the lock and disappeared into the Home.

"Renzie."

She'd almost passed out with shock. She whipped around. Her mother, Margaret, stood behind her.

"What do you think you're doing?" Margaret asked.

Renzie hadn't been able to answer, she was gasping so hard. Margaret didn't ask her again, didn't push her. She'd sighed instead. The resigned look on her spare, sharp face told Renzie that she knew the answer anyway.

She held out a hand to Renzie. "Well, now that you're here, come on. Come with me." Renzie took her hand and let her mother pull her up from where she crouched.

"I've been trailing you since you headed out past the Watchers' Domes," Margaret said. "You looked like a crazed little squirrel on drugs, zapping around like that. Come on in here. You might as well see what you came to see."

Instead of walking Renzie back to the House, Margaret had brought her around to a side door of the Home she'd been hiding behind. Margaret pushed it open. The door wasn't locked.

The Home smelled musty. Books and magazines lay piled everywhere. Margaret led her through to a room on the opposite side of the Home. Gauze-curtained windows faced the Home Old George had gone into.

"Do you think you can sit here quietly and just watch?"

Renzie nodded yes.

Margaret pulled up a chair for her to sit on; it was just high enough for Renzie to rest her chin on the sill. "You can see through the curtain. Do you promise not to pull the curtains back?" Renzie had promised. Margaret left her to sit there by herself.

Windows slammed open at the Home next door. Old George was airing the place. In a while he came out through the garage doors dragging a long ladder. He set it up against the roof, climbed it, and began cleaning out the gutters. A middle-aged lady came out of a Home across the street. She called out something to him that Renzie couldn't hear. George waved back at the lady and kept working.

He was sweating heavily, staining his ginger-colored hair a darker brown in wet streaks. Every once in a while he stopped to wipe his brow. When he finished with the roof he climbed back down and put away the ladder.

He came out of the garage again wheeling two dusty children's bikes. The red one with training wheels he parked by the garage door. The bigger one, in Renzie's favorite shade of purple, he kickstanded upright in the middle of the driveway, dusted it, then washed it lovingly with a hose and bucket of sudsy water. He did the same for the smaller bike. Then he sat down in the middle of the lawn and cried for a long, long time. When he was done he put the two bikes back in the garage. Next he pulled out a lawn mower and began to mow the lawn. Renzie lost interest.

She looked around the room she was spying from. Cobwebs laced its corners. A four-poster bed was backed against one wall. A dresser stood along another wall, framed photographs scattered randomly on its top. Renzie looked at the photos.

One was a picture of a bride; a slender young woman with dark hair, wearing a long white dress, lips painted bloodred. She was strikingly pretty in spite of her angular features. Other photographs were pictures of family gatherings. In one of them Renzie thought she spied the bride again, a little bit older now, with one arm around the waist of a short man with wavy, greasy black hair. Another picture was of the woman with a bunch of men and women, posing against a dark panel van, all of them wearing brown jumpsuits and smiling.

Renzie wandered out into the living room of the Home. Margaret sat on a plastic-upholstered sofa. She was smoking, as always, and reading a magazine she'd pulled from one of the piles. The room, filled with cheap furniture and piles of reading material, felt empty. Renzie explored the rest of the Home; another bedroom, the kitchen, the bathroom. It didn't lead anywhere. It meant nothing. Compared to the House it felt truncated and without meaning, like an amputated limb.

She returned to her mother. The lawn mower still whined outside. Margaret looked up at her. "I know you're bored," she said. "But we can't leave until he's finished and gone."

"I know, Mommy."

"How about if I find something for you to read while we wait?" Margaret walked over to one of the bookshelves, paused to scan the titles for a bare second, then with surety pulled a volume out.

"Okay," said Renzie. She sat on the floor, spreading the book out in front of her. It was by a man called Dr. Seuss and was all about a boy called Bartholomew Cubbins, who owned a magic hat. Every time the hat got knocked off his head a new and more beautiful hat appeared. It was a wonderful book. Renzie had become lost in the pages when a shadow crossed over the book. She looked up at Margaret standing over her and at the same moment noticed that the lawn mower had stopped.

"He's finished," her mother said. They went together to peer through the curtains. Next door the windows slammed shut. Then

George came out and locked the door behind him. Renzie had never seen anyone look sad and happy at the same time. She'd never seen her father look *either* sad or happy—just tired, or angry, or scared, or blank. In that moment she began to hate whoever had lived in that Home with him.

George walked out to the sidewalk. Across the street a man opened the front door of the same Home the lady had come out of earlier. George went over and started talking to him. The two men stepped around the side of the Home.

"Let's go," said Margaret, tugging at Renzie's hand. They crept out the side door.

"Now!" said Margaret, ducking low. They scuttled past the Home. On the other side they broke into a run clear to the end of the block. They reached a Home on the corner, stopping for breath out of sight behind its hedge. Margaret was laughing like a kid who had gotten away with something. She wiped her forehead with the back of her shirtsleeve.

"I want to show you something else." She drew Renzie to a break in the hedge and squatted down, drawing Renzie with her, so that they had a good view of the Home on the corner, a beige place with badly flaked paint. The front door had been smashed in, then boarded over; same with a kitchen window in the front. Although deserted, the place didn't look completely neglected. The roof didn't sag from flooding. Someone must be cleaning the gutters. Bushes had been tamed back from obscuring the picture windows. Renzie wondered who took care of the property—her father, or the man he'd been talking to?

"This was where Ginny and Brad lived. Ginny was only three and Brad still a baby when their parents Vanished. Your father broke in here and saved them. They were so little they could have starved to death. Your father took care of them from then on."

Margaret tipped up Renzie's chin so that they were eye to eye. "Do you understand?" Her usually deadpan face held a rare softness.

"I think so," Renzie said.

Margaret rolled herself another cigarette. She took a long drag, then got to her feet, brushing dried grass from her rear end.

Renzie knew Margaret told her this so that she'd see a good side to Old George. Maybe it worked for Margaret, but it didn't make Renzie feel any better. Old George didn't yell at Brad and Ginny the way he yelled at her and Tuck. He didn't wake them up in the middle of the night to scare them. And it wasn't just Ginny and Brad. She knew he'd never cry over her and Tuck's toys the way he'd cried over the bicycles of his first, Vanished children.

Walking back to the House with Margaret she'd been so tired. It wasn't till they were halfway that she recognized the sweetened, softened look on her mother's face when she'd been talking and realized that Margaret was the bride in the photograph in the Home next door to her father's place.

CHAPTER FOUR

"Are you okay?" Tuck leaned over her, hands braced on the table, forehead knotted in concern.

Renzie's temples pulsed with the beginnings of a headache. She rubbed them hard. "More or less. I'll survive."

"Hake's already left for the lab," Tuck said. "He wants you to meet him there for your tests. He'll give you something for your head, too."

Renzie pushed back her chair. She'd have liked to say hello to Eric, but he was still dealing with the Homer family. "Let's go," she said.

They left the main part of the House and crossed the courtyard. There they skirted around the old gift shop, home now to a pack of adolescents. It also contained the House computers and the remains of an old video arcade that the children mauled and played with the way the House cats toyed with mice and other small creatures.

They stopped to part company at the path between the gift shop and the lab, a narrow causeway that afforded a glimpse across the communal gardens to the Watchers' Domes.

Renzie leaned against the lab door. "It sounds like you and Hammer were up till all hours. Don't work too hard, and get some sleep this afternoon," she advised him.

Tuck pecked her a kiss on the cheek. "Lordie, how did I ever survive these weeks you were away?"

"Tuck? Are you busy?" came a voice like the purr of a saxophone. A lithe, highly freckled young woman was walking toward them from the direction of the Domes. If she thought that ducking her head shyly would make her unobtrusive, she might as well have not bothered—her long, carnelian-colored hair had always drawn the eye like a moth to flame. Renzie was bemused by the Watcher girl's coy behavior. Le Chell had always been a hoyden, racing when others walked, whooping when others whispered.

"Hi, Le Chell," Renzie said.

"Renzie, you're back! We all missed you," Le Chell said, brushing stray strands of hair bashfully back from her face.

Although Le Chell's greeting sounded sincere, it was clearly apparent that Tuck was the main attraction. Renzie's eyebrows raised. She shot a glance at Tuck. The set look in his eyes said clearly as words, "Don't you dare."

"Uh, well, Hake's waiting for me for tests," Renzie excused herself. She smiled sweetly at Tuck and murmured, "I guess surviving the last couple of weeks *was* rough." Now she knew the reason for Tuck's blushing earlier in the morning. Renzie wondered how her brother was enjoying the merry chaos of the Watchers' Domes. Probably having a little difficulty with it—which would explain why he'd ended up last night working with Hammer back in the House.

Renzie emerged fifteen minutes later from the lab, rubbing the punctures in her arm, and headed for the low-slung sheds lining the garden.

Somewhere between the sheds someone shouted angrily. Renzie recognized the voice. She sprinted toward it. Other adults working in the garden looked up.

Renzie rounded the corner of one of the sheds. A worn old drying frame lay on the ground. The cheesecloth stretched over it was torn and dragging in the dirt. Several children stood around in a mute circle. In the middle Sun held Minda by one of her thin little arms, almost lifting her off the ground, at the same time bending down and spitting out words into her astonished, upturned face.

"I *told* you not to stretch the cloth like that. If it's too tight it'll warp, and if it's too loose it'll touch the ground and the dirt will rot the tomatoes. What's wrong with you, you little moron?"

He looked like a gargoyle carved from some hard, oiled wood. His sweat held the acrid smell of anger, rather than of work or heat. "Why don't you listen to me? You never listen. You never listen to anyone. How are you going to learn anything that way?" He shook the little girl to emphasize his words. She flopped in his grip like a dead rabbit. "What are you going to do if there's another Vanishing? What if there's only you left? Do you think you could take care of yourself? Do you think you could survive?"

He shook Minda again.

The scene that Renzie had blocked earlier up in the tower sprang into her mind's eye. She saw again a young, terrified Tuck, no more than five years old, struggling with the confusion that comes from being ripped out of a deep sleep. His small pale face was harshly lit by the lamp looming over him, held high by Old George. The words booming down on Tuck like stones were the same as those Renzie was hearing now. The sounds of the present and her memory overlapped each other in a jangling echo.

"What if you wake up tomorrow and it's happened again and everybody's gone and there's only you left? Do you know enough? Could you take care of yourself?"

There was an even older memory, stronger but unpictured, of the endless nights she'd been yanked from her own bed in the same way to face the same frantic interrogation. Until the night she'd woken to those words raining down on Tuck, not her, and the memory of outrage, the image of his innocent terror . . . she remembered jumping from her cot and thrusting herself between Tuck and their dark-silhouetted roaring father.

Renzie was now almost on top of Sun, too caught up in his tirade to notice her. She punched him hard in the shoulder of his free, gesturing arm.

Sun yelled in pain and surprise. Renzie slid her right hand down to wrap viselike on his fist. Sun dropped Minda and turned. As he cocked that arm, now free to strike, Renzie spun back to back with him, out of his line of fire, not surrendering her grip on his fist. She took one more giant step back, stretching him out and pulling him around. Sun spun about off balance to face her. Sandwiching her left hand down on top of her right, locking in his fist, Renzie twisted her hips and dropped to her knees. All of her weight went into the motion. Sun hit the ground hard. In spite of her fury Renzie winced at the impact his ribs and back made with the packed earth.

Even with the breath knocked out of him Sun rolled over, got to his knees and started to come up. Renzie let him get halfway, simultaneously sliding behind him. She grabbed his far shoulder, pulling him backward as she hit sharply down on his face, the edge of her hand held like a knife blade.

Sun lay gasping for long moments as Renzie, Minda, and the other children stared down at him. A few adults filtered up to the edges of the circle. Bracing himself on his elbows, Sun struggled into a sitting position. He cupped the back of his head and blinked up at Renzie.

"What in the hell was that for? I wasn't doing anything wrong, just shaking some sense into her."

Renzie's anger rose again like scalding steam up through her chest, tightening her throat. "Minda is just fine the way she is. None of the children need to be terrorized like that," she spat at him.

Sun glared at her. "You're stupid. All you Housers have your heads buried in the sand. You're not doing the kids any favors, letting them coast through life half-asleep. What do you think is going to happen to them if there's another Vanishing? They're not going to know what hit them. They need to know what it'll be like when It happens."

Renzie started to kick him, then stopped herself. "You didn't grow up here. We've been through that kind of fear already. It isn't needed." She waved her hand at the children. "They know perfectly well how to survive without that."

Sun sneered. "How would you know? You were born after the Vanishing."

"So were you. You wouldn't know any better than me." Renzie stared at him. What an odd point to make.

Sun flushed. "Maybe so. But I kicked around some before I came here. You don't know how protected the House is . . . like some sort of fairy tale."

Hot Rod came over to help Sun up. "You'd better get checked out at the lab," he told the younger man. "When Renzie blows you've got to learn to say 'Uncle' fast or duck." He winked at Renzie. When he pulled on Sun's hand Sun flinched and sat back down. Hot Rod examined the hand gently. "Looks like a sprain, maybe." He supported Sun under his arm and drew him to standing.

"I'm acting foreman. Eric has to know about this," Sun threatened.

Renzie turned to a stocky youngster. "Quill, go get Eric."

Hot Rod grinned. "Eric got done with those Homers and finally left for the distillery. He won't appreciate being called back just for this."

"Take a bike and go tell him, then. We'll deal with this tonight," Renzie said. The anger in Sun's eyes at her taking control was all too evident, but before he could protest Hot Rod turned him away and helped him hobble off.

Renzie suddenly realized that her own hand was sore from hitting Sun. She shook it out a little. The children still circled her. With a start Renzie saw that they were waiting for her to put them to work. They had readjusted so quickly. She still shook, coming down from her anger.

"Set up the kettles for blanching." She directed them with hand motions, like a conductor. "And you guys borrow cutting boards and very sharp knives from the kitchen. You'll be the slicing team." She picked up the torn frame at her feet. "Most of the trays look good, except for this one. Stack them over there. That's where we'll start the drying . . . it's good and hot this morning." The act of organizing calmed her. "With any luck we'll be out of here in a couple of hours and not have to come back till late afternoon to check up on things."

Someone tugged at her arm. Minda stood next to her. "Renzie, are you all right?"

Renzie knelt beside the little girl, and remembered Margaret kneeling beside her. "I'm okay now. I was just worried because I thought Sun was hurting and scaring you."

Minda shrugged. "Sun's like that. If he'd hurt me I would have started yelling. It was scarier that you got so mad."

"Oh, Minda. I didn't think of that. It all happened so fast." She'd responded automatically as a reaction to her own past, but Minda was neither herself nor Tuck. Renzie felt stricken. She could have done as much harm as good.

Minda tapped her on the shoulder. "Don't feel bad. It was real stance having you rescue me. Honest." She hugged Renzie and then skipped off to join the other children.

All alone, Renzie felt dejected. She wished she could disappear. She wished she could Vanish. She smiled wryly.

Whenever her father had ranted and raved at her, threatened that he might Vanish some night, Renzie had thought back at him hard, silent anger punching at him as if she were using her fists: I hate you.

I hate you. Just you wait. You won't Vanish. *I* will. Then you'll be sorry.

Renzie sighed. What a haunted day it had been.

"Renzie, where do you want us to set up this stuff?" A few of the children stood there, their arms filled with cutting boards. Their return exorcised Renzie's ghosts for a while.

By late afternoon they'd turned the tomatoes over once on the drying racks, gone down into the basement to select mushrooms to start drying the next day, then returned to the tomatoes, storing them in a shed until the next morning when the drying would be completed. Renzie sent the kids to clean up before supper while she finished putting away the equipment.

She bent over the cases, sleeves rolled up past her elbows. She looked at her bare arms, her bare wrist. There would be no lab clearance and red plastic bracelet for her for two weeks. She wanted so badly to lie next to someone again, to stretch out and feel the comfort of someone beside her.

As if conjured by her thoughts warm arms enfolded her from behind. A spill of silky hair stroked her right cheek. Startled, Renzie threw her head back, connecting solidly with someone else's skull. She yelped.

"Ow! Sorry. I didn't mean to make you jump," Eric's voice said in her ear. He started to release her. Renzie grabbed his forearms and held him to her.

"No, I'm the one that's sorry," she said. "Hang on to me. I could use it."

"It's been a rough day for you, hasn't it?" Then he chuckled. "Though not nearly as hard a day as Sun's."

Renzie flinched. "I really screwed up this morning."

Eric shook his head against hers. "I've talked to Hot Rod, the kids, even Sun himself. He was out of line. You can snap a child's neck shaking them like that. You did the right thing in stopping him."

Renzie relaxed a little.

"But what concerns me is how angry everyone said you were, how out of control—almost like Sun himself. I've seen you get like that before, but only in extreme circumstances."

Renzie cringed. She knew exactly the incidents Eric was referring to.

"You need to ease up. Sun is a pain in the ass, but do you think he's worth the kind of energy and anger you spend on him? Or is it something else?"

Sun's screamed words came back to Renzie, sounding even in her memory just like Old George.

"No, it's not all Sun," she said, ashamed. "In fact, it's hardly Sun at all. I'll apologize to him tonight."

"Renzie, you don't have to apologize to Sun. He had it coming and he knows it. The reason I'm harping on this is because I'm worried about you. Tell me what's going on."

Renzie picked at the red plastic bracelet around Eric's wrist regretfully and leaned her head back against his collarbone. "I don't know. I guess I'm still tired from the roadwork. I came back and everything is in an uproar because of the trade fair. I wasn't ready for it. I'm a little short-fused."

Eric rocked her back and forth till she felt lulled. After a long silence he said, "You're the one who's owed an apology. I shouldn't have unloaded a project on you again so quickly. You deserve some time off first. It's true—roadwork is grueling and the fair is going to be exhausting. Especially for you and Tuck. I know about Old George and his whole gang coming."

She flinched again. He'd caught her off guard. He was good at that.

Eric turned her to face him. "I thought that might be it. Look, the kids can finish up this drying project. Quill is old enough to oversee them. Sun suggested you for the job because he thought you'd like it and we prefer to have someone teach the kids something while they work. But that's not crucial. Let them be ignorant for a couple of days."

Renzie started to protest, but Eric hushed her. "I *order* you to do whatever you want for three or four days to unwind. Maybe hang out at the Hackers or go do some hunting. Okay?"

"Hunting sounds wonderful," Renzie grudgingly agreed. Time to be just by herself. Time for the aching and stiffness in her body and heart to mend.

CHAPTER FIVE

Nesta saw the girl walking down the street just as she was ready to give up on the garden for the day. She'd been struggling with the weeds and dried-out ground for hours, cursing herself for being an incompetent old woman, then turning right around and excusing herself for the same reason.

After all, she thought, I've planted, grown, and harvested crops every year since the Disappearance in my garden back home.

But here the plants had grown in an enthusiastic undisciplined fashion for thirty years. Nesta couldn't deceive herself—the big, capable body she'd always been so proud of had dwindled. She was no match for the garden. When she pulled up on the clumps of desiccated grasses their stalks snapped, exploding puffs of dusty chaff that parched and irritated her nostrils. Small cushions of blisters were raising on her palms. They would pop soon, leaving her hands fluid-slicked and sore.

Her old garden back home would have yielded to her efforts with a damp, easy pleasure. It was the least of the things Nesta had expected to miss. She was already tired of the tenacious dryness of the California soil. The girl was a welcome distraction.

She'd seen no one since she'd arrived, unless she counted the wild-eyed old man, bundled up like a mummy, who'd run off as soon he caught sight of her. Which was fine with her. She'd wanted to avoid people for a few more days until she'd gotten a sense of the lay of the land, recovered from the journey, built her strength back up and prepared herself for the hierarchical jockeying inherent in moving into new territory, a new position. It had been easy so far.

Nesta squinted her eyes, trying to focus. From this distance the girl's silhouette looked intriguing—peculiarly fat-hipped and particolored. Nesta wondered if it was some new post-Disappearance aberration. Her caution fell victim to her curiosity, as it always did. She decided that maybe it was time to start meeting her new neighbors after all.

But as the young woman drew closer the deformity sorted itself out into clumps of dead rabbits tied by their heels to her belt. Nesta had to laugh at herself. Aberration, indeed.

The girl wore tiretread-soled shoes, a long homespun shirt, and threadbare denim pants. Sunlight glinted off the barrel of a .22 slung over her shoulder. Her hair had the metallic shimmer that marked all the first generation born after the Disappearance, so in age she had to be under thirty. Its colors reminded Nesta of bronze Roman statues dredged from the sea, cleaned up and polished to their intended patinas—brown-golds, burnt and raw umbers, all overlaying streaks of bluish-black—a miracle of chemical interaction. A red bandanna covered just the crown of the young woman's head.

"You, girl," Nesta called out as she drew abreast. The girl looked at Nesta expressionlessly; slowing down but not halting.

"Wait. I'd like to talk to you if I could."

The young woman stopped. With her last few steps she'd drifted to the far side of the street, getting her distance.

"What's your name?" Nesta asked.

She stared at Nesta, then at the dilapidated and uncared-for house, then Nesta again. "Who are *you?*" she asked in kind.

Mentally Nesta chided herself. An old, unfamiliar woman mysteriously appears at an abandoned home—I could be crazy, or I could be an outlaw of some sort, doubtful though that might seem at my age, or I could be one of the Disappeared returned, she thought. No wonder the girl was wary.

"My name's Nesta."

The girl shook her head. "I've never seen you before," she said. "I'd recognize any Homers living this close to the House." She motioned down the street to the bizarre, sprawling mansion that rose over the crumbling housing developments.

When Nesta had lived here as a child that building had been collapsing genteelly into decay, ever more encroached upon by suburban sprawl, the tide of tinny new houses threatening to roll over it.

"You must be another Drift-back Homer," the young woman said. Her tone of voice indicated that this was not an advantage. "We've been getting more of them lately."

"No, I'm not. Or at least not exactly," Nesta said.

"Then what are you?"

Nesta shrugged. "I lived here years ago, before you were born. Then the troubles came. I left, got old, wanted to come back to where things were more interesting and the weather warmer. So I did." Not the exact chronology, but it would do.

"The weather is warmer? Where did you come back from?"

"Pennsylvania."

"Pennsylvania? That's a long way, Nesta. Whereabouts in Pennsylvania?"

"All over the place," Nesta lied. All of a sudden the young woman seemed too interested. "Now that you know my name, what's yours?"

The girl favored Nesta with a grin and stuck out her hand. "My name's Renzie. Welcome back to San Jose." She looked behind the older woman to the ranch-style home. "So you lived here as a kid?"

Nesta nodded. "I even went on tours in your House. That was before they renovated it. It's much grander now than then. It looks bigger."

Renzie gave her an appraising look. "That's because it is. If you visited the House as a kid, you know the legend . . . why the woman who owned it kept working on it."

"Of course. All the children around here made up ghost stories about the place. The old lady believed in spirits, and the spirits told her to have crews building onto it night and day."

Nesta's new neighbor nodded as if she'd passed some test. "That's right. Well, we've got a man who calls himself Carpenter living on the property. He believes that the old woman was onto something. He thinks if he never stops building, it will prevent any more Vanishings. He's got his own little work force that thinks the same way. They do repairs and keep adding on to the House, just like the old lady did, years and years ago. The rest of us help too, off and on."

"Sounds like a cult," Nesta said.

Renzie shrugged. "Almost got that way at one point."

Nesta wondered if this might indicate another anomaly, something to add to her list. "Do you believe that too—that as long as your
man Carpenter keeps building on the House, there won't be another
Vanishing?"

"No, but it's nice for the House; sort of in its spirit, to keep
working on it like that." Renzie looked down the street at the mansion
and scuffed at the layers of dirt and eucalyptus leaves that made up the
surface of the street.

When Nesta first refound her childhood home she couldn't believe that after thirty years the road hadn't been buried by under-
growth. There were no inhabitants for blocks, that she could tell; no
traffic of any kind to keep the streets so clear. Then she'd remembered
how nothing grows beneath eucalyptus trees; the soil below them satu-
rates with their pungent, barrening oils.

So many things were not as changed as she'd expected. And other
things were completely and unexpectedly transformed, as if the magical
strangeness of the House had been unleashed from its boundaries by
the Vanishing and now blanketed the area.

"When did you move back?" Renzie asked. She'd turned away
from the House toward Nesta again, the rabbits shifting on her hips like
a lumpy brown bustle.

"About a week ago."

"And you really came here all the way from Pennsylvania?"

The older woman nodded.

"How did you do it? How long did it take?"

Nesta hedged. "Someday maybe we'll sit down and talk about it."

Renzie grinned more widely. "So, what have you been eating
since you moved in? Your garden isn't exactly producing yet."

"I ate off the land a lot getting here, so I've still got some dried
supplies from traveling. The orange and avocado trees in the backyard
are bearing right now. Dandelion greens are always good."

Patting the rabbits with one hand as if they were pets, Renzie said,
"You could probably use some fresh protein. Come on up to the House
for supper."

Nesta brushed dirty hands against her overalls.

"Don't worry about that. You can wash up at the House." Seeing
how Nesta brightened the younger woman added, "You can even take
a hot bath, if you want."

Nesta's intention to keep her distance a little while longer was
weakening fast. Not too much too soon, she reminded herself. How can

you stay a detached observer if you plunge—literally in the case of a bath—into the middle of things?

"Not today," she said. "I need to get myself more organized here."

Renzie looked amused. "Suit yourself. When you get hungry and dirty enough, just come around. I'll describe you to the kitchen crew. Have fun with your gardening."

She turned and headed off. Nesta imagined the smell of roasting rabbits. At the end of the block Renzie must have had an afterthought, for she turned around and yelled back. "Hey, Nesta! In three days there's going to be a big get-together to plan a trading fair. Be ready to come up to the House by then, or else I'll come and get you." She rounded the corner and was gone.

Nesta glared and twisted the faucet, cutting off its paltry trickle of rusty water. She knew she shouldn't feel so peevish. She was lucky that this home hooked up to one of the old artesian wells and that she had water at all, though she knew she was taking chances using it before testing it. She was just crossing her fingers and assuming that after thirty years the aquifer had had time to cleanse itself of the toxic seepage from the computer industries.

She shook her head. That kind of risk and lack of procedure— how unlike herself. She looked back up the street, as if she could still catch a glimpse of Renzie. Her eyes came to rest on the House.

———

On the day of the meeting Nesta could have arranged to be absent— she'd certainly thought of it. She was hesitant about meeting her new neighbors and colleagues-to-be.

But her reluctance was matched by her attraction to the House, the Mystery House that had loomed so marvelously over her childhood. And since she couldn't precisely define the House's allure, she was afraid of that, too. She waited to see if Renzie would indeed come fetch her. Renzie would be the deciding factor. She half hoped the young woman wouldn't come.

Still, early that morning Nesta coaxed a dribble of dirty water from the outdoor faucet to wipe herself down with. She hated not being able to bathe.

The hours passed and Renzie didn't come. By early afternoon

initial relief passed into growing anxiety. Nesta began to fuss with the
storm drains to distract herself. A section of drainpipe crumbled in her
hands as she tried to poke debris out of it. "Goddamned piece of
manure," she growled at it.

"You don't need to do that now. It's summer. Doesn't start
raining around here for another month or so." Renzie's voice interrupted her.

"I was just killing time till you got here," Nesta said lamely,
turning around and putting the corroded aluminum down.

"Well, if you're ready then, let's go," Renzie said. They set out,
walking the few suburban blocks to the House.

Nesta heard a noise overhead like a deck of cards being riffled. A
scattering of leaves fell from the plum trees to the right. Flying foxes
grazed there, moving eerily from branch to branch like animated bundled bags of bones, lapping at fruit with tongues as leathery as their
wings, their enormous eyes almost the bronze of Renzie's hair. Ahead
rose the House. Nesta wondered if it was waiting for her. But what the
truth probably is, she thought, is that I've been waiting for it.

CHAPTER SIX

To Nesta's relief Renzie didn't try to take her directly inside. They wound around outbuildings till they arrived at a huge porch cradling a courtyard.

Nesta was surprised to find herself feeling self-conscious, both anxious and nervous to meet the House's denizens. She told herself that that reaction was natural; she was about to meet the people who would probably be her neighbors for whatever time was left to her in life. And she was about to meet them feeling less than herself, scrawny and dusty.

Nesta had always been a big woman and liked it, even in the days when her kind of body had been deemed less than fashionable. She'd always been conscious of the way she moved as a presence in the world, the stability and rootedness she felt and projected. But now as she walked her arms swung freely past her sides, where they had once brushed reassuringly against full hips. She felt light and insubstantial, off balance. But not defenseless, she told herself fiercely. She still had an intellect to be reckoned with.

A group of Housers lounged on the porch steps and sun-warmed concrete of the patio. Their attention was focused on a stocky white male terrier standing immobile on the pavement before them. In, out, and around the dog's stiff legs a cat entwined itself, arching its back against the terrier's legs, rubbing its face along his flanks, feline features rounded in a wickedly happy smile. It seemed to Nesta that the audience, laughing at the dog's discomfort, was taking risks with the cat's life.

Renzie introduced the older woman. "This is Nesta. I told you guys about her." Nesta wondered what she'd told them. "Nesta, this is Kip, Hot Rod, Hake . . ."

Nesta couldn't keep track of them all.

"This is Grendel," Renzie said, indicating the dog. His big triangular ears pricked up at the mention of his name.

"Grendel belongs with Pel here." She waved at a Chicano-looking fellow with bedroom eyes leaning against the bottom rail. "Pel is from the old amusement park just north—he runs sheep up there—but we count him as an honorary Houser."

Pel took Nesta's hand in both of his. When he stroked his fingers suggestively up the middle of her palm she started, almost pulling her hand back. This one is a serious Romeo, she thought, suppressing a chuckle, if he automatically puts himself out there for even a woman of my age.

He relinquished his grasp. The pressure of his hand leaving hers suggested regret.

A middle-aged woman came out of the House carrying a tray piled high with empty bowls. A young man in his twenties came after with a pewter pitcher filled with something cool enough to sweat the molten colored metal. And following on his heels a silver-haired giant of a woman wearing thick kitchen mitts lugged a huge stewpot.

"You're just in time. We're having midday supper before the meeting begins," the first woman said as she set her burden down.

"That's Jorda," Renzie said. "My brother Tuck is carrying the lemonade. Chloe's behind him."

Nesta and Renzie sidled around the animals and mounted the steps. When Nesta passed, Grendel looked up at her out of the corner of one black-bead eye as if begging her to plead his case.

The pot held stew savory with fresh vegetables and chunks of rabbit meat. The cat left off tormenting Grendel to mooch for tidbits. Cold lemonade from the pitcher washed down the stew. Nesta hadn't tasted food so hearty and sustaining since before she'd left Pennsylvania. Perhaps if I could eat like this for a while, she thought, I'd gain myself back. All of me I've lost to hard Eastern winters, the trip out, old age.

Two men wearing leather carpenter's aprons crossed the courtyard. One was sallow and bearded with a cadaverously lean face. The other was clean-shaven, blond and robust.

"Eric!" Renzie gestured the blond fellow over. "This is Nesta."

Eric pulled off a leather work glove to take her hand. "My pleasure, Nesta. Renzie told me you're newly arrived. Do you need a place to stay?" He waved the glove in the direction of the other man, who'd kept on going. "Carpenter's almost got some expansions finished. Nice spaces, though a little snug."

Nesta liked his manner. At the same time, intentionally or not, his offer constituted a trap. She couldn't study the House objectively if she were living in it. On the other hand, she didn't want to give the impression that she was sleeping out in the streets.

"I've got a place to stay for now," she said. "But it would be nice to move in here eventually." She looked at the gingerbread detailing hanging from the porch eaves and realized she *did* want to live there. The feeling was warm, seductive, and completely unexpected. Nesta shivered at its sudden insidiousness. She distrusted irrationality, especially in herself.

"Renzie said you came from all the way back East. Where was it? She told me, but I forget."

"Pennsylvania."

Nesta knew he was taking her measure. She wondered what else Renzie had told him.

"That's a long, hard trip, Nesta. If you need any help, let us know and we'll lend you a hand."

"Pipes." Renzie put in her two cents' worth. "She's got drain gutter problems and I'll bet the plumbing is in even worse shape."

The older woman glared at her. Eric smiled. "We'll send someone over to check it out. Maybe even Renzie here." He shook Nesta's hand again. "It's been a pleasure meeting you. I hope that you plan to stay." He excused himself and left.

People filtered into the central courtyard. Renzie pointed out representatives from the old movie theaters next door (which she called the Watchers' Domes), the office buildings across the street, and the department-store complex further down Winchester Boulevard.

She nodded at a group of four people drawn tightly together apart from the rest of the crowd. "That's Abel and the rest of the Homers' Council. If you're going to stay in that Home you'll want to meet them. They have jurisdiction over all the Homes."

In that case, it was good for Nesta to know who they were so she could avoid them. Her claim to the split-level as a legitimate Homer wouldn't bear up under scrutiny.

Nesta tracked another group, all men, a regular pride of academic-looking lions. "Are those the Hackers?" she asked.

"You got it," said Renzie. Nesta felt Renzie studying her reaction to them.

Eric had called the meeting to order. He reviewed the logistics for the trade fair. Representatives from different communities in the Valley took turns explaining how their group would handle its responsibilities and coordinate with the other contingents. It was the first time Nesta'd had a chance to see who else in the area had survived the Disappearance.

She wasn't surprised to see a party of Vietnamese, or another of Chicanos. The Hackers she already knew of, from long before she left Carnegie-Mellon. The other groups were heterogeneous but predominately white. She assumed that most of them, including the people who lived here in the House, had started from a nucleus of survivors who had lived near to whatever building or set of structures they ended up colonizing.

"What about security?" someone called out to Eric. "Have any special-interest groups said they're coming?"

"So far, no one that's a problem," he said. "Some Apocalyptics from Palo Alto hammed us that they've got a party of traders they'd like to send down, and we've also heard from the Neo-Christians in Morgan Hill. They might proselytize a little if they get loaded"—everyone laughed at that—"but that would be as bad as it'd get."

Apparently the term "special-interest groups" was a euphemism for "cults." And apparently some of the attendees present, like the Watchers and the Homers, didn't include themselves in that category. That didn't surprise Nesta. Such is the nature of cults—they're the normal ones; anyone *else* with a dogma is a cult.

"Has there been any word of the Heaven Bound?" one of the Homers asked with concern.

"No, that wouldn't be likely. If they needed goods desperately enough to come to the fair, they'd send members in disguise. Luckily, we haven't heard of any bands of them in the immediate area." Was it Nesta's imagination, or did he glance her way?

He briefly reviewed various security measures. Then he asked about lab test results.

"Lab tests?" Nesta asked Renzie.

"Yeah. For all kinds of communicable diseases, especially sexual. These get-togethers generate serious partying. Don't they do stuff like this and take precautions beforehand back East?"

The older woman thought of the isolation of snowbound, claustrophobic winters and the spring bacchanals that followed. "Yes, something similar," she replied dryly.

The meeting wore on. Nesta drank more lemonade, patted Grendel and studied people.

"That about does it for now for the trade fair," Eric finally said. But as people began to stretch and rise to go, he halted them.

"Wait just a minute, please. There's one matter that still needs to be addressed. It doesn't have anything to do with the trade fair, but since we're all gathered together it seemed a good time to bring it up." He looked over at the group on the porch. "Renzie?"

She stood up. Everyone turned to stare. Nesta slid behind Renzie's brother.

Renzie raised her voice. "I've been working as bosun for a repair team on the roads north of here, up until almost a week ago. Some of you already know that—you contributed members to work on the crew." She paused, looking grim. "One day when I went out hunting I came across a Home that had been fired." The crowd, already quiet, became mortally still, especially the Homers. "I explored around and found three more. For all I know, there could have been others."

"Maybe they'd collapsed and someone from up north took care of them," one of the Vietnamese volunteered.

"I thought of that, but there weren't any traces of the kind of crew work or campsite you'd expect. And it was a deserted area. There isn't anyone there to notice if a Home needs to be torn down."

"None of you people have the right to judge when a Home should be torn down," one of the Homers yelled angrily. She started to say more, but the rest of her group hushed her.

"That's what I'm trying to say," Renzie agreed. "A Homer should judge that, and there aren't any left in that area that I could see. That's one of the reasons I'm concerned."

"Are you sure it was fired?" a tense, lean young man asked in a somewhat sarcastic tone of voice. "Couldn't it have been an accident . . . lightning, or a careless campfire?"

Renzie stared at him for a long moment before replying, evidently controlling her temper. "No, Sun. Whoever did it was very careful, set the fires not to spread. We'd have seen the smoke from a big blaze down here. They'd been set in the spring, during the rainy season. There was considerable new plant growth already started over the burns when I found them."

"Heaven Bounders," someone guessed.

"No, we don't think so," Eric said. "As soon as I heard about this I checked around as thoroughly as I could on such short notice. That's why I mentioned earlier that we're pretty sure there's no 'Bounders nearby."

Renzie nodded, backing him up. "And it's not their style," she said. "They'd have set as big a burn as they could and then taken off."

"What do you want us to do? What kind of danger are we talking about here?" The question came from a big, slothlike fellow that Renzie had pointed out to Nesta as the head of the Office Buildings.

"If this happens again, we're betting whoever is doing it will follow the same pattern, which means we have until the rains start," Eric said. "We can all keep our eyes open to anything suspicious here on in, and the trade fair will give us an opportunity to find out if any of the outlying communities have experienced anything similar. I'd like to ask the Hackers to coordinate data."

One of the Hackers made a gesture of assent.

"In that case, it's getting late. I'd like to adjourn the meeting," Eric declared.

Nesta helped Renzie stack the bowls back on the tray. The sky layered into a parfait of colors as it began to melt into night. Pel fed stew scraps to Grendel.

"Who are the Heaven Bound?" Nesta asked.

"Not good news, as I'm sure you gathered," Renzie said. "They believe that everyone who Vanished ascended to 'heaven,' and that anyone who got left behind must have done or not done something to get excluded. They think there would be another Vanishing except that the rest of us are holding it back. Especially the Watchers, who actively resist Vanishing, and the Homers, who want to bring the Vanished back instead of the other way around. The 'Bounders would like to flatten all the Homes, one way or the other.

"Everyone you see here wants to survive." Renzie gestured to the courtyard still teeming with people. "That makes the 'Bounders our natural enemy." She grinned. "One of the few that can make us all get along together."

"Excuse me for interrupting." Eric had come up behind them. "Nesta, could I see you for a minute?"

She turned around. Two of the Hackers flanked Eric. Oh damn, she thought. Caught. Renzie continued stacking bowls and glasses, but she was looking over her shoulder at Nesta.

"This is the woman I mentioned," Eric told the Hackers. "She just arrived cross-country from Pennsylvania. Nesta, this is Ernest Yorheim and Pax Willster, co-supervisors of the Silicon Valley research and educational complex—more commonly known as the Hackers' Center."

The two men's names and work were certainly familiar enough to Nesta. This wasn't how she'd imagined her first meeting with her future associates. She glared at Renzie and wished she weren't so scruffy and dusty, like an old bag lady.

Making the best of it, Nesta stuck out her hand at Pax Willster. "It's a pleasure meeting you. I've been looking forward to this," she said. "I'm Dr. Nesta Christiana Easterman."

Ernest Yorheim turned his head away, his face tightly set. Pax Willster, looking bewildered, took her hand and shook it. "Dr. Easterman, I'm so relieved," he said. "We hadn't had any word of you in such a long time that we were becoming quite worried. How long have you been here?"

"Uh . . . a few days."

Renzie rolled her eyes. Willster's expression changed to one of dismay and irritation. "Why didn't you let us know? We'd begun to organize search teams to look for you. Why didn't you come to us?"

She'd traveled all the way from Carnegie-Mellon to work with these people and had already alienated them. Her strategy of taking the time to check them out first had backfired.

"My family used to live here when I was little—just a few blocks away, actually," she said. "My first instinct when I arrived was to find my home, see if it still stood and get settled in. It took me so long to get here that I didn't think a few more days would concern you."

There was an awkward silence. Dr. Yorheim started to say something but it turned into a cough.

Pax Willster sighed. "Well, we're glad that you're finally safely here. We didn't know you'd had family in the area. We assumed you'd be staying in the Center. All the researchers live in-house."

An undercurrent of pain ran through his words. Nesta studied his face. She knew that most of the Hacker Center people came from this area. Somewhere out in the suburban sprawl lay their deserted former Homes. She wondered if either of these two men who'd dedicated themselves to their work and the future, not to the past, slipped away at times to sit in their old dwellings emptied of loved ones.

"I'll probably move in eventually. I just need to get my bearings a little more first," she told him.

"And don't forget that you're always welcome to move in here," Eric said. "A van drives a load of kids up to the Center every day, so you'd have transportation."

"When do you think you'll be ready to come up and get introduced around?" Yorheim asked.

"How about tomorrow?" Now that she'd been exposed, she might as well jump into it. Nesta turned to Eric. "Would it be possible to catch a lift with that van tomorrow morning?"

"I don't see why not." He looked at the light-colored black man Renzie had introduced her to earlier. "Hake, what time are you leaving?"

"Eight o'clock. Just meet us here in the courtyard, if that's not too early for you," Hake said.

"That would be fine."

"Then we'll be expecting you tomorrow," Pax Willster said.

CHAPTER SEVEN

Night finished creeping up to claim the sky. Chloe, Tuck and the others had carried away the rest of the kitchenware. Only Renzie and Nesta remained.

Nesta leaned back against the porch rail and sighed. "I wish you hadn't figured me out and turned me in so soon. I wanted to feel my way around more first."

Renzie shrugged. "I gathered you had your reasons for lying low, but when Pax said they were about to send out search teams, he meant clear to Warm Springs, up to and including confronting the 'Bounders. Yorheim can be a jerk, but they've been sincerely worried about you. 'Bounders are notably unenthusiastic about scientists—they feel that scientists are only interested in bringing the Vanished back and preventing another Vanishing. If they'd gotten their hands on you . . ." She shook her head.

"Maybe you should have told me all that," the older woman said with some asperity.

Renzie shot her a sidelong glance. "I thought about it," she said. "But you threw me a loop when you said you were from here and then knew so much about the House. No one knew the physicist from Carnegie-Mellon originally came from these parts. By the time Eric and I figured it out, it was time to come fetch you for the meeting."

"Well, I guess I'm actually grateful," Nesta said. "My future colleagues may not be happy with me now, but they'd have been far more displeased if they'd taken off hunting for me and *then* I showed up on their doorstep. It's going to be hard enough convincing them of my theories without completely alienating them beforehand. I just don't have that much energy."

Renzie looked at her closely. "You look exhausted right now."

"I am."

"Would a hot bath help?"

"Yes!" Nesta brightened, then looked at the House. She wasn't quite ready for it. "Where?"

Renzie laughed. "Don't worry—the tubs are out in the garden."

"Let's go," Nesta said.

As they walked over, Renzie kept glancing at Nesta sideways.

"Go ahead," the older woman finally said. "Whatever it is, ask it."

"These theories of yours, are they a big secret, too?"

"Not at all. Some of them aren't going to be particularly popular, but I'm not going to keep them to myself."

"How about me?"

"Renzie, if you're willing to hang around me long enough for me to explain them, I'll tell you anything you want to know. But not tonight. I'm too damned tired."

"What about Pennsylvania? And what it's like traveling across the country? Could you tell me that, too?"

Her insatiable curiosity was amusing. "You're merciless! Yes, eventually."

The baths were old wooden hot tubs perched in a communal row on a ridge surrounding the gardens. From down below they looked like witches' cauldrons. Steam wraithed up from them into the moonless night. Nesta could just barely glimpse heads bobbing on their surface like apples. People perched on the edges, boiled ghosts cooling.

Along the outer, nongarden side, showers ringed the ridgeline. Renzie stripped, rinsed, soaped, and rinsed again. She waited for Nesta to follow suit. Nesta wanted to bathe, but was suddenly shy. She didn't want to expose her depleted, age-scrawny body to strangers.

Renzie clambered up the embankment. She picked a tub with no occupants and pulled its solar cover off.

"C'mon. It's okay," she said. The air had cooled with the advent of evening. She must have been chilled, standing there naked, wet from the showers.

The night sky, although brilliant with stars, shed little light downward. Without a moon out everything looked obscure, the other bathers no more than white smudges behind the steam. Maybe it's better that they're still strangers, Nesta thought as she pulled off her overalls. Who cares what strangers think?

They soaked till her skin felt like it was pulling loose from her flesh and ready to shed like a snake. She wished it could have. She'd have enjoyed being that sleek and new. Putting on her dusty gardening clothes again would be a distasteful act.

"Why don't you want to come live in the House?" Renzie's question hung suspended over the clear silence of the water.

"It's not that I don't want to," Nesta said. "Just not yet."

Renzie shrugged. Nesta's answer obviously didn't make sense to her. It wasn't rational to Nesta either, for that matter. "Why would you want to live in that—" Renzie stopped.

Nesta didn't need to see her face to sense her embarrassment. As far as Renzie knew the ranch house was Nesta's long-lost family Home, reliquary of old, cherished memories. Nesta didn't want to explain that she was staying there under almost false pretenses. Her family hadn't lived there for years before the Disappearance. Vanishing, she corrected herself. They call it the Vanishing out here.

She didn't want Renzie to feel uncomfortable. "I'm not particularly attached to the place. And I do want to move into the House. But not yet. Not *quite* yet," she reiterated, struggling to find words that would explain what she was feeling. "There's something about the House that's so . . . strong."

"Are you afraid of the House?"

"No, it's not like that. Nothing frightening in and of itself. More of an allure, a glamour. I've always been cautious around charismatics." Nesta tried to make a joke of it.

But Renzie considered her comment seriously. "Yes, I think I understand that," she said. Nesta had sat with her back to the House. Renzie was looking past her at the sprawling manor. "Just take your time until you're ready. We'll always find room for you."

Nesta turned to look too. Muted orange-gold light melted out of its windows, highlighting its dark-silhouetted shape. It made her think of some sort of fabulous, absurd jack-o'-lantern, both merry and ominous at the same time. "It's getting late," Nesta said. "I'd better be getting back."

———
———
———
—

The sky had turned almost black. "May I borrow a lamp to walk home with?"

"You could stay over for the night," Renzie said, laughing. This interchange had already become a game between them. "No? Then I'll walk you home."

The road was relatively smooth. Still, Nesta was amazed by Renzie's sure footing. With the lack of light fooling her eyes she found herself taking missteps even on firm, flat surfaces.

"How do you do that?" she asked Renzie.

"Do what?"

"Walk in the dark without stumbling at all. I wouldn't have thought you'd know your way among the Homes *that* well."

"But there's plenty of light." Renzie sounded puzzled. Nesta could see the dark silhouette of her arm gesture against the lesser black of the sky. "The aurora is good and strong tonight."

All Nesta saw were the usual stars, unhelpful pinpricks.

CHAPTER EIGHT

Nesta found the evolution of the district that had become the Hackers' Center fascinating. In her youth Silicon Valley had consisted of an unintegrated series of low-slung monolithic corporate buildings tamped down onto the flattened terrain. It resembled a vast, fragmented enlargement of a computer chip schematic. The Hackers had taken a central chunk of this real estate and finished integrating its circuits.

Outer buildings stood empty and neglected. All activity had condensed to the inner buildings. These were now connected by tunnels, enclosed walkways, and "fill-in" structures.

The Center devoted itself not only to research but also to education. Children from all over the San Jose area swarmed the place like clouds of nuclear particles.

Hake and Pax Willster gave her an initial tour of the research facilities—just the central offices. The actual laboratories, computer stations, and living quarters were too extensive to cover in a single day.

"How do they sustain all this?" Nesta asked Hake.

"They have their own gardens, which everyone works in," he said. "The rest of the Valley contributes what's needed in exchange for educational and information services and some electronic and medical products. It's similar to the role monasteries played in the European Dark Ages."

Nesta thought of the "classroom" sections and the children bouncing around like electrons gone wild. Some monastery.

Once she'd been thoroughly disoriented by the tour they took her to a lounge for lunch and to meet with some of the project coordinators. Ernest Yorheim was already there, organizing things.

Over the course of the morning Nesta had come to like Pax Willster. He reminded her of Woody Allen in films she'd loved in her college days. That is, if Woody Allen had possessed a full head of straight, black hair just beginning to gray. Woody Allen before the scandals. Dr. Yorheim was another matter.

Once they'd selected their food and sat down, Yorheim addressed the group of perhaps fifteen people. "I'd like to present Dr. Nesta Christiana Easterman, noted physicist and our new colleague, *finally* arrived from Carnegie-Mellon. We're very pleased that she made it here safely."

"Thank you, Dr. Yorheim." Nesta smiled benignly at her new associates. Maybe if she held her temper and just let him get it out of his system they could get off to a fresh start.

"Actually, these days my studies could be more precisely described as ontological." She thought this would be a good lead-in to introducing herself.

Dr. Yorheim chose to interrupt. "Ah, so perhaps—ha ha—I should have introduced you as a noted *metaphysicist.*"

A few people chuckled. Nesta sighed. They were already off to an adversarial start. So be it.

"Hardly, Dr. Yorheim. Almost thirty years ago ninety percent of the human population, as closely as we can tell, disappeared overnight. Since then, the investigation and definition of existence itself can hardly be considered occult. It now falls squarely into the realm of physics." Nesta spoke quietly, but a pin drop could have been heard in the silence that followed.

"Uh, John, Susan, Laird, why don't you and the rest of the department heads give Dr. Easterman a current overview of your work?" Pax Willster tried valiantly for a diversion.

All of the assembled were investigating potential origins of the Vanishing. Little of it was new to Nesta—there had been work along similar lines at Carnegie-Mellon, albeit without such extensive facilities.

They summarized their virtual-particle interactions research (which had been her field of expertise), mass/energy breakups and freeze patterns, recurrent global extinction cycles, electromagnetic polar switches, temporal shifts, dimensional shifts. There were data coordinators trying to determine if the Vanishing was human caused or "natural." Mass teleportation and extraterrestrial contact hadn't been ignored.

One concept new to her was shadow theory. "A shadow is a projection of points in three-dimensional space onto a two-dimensional plan," a stout man explained. "You can make the shadow disappear by directly altering the photons cast on the points or by removing the source of the shadow. So, if our reality can be considered as a projection of 'points' in higher-dimensional space into or onto three-dimensional space, what could make those 'shadows' disappear?"

After about two hours of this Pax and Hake ushered Nesta to the office she'd been assigned to. She slumped into a chair.

"We put you just down the hall from the team involved with the virtual-particle work. I know they've got questions they'd like to run by you," Pax said, then caught himself and looked away, embarrassed.

Nesta guessed that Pax was one of the few in the Center who knew that part of the reason the Hacker oligarchy had been so supportive of her arrival was the role she was to play in pulling the rug out from under that particular line of research. Bringing up the subject in front of an outsider like Hake was quite a faux pas.

She twiddled her fingers over the mute keys of the desk's computer keyboard. "I'll help them in any way that I can, of course," she said. "But most of my efforts have to go into assembling a team for my own research. I need to draw from a pretty eclectic assortment of disciplines, starting with at least one biologist, a chemist, an astronomer, and some data technicians. And I want Jan, that socioanthropologist."

"A biologist? And a socioanthropologist? You? Why?" asked Pax.

"Because the Vanishing happened to human beings—and maybe some other species too, for all we know. Anybody do a census study on ants lately? Therefore—biology. We need to run checks on DNA cueing. We need to know what other people out there have been noticing, whether they're scientists or not."

"But your work involved the projection of virtual-particle theory on a macroscale, baryon jump integration and the like. What you're working on now must have emerged from that research. How do you plan to tie biology in to find the source of the Vanishing?" Pax asked.

Nesta took a deep breath and prepared to launch herself into heresy. "I'm not looking to find the source of the Vanishing."

There, it was out. She wondered if Pax would run to Yorheim with the news. "If I do find the source, it will be the icing on the cake."

"You're not? Then what the hell are you doing?"

Hake held out a restraining hand to Pax and asked a question of his own. "If finding out what caused the Vanishing is the icing, what's the cake?"

"Let me put the matter in context first," Nesta said. "I think all the inquiries relating to the Vanishing have been misdirected."

The set of Pax's face was beginning, Jekyll/Hyde-like, to resemble Ernest Yorheim's.

"You asked me," Nesta reminded him. "So let me finish explaining. The Vanishing began . . . Something. And that Something is still going on." She stretched back in the chair. Pax hunched forward. He still looked unhappy, but she could tell she'd at least caught his interest.

"Thirty years ago," she continued, "when folks woke up one morning to find that a major chunk of the population had disappeared overnight, including their loved ones who'd been sleeping right next to them, it naturally generated certain self-protective responses which have continued to this day. Something that had never happened before had happened; something beyond any scientific or religious concept. And if it had happened once, why shouldn't it happen again?

"So some people disintegrated into suicide, violence, or existential indulgences. The survival-oriented adapted in various ways. Adults began force-feeding knowledge to children to try to increase the kids' chances of survival if there was another Vanishing. Groups similar to your Watchers' Dome folk cropped up everywhere. And so on and so forth."

They already knew all this, of course. Nesta made herself quit fiddling with the computer, wondered where she could get the disks she'd brought with her converted. She stalled for a moment, knowing she'd probably get upset when she continued.

"But it's been thirty years now, and for a number of reasons I think the Vanishing was a singular occurrence. We can get into that later. I don't believe the conditions necessary to duplicate it exist anymore and won't occur again for thousands or millions of years, if ever."

"So you think all the research of the last thirty years is pointless?" said Pax.

"No! I believe it's vital. But as I said before, I think it's been misdirected."

Nesta could tell from their baffled faces that she'd lost them. "The Vanishing didn't just happen and stop. We're so overwhelmed and distracted by its psychological consequences that we can't see its actual, physical effects. It started chains of events that continue, have maybe accelerated, that haven't been examined except as possible clues to the Vanishing's source. That's what scares me to death. We've got our heads buried in the sand and don't even know it."

"For instance?" asked Hake.

"Allow me to be blunt, even obvious. All of the first generation of post-Vanishment children have unusual hair."

Pax shrugged her sarcasm aside. "Prismatic-metallic effect. That's been researched. It didn't lead anywhere."

"It didn't lead anywhere as far as indicating a direct cause of the Vanishing. Now, what if it was caused by the Vanishing? What is the explanation of this phenomenon?" She held up one finger. "Maybe there's a thicker clear protein sheathing the individual hairs, allowing something like a lens-refraction effect. Is that what they found?"

Pax frowned, thinking hard, trying to remember. "No, it was some sort of molecular or submolecular shift."

"Try subatomic. I know. I looked."

"So what?" he said, nettled. "The next generation after that is already in progress, and their hair looks fine. Maybe it was a temporary mutation."

Nesta waggled a finger at him. *"Temporary* mutation? Tsk, tsk. Not up on our biology, are we? There are questions that should have been asked: What's really going on here with these kids? Why didn't the next generation express the gene? Even if it's recessive, in this case with both parents expressing it, it would still show up in the children. Why *don't* the next batch of kids show it? Or is it being expressed, but not within *our* visual range?"

Pax reddened at her words.

I'm getting too carried away, she thought. I could pass as one of those cult maniacs. Easy, go easier. I need allies, not enemies.

"Wait a minute," said Hake. "Back up. What did you mean by 'within *our* visual range'?"

"Hair color for one generation isn't the only transformation. Last night Renzie walked me back to my place. She seemed to have perfect night vision, in spite of no moon and no human illumination within a couple of blocks of the House. When I asked her about it, she said there was plenty of light from the aurora. I didn't see any aurora, but it was there . . . for her. We can see them back East, under the right conditions, but in California . . . ? One of the first things I want to do is make a spectroscopic check of the night sky here.

"And what about you two? Can you see the aurora?"

Pax Willster looked queasy. "No . . ."

"And you never noticed that they could?"

Hake rubbed his brow. "Yes, but it didn't seem as though it had anything to do with the Vanishing."

"Head in the sand?" Nesta said.

"Head in the sand," he agreed. Ah, at least one ally.

"The effect is endemic on every level of reality, however you define reality these days. It's not just us . . ." Nesta's gaze dropped to the computer. She felt as though a bar of lead had been dropped into her gut. She hadn't thought about the computers. "But everything."

CHAPTER NINE

Preparations for the fair interrupted Nesta's research before it even began. Pax had assembled a list of available researchers, but all of them were temporarily drawn away to other duties. Only Hake came up from the House each day to help her set up the computers.

One morning as a break Renzie and Jan the socioanthropologist took Nesta to see the trade fair being set up.

A fine mist of dust hung suspended in the air as people filtered into the Valley. They traveled on vehicles piled to overflowing with goods—horse- or cattle-drawn wagons, tandem bicycles pulling along small carts, peddlers with huge packs on their backs, vans and trucks fueled by either wine-reeking alcohol or solar batteries or panels.

Renzie dragged Jan and Nesta along behind her, squeezing between tables setting up in every space imaginable between the Watchers' Domes, the House, and the neighboring Office Buildings. Old friends called greetings to each other. Trading rivals exchanged good-natured catcalls. Nesta thought it resembled a giant flea market as much as it did a country fair.

Renzie and Jan introduced her to locals and visitors alike and gave her a crash course in the customs and economics of the area. Nesta tried to stay alert to everything. It wasn't impossible that if she kept her wits about her that she might find direct evidence of aberrations.

"If you think this is crowded," Renzie said as they ducked around a group of weavers flapping out blankets, stringing some of their wares onto poles to form an open tent, "tomorrow this chunk of roadway will be completely closed off to traffic. This will all be wall-to-wall stands."

As Nesta looked around at the hustle and bustle she remembered this same boulevard from her youth. Then it had been truly filled, saturated with a metallic river of automobiles, their swift flow interrupted only by the occasional red of a stop light. When the lights turned green again the cars would surge forward en masse, spewing out leaden fumes, anxious to depart before the next wave of vehicles exited off the nearby grid-locked freeway.

Glancing at Renzie, Nesta felt the huge gap between them, a gap greater than the mere decades that separated them by age.

"This isn't where the big deals are made," Renzie was saying. They passed tables loaded with tools and odds and ends of machinery. Jan trailed behind, watching for old contacts who would be useful to the project. "The livestock trading goes on down at the Department Store stockyards, for example. If there's time we'll stop by there later."

Renzie's chatter verged on the manic. She too seemed to be on the lookout. Although her conversation focused on the physicist, her attention did not. Her eyes darted back and forth, her gaze settling momentarily on vendors, then moving restlessly on. Nesta couldn't tell if it was simple excitement and anticipation, or something else.

"The Orinda glass and solar magnates will go directly to the Hacker Center for solar-cell technology and computer chips," Renzie said. "Eric and the wine co-op will meet with some of the Orindans at private dinners in the House to haggle over the vineahol harvest. Medical supplies and drugs, on the whole . . ." Nesta's itching curiosity found itself relieved, then numbed, then drowned in the deluge of information.

The machinery had heralded the beginning of a salvage section. Many "booths" were simply blankets thrown out on the tarmac with mounds of items piled high upon them: here a hodgepodge of every imaginable size and shape of nuts, bolts and screws; there a jackstraw heap of tire irons. Even stacks of mildewed fancy wallpaper samples, drapery swatches and pails of decorator paints (undoubtedly mostly dried up after all these years) were displayed in the belief that some use might be made of them. Nesta thought that as likely as the absurd names embellishing the paint cans. Puce, Coquelicot, Madder, Chartreuse, Serpentine, Abelard, Solferino, Magandá, Croze—she thought she recognized the names of one or two of the colors, but the baroque nomenclature gave her no idea of what they actually looked like. They were the extinct, flamboyant relics of an era of overrefined sensibilities and manipulative commercialism. At least there were some things the Vanishing could be thanked for.

"Sepulveda!" Renzie's yell interrupted Nesta's reverie.

Just beyond the pyramided piles of paint began a long row of card tables covered with spare parts. Behind the tables stood a file of rebuilt bicycles. A thin young woman bent over a mountain bike looked up. "Renzie!" she called back, waving a sprocket wrench at them. She crawled under one of the tables to get out, then gave Renzie a big hug.

"Old friends?" Nesta asked Jan.

"I guess," Jan said. "I think she's one of the Orindans. Renzie, why don't we leave you to catch up? I'll take Nesta through the rest. We'll pick you up later, okay?"

Renzie agreed happily. What Nesta had thought might be nervousness must have just been the expectation of reuniting with old comrades. Jan and Nesta continued their wandering.

Jan was middle-aged, probably in her mid-fifties, neither fat nor thin, with short-cropped, fading brown hair. Her manner was restrained but not shy or retiring. From the little Nesta had seen of her so far she possessed the best traits of her chosen field: She was intelligent, didn't leap to judgment, and had the quietly inviting manner of a good listener.

Nesta hoped that she would prove to be one of the most important members of her team. While the rest of the crew worked out models on the computers, whose reliability Nesta mistrusted more and more, Jan would be out researching, gathering information and clues on the anomalies the physicist hoped to find.

Nesta thought, And if I prove my case, what then? She pushed her concern aside, as she'd been doing for months. If she proved her case, she had to hope that the information she gathered would suggest the next step. If there were, in fact, any next steps to be taken.

"What Renzie was telling you—about the wheeling and dealing at these events—was more or less true, but the setup of these fairs isn't that simple," Jan said. "Some of these innocuous little stands are more than they might seem at first." They'd come to an aisle of farmers' bulk goods. "See that man with a few bales of cotton?"

Nesta had to laugh. "Who is seriously going to bring three bales of cotton to a big trading fair?"

Jan nodded. "Exactly. In point of fact, he represents a big cooperative from way out in the Valley, past Pleasanton. His three bales are just samples. Watch this."

A group of women from the Watchers' Domes approached the cotton dealer. Nesta recognized Tuck's red-haired girlfriend, Le Chell, among them. The man cut off some snippets of cotton from one of the bales. The women inspected the fibers closely, drawing the filaments apart, felting bits of the cotton into pellets between their fingers. Then they settled down to serious dickering with the man.

"I didn't know the Watchers' Domes were weavers," Nesta said.

Jan smiled. "They're not. Like everybody else, the Watchers' Dome folk are pretty self-sufficient for bare necessities. And like everybody else they also produce a few specialty items. In their case they manufacture sanitary pads and tampons—they've got a minifactory at an old shop in the mall across the way. They practically have a corner on the market."

From the fustiness of cotton Jan led Nesta to the yeasty scent of fresh-cut hay and oat straw. On the way they passed a young man standing on a chair in front of a tall kiosk. He was writing in a schedule for workshops that would be offered over the five days of the fair. Jan let Nesta study the list for a few minutes, then steered her on to the garden produce section.

"Those folks over there"—Jan indicated a handsomely robed group—"are 'Rosies,' Rosicrucians. They were experts on medicinal herbs long before the Vanishing. The woman who is bargaining with them is from the Women's Brigade. The Brigade deals in medical services and provisions." Jan looked at Nesta meaningfully. "They're the major supplier of estrogen for this end of the Valley."

The fragrance of ripe tomatoes, braids of garlic, summer squash, pungent basil and cilantro overlapped in a rich aromatic stew. A woman dressed in shirt, overalls, and apron all dyed a deep indigo blue looked up from arranging a display of vegetables as rich in color as it was in smell. She offered a flowerlike bouquet of coriander, dill and borage to Nesta, saying,

> "To pick a blossom
> From the shadow of the water.
> Gaze and gaze in vain."

Nesta politely declined, confused, well aware of Jan's amusement.

"The Koanites do some of the best truck gardening in this area,"

Jan said, indicating other indigo-garbed farmers pushing handcarts heaped high. The vegetables were followed by perfumed arrays of fruit: oranges, peaches, melons, and grapes.

"Are they Koanites too, or Rosies?" Nesta asked, pointing to several people helping unload crates of vegetables. The roustabouts' gender was indistinguishable beneath hooded undyed brown wool robes.

Jan shook her head. "No, those are Penitents. They're sort of the flip side of the Heaven Bounders. Both groups share the same basic belief: that the Vanishing was the actual end of the world and that humankind was whisked away by God for judgment."

"And those of us left behind?" Nesta asked. She noticed that the Penitents were barefoot, though the pavement must have been horribly hot.

"It depends on which faction of which group you talk to, but basically the Penitents believe that those left behind were neither good nor bad enough to make it to heaven or hell. That we're stuck in a kind of purgatory, doomed to die and reincarnate here till we make the break one way or the other. That's why they live as they do; making penance, doing good deeds, trying to demonstrate to God that they're unattached to life here, hoping they'll eventually make the upward-bound cut."

"And probably arguing your ear off in the process to do you the favor of taking you with them," Nesta said. "There's a group with similar beliefs in the Northeast that call themselves the Redemptionists."

"The Penitents don't do as much proselytizing as you might think," said Jan. "They have faith in conversion by example. They believe too much gab and not enough action to be a major weakness. That's why they call the remaining evangelical Christians the 'Talkers.'"

Nesta laughed. "At least they've got a sense of humor."

"Not really. That's funny to you and me, but they mean it seriously. They are a rich source for our research, though. They're always searching for signs and portents, miracles, to signal that ascension is near."

"What about the Heaven Bounders? They're supposed to be bad news, but if they're actively searching for omens, too . . ."

"Too risky," Jan said flatly. "The Penitents believe in individual deliverance. The 'Bounders differ in that they believe in another wholesale Vanishing. That they alone are on the right track and that no one gets to Go until *all* have faith in the Second Ascendance and live their lives accordingly.

"Groups of them go out on jihads to burn down granaries, crops, orchards, anything that smacks of planning for an earthly future. What makes them particularly dangerous is their belief that it's all—everybody—or nothing. Therefore the rest of us are standing in their way to salvation. If *we* don't convert, *they* don't make it to heaven. Consider what that means as far as behavioral motivation."

Nesta shuddered and thought of how nonchalant she'd been about the concern Eric and the Hackers had expressed at her delayed arrival, how cavalier she'd been about the people they'd almost sent searching into 'Bounder territory after her.

Renzie came down the aisle. "The Office Building is hosting a welcoming party tonight," she said. "I think they want to do it before the crowd gets too huge and unwieldy. Nesta, you should definitely attend. Jan, you too if you can. What about it?"

Jan shrugged. "Perhaps. I need to make the rounds a little more here. My plans will depend on who I run into."

There were gaps in the aisles where vendors hadn't yet arrived. A rift several tables wide breached a section of stalls laden with cured hams and beef and venison jerky.

"What'll be here?" Nesta asked.

"I don't know," said Renzie. *"Quién viene aquí?"* she asked the Latina minding the next table over.

"Pescado de Santa Cruz." Fish from Santa Cruz.

"Drovers will be bringing them in," said Renzie. *"Conoce usted las personas?"*

"No." The woman didn't know who the merchants were. *"Pero pienso que ellos vengan en poco tiempo."*

Renzie shrugged. She seemed anxious to move on.

The three women continued on their way. The spicy, bloody stench of meat changed to that of mildew and the distinctive odor of old cardboard and leather bindings. The next row of tables down were stacked high with salvaged books. Nesta recognized a few Hackers grazing through piles of science books, looking for volumes to supplement the Center's library.

After that came table after table of old art books. Some of the names heralded on the spines were familiar to her from Pre-Vanishment days, others not: Picasso, Edvard Munch, Rembrandt, a thick two-volume set of the collected erotic works of Norman Rockwell, Emily Bonnard, *The Bauhaus Days Of Alexander Calder,* Salvador Dali, George Grosz, the working sketches of George Sand, Michelangelo's Sistine Chapel.

These were the names of those who spent their entire lives doing nothing more than laying pretty dabs of pigment or strokes of graphite on paper or canvas. Nesta shook her head.

The art books segued into displays of literature. *A Tale of Two Cities* by Dickens, *Moby-Dick* by Melville, *Silas Marner, Treasure Island, The Mayor of Castlebridge* by Thomas Handy.

"Make way please, make way," a child on a pony cried out, clearing a path for two rattling wagons drawn by sweaty oaken-thighed draft horses. Jan and Nesta crowded to the side to let the procession pass. An iodine reek of fish swept by.

Like most of the wagons these were chopped, decapitated, and converted old panel vans. A man in his early to mid-sixties sporting a thick mustache drove the first one. A much younger frizzle-haired woman clung to him. Their plushly upholstered bodies and light brown hair put Nesta in mind of a pair of elephant seals. The second wagon was piloted by a lean man in his early thirties.

Ragged children ranging from toddlers to almost-teens hopped like fleas around the two vehicles. Some bore the shimmer-haired birthmark of the second generation, others did not. A tall woman with radiant black hair tried without great success to shepherd them.

Renzie barely turned to let the boy on the pony brush past her, then stood solid against the wagon, forcing it to stop. She and the mustached man stared at each other.

"Heard you were coming," she said, no welcome in her voice.

The man nodded. "Big fair like this means a lot of business for us, too much to pass up."

Renzie swept a long, deliberate gaze over the two wagons, their occupants, the pack of children. With the halting of the wagons a crowd began to gather to see what was happening. Le Chell's red hair bobbed in and out of Nesta's line of sight as she jumped up and down toward the back of the throng, trying to get a clear view.

The man looked uncomfortable, defensive. "Needed a lot of hands to deal with all this. Couldn't leave the kids behind."

He and Renzie eyed each other for another lengthy moment, then came to some hidden agreement. Renzie stepped aside.

The ginger-haired woman looked down from her roost. "Nice to see you again, Renzie. The children have been waiting to come up here and visit for *years,"* she said. "Isn't it lovely that George said we could finally all make it?" She and Renzie glowered at each other as the wagon began to move. Ginger Hair called down to the tall woman herding the children, "Sara, this is Renzie, whom you've heard *so* much about. Renzie, this is Sara, Brad's wife."

The other woman left off minding the children, her attention riveted.

"So *you're* Renzie."

"I'm Renzie."

The taller woman put her hands on her hips. "So you're the one that drove them off, that kept them from their Homes." She looked Renzie up. She looked Renzie down.

Renzie turned away from the woman, her expression stony.

"I'm talking to you," the woman said. "Don't you walk away from me." She grabbed at Renzie's shirt to pull her around, cocking her free arm back to slap.

Renzie brought her right hand up the middle fast, straight under the other woman's chin. Simultaneously she slid one leg in deep behind her opponent, tripping Sara, and pulled downward and out to the left on the woman's trapped arm.

Sara's head snapped back. She stumbled backward, her spine arching in an exaggerated curve. Renzie's hand under Sara's jaw projected forcefully along the trajectory of the woman's fall, propelling the back of her head toward the ground. Nesta flinched, expecting to hear the woman's neck crack.

"Renzie, no! Don't!" the man in the second fish wagon screamed.

At the sound of his voice, Renzie's force slackened. Sara tumbled, grabbing at Renzie's arm in a panic, pulling Renzie off balance with her as she fell. Renzie rolled clear over Sara, and was on her feet and in back of the other woman before her opponent could finish scrambling up. Renzie grabbed hold of the collar of her attacker's jumpsuit and pressed down or pulled backward, keeping Sara scrabbling helplessly in circles on the ground.

"Stop it, Renzie, stop it!" The younger man had come up behind Renzie. He hunched over and grabbed at her arms, trying to pin them behind her.

"Let go of me, Brad," Renzie growled. She managed to hang on to the other woman briefly: for a moment the three of them were frozen in a tableau that resembled a violent orgy—Brad spooned up against Renzie, Renzie welded to Sara.

Then Renzie dropped her center of gravity and ducked forward, apparently trying to throw Brad over her head onto the woman. Brad dropped too, outmaneuvering Renzie. He yanked her to the right and she had to let go of Sara.

"Damn it, Renzie, cut it out," he said, staggering from his knees to his feet, bringing her up with him.

"Get her to cut it out," Renzie panted. "She started it."

As if that were a cue Sara surged to her feet, punching out at Renzie. Brad swung Renzie out of reach.

"Lay off, Sara," he yelled at the other woman.

The puffy-looking older man had finally decided to get in on the action and clambered down from the first wagon. He grabbed Sara's arms and pulled her back.

Still held by Brad, Renzie muscled her position around to face Sara again. "You think these are such wonderful people, worth starting fights for?" she spat. "You seem pretty impassioned. Has Old George indoctrinated you into a little incest, too?"

The woman turned fish-belly white and almost wrenched herself free. George tried to reach out with one hand to slap at Renzie. "Shut up," he said. "Shut your filthy mouth."

Renzie didn't move. She just laughed at him. "Shut up? Why? You think people don't remember? You forget it's not a big secret. You just wish it were." She turned her head back toward Sara. "Don't take my word for it. While you're visiting you can ask anybody who lived in the House back then. They'll tell you." She shook her shoulders against Brad's grip. He looked around at the gathered crowd and let her go.

Brad pulled Sara away from George. "Come on," he said, pushing her before him onto the seat of his wagon.

The older man stood for a moment staring at Renzie. Then he too climbed up and the small caravan headed down the aisle. The throng of people ebbed away.

Jan examined Renzie's face. Renzie's lip was cut and bleeding, beginning to puff up. Her jawline was abraded too, probably from when she'd rolled off Sara.

"It doesn't look as though you're going to need stitches for that," said Jan, "but I think I'd better get ice and rubbing alcohol, maybe some poultices, too. Sit down here till I get back."

"Who the hell were they? What was that all about?" Nesta asked.

Although Renzie held herself rigidly, she couldn't stop shaking. "I've never met that woman before. The others were the rest of my family."

The older woman studied Renzie, trying to grasp this new aspect of her. A capable, outgoing, take-charge young woman; Nesta would never have suspected her of being an incest victim. "Your father molested . . . ?" She couldn't make herself finish.

"Shit. All that dirty laundry aired in public." Renzie groaned and rubbed at her scalp where a lump would probably rise. "It's not *quite* as bad as I made it sound. Ginny and Brad's parents Vanished. Old George took them in. Later he and my mother Margaret ended up together and Tuck and I came along."

Renzie whacked at the dust on her pants and shirt sleeves. "Would you brush the dirt off my back?" she asked.

As Nesta obliged, she continued. "Old George thought he was raising us as one big happy family. Except that he always treated Ginny and Brad differently from me and Tuck. As if because they'd lived through the Vanishing they had some sort of exemption, like they were born holy or something.

"When I was fifteen, I . . . uh, had an affair with Brad." She looked down for a moment. Nesta couldn't see her face. "Old George walked in on us one day, threw a real scene. Accused me of being incestuous with Brad, like it was fucking my brother, fucking Tuck. Things got worse from there. Anyway, a couple of months later they packed up and moved to Santa Cruz, started a family cooperative as fish drovers. Tuck and I stayed here."

"Here we go." Jan had returned with clean rags, bandages, and alcohol. "Roll up your sleeve and let me get at that scrape."

Renzie let out a long, pained sigh as Jan swabbed her with the alcohol. "Anyway, it's old news. They took off . . ." She thought a moment. "I guess about thirteen years ago. We've seen Old George maybe three times since, but this is the first time he's brought the whole brood with him." She rubbed at her arm. "I'd better go back to the House and get cleaned up. You two don't have to leave off here just because of me."

Jan shrugged. "We've made a pretty complete circuit except for the livestock exhibit. I'd like to rest up if I'm going to be collecting data tonight."

"Me, too," Nesta said.

"A crash pad's been set up in the Grand Ballroom for visitors," Renzie said.

"Sounds good to me," said Jan.

"My Home's just a few blocks away," Nesta said. "I'll be able to rest better in my own surroundings."

Renzie finally smiled at Nesta's usual skittishness where the House was concerned. "Suit yourself," she said. "But don't forget, the party's still on. Just come to the courtyard around sunset and we'll go over together."

"What about your family? Aren't you afraid of running into them?"

Renzie shook her head. "They won't have been invited."

"All right then, you're on." As Renzie stood up Nesta looked around. The crowd had long since dispersed and the smell of dried fish, wet seaweed, and horses had given way to the musty odor of the book stalls again.

She scanned the volumes disinterestedly as she helped Renzie up, dusted her off a little more. Nesta thought she remembered something of *The Mayor of Castlebridge;* that it was a tragedy about a deserting father who later tries to make amends to his abandoned daughter. Nesta looked after Renzie, trudging her way back to the House, and wanted to weep for all the children scarred by their parents in the aftermath of the Vanishing.

CHAPTER TEN

Renzie managed to commandeer a hot tub for herself, although the baths had begun to fill up with travelers anxious to rinse off the grime of their journey and soak away the aches of hours of walking, riding, or driving. She didn't have to defend her privacy. Her surly expression and the cuts and scrapes kept other bathers at bay.

She tilted her head back against the rim of the tub, slid her body across its length to rest her feet on the opposite seat, and sighed to herself. The heat of the water seeped deep into muscle and bone.

She'd referred to the incident as old news, but it wasn't. Something always brought it back: passing through a déjà vu spot in the House, a hunching, defensive gesture from Tuck, or just waking in the middle of the night, open and vulnerable to thoughts and remembrances normally walled out.

Old George had made the issue of love and sex confusing. Sometimes he harangued them that they must never fall in love—to give your heart to someone meant losing it along with them in the next Vanishing. Better not to risk it in the first place.

But George suffered from selective amnesia. At other times he'd expound at length, saying that in any form of involvement, whether in friendship or love, they should connect, commit, and love fully each and every time they were with others. Because after all, those others might Vanish the next night, and the time you spent with them now might be the only time you'd get. He never actually mentioned his lost first family, but the source of his anguish was clear.

All of this had been force-fed to them with the rest of Old George's paranoid philosophy of survival. Margaret's presence tempered his extremes. Just to look up and see her leaning in the doorway, smiling sardonically, was often enough to silence him. At other times he'd keep going. Margaret would frown or say, "Enough, George," or at her sharpest, "Quit being such a fucking terrorist, George. They're only children." Renzie thought later that much of what George said must have hurt her mother. For if Margaret had Vanished he might have been sorry, but not devastated. Renzie thought that was one of the reasons he'd stop, embarrassed, when she appeared.

By the time Renzie entered puberty Margaret was gone. Ginny had assumed the role of big sister/little mother. Old George at last held sway alone and unchallenged. For a few years he seemed quieter. Renzie believed he felt guilty for the way he'd treated Margaret.

Renzie was concerned with other matters than her father by then.

She knew about puberty, of course, just as she knew about midwifery, how to perform a tracheotomy, CPR and menopause.

But knowing that her breasts would grow didn't prepare her for the aching and swelling. Or that hormones kicking in would change everything about her body, making her acutely self-conscious. To be told that she'd go through mood shifts didn't equip her for the soaring highs and plunging bleak lows. At her most despondent she thought her adolescence to be different from everybody else's: a genetic factor must have kicked in, causing her to mutate into an emotional monster like her father.

Puberty was supposed to be accompanied by an interest in boys. As if proof of her deviation, Renzie instead experienced shyness, fear, and revulsion of even childhood friends like Kip, and men she'd always looked up to and adored, like Eric and Hake.

The only males she felt comfortable with were Tuck and Brad; Tuck because he was her little brother. Brad, because in this, as in everything else, he was exempt.

Renzie knew when and how it started. One afternoon she, Tuck, and Brad were hanging around, doing nothing in particular. They'd spent the morning together in the lab with three or four other House children monitoring penicillin cultures. Afterward the three of them grabbed sandwiches from the kitchen and gravitated to the family's living area, a remodeled suite of servant quarters on the far side of the Northern Conservatory.

"Where's Old George?" Renzie asked, lounging back on a raft of floor cushions.

"He's away 'doing maintenance,' " Tuck said, their euphemism for the times when Old George went off to caretake his shrine of a Home.

Renzie wrinkled her nose but let it go. Her father's obsession with his past still rankled. But since it was unavoidable and unchangeable, dwelling on it only punished herself. The sweet side of it was Old George's guaranteed absence for hours.

She looked around for her other source of irritation—Ginny. "Where's your sister, Brad?"

"George took her with him to work on both the Homes," Brad said. "They won't be back till late."

George did that sometimes. He often took Brad too, determined that his foster children's upbringing included knowledge of their pre-Vanishment heritage.

Tuck and Renzie didn't have a Home they'd be expected to enshrine, no expectations of a glorious Great Return. If Old George's first wife and children ever did Return, Renzie and Tuck knew that the two of them would be expected to disappear from Old George's life as completely as if they themselves had Vanished.

When she felt Brad looking at her, Renzie realized her face must have twisted into a reflection of her resentment. Then she felt *how* he was looking at her; with sympathy, as if he understood how orphaned she and Tuck often felt.

No one had ever looked at her like that, that she could remember.

Over the next few weeks Renzie noticed things about Brad she'd never paid attention to before. His patience. His gentleness. How calm he was, not allowing himself to be touched in any way when the rest of the family lashed out at each other. She found herself trying to copy him. She couldn't understand how she'd thought of him before as bland and indifferent. Now she realized that he was the only one of their family who'd found a way to survive intact.

Then there was the not unpleasant, prickling sensation when she saw that while she studied him, he was studying her.

They began to run into each other at places and times outside the usual family trajectory, as if they were two planets linked in an erratic orbit. One evening they encountered each other behind the machinery shed. They dazedly sank into a kiss as if plunged together down a gravity well.

After that their paths synchronized and aligned. They met in private and hidden places. They patiently and impatiently surrendered a little more of their souls, a little more of their flesh to each other each time, until they'd gladly relinquished everything.

After making love one night in the backyard of a deserted Home, Brad amazed Renzie by dancing around her buck naked, penis flapping like a handless puppet, chanting-singing, "She loves me, I love her, Renzie loves me, I love Renzie," absolutely proud in his ludicrousness.

"What on earth are you doing?"

"I'm telling the universe I love you. The universe has got to know."

"Oh, yeah?" Renzie giggled, at her age unable to find any other way to express the overwhelming tenderness she felt for him. "Come here and prove it."

Brad may have proclaimed his devotion to the universe, but only that single night's universe and Tuck ever knew. They went to laughable extremes to keep the relationship hidden. Not because it was something to be ashamed of, but because it was so vulnerable, precious and fresh.

"How can you love me?" she asked Brad. "You're perfect, so gentle and patient. I'm always so angry."

"I like your rages. They're magnificent. They're a force of nature, like you. Just don't ever get angry at me."

—————
—————
—

It was the middle of a mellow fall morning when Old George walked in on them.

Renzie was curled up in her little room with a pile of textbooks, the door ajar to the family room to let in light and air. Behind in his homework, Tuck had shut himself into the room that he and Brad shared. When Renzie heard someone moving around in the living quarters, she didn't let the sounds interrupt her concentration, assuming Tuck had stopped to take a break.

The door to her room swung open. Brad peered in. "Recess time, schoolgirl," he said as he plunked himself down on her mattress and tugged at the drawstrings on her pants.

"Cut that out!" Renzie slapped at his hands. "What are you doing here? You're supposed to be bulldozing a Home."

"Funny thing, my machine all of a sudden stopped working. I came back to retool a part at the tool and die shop." He stood up to slide her pants off, simultaneously reaching behind himself to shut the door.

"Stop it!" Renzie kicked at him, laughing. "What about George?"

"He's busy elsewhere." Brad had knelt beside her, worrying at the buttons of her shirt. He grabbed her and rolled her over so that she lay on top of him. He licked along the side of her face.

Renzie sat up, reached for her pillow, and hit him with it. "You're obscene!"

Hands stroking Renzie's thighs where they framed his hips, Brad's face became wistful, serious. "Only with you." He sat up against her to shed her shirt and kiss her in the same motion.

They'd never made love in the daytime before. The warmth of the Indian summer day had already risen to the third-floor rooms. Their bodies were soon slick with sweat. Renzie shut her eyes tightly to block out any sensation other than movement and touch.

The door crashed behind them. Renzie's eyes flew open. Brad half rose and turned to look over his shoulder, disengaging from her as he did so. Then he was pulled backward and off her, crashing into the wall, the top sheet tangled about his legs. Old George stood between them, a look of revulsion stamped on his face as he wiped the sweat from Brad's shoulder off on his pants.

"How could you?" he roared. "The two of you! Sick . . ." He back-handed Brad.

Brad turned white as milk, pulled up the sheet to cover his groin. "George, I'm sorry," he gasped.

George leaned forward as if he were going to pick Brad up by his collar and punch him, then hesitated, stymied by Brad's lack of clothing. He raised his hand to slap Brad again.

"Stop it!" Renzie screamed. "We haven't done anything wrong! What's the matter with you?"

Her father turned on her. His arm shot out. He grabbed a thick handful of her hair and pulled her to him. She drew her fists up to punch him. Old George batted the blows away with his free hand.

"Haven't done anything wrong?" His scream matched hers. "Look at him!" He swung her around to look at Brad. *"He* knows the two of you did something wrong. Why don't *you,* you little whore?" George tried to slap Renzie too, but she kept her forearms up and in the way, so he shook her by her hair, cranking her neck tight. "I raised you as a family, like brother and sister, and this is how you end up, fucking like weasels? Like dogs? Dogs don't care how they fuck each other."

Horribly, most horribly of all, Old George began to cry. "Incest, haven't you ever heard of incest? I-n-c-e-s-t." He spelled it out, spitting the words in her face.

Behind him Renzie saw Tuck and Ginny crowd into the narrow doorway. The look on Tuck's face made her feel ill. Suddenly she was conscious of her naked, sweaty body. She heard running footsteps approaching in the distance.

"Stop it!" she shouted, trying to reach Old George through sheer volume of noise. "That's not true! We haven't done anything wrong. We're not brother and sister."

"That doesn't make any difference!" He commenced shaking her again and finally managed to get in a solid slap to the side of her face. Renzie wondered dizzily if he'd snap her neck before he stopped yelling at her, wondered if he'd even notice. "I raised you as brother and sister, you've lived as brother and sister, you're the same as brother and sister."

Renzie'd thought Old George was unconscious of Tuck and Ginny's presence, but suddenly her father reached behind, grabbed Tuck and hauled him around, oblivious to Tuck's punches and kicks as the boy struggled to free himself. He shoved Tuck up face to face with Renzie.

"So what were you going to do, fuck him next?" He shook Tuck in Renzie's face as if her brother were an overgrown marionette. "Is this what you were working your way around to next? Want me to help you? Want me to pull his pants down for you?"

Tuck thrashed like a trapped animal, eyes blanked in blind panic, face blushing scarlet. Renzie started to cry, miserably conscious of being jammed up naked against Tuck as if in proof of Old George's rantings.

"Stop it, stop it, stop it," she screamed.

At some point her litany became a chorus. A deeper set of "Stop it, stop it," overlapped her own.

"All right, George, if you *won't* stop it and drop those kids right now, I'm going to have to brain you with a two-by-four." It was Hake's voice. George turned. Hake and Eric stood behind him, Jorda peering between them. Eric grabbed George's arm and began prying his fingers loose from Tuck.

George dropped Renzie and Tuck. As Renzie started to fall to her knees on the bedding Jorda slid past Old George and braced her up.

Eric turned around to the family room now crowded with House folk. "It's okay, it's over," he said.

Ginny started fluttering and shooing people out.

"It was just an argument, nobody's hurt," Renzie heard Ginny say, even though over Jorda's shoulder Renzie could see that the side of Brad's face looked swollen and bruised, George's cheeks were scratched and bleeding where she must have reached him after all, and one of her own eyes felt puffy and was beginning to close.

Jorda pulled up the bottom sheet of the bedding and wrapped it around Renzie.

"Jorda, bring her here," Eric said. "George, you owe your children an apology. You were born with a brain, man. Use it."

George didn't defend himself. He wouldn't say anything. Tuck sat slumped on the floor, staring at the ground. Renzie couldn't stop weeping, which made her furious with herself. She buried her face against Jorda's shoulder. Above the sounds of her own sobs, she heard Brad crying too, saying over and over, "George, I'm sorry, I'm sorry."

Renzie shifted in the hot tub. Her neck ached—she'd left it resting against the edge of the tub too long. She raised her hands to rub the back of her neck.

Old George visited every few years on business, and that was bad enough. But having the whole clan descend was unbearable. Thirteen years had passed and the wounds were still fresh.

Someone was climbing the side of the embankment approaching her tub. Renzie prepared herself to glare again. She was brought up short when Nesta leaned over the edge.

"You said you were going back to your place to rest."

"I did," Nesta said. "And I did. But I decided that if I was going to attend a party tonight that I wanted to get cleaned up. May I join you?"

Renzie was intrigued at the thought of Nesta willingly bathing in broad daylight. "Sure."

Nesta carefully slid into the steeping water. "I could get used to this," she sighed.

Renzie opened her mouth, but before she could speak Nesta waved a hand at her. "You can save the pitch. Yes, yes, yes, I'm sure I'll move here eventually."

Renzie closed her eyes, grateful to have her bitter reminiscences interrupted. They relaxed in silence for a while. Nesta was so quiet that Renzie wondered if she'd fallen asleep. When she opened her eyes to check on the older woman she found Nesta studying her.

A trace of Renzie's irritation returned. "Have I sprouted wings in the last few minutes, or broken out in polka dots?" She remembered the abrasions on her jaw and touched the area gingerly, feeling the welts that had risen. "Well, maybe the polka dots, I guess."

Nesta was already red enough from the steam that Renzie couldn't tell if she blushed or not, but she did have the grace to look embarrassed.

"I was worried about you," the older woman admitted. "I wanted to see how you were. When someone takes a hard fall like you did, onto asphalt, they can sustain injuries to their neck and back and not know it for hours."

Renzie turned her head to the right and left. Was her neck sore from the tub rim, or from the fight? She was touched by Nesta's concern.

"I think I'm okay."

Renzie studied Nesta in turn. In her sharp-faced thinness and constant curiosity, Nesta reminded Renzie a bit of her mother, Margaret. There was always that desire to know everything.

"That's not all, is it?" Renzie asked.

"No," admitted Nesta. "I've been thinking about what happened today, the fight. It's been bothering me. You said that things got worse before your father finally left, but I can't imagine, after what your father laid on you and Tuck . . ."

Renzie hunched in on herself.

Nesta touched Renzie's arm. "I'm sorry. I shouldn't have brought it up. Please forgive my curiosity."

Renzie shook her head. "It's not like it's any big secret. Everybody living in the House at the time knew about it—couldn't help but know about it. That's why Old George backed off today when I threw it up to him."

She shifted on her perch in the tub. The movement drew a current of hotter water across her chest.

"I ran away for a while, a little over a month. But I kept worrying about leaving Tuck with George, especially after the things Old George had said, so I came back. But for that same reason it was uncomfortable at first. I'll never forgive Old George for making Tuck and me feel that way about each other." Renzie riffled her fingers through the water, raising small fretful waves.

"I moved into a room down the hall from the rest of them. Old George had been humiliated by the whole House knowing about the fight. Tuck said that George was also scared when I ran away—I might have come to harm and it would have been on his head. So somehow or other we declared an unspoken truce. No one, but *no one* ever talked about the incident."

"What about Brad?" asked Nesta.

"Nothing about Brad. He acted as if I were invisible. I acted as if he were invisible. Tuck was furious. He told me later, after they'd all moved away, that Brad never once stuck up for me, even when I was missing." Renzie couldn't keep the bitterness from her voice.

"Things were quiet for several weeks. I even began to believe that maybe in a horrible way the blowup had been a good thing. That it was so awful that it had scared us all into changing, even Old George.

"One morning about three weeks after I got back Old George called us all together, sent Tuck to fetch me. Brad brought up coffee, tea, and muffins from the kitchen. George had us all sit down together and get cozy.

"Once we did that he launched into one of his long lectures about the Vanishing. But this one was different. It started out as a confession.

"Old George said he'd been crazy ever since the Vanishing, that it had changed him into someone completely different from the person he'd been before. He talked about his first wife and kids and started crying . . . said they wouldn't recognize him, wouldn't want him the way he was now." Renzie shook her head. "Old George had *never* talked about them directly before.

"After that he—no surprise—justified himself: He'd changed in order to survive, so he could protect all of us. Now he wanted to change back to who he was before, the person he *really* was. He said he'd needed something outside of himself to jolt him. That's why he'd brought us all together, to acknowledge that.

"For a moment I actually thought he was going to apologize to me and Tuck and Brad. That the old monster was going to admit he'd been wrong. Next to me, I could feel Tuck tensing up. I remember putting my hand on top of his and almost yanking it back, his hand was so cold. *He* knew better.

"George said he owed this big change he was going through to one event, one person. Then he turned to Ginny and started blubbering like an infant. He told us that he was in love with Ginny . . . he actually used the words 'transformed by love.' She'd made him realize he could 'finally leave his past behind.' I wanted to jump up and start screaming, but I was too numb.

"Then Old George said, 'There's more.' I thought, please dear God, not more. George looked at Ginny again, both of them as happy and moist as a pair of overfed walrus. 'Ginny's expecting,' he said. 'She's carrying my baby.'

"I wound up tight as a spring. I remember asking how long till the baby was due.

"Old George was in such a syrupy fog that it went right past him. But I could see Ginny's antenna pick up, and Brad practically disappeared inside himself. 'Only five more months,' Old George said, all moony."

For a few minutes Renzie couldn't speak. She became so still that the surface of the water flattened to glass.

Then, at last, "I exploded. I jumped to my feet and started screaming that if two months ago I had been accused of incest for sleeping with Brad because he was supposed to be 'just like a brother' to me, wouldn't that make George's relationship with Ginny the same as father and daughter? So who did he think *he* was to have beaten me and given me a hard time? And if by his own logic *my* next step would have been to sleep with Tuck, my real brother, then did he intend to move on from Ginny to me, his real daughter?

"By the time I finished I could hear people running up the stairs and down the hallway toward us again.

"Apparently Old George didn't hear them. He leapt up and grabbed me. This time I was ready for him." Renzie started laughing. "I hauled off and punched him in the nose as hard as I could. Broke it, too. There was blood all over. Hot Rod and Eric came crashing through the door. They found George hanging on to me with one hand and his nose with the other.

"I was still shrieking like a banshee telling him to go on, to put his hands all over me, and did he want me to lie down right there and spread my legs for him? Old George dropped me like a scalded cat.

"That should have been it. It should have been over right there. I was laughing and crying at the same time. I hugged Tuck so hard his feet left the ground.

"Then I turned to Brad. I started babbling at him: I knew that it was going to be okay now for the two of us. That we could be together again and Old George couldn't stand in our way.

"Brad didn't say anything. He wouldn't look at me. I was the last person in the room to figure it out; after Tuck, Eric, Hot Rod . . . even Old George.

"You could tell by the way Brad just sat there that he'd known about Ginny and George all along. Of course he would. Tuck and I shared all our secrets. So had Brad and Ginny. How else would he have always known when it was safe to be with me?

"I just stared at Brad as the light dawned. Brad had said he loved me. Yet Brad had let George beat on me when he knew Old George had no right to, even by George's own standards. It suddenly struck me that Brad was worse than George.

"I grabbed the edge of the table and heaved it over. Hot coffee and tea went soaring. The plate of muffins flipped onto Ginny's chest. I snatched up a chair and tried to smash it over Brad's head, but he rolled out of the way just in time. I grabbed every loose object I could lay my hands on and let fly.

"Hot Rod and Eric must have yanked them all out of there because after a while I realized I was alone in a room that looked like a cyclone had hit it. I'd broken the windows, left holes in the wall. I sat down in the middle of the wreckage and sobbed and sobbed. Tuck must have been waiting all that time out in the hallway. He came in and held me for hours while I cried."

The water was slapping in agitation against the sides of the tub.

Renzie looked up at Nesta. The older woman's face was drawn. Renzie could see that she wanted to ask "And what then?" but couldn't bring herself to say the words.

"After I wrecked the room, George and Ginny and Brad didn't have any place to stay till it was repaired. The House was occupied full-up at that point. People here never particularly liked my father, except for Eric, who knew him from before the Vanishing. So no one would take them in. Old George saw the writing on the wall. The three of them took off for Santa Cruz, set themselves up as drovers."

"I'm sorry," said Nesta.

"Don't be. Me and Tuck were happy to see them go."

"No, I'm sorry that they're back."

Renzie massaged the tension in the back of her neck again. Her hands as she raised them were wrinkled as raisins from the water's long poaching. She smiled. "It doesn't matter. That's where I was so stupid today, getting into that fight, because they aren't back for long."

"Who's not back for long?"

Both Renzie and Nesta jumped. Minda, naked as an eel, leaned over the edge of the tub. There'd been no sound of her scrambling up the slope toward them.

She hopped into the water, not waiting for an answer.

> *"Rub a dub dub, six men in a tub,*
> *And who do you think they be?*
> *The butcher, the baker, the candlestick maker,*
> *And Renzie, and Nesta, and me.*

You look like two prunes," she declared. "How long have you been sitting here? Don't you know it's almost time to get ready to go to the party?"

CHAPTER ELEVEN

Tuck woke to a soft gliding sensation. Le Chell bent over him, sweeping his face with the tip of her auburn pigtail. Not fully emerged from the velvet of sleep, he gently brushed a stray strand of hair away from her forehead, let his fingers linger against her freckle-dappled cheek.

Le Chell grinned down at him. "Wake up, sleepyhead. That was some nap."

Tuck stretched. "You wore me out, insatiable wench." He turned his head dreamily to look out the window. His room perched over the long limb of the greenhouse, with a view of the tops of a row of date palms. The sky held the softened late-afternoon glow that at this time of the year—the downhill side of summer—meant it was very late indeed. He sat bolt upright. "Oh Lord!" he said. "What time is it?"

Tuck noticed guiltily that Le Chell had already dressed.

"Moving on toward seven o'clock, I'd guess," she said. She unbraided her hair and carefully unmatted the tangles she always collected during lovemaking. "I need to be getting back before I go on duty." She tapped his chest with one finger, turned it into a caress. "And you need to pull yourself together for the Office Building party. You should look up Renzie and see if she's okay, take her with you." Le Chell had run to fetch him at the beginning of the fight that afternoon. By the time they returned to the scene the fray was over and Renzie gone.

Tuck pulled Le Chell back against him and nuzzled her. "It's still light and you've got a long evening to go," he said. "Rest here—I'll look after you. There's time for that." He knew she'd made herself stay awake to guard him when he'd fallen asleep after they made love; and that she'd need to take a nap herself before her Watch began.

Le Chell shook her head as she drew away from him. She never stayed to sleep with him in the House. She grinned at his expression. "Don't look so wounded. You know I trust you. I know you wouldn't conk out on me or leave me while I slept." She gestured, taking in the small room, its privacy. "I just can't get . . . comfortable enough to sleep here."

He understood—just as he couldn't feel comfortable enough to sleep when he tried staying with her overnight in the Domes. He'd lie there holding her, surrounded on all sides by the other sleepers, far too aware of floating like part of some spreading Sargasso Sea of humanity. Le Chell would wake sometimes and laugh at him drowsily.

"You don't have to stay up to look after me. We're being Watched over. We're safe here. That's the point." She'd nestle up against him and go back to sleep.

Tuck would lie staring at the ceiling all night; making an hours-long study of the fineness of Le Chell's bones as he held her, light as those of an injured seagull he'd once rescued on an outing to the Alviso Slough.

In the morning he'd stagger back to the House to catch a few hours' sleep, in the same way that Le Chell was returning to the Watchers' Domes now for rest.

He watched as Le Chell brushed her hair straight back over her shoulders. Its iridescence cast scarlet shadows on the white pullover she wore. "Why don't I come over to the Domes tonight and party with you instead," he said, "help you Watch?" He gestured to her for the brush. She handed it over and rearranged herself so that she sat with her back to him. Tuck stroked her hair with one hand as he drew the brush's bristles through the thick red mane with the other. It flowed through his palms with the soft, smooth, heavy weight of water.

Le Chell sat straight-backed, holding herself still for him. "No, you go over to the party," she said. "This is the time to catch up with old friends. We're busy at the Domes too, you know. Other Watchers from as far away as Union City and Monterey are staying with us during the fair. The sleeping floor is completely jammed and we've all got extra duties. You wouldn't have any fun. You'd just be in the way."

She turned around, kissed the tip of his nose, then got up and stretched. "Go to the party and have a good time." She grinned at him. "Just be sure to tell me all the gossip tomorrow."

Tuck went looking for Renzie in her hayloft eave rooms. She wasn't there. He sat back on her bedding, made himself comfortable and cleared his mind. Sometimes he swore he could sense his sister, triangulate her whereabouts, as if the House somehow acted to amplify and home in on her presence.

But today Tuck felt nothing.

He headed for the kitchens. Maybe someone there had seen Renzie. Besides, he was hungry. His hours with Le Chell had carried them through the regular dinner hour and the Office party would be long on beverages, short on food.

Jorda had Chloe, Sun, and some newcomers hard at work kneading dough. The House would be preparing food around the clock for the duration of the fair.

"Any leftovers you can spare?" Tuck asked.

"Check the pantry," Jorda said as she measured out ingredients for a batch of cinnamon sticky rolls. Tuck sniffed at a jar of the sienna-colored spice and thought of Le Chell. "Seen Renzie around?" he asked. He scooped brown rice into a bowl and poured some ratatouille over it.

"A long time ago, in the baths," said Jorda. "Even from a distance she looked to be in a foul mood. Sure you want to find her?"

Tuck thought of Renzie confronting Old George's clan alone without him. "Yes, especially now."

Sun looked up from pummeling a huge, mealy lump. "She ate dinner with the old lady and that kid. They ate out on the porch together." Sun turned back to his task and dealt the wad a vigorous blow. "Looked like someone had given your sister a real hard time, bounced her around a bunch," he said with satisfaction.

Tuck sighed and wished that Renzie and Sun weren't antagonists. But if anyone was likely to know Renzie's whereabouts it would be Sun, if only to avoid her. "Thanks," he said to Sun. "That kid . . . you mean Minda?"

"That's the one," Sun said without turning around.

Minda's room was close by—just out the hallway from the kitchen, around the concrete-floored area where long ago horse-drawn carriages had entered the House to discharge passengers safely out of the rain. Tuck walked past and then through glass doors and down another hallway. As he made an abrupt right-hand turn into a last short passageway he listened for voices. Even if Renzie wasn't there, Minda might be able to tell him where his sister had gone to.

"Minda, you there?" he called out. She didn't answer. Maybe she was napping.

Most of the other children lived together in the old gift shop. Minda had chosen otherwise, picking a space almost as unlikely as the Krit's drafty aerie. As far as anyone knew, in the whole history of the House she was the first person ever to live on the Stairs-to-Nowhere.

Tuck peered around the corner at the end of the hallway. "Minda?" he whispered.

Bright-colored cushions lay piled deeply at the base of the stairs, obliterating the first six or seven steps. A section of sturdy railing nailed across the base of the stairs kept the pillows from avalanching into the hallway. Tuck had thought he might find Minda curled up asleep like a dormouse in this nest, but the pillows were empty.

The remainder of the stairway marched straight up to end abruptly at the ceiling. Clothes, books, and the collected knickknacks so precious to children perched tidily along the right side of the steps, the left side remaining clear to serve as a pathway. A net of acrylic loops slung from the ceiling provided the only light in the stairwell.

Tuck imagined Minda sitting as neatly on the steps as her possessions. He smiled. The thought reminded him of one of the nursery rhymes his mother, Margaret, used to recite to him and Renzie.

> *Halfway up the stairs*
> *Is the place where I always sit.*
> *And there's no other place*
> *Quite like it.*

CHAPTER TWELVE

By the time Tuck walked over to the Office Buildings the day was releasing its final stored residues of heat. Trading for the day had wound down hours before. Stalls were covered up. Visiting vendors gathered around barbecue pits cooking their evening meal or unrolling bedrolls in preparation for camping out. The asphalt roadway exhaled its hot, pungent breath, toasting Tuck's toes where they overhung the edges of his sandals. A few merchants, recognizing Tuck, called out greetings. He hailed them back with a wave of his arm. Ahead of him a boisterous group of Orindans made their way to the Office Buildings, laughing and joking.

A derelict garden restaurant hemmed the first floor of the closest Office Building like a torn, bedraggled skirt. Tuck walked around it to the south side entrance and pushed open the heavy metal doors. The room they swung in on must have been a sleekly spacious lobby once. Now it resembled a cubistic jungle bisected by a single clear corridor.

When survivors of the Vanishing initially settled into the building they'd needed to protect themselves from marauders, looters, and the grief-mad. For their first line of defense they'd dismantled office partitions in some of the upper floors, reconstructed them into a maze in the lobby and mined the passages with booby traps.

Years passed and life stabilized. Eventually the Office dwellers felt secure enough to remove the snares and dismantle the maze's central set of panels, cutting a swath straight through it to the back hallway and stairwells, opening up the labyrinth and revealing its secrets for all to see, like the honeycombed entrails of a halved pomegranate. Partitions were cannibalized as needed. The remnants filled up with debris and stored junk. As he passed Tuck heard the rustling of the maze's current tenants—bandicoots, palm rats, and lemurs—in its far corners.

Tuck opened another unwieldy metal door in the back hallway and trudged up three flights of stark concrete stairwell.

Lively noises muffled by distance greeted him on the third-floor landing. Tuck opened the door and peered down a dimly lit corridor. He slipped off his sandals, tossed them to the edge of a big pile of shoes accumulated inside the door.

He made his way down a "hallway" created by rows of office cubicles and filing cabinets, resisting the impulse to track his progress by counting off sets of modules as he passed. Like most House dwellers, Tuck felt off balance when he visited the Office Buildings. The anonymous repetitiveness of the passageways mesmerized and confused him.

Sound and an increasing glow led him to a huge conference room constructed of thick, water-quavery glass bricks. Light wavered out of it, illuminating a few people sitting outside in the dim hallway, their backs propped against the wall—the usual refuge for anyone wanting private or quiet conversation. When Tuck opened the conference-room door paint-thick light and sound washed out over them, further muting their presence.

Inside, a good mix of people of all ages milled about laughing and joking, hoisting earthenware mugs filled with wine, juice, or punch. Tuck saw Renzie immediately, sitting with Nesta, Hake, Hot Rod, Kip, Pel and some of the Orindans on bleachers jerry-rigged from stacked and carpet-covered filing cabinets. Pel had brought one of his bull terriers with him, the female—its stark white bat-eared face bobbed up and down with excitement between the Chicano and Hake.

Tuck started to climb up to join his sister. A heavy hand stopped him. "You can't go any further without libation, son. Party rules. You know that." Templeton, a large man in his late forties built like an amiable sloth, was the spokesperson for the Office Buildings. He flourished a mug toward three water coolers parked against the wall. The fruity red, orange, and rose colors of their contents reflected along the glass partition like a fluttering cool fire.

"I'll take wine, thanks," Tuck said.

Templeton leaned over to fill the mug, gripping the handle in his fingers and stretching his long thumb to trigger the spigot. He didn't relinquish his grip on Tuck with his other hand, as if afraid Tuck would escape his hostmanship. Not till the wine trembled right at the rim, held in only by surface tension, did Templeton present it to Tuck as if in blessing.

"Thank you," Tuck said.

Templeton didn't let go. "Honor the Buildings," he chided.

Tuck sighed and downed the cup in three gulps. Templeton beamed his approval. The big man took the mug from Tuck and filled it again. Only then did he release Tuck.

Tuck slurped enough of the wine so he could climb the risers without spilling, but he still had to balance gingerly as he clambered up the bleachers. The wine coated the back of his mouth with a pleasantly gritty, grapey film, warming him.

From several risers away he could see Renzie's swollen lip and the abrasions on her jaw. In spite of the room's warmth she wore a long-sleeved shirt with the sleeves rolled down—Tuck guessed to hide new bruises.

A young woman on Renzie's right, twisted around to talk to Kip and Nesta, turned as Tuck joined them. Tuck recognized the dark curls and narrow-boned features. "Hi, Sepulveda," he said.

"Hello, stranger! Where have you been? We kept expecting to run into you all afternoon," she said.

Tuck thought of the hours spent in bed with Le Chell. His cheeks burned. The blush spread and deepened as Sepulveda leapt up and hugged him. When she sat back down she squeezed over to make room between herself and Renzie.

"Uh, thanks," Tuck said as he wedged himself in.

Renzie arched her eyebrows. Tuck wanted to elbow her in the ribs but he was pinned in too tightly. He tried to shift around. Sepulveda adjusted herself to give him more room by turning sideways toward him and draping her arm over his shoulders. Renzie watched with evident amusement.

"Hi, Tuck, it's good to see you again." Sepulveda's brother Bolivar had clambered up and around them to sit behind Renzie. The big Orindan leaned Renzie back against his knees and began massaging her scalp, combing through her hair with blunt, strong fingers. Renzie let her head fall back and closed her eyes. "Lord, that feels great," she sighed.

Snakelike, Sepulveda had twined herself around again to resume explaining the Orindan economics of solar "barons" and glass technicians to Nesta, with Kip's help. Her arm still rested across Tuck's back. Her hand stroked his shoulder. The sensation was pleasant; pleasant enough to make Tuck feel uncomfortable. He studiously sipped at his wine.

"Are you ready for a refill?" Bolivar was asking Renzie. He turned to Tuck. "You look like you've hit bottom, too."

Tuck looked down at his empty mug with surprise. "Sure, thanks," he said and handed it over. "Can you handle three cups okay?" He remembered Sepulveda belatedly. "How about you? Are you ready for some more, Sep?"

"I am, but I think I'd like to go down with Bolivar. I could use to stretch my legs a bit." She caressed Tuck's knee as she stood. "I can take your mug with me," she said.

As soon as Bolivar and Sepulveda left, Renzie pounced on Tuck. "Where's Le Chell?"

"She's on the Watcher's shift tonight," Tuck said.

"Has she got you on a leash or something?"

Tuck watched Sepulveda and Bolivar walk past the coolers and approach Templeton. They talked with him briefly, then Templeton led the two Orindans out into the hall.

"No, no leash." Tuck put his head in his hands.

"You look miserable," Renzie said.

"I'm just confused. I've never felt like this before. I'm scared to death of . . ." He couldn't say, didn't know, of what.

Renzie huddled up to him and Tuck leaned against her in an old and comforting gesture. Renzie reached over and brushed a stray strand of hair away from his eyes. It reminded Tuck of the way he'd stroked Le Chell's face earlier in the day.

"Scared of losing her to a Vanishing?" Renzie asked softly.

Tuck snorted. No one believed in another Vanishing, not really. But when Renzie said that he felt faint pincers twinge his heart. "To another Vanishing, to somebody else, to getting bored with me . . . to anything."

Renzie whistled. "She must pitch a pretty witchy woo."

Tuck shrugged himself out of Renzie's embrace, then looked back apologetically so she'd know the impatience was for himself, not her. "When I sleep over there with Le Chell—" He corrected himself. *"Try to sleep with Le Chell, I can't. I love the way the Domes are part of her,* but I can't accept that Le Chell and I will never get to sleep alone, be alone there. And"—he hated to admit it—"I'm jealous of her fearlessness. I feel left out by it."

Renzie arched one eyebrow at him. "Does Le Chell know how you feel?"

"She thinks *I'm* the one who's courageous, because I sleep un-Watched. She doesn't feel any more comfortable in the House than I do in the Domes." He thought of Le Chell forcing herself to stay awake to guard him while he'd napped that afternoon.

Renzie reclined against the back of the riser, knotted her hands around one knee. "If you give it enough time . . ."

"That's just one small thing. The list goes on and on. I keep thinking, way behind it all . . ."

"What?"

"Nothing." Tuck shook his head.

Renzie leaned forward and cuffed him. "Tell me."

"You know. All that stuff Old George used to tell us, about partnering, falling in love, about getting wounded. I know it's all bullshit, but . . ."

"Tuck, Old George was the way he was because of the Vanishing, because his first wife and children Vanished." Renzie pulled him around to face her fully. "Don't let anything Old George said stop your life, okay?"

She poked him. "What are you smiling about? Am I amusing you or something?"

"No. It's just that you look exactly the same as when you used to stand up to Old George for me. You always seemed so big and ferocious. You'd fluff up to three times your size like a cat. I just realized how young, how little you really were."

That broke Renzie's stride. She reluctantly released a wry smile, but the sadness didn't ebb completely from her face.

A wave of heartsoreness for Renzie curled over Tuck. The closest Renzie had ever come to what he and Le Chell had was her affair with Brad.

Renzie nodded her head downward. "Looks like we're going to get something more to drink—at last." Bolivar and Sepulveda were finally climbing back up the bleachers.

The Orindans' knees knocked into Tuck's calves as they reached across to distribute the drinks.

"Templeton showed us a nice, untenanted suite of rooms," Sepulveda said. "A few of us are going to pick up and party over there for a while. C'mon."

Behind Tuck Bolivar bent over and murmured something to Renzie. She let the Orindan pull her up. Pel had caught on, too. He threw his dog's leash to Hake. "Watch out for Grendelyn for me." He winked at the black man. Hake accepted custody, sending Pel off with a resigned wave.

Tuck couldn't think of a quick, acceptable excuse. He buried his face in his wine cup. Renzie looked back at him. He shot her a pleading look. She plucked at Sepulveda's shirtsleeve and whispered in her ear. The Orindan nodded as she listened. She looked puzzled but was still smiling as Renzie drew her away. She waved goodbye to Tuck. "Guess we'll see you later," she said.

Hake had shifted to Tuck's other side. "Young as he is, I don't know how Pel manages lugging his dogs around. They're like stiff little overstuffed sofas," he said, lifting the bulky Grendelyn to sit between them.

She promptly laid her head on Tuck's lap and gazed at him adoringly. Tuck scratched behind her ears. "Yes, it's true," he told her. "You're a gorgeously ugly dog." Grendelyn wiggled with pleasure.

Down on the floor Templeton supervised the unloading of more beverages. A swarm of children played tag using clumps of tolerant adults as buffers. Tuck caught sight of Minda among them. Trailing the youngsters, not really included in their play, was a girl who looked vaguely familiar. The pack of kids streamed out of the party room and down away through the hallways, leaving the child drifting behind. Tuck remembered where he'd seen her before. She was the daughter of the Homer who'd fought with Sun in the dining room several weeks before.

Tuck tried to pay attention to Hake and Nesta's conversation—something about the physicist's work. But his thoughts kept drifting to the Watchers' Domes. He wondered if any of the visiting Watchers were old lovers of Le Chell's. Was that the real reason she hadn't wanted him to stay with her tonight?

Tuck looked down at his cup. He'd drained it again without realizing it. How much time had passed?

A cheerful commotion at the doorway caught his attention. Renzie, Sepulveda, Bolivar, Pel and the other revelers had returned.

"Have a good time?" Tuck asked Renzie. He noticed that Sepulveda had returned arm in arm with Kip. He thought of Le Chell and

felt a pang of jealousy: not of Kip and the Orindan, but at the thought
that Le Chell might be with somebody else.

"It's getting late," Hake observed, looking at the romping children.

"I'm ready to go," said Hot Rod. "I'll round them up." Although
it had been years, no one had forgotten how children had been stolen
as investments after the Vanishing.

"If you'll escort the batch from the Mall I'll take responsibility for
the House brats," Jorda said.

Hot Rod shook her hand. "You're on."

He called down to the children. "Listen up, you little yahoos.
Time to leave. Bedtime."

The youngsters wailed in unison, then jeered him good-naturedly.

"A story first," yelled Quill.

Hot Rod shook his head.

"Story, story, a story," the children chanted. "We won't leave
without a story."

The other adults in the room glanced around, distracted by the
excess noise.

"Okay, okay." Hot Rod threw up his hands. Jorda glared at him.
"Hake will tell you a story," the ponytailed mechanic said. The children
cheered. The other grown-ups relaxed. Like animals returning to graze
after an alarm, they bent their heads to their discussions again.

"Thanks a lot," said Hake. The children scrambled up to sur-
round him. "All right," he said. "What do you want? An old story, or
are you going to force me to make up a new one?"

"The zoo story," Minda piped. "I want the zoo story."

"Yeah, the zoo story," the others agreed in a chorus.

Hake's cheerful expression changed. "But Minda, you've all
heard that one before. It's a sad story."

"No it's not," said Minda. "It's just right. It's a good story."

Chupa, still set a little apart from the others, spoke up. "I've never
heard it before, but if it's a sad story, I don't want to hear it."

Good for you, thought Tuck. The other children drew further
away from her, stared her down.

"All right, all right." Hake resigned himself to the task.

"Right after the Vanishing," Hake began, "things were real quiet. The few people left sat around stunned with shock. After a couple of days things looked as though they were going to stay quiet.

"I got to thinking a lot—not much else to do. I didn't have to go to work anymore; nobody even came to unlock the building I worked in. I didn't have anyone to talk to. I lived up in San Francisco at the time, but I hadn't lived there long. The few people I knew well had been Taken. Didn't have to worry about sustenance, at least not for a while. Fresh food just sat around in the markets and other folks' houses and apartments, if you didn't mind unhinging your neighbor's doors.

"There seemed to be just me, a few muted folks drifting like ghosts, and the quiet. No streams of cars honking and screeching, crashing into each other. No sirens. No jets booming."

The children's eyes got big at this point, as they always did. They'd seen old movies made before the Vanishing, but it still seemed like make-believe. In their own lives, masses of cars brought to mind the image of slow, quiet, rusting decay.

"Of course, it wasn't completely silent," Hake continued. "I heard the empty rattling of garbage cans and trash clattering down the streets. Glass smashing or the wood of a door splintering when some survivor broke into a store; sometimes someone crying. This was *right* at first, you understand, before some of the survivors pulled themselves together and the rest went off the deep end."

He sighed and scratched Grendelyn's back down near the base of her tail. She tipped her blunt-pointed head up and skewed her eyes around in pleasure, licking the end of her nose spasmodically.

"But the worst of the sounds came from the dogs." Hake slapped Grendelyn's coat hard a couple of times to let her know the scratching was over. She banged her whiplike tail against the riser. "A lot of them were shut up in apartments and houses, scared to death without their owners, getting hungrier and hungrier, crying their hearts out. There were cats too, but not so many or so loud. A lot of them had been outdoors That Night. You could look out and see them going about the business of surviving, as they always do. But the dogs stayed a problem. No way to set them all free, which wouldn't have been a good idea anyway, as you know."

The children nodded. With the exception of the few working dogs like Grendelyn, most of their experiences with dogs stemmed from feral packs.

"It wouldn't have been practical or safe to try to put *all* those dogs out of their misery. Knowing that didn't make me feel any better when they'd commence their moaning and howling. Knowing they'd die of thirst or starve to death in a matter of days didn't help how I felt either, though I knew that at least they'd be beyond misery then. So I decided to pack up some supplies and gear and go camp out at the beach until it was over. I got up before dawn the next day and left.

"But as I drove out I-280 I passed the Ocean Boulevard exit. That made me remember the zoo, since that was the route I'd gone the few times I'd visited the place. I pulled over to the shoulder of the freeway and stopped right there. I sat and thought a lot more. The whole situation with the dogs had bothered me, but you know . . ." He stopped to stroke Grendelyn's head. She turned to look at him with a happy, shark-toothy grin. "The fact of the matter is, dogs decided thousands and thousands of years ago to throw their lot in with ours. They made their choice to share fates with us, come what may.

"The animals in the zoo were a different matter—each and every one of them a prisoner: a kidnapee or offspring of kidnapees. I hadn't thought of them at all before, but suddenly knowing that they were there in the zoo, starving to death, was more than I could bear.

"I figured the gun stores might already be ransacked. Even though I hadn't lived in the city long, I knew people who owned guns. A lot of guns. And I knew how to use guns." Hake always seemed ashamed when he got to this point of the story. That had puzzled Tuck when he was young, and he knew it puzzled the children here, all of whom could safely handle at the very least a .22.

"I took the next exit off the freeway and drove to one of those homes, hung around till I felt sure the man who lived there had Vanished. Then I broke in and made off with every rifle, gun, and round of ammunition I could find.

"It was mid-morning by then. The sun shone down mad and hot when I arrived at the zoo. The heat of it and the sounds of the animals beat upon my head. At a lot of the cages they came running to me at first, trusting, thinking I might be one of their keepers finally come to feed them. In those cases it was easy, over fast.

"When I killed the antelope and camels the noise and the smell of the blood drove the meat-eaters crazy.

"Wallabies, jackals, the binturongs; they all went down. When I got to the elephant enclosure I found a woman there, trampled. She must have been one of their trainers. She'd survived the Vanishing and come to care for them. She still clutched a hayfork. Straw was tangled

in its tines. I don't know what happened, why they killed her. Maybe
they panicked. Now they wandered unconcernedly around her flattened, crushed body. I don't remember feeling anything when I killed
them, except that it took a long time, a lot of ammunition, and then I
went on.

"Some of the monkeys were housed in elaborate jungle habitats.
I went in after them and thought I got all of them. But some must have
been hiding in the foliage. That's where all the little varmints you see
around here probably came from—the squirrel monkeys and the
lemurs. Over the years they could have slowly made their way down
along the Peninsula to here where it's warmer. Or maybe they just came
to haunt me.

"I cried when I killed the orangutans, cried so hard I could hardly
see to aim. Cried that hard, I think, so I wouldn't have to see their faces.
They looked at me with those more-than-human eyes out of those big,
weird, more-than-human faces, and they knew. With them, more than
with any of the other animals, I understood that even though I believed
I was being humane, it was still murder.

"When I killed the tigers, that was hard too, in a different way.
They paced their enclosure and glared at me, all rage and gleaming
gold, stripes sharp like long, black curved daggers, teeth shorter white
ivory daggers. It was like destroying a powerful magic, the glue that
keeps everything together: like annihilating the very force of nature.
But that glue had already disintegrated three days before with the
Vanishing. Just when I shot them, for just a moment, I suffered the
illusion that their power and magic washed over onto me—so that I
would forever be burdened with it and responsible for its continuation
in the world. But that passed, leaving me and the world empty.

"I came upon the aviary, a glorious walk-in habitat with its own
little lagoon. I gave up on that one. I could have sat there blasting at
flying hiding birds all day. I finally left them there, knowing it would
take them longer to die, since the habitat might support them for quite
a while.

"Do I sound cold about all this? I didn't feel cold—just numb and
real bad about it all. I comforted myself thinking that in the lands those
creatures came from, maybe now with most of the people gone their
species would finally have a chance to reestablish themselves in the wild
and survive."

He paused to drink. The mood of his audience shifted in anticipation of the shift they knew was coming in the story. Tuck noticed that many of the adults had fallen silent, listening clandestinely.

"So for that same reason I didn't kill everything," he resumed. "Animals that belong here in this country I set free. I didn't know if they'd survive or not, but I figured they deserved at least a chance. I freed the pronghorn antelope, the otters, the red foxes, coyotes, the wapiti and moose, the wolves, pumas, and native bears. I knew some of them would likely get killed trying to get out of the city—what was left of the people panicking and shooting at them. But I figured some of them would make it. I left the door open to the cages where I'd killed so the predators could get to the carcasses and feed and get strong again first.

"Some of the deer behaved unbelievably. In the middle of all that carnage, with the smells of gunpowder and blood and animal fear so thick it coated the inside of your nostrils, with wolves and bear wandering around—those deer went out to the green lawns between the cages and settled down to graze. I don't know if they'd been crazed into stupidity or were just plain stupid."

"What about you? Even if you had guns, it sounds like most of the time you were wandering around in a daze too," Chupa heckled from her exile on the next set of tiers. "Weren't you afraid a bear would come after you? Doesn't sound as if you were much smarter than the deer."

Tuck leaned forward. Each time Hake told a story, different details were challenged, forcing him to garnish, adapt, or explain accordingly. Tuck believed it allowed Hake the opportunity to forge and hone each story into a sharp, immaculate sword that would slice life into translucently thin cross sections of meaning.

Hake accepted Chupa's challenge good-naturedly. "That's a good observation. Truth to tell, right then I didn't care. You kids, you've heard stories all your lives about the Vanishing, so that you can survive it if it comes again. But until it does you'll never know what it was like, how you'd react."

Tuck thought of all the things Hake never included in his stories—whether he'd had a family that he'd lost, what kind of work he'd done before the Vanishing, where he'd spent his life before coming to San Francisco, why he'd been the kind of a man who would visit a zoo.

"So if a bear had laid me low," Hake was continuing, "I wouldn't have cared. I was that anesthetized. But none of the animals I released attacked me. I was carrying all those rifles strapped to me, rattling like a tin man, with shiny cartridge belts slung every which way on me. I stunk of sweat, gunmetal, and gunpowder. But I didn't smell of fear. The animals that didn't hightail it right away slunk off when they heard or smelled me coming. The hungrier ones, feeding, ignored me. And sometimes I took to the rooftops to get at some of the cages."

"Wait a minute," Chupa cut in, her voice mocking. "The animals you let go—what did you do, just wish the doors open?"

"Shhh!" Minda hissed at her. "Quit interrupting the story."

Chupa glared at Minda.

Hake looked at Chupa. Although the girl's attempt to trip Hake seemed like an exercise in sarcasm, a child's desire to best an adult, Tuck could tell that wasn't so. Chupa needed to prove that Hake's story couldn't possibly be true for herself.

Hake wouldn't give her that. "Well, if I'd been in any state to think about it, I could have gone looking for keys to unlock everything. I imagine they were kept in offices or the zookeepers' supply rooms between the cages. Wouldn't have been hard to break in and find them, though it would have taken a lot of time. As it was, as soon as I'd gotten there I started firing, like some sort of robot. I opened the cage doors by blasting open the locks. If animals came running up that I didn't want to shoot, like the otters did, I fired a shot into the air to scare them back first."

Chupa retreated. Her stubborn unconvinced expression barely masked tears. The other children nodded in agreement with Hake's explanations. Tuck caught Nesta's eye. She gave a sad grimace. Hake wasn't trying to be cruel to Chupa. He'd met her challenge fairly. His tale continued.

"I wasn't aware of when it became night. Being midsummer, the light seemed to last forever. I just remember this dream of moving and shooting, animals lying twitching, then still. The noise had escalated for a while—hours, I guess—as they panicked. Monkeys whooped and shrieked. Big animals crashed around in their cages. Then the heat and the sounds tapered off as the day and the beasts died. Those animals that were left alive were busy feeding." He thumped Grendelyn's coat again. "I'm sure I missed a lot. Some, like I said, probably escaped. Others must have starved to death after all. I was frenzied that day, not thorough. A lot of cages that looked empty might not have been.

"I came to in the middle of the night, walking down a path between two rows of cages. Most of the cages had stiffened bodies in them, so I'd been there earlier, though none of it looked familiar to me.

A few stood empty with the doors open. When I peered in the moon-light at the placards in front they read 'Jaguarundi' and 'Ocelot'—small wildcats that I knew up until recently had lived in the Southwest, so I must have let them go, though I didn't remember doing so.

"The cartridge belts I'd worn were gone—used up, I guess, and I only carried one rifle. I felt so tired, stripped to the bare bones of nothingness. Standing there, regaining consciousness, was the most naked, exhausting thing I've ever done.

"In that state I heard a whisper of sound from an empty cage behind me. If it had come just minutes earlier I would have spun around blasting. Instead I turned toward it slowly.

"At first it seemed as though something was materializing out of gunpowder smoke and shadow in that empty space, like a revenant dream. Chills ran up my spine to splinter like icicles in the base of my brain. Then I saw that it was a cat, a big cat, its fur so soft, gray and diffuse that its form stayed indistinct no matter how hard I tried to focus in on it. My breath caught in my throat and stayed there.

"There was another *shuush* of sound. Something dimly silver slid like mercury from a dark opening at the back of the cage, coalescing into another cat. It came to sit by the first.

"They were snow leopards, the rarest cats in the world. I raised the rifle, leveled the sights between the first one's eyes. He just sat there . . . they both just sat there . . . calmly looking at me. I lowered the rifle, then raised it again.

"I couldn't do it. There were so few of them left in the world. There never *had* been very many. Even if I let them go, the likelihood of their making their way to the nearest thing like their natural ecosys-tem, the Sierras or Mount Shasta, was impossible. They'd have to travel around the Bay or across the bridges, then over more bridges and rivers and the openness of the Central Valley. And even then, if they both miraculously survived, their chances of reproducing and flourishing were slim.

"I really thought all those things. I wasn't just rationalizing. But another thought took hold of me. They had a presence like the tigers'—a strong, strong magic. When I thought that, I raised my rifle again.

"A weird collage of images rushed through my head: the tigers all gold like fire, *on* fire, like Shiva, running and dancing on the turning rim of the wheel of destruction, bursting into flames along with it. The snow leopards all cool, silvery smoky blue like Vishnu, breathing the first breath of an icy new air that had never existed before, the first step of creation. They belonged to this new time, the slate wiped clean by the Vanishment: As if their sparse numbers had always existed as dormant seeds buried deep in the earth, waiting to germinate to the echo of distant heat as fire scoured the surface to pristineness.

"I lowered the rifle, just a little this time, stepped off at an angle, and blew the lock to nothingness. Then I threw away the rifle.

"The cage door creaked open, all on its own, probably from the shock of the blast. They walked out and away, not even looking at me, as if that was all I'd ever existed to do, that one act. Their shadows blended with the shadows of the bush and then they were gone. That was all."

Hake's audience absorbed the ending in silence. Tuck saw some of the older listeners turn away, their faces strained masks. What did the story mean to them? A myth of great horror and grief, followed by hope? What did Hake think this story would teach the children? That compassion can take grim forms? Tuck didn't know if these youngsters would understand. These children were so different. As different from him as his and Renzie's generation was from the pre-Vanishment generations.

He glanced as unobtrusively as he could around the circle of still spellbound children. An ecstatic calm saturated their faces, as if they'd just been validated in a religious experience.

And what did mavericks like Chupa feel? He looked over at the girl. Her face was a wall.

"Of course, I wasn't the only one to saddle myself like that at the time," Hake said, breaking the spell. "Jorda here, she did her little bit too." He looked as though he were forcing his brown face to split over white teeth in a grin. "Tell them about the cows, Jorda."

Tuck didn't remember ever hearing any story about Jorda and cows.

A rather sour look disrupted Jorda's serene features. "It's nothing," she said. "It's not a story."

People sat up straighter. Hake was a fabulist. You never knew if his stories were true or not, not that it mattered. Jorda, on the other hand, was down-to-earth.

Jorda saw that protesting would only keep them after her. "All right, all right, but it's nothing. You'll see. Two days after the Vanishing, I remembered there was a huge cattle holding pen out on I-5 near Coalinga. I drove out there. The stockmen must all have Vanished, because no one had been taking care of the cattle. So I let them go. That's all. I told you it was nothing."

"Wait a minute," called out one of the livestockwomen from the Department Store. "Why did you do that? At that point, as far as anyone knew, the Vanished might have come right back. How would you have explained to the stockyards about the cattle being gone, and to the local farmers how their crops got trampled?"

Jorda shrugged. "They'd have no way of knowing it was me. Either way there'd have been damage—dead cattle or stripped fields."

"But I still don't understand why you let them go," Quill said, from the circle of youngsters. "It's not at all the same as Hake's story, so the reasons can't be the same."

"For food," Jorda said flatly. "Where I lived, grocery stores were already being looted. Some of the survivors were jockeying for power by stockpiling and monopolizing canned goods. There was no way of knowing how long power sources would continue, and when refrigeration went . . . Sooner or later, maybe in months, maybe in years, food—especially protein—might prove scarce. The cattle had a good chance of surviving. And I'd know the general vicinity where beef on the hoof could be found. That's it, end of story." Jorda had not been pleased to have been put on the spot.

Again the room lapsed into silence.

Minda broke the tension. "Well, *I* have a story. When I woke up this morning . . ." Most of the audience adjourned back into small conversational groups. Frustrated but undaunted, Minda continued. "I woke up real early and knew it was going to be one of those 'probably' days."

"What do you mean by a 'probably' day, Minda?" Nesta asked.

Minda looked at her impatiently. "A day with lots of chances for probablys. A slipping day. So anyway, I got up and climbed my stairs to the next floor, and the next, all the way up to the tallest tower, like I do a lot of mornings. And I looked from there from that probably down to this probably, and heard all kinds of things sliding back and forth."

Against his knees, Tuck felt Renzie stiffen.

"That's a dumb story," Chupa scoffed. "I've seen your room. Your stairs don't go anywhere but up to the ceiling."

"I *told* you it was a 'probably' day," Minda said with great scorn. "It's not my fault you're nothing but a stupid ghost and can't see that." She started to flounce off in a sulk.

"Wait a minute, young lady," Hot Rod called after her. "Hake told his story, so now it's time for you rug rats to call it a night."

"I'll help you round them up and take them back," said Nesta. She was looking after Minda thoughtfully. "It's past my bedtime, too."

Tuck shook his head. "They've got even wilder imaginations than we did. I haven't a clue what all that stuff means, do you?" He nudged Renzie with his knee.

"No," she said, her voice low.

"It does remind me of something, though, an old nursery rhyme. Remember the morning a couple of weeks ago, when you'd just gotten back from the road gang and Minda was teasing Kip with her rendition of that old Dr. Fell poem? I think I'll tease her with a rhyme version of my own. What do you think of this?

> *"As I was going up the stair*
> *I met a Minda who wasn't there.*
> *She wasn't there again today—*
> *I wish, I wish she'd go away."*

That seemed to jar Renzie out of her mood. She must be trying to stifle a giggle, Tuck thought, as her back trembled against his legs.

———

Much later, Tuck walked back toward the House with Renzie and Hake. Renzie nodded to the bicycle Hake was walking and the knapsack on his back. "Did you come straight to the party from work?"

Hake peered at her as if he could just barely make out her features, although his own dark face stood out clearly in the light from the aurora. "With all the preparation for this"—he gestured at the setup lining the road, the vendors asleep now behind their tables—"I guess you haven't had a chance to notice, but I moved out of the House a couple of days ago. I'm living up at the Hackers' Center now."

Tuck stopped. Hake had lived in the House as long as he could remember. Hake was part of the House. Tuck felt shaken.

"Hake, why?" Tuck could tell by the strain in her voice that Renzie felt the same way.

"It was time," Hake said. "Ever since the Vanishing I've spent my life trying first to survive, and then to rebuild the world. I want to pass some time before I die trying to help figure out what happened."

Hake rummaged in his pack. He pulled out a strap-on light and attached it to the front of his bike. "I want to eat, sleep, and breathe all those unanswered questions, even though I know they'll probably stay unanswered, just as they have the last thirty years. I want to hook up more with the others that have been asking those questions all along, like your friend Nesta." He looked at her. "Renzie, I'm entitled."

He swung his leg over the bike. "I've already suggested to Eric that once the fair is over you be assigned semipermanently to bussing the kids up to the Center, so that you can keep on working with Nesta. And me."

Tuck felt as though Hake and Renzie were leaving him far, far behind.

"So you see, it's not like you won't see me all the time anyway. It's not like I'm Vanishing," Hake said. He switched on the bike's headlight. It blazed a clear trail for him down the roadway. "Good night, Renzie. Good night, Tuck."

"Good night, Hake."

Renzie and Tuck went into the House. At least the House is always the House, thought Tuck, separate from all its changing occupants, a permanent being.

CHAPTER THIRTEEN

Tuck watched while he waited. The trueing stand snugged the bicycle's hub in place, allowing Sepulveda to turn the tire as freely as if it were a spinning wheel and she some latter-day Rapunzel. An already shorn Rapunzel, Tuck thought, standing at the edge of the crowd gathered for her workshop.

"All right, now we'll move on to adjusting the rim," Sepulveda said, demonstrating with deft, agile motions. Her audience consisted largely of younger children who hadn't had a chance to take the advanced bike maintenance and repair course before. A narrow line of adults crescented behind the youngsters. Some looked as if they were outlanders on their first visit to the Valley, hunkered down and staring with the same concentration as the children. The other grown-ups looked more relaxed, probably observing as a review. Among them Tuck noticed Jan, the socioanthropologist on Nesta's team. But rather than watching Sepulveda, Jan studied three Penitents clustered together nearby. They in turn appeared to focus more on Sepulveda herself than the lesson. This was true of Tuck too, although he knew his reasons would be different from theirs.

Tuck had counted six or seven Penitents attending the festivities and noticed that they'd concentrated their penance-assistance primarily toward the Orindan and House contingents—helping the Orindans with drayage, the House with cleanup chores, asking questions about township and Valley, socializing more than the ascetic Penitents usually did.

Tuck smiled to himself. Every once in a while the Valley saw elderly Penitents passing through. Most of this group were younger. Perhaps they'd become tired of the deliberate harshness of their lives and sought gentler locales in which to discharge their atonement this coming winter. What better place than the House environs? Or Orinda, one of the few places only lightly blighted by the Vanishing, a township rich in food and energy-affluent with its banks and banks of solar panels? If he were a Penitent, he would be willing to curry favor and make a good impression on these potential patrons. Tuck had no doubt that the hovering drab brown trio waited for the end of Sepulveda's workshop for just that purpose.

Which meant that they'd monopolize Sepulveda for an indeterminate amount of time if they got to her first. He intended to outmaneuver them.

Only one more day remained of the trading fair. The air felt laden with the weight of matters drawing to a close. It had taken Tuck all this time since the party to sort out his thoughts and feelings, shuffle them over and over in his mind like a deck of cards, mentally dealing himself hand after hand, trying to arrange the shifting suits of his life's circumstances.

For weeks before the trade fair he had looked forward to a reunion with old friends. Then he'd spent the entire fair jealous, lonely, embarrassed by his conduct and miserable. This rare visit was passing him by, snared as he was in the grip of a self-imposed fugue, unable to change his behavior.

At the least, he owed it to Sepulveda to try to explain why he'd distanced himself from her for the last five days.

Since the final estrangement from his father, Tuck had sworn he wouldn't allow his actions to be guided by the blackmail of another anticipated Vanishing. But Tuck also knew that connections could be severed by things other than a Vanishing. Things as final as death or as rending as neglect.

He shrank inside when he thought of Sepulveda. Although they were long-time friends and intermittent lovers, he had treated her with less courtesy and kindness than he would a stranger. Even so, only the fair's impending end had finally forced him to seek her out to apologize and make amends.

"All right, that's enough for today. Go try it out on your own bikes." Finished, Sepulveda freed the wheel from the trueing stand. The children slowly dispersed. Tuck edged against their outward current, keeping an eye on the Penitents as they also tried to reach the Orindan. But with three of them maneuvering as a single larger unit they made slower progress. One of them spotted Tuck's trajectory toward their target and said something to the others. They tried to press forward more quickly, but compacted against the mass of youngsters. Tuck grinned, enjoying the miniature drama.

Then two things happened simultaneously. The Penitents themselves were overtaken by Jan; and Sepulveda, turning around from packing up her tools, caught sight of Tuck and moved toward him. With a view over her shoulder Tuck saw the Penitents' pantomimed frustration and defeat; broad, almost ritualized gestures magnified by the abstracted volume of their robes.

"Hello, Tuck," said Sepulveda, unaware of the mute theatrics behind her. "Don't tell me you're actually here to see me?"

"Hi, Sep," Tuck said. "Yes, I am." The charm of the farce playing out in back of her faded as he tried to remember how he'd intended to initiate his apology and explanation.

"Must be my sultry ways. You've been killing yourself trying to resist me the whole week." Sarcastic words, but her tone of voice was mild and her face neutral. Tuck knew underneath that flat expression lay at least a ripple of hurt.

"That's true. That's part of it, part of why I've been avoiding you," he said.

"At least you admit it," she said, finally showing some irritation.

"The night of the party at the Office Buildings—what did Renzie say to you?" he asked her.

"To ignore you. That you'd been distracted. That you'd been unmanned by a succubus and she'd explain more later."

Tuck rolled his eyes and groaned.

The corners of Sepulveda's mouth twitched, but she neither smiled nor said anything more as she waited him out.

Tuck took a deep breath. "I think I'm in love with someone."

"You *think*?"

He shook his head in angry confusion. "How would I know? Falling in love is something people used to do, before the Vanishing. Nobody 'falls in love' anymore, except my father, according to him."

"But now you have, too?"

"I guess so. I'm miserable and jealous. I'm lonely when I'm not with her."

"I see," Sepulveda said. "And you didn't know how to go about rejecting me when I showed up."

Tuck squirmed in discomfort. "I haven't seen you in over a year. I didn't know how to come out with it all at once. How could I explain something I'm so unsure of anyway? And then at the party you were so . . . very . . ."

Sepulveda looked stung. "Do you think I've been celibately pining away for you since the last time I saw you—as you pointed out, over a year ago?"

"No, no!" Tuck said. "I didn't know how to explain about not being able to be lovers anymore in such a way that I wouldn't lose you as a friend. I didn't want to say *anything* till I'd figured out a way to do that. And because I *am* still attracted to you I was having trouble sorting out having just a friendship with you. But the more I *didn't* talk to you, the more it became obvious that that was worse than if I *had*. I should have said *something*. That's why I had to find you now before you left to go back to Orinda."

To Tuck's amazement, a small smile shadowed Sepulveda's lips. Was it possible that in spite of his incoherence he'd made himself understood and Sepulveda forgave him?

"Tuck, anyone as messed up as you deserves compassion. Renzie was right. You are possessed. So, are you going to explain about 'her'?"

Great, it looked as though Sepulveda was going to absolve him *because* of his muddledness. "Sep, the main thing is that I didn't mean to hurt you or be rude to you."

"All right, apology accepted. So, if you're such a friend, are you going to tell me?"

Tuck resigned himself to explaining about Le Chell. Past Sepulveda he saw Jan talking to the Penitents in an animated fashion. He let the puppetlike show distract him a little from the confession he'd maneuvered himself into. "She's one of the Watchers, tall and slim like you, with long red hair and freckles . . ." The anthropologist grabbed at the sleeve of a Penitent, who yanked him or herself away. Another Penitent stepped in, obscuring Tuck's view. This time Jan pulled apart from the group, doubled over and clutching her side. The brown cassocks closed in around her.

"Oh shit," Tuck said, slamming past Sepulveda. "There's trouble!" he yelled back as he vaulted over a pile of bicycle tools. At the sound of his voice several of the robes whirled around, allowing Tuck a glimpse of the continuing dumbshow.

One of the Penitents had grabbed Jan by the shoulder. Jan's attacker was a young woman—her cowl fell away from her face as she tried to stab Jan in the throat, revealing gold-shot hair. Jan's forearm sluiced with blood as she blocked the blows. One of the other Penitents maneuvered around, trying to grab that arm so the blond girl could deliver a killing strike. Jan kept kicking out at this second assailant, keeping him momentarily at bay. As soon as she saw Tuck, Jan screamed out, "They're 'Bounders, not Penitents! They're scouting for a raid!"

Defeated in trying to silence Jan, the blond woman swore and stopped trying to slice her.

Tuck closed on the nearest robed figure, who stepped aside and drew a knife just as Tuck reached for him. Coming up hard behind Tuck and shrieking like a demon, Sepulveda smashed the trueing stand across the man's arm, knocking the knife onto the tarmac. The man slid to the ground and reached for the weapon with his other hand. Thanking the fates that Sepulveda had more presence of mind than he did, Tuck kicked the man in the face and snatched the blade up for himself. Clutching head and arm, the 'Bounder rolled over and over back to his comrades.

The 'Bounders regrouped in a tight circle back-to-back as an alerted crowd of fairgoers gathered and hemmed them in. Older folk came running at the commotion, automatically arranging themselves, the patterns of defense learned at such hard cost during the days of the marauders never completely forgotten. Dozens of rifles pointed at the 'Bounders' heads as inexorably as compass points attracted to the North Pole.

The young woman had controlled Jan at last and pulled the scientist completely across her own body, hunting blade edged to Jan's jugular, jamming even her golden head behind Jan, so that she had to wedge her face sideways to speak.

"You can shoot us if you want to," she shouted from that awkward angle. "But not before I can kill her."

Her threat was a needless warning. The old drills were for containment. Contained the 'Bounders were. "Someone's gone to fetch the House foreman," Tuck heard a Koanite say. The throng settled in to wait.

Tuck turned to Sepulveda. "Thanks," he said. "Since you saved my ass, does this mean you accept my apology?"

Sepulveda grinned hugely and Tuck knew he was forgiven. "No," she said. "It means if your love affair doesn't work out that I'll *own* your ass."

A line rippled as four people wedged their way through the packed crowd—Eric in the lead, a livestocker's jacket flapping about his hips, Ernest Yorheim, Abel Howe of the Homers' Council, and Dora Whitcomb, head of the Orindan contingent.

Eric walked up to ten feet of the pack of 'Bounders. The leader yanked meaningfully on Jan to indicate he'd come far enough. Jan's eyes were closed, although her legs still braced her up. Fresh blood stained slowly through the darker red splotches at her side and forearm.

"Terms," Eric said, not bothering with challenges or admonishments.

"Us out of here, and you get her back."

"How?"

The blond girl thought for a moment. "There has to be cover, a lot of it, or you'll mow us down when we release her."

"Then I have to be right there with you, otherwise you'll off her as you go to ground."

The girl shook her head. "No I wouldn't. I don't have to." She smiled, a real smile, chilling in its friendliness. "I'll get her later when we come back to finish you all off." The smile dissolved into blankness. "Especially them"—she jerked Jan in the direction of the Watchers' Domes—"and *your* obscene hovels," she said, as she hawked and launched a wad of spit at Abel.

"I'm going to be right on top of you when you hit the woods," Eric said.

The girl nodded. "Understood."

Eric pointed to the northwest. "The nearest cover, the closest neck of forest, is in that direction," he said. The 'Bounder leader's eyes flicked elsewhere, then along the bearings he indicated.

"How far?" she asked.

"About a ten-minute walk at a regular pace."

"We'd better get going then," she said. "I think your friend's going into shock, and it'll take a lot longer than ten minutes to get this circus there." But she didn't look as though she wanted to start—she seemed to be gathering her thoughts.

Eric considered Jan's whitening skin, the involuntary shaking beginning to shiver her body. He turned, scanning the crowd around him till he spotted Tuck. "Come here, Tuck." He gestured him over, met him halfway. "I want you to arrange to follow with a stretcher for Jan. Also the full med kit."

Tuck nodded.

"Good boy," Eric said, turning his back on the 'Bounders to slap Tuck's arm in confirmation. "And some plasma from the lab." Then he muttered, under his breath, "They've got to have guns, but they wouldn't risk bringing them to the fair. They'll have hidden them first. My guess is somewhere to the east. Send a party to head them off in that direction." Then loudly again, "And don't forget blankets for shock."

Tuck sprinted for the House. Renzie and Sep caught up with him midway. "Put together a crew to cut the 'Bounders off if they veer, especially to the east," he told them. "Eric thinks they've probably got guns stashed nearby."

Sep and Renzie loped away, efficient as hunting wolves. By the time Tuck reached the lab, Hake was there stuffing a large backpack with medical supplies and a couple of blankets, and had already hauled out a stretcher. "Grab one of the Orindans' little electric carts," Hake said. "It'll get us there just as fast as running and in better shape."

They bounced along pockmarked streets blemished with the usual debris of shredded eucalyptus bark and leaves. Tuck clutched the stretcher, which hung out the back end. With each jolt it banged against the roadway, threatening to dislodge and take wing.

In a few rambunctious minutes they caught up with the crowd.

Like a gigantic obese crab the procession scuttled in a slow, lopsided fashion toward an overgrown park a block away from where Tuck and Hake found them. Sharpshooters still ringed the 'Bounders, the far side of their circle having to walk cautiously backward on the uneven roadway to keep their guns trained on the fanatics' heads. The 'Bounders had their knives out and shuffled along in their tight back-to-back clump, equally awkward. On the far side of the park stood the goal, a dense stand of bay laurels.

Hake grunted. "Made it in plenty of time. Be obvious. Make a lot of noise unloading so that the 'Bounders don't spook." He raised his voice and yelled, "Medics! We've brought the stretcher!"

It took another five minutes for the ungainly cavalcade to reach the woods' border.

"Get back," the 'Bounder leader yelled at the rifle bearers who'd reached the trees' edge. "Don't even think of slipping in ahead of us.

And there'd better not be a reception committee in there waiting, because I'm going to stay here long enough with your friend to be sure."

The sharpshooters reluctantly peeled away. The 'Bounders sidled to the breach in the blockade.

"Stop right there," said Eric. The blond woman glared at him, but the fanatics stopped. Eric walked up to them, arms out, hands open. Tuck drew his breath in and held it. Eric could handle any one person with a knife, maybe even two or three, but if all the 'Bounders jumped him at once . . . All around him Tuck heard rifles clicking as safeties were released. In the tight sullen silence weighting the clearing, the 'Bounders couldn't help but hear them, too.

Eric reached the leader and with deliberate care raised one hand and firmly grasped one of Jan's arms, cautious not to jar the blond girl, whose knife was still wedged to Jan's throat. Eric and the fanatic stared at each other. Then she nodded. Without dropping her gaze from Eric she said something to her compatriots that Tuck couldn't hear. They slid into the woods in an interminable process, one after another, waiting long moments between each furtive departure. At last only the leader, Jan, and Eric remained, the blond woman backed up to the closest tree to support the half-unconscious Jan. The 'Bounder seemed to wait longer than necessary, glowering at Eric, not bothering to mask her loathing. Tuck would have bet that she was weighing her chances of slitting Jan's throat, shoving the anthropologist into Eric, and still making off into the woods.

The same thought must have occurred to Eric. He appeared to shift for a second to get a better grip on Jan. As he did so he palmed something from inside his jacket with his other hand in a smooth, effortless motion. He and the fanatic's eyes had never left each other's face, never changed expression, so the presence of the small pistol pointed at her temple entered the 'Bounder's consciousness like an intrusion into a dream. Her expression slackened peculiarly into something like a peaceful trance. She said something to Eric, again in tones too low to hear. Suddenly she lowered the knife, dropped behind Jan and shoved the older woman as hard as she could onto Eric, and was gone.

The crowd whooped and headed for the forest. Hake and Tuck raced forward with the stretcher. Trying not to drop Jan, Eric shouted after the mob. "Slow down, damn it. You know better than that. Come back here and get organized."

Eric helped Tuck lower Jan onto the stretcher while Hake opened up the med kit, then faced his sheepish troops. "Fan out first and go slow. They may try to rush off to a weapons stash or they may lay ambushes for any stray fools that just go plunging in after them. Pel, get back to the House as fast as you can and take at least four off-road vehicles and drive around to head them off in front. Get more than four if you can. Make sure you've got full emergency equipment in case they start any brushfires as a diversion. Tuck, did you have time to send someone around to the east?"

Tuck, ripping Jan's shirt away from the first wound where the 'Bounder had slashed her chest, nodded. "Renzie and Sep are taking care of it. With their head start they'll have plenty of folks closing in from that direction by now."

Eric grinned. "Perfect." He turned away to direct his ad hoc brigade.

Hake cursorily examined Jan, then filled a hypodermic from the kit. "She may have a nicked lung, but other than that, her biggest problem right now is shock and loss of blood," he said as he squirted the needle clear. Tuck watched the older man slide the needle into Jan's skin as easily as if he were lancing soft butter.

"So she'll be all right?" Tuck asked.

"Most probably so."

"I guess we're lucky no one got killed," Tuck said.

Hake's face saddened. "I don't think we can assume that," he said. "Those Penitent robes the 'Bounders wore—they were the real thing. You know the 'Bounders grow nothing, raise nothing, make almost nothing themselves, except ammunition. The Penitents weave those robes themselves as part of their faith, and they never sell or give them away to anyone—willingly."

CHAPTER FOURTEEN

The scarred, scalded-looking man stood like a lost statue in the middle of the street, his senses sieving for anything familiar that might provide a clue. He hadn't thought it would be so hard to find his Home again. He and Jennifer had moved into it three years before the Vanishing—their "dream house," they'd called it then.

He still remembered that the closest intact thoroughfare was the Lawrence Expressway. But linking segments of streets and landmark Homes had disappeared as almost thirty years of age, weather, small earthquakes and demolition squads took their toll.

Hoping to get a bearing, make out some familiar landmarks, the man turned his head with a mincing, tentative motion, taking care not to pull too hard or quickly against the scar tissue along the left side of his neck. Since the fire in the spring he'd done little but lie in agony and try to heal. Burns spidered down most of the length of his arm in a thick-stranded webbing, impeding and slowing his every movement. It had taken months for them to fade from suppurating purple to dead white.

A racket of thrashing branches and the soft pounding of feet on dirt intruded on his silent, motionless investigation. He scuttled for cover.

This street terminated a short block south, where the roadway and a number of Homes had been reclaimed. The land there now supported an adolescent copse of dwarf fruit trees. Instead of the family of deer he'd expected from the noise, a ragtag mob of brown-robed people burst out of the grove like monks on a drunken spree. He counted seven of them.

"Quick, climb up and see if they're still following," the smallest one, a woman by her voice, commanded.

"These trees are too little," the man she'd given the order to said. "I can't even get into them, and they're too short anyway."

"Over here, then," the woman said. She and another man gave him a leg up to a patio wall that butted into the side of a Home. From there they pushed him onto the roof of the building. He snaked along till he had a clear view along the way they'd come, then bellied his way back and slid down while they braced him.

"We gained some distance, but they're still on our trail. I can see bushes thrashing around pretty far back."

"Not good," the woman said. "They know this area better than we do. They should be moving almost as fast as us, without having to kill themselves the way we're doing. If they've dropped back a little, it means they're taking their time to make sure we don't fan out and double back on them, and they've probably sent others around to try to outflank us. It's time for a little strategy. Let's give them something else to keep them busy." She trotted down the street. The burned man tried to shrink himself into a shadow as she passed the garage and bushes he hid behind. "Here. This one will do," he heard her say. He almost bolted until he realized she'd stopped at the Home next to him. As her followers gathered around her, he sidled two more houses away and found an overgrown backyard fence he could peer through to keep them in sight.

Two of the men were trying to break down the front door. The others, two men and three women, counting the leader, were yanking up fistfuls of dried grass and twisting them into messy ropelike strands as fast as they could.

"Not like that," the woman called out to the would-be door bashers. She picked up an earthenware planter, the shrub it had once housed long since shriveled well past mummification, and threw it through the Home's picture window. It punched a head-sized hole in the glass, crazing the entire surface of the window with angry fractures. "Like *that*," she said with evident satisfaction. The men took her cue and began flinging anything heavy they could find at the glass. The gap enlarged to a sharp-toothed portal.

In the meantime the rest of the brown robes had brought up their twined and tangled strands of grass. The leader ferreted out a tin from deep within her robes, opened it and withdrew some matches. The crude, handmade lucifers sparked crankily as she lit the brands. One after another, her followers thrust the torches through the window's break, waving them until the desiccated curtains embroidering the windows caught fire. The scarred man pursed his lips at their shoddy, risky technique.

"Hang on to a couple of brands," the woman ordered. She pointed to the tinder-dry grasses of what had once been the front lawn. "There." A man and a woman pitched their torches where she pointed. The turf began to ripple and crackle. The scarred man flinched back from the too-familiar sound.

The arsonists were beginning to look around worriedly for signs of their pursuers. "Hurry, hurry, take off the robes," instructed the woman, shedding her own and throwing it onto the flaming lawn. Underneath she wore nondescript salvaged pants, a pullover, and a light utility belt garnished with small leather pouches and a knife sheath. "It'll leave them lots of smoke to find." The others followed suit. At first the weight of the garments almost smothered the infant blaze. Then a black cloud billowed upward, reeking of the acrid fumes of burning wool.

"Okay, this way. Spread out, keep to cover and go slow. Once they find this they'll be too busy to keep chasing us." She crossed the street and headed out at an angle between the Homes. The others followed.

The burned man found himself short of breath. His heart pounded. Primitive though the fugitives' methods were, the whole operation had taken less than ten minutes. It wasn't how he would have done it. If its interior was rife with mildew and damp-rot the Home might not catch right away unless other furniture was close to the flaming curtains. Its moldy carpet might barely smolder, only slowly building up heat to a flash point. More likely the grass fire on the outside would overtake the building first. Still, for their purposes, he had to admit the brown robes had been effective.

He looked at the Home sadly. For all he knew, it was untainted. Somebody had lived there once, probably been happy there. It was criminal to destroy an undecayed and uninfected Home.

After all the places he'd torched, it would be ironic to be caught at the site of someone else's crime. He expected from what the incendiarists had said that their pursuers would arrive shortly, possibly from several directions. He'd have to take care leaving.

The lawn had begun to blaze in earnest and was rippling toward the House. The boundaries of driveway and street might impede it a little, but once it reached around to the backyard it would gain impetus. He'd have to be careful of that too.

As he hesitated, deciding on his bearings, someone stepped into the street from the Homes that kitty-cornered the fledgling orchard. The burned man froze into camouflaging stillness.

The newcomer was a young man, lean and tanned like leather. He strode up the street with stiff, calculated steps. The burned man waited for him to sound the alarm and bring the rest of the pursuers.

But the youth hardly looked at the smoking Home. He cast a long and wide glance over the scene, taking in the length of the street, the cremated robes, the foliage the burned man hid behind. There was something about the younger man's deliberateness, his lack of dismay and surprise, that suggested that he too had witnessed the torching. The burned man trembled. Had he been seen? Should he run? But before he could break out of panicked stasis, the young man turned and slipped off in the direction the arsonists had taken.

Above the growing roar of the flames the burned man heard shouts from the orchard as over the low crest of the trees the approaching hunters caught sight of the smoke. A rumble came to him from the opposite, far direction. The arsonist leader had been correct—four-wheel-drive vehicles had circled around to catch them in front. The woman had also been correct about the effect of her diversion. With a fire on their hands, the pursuers wouldn't be concerned about continuing their hunt. The burned man crept off through the backyards, in the opposite direction to that taken by the arsonists and the stalking young man.

CHAPTER FIFTEEN

Renzie leaned against the back of a refreshment booth, sucking thirstily at her third fruit ice. The night had brought some coolness to the air, but not to her skin, parchment-tight after hours of firefighting. The ices only soothed her smoke-parched throat briefly in passing, then settled in a solid frozen lump in her gut. She shivered to her core.

The concession stand's single dangling bulb strafed her with a lance of stark whiteness through its back vent, rendering her exhausted face into a landscape of harsh planes. Just beyond the border of light a man slouched against the booth too. His black silhouette could have been Renzie's shadow.

"Is she going to be okay, the woman who was stabbed?" the man asked.

"Slashed," Renzie corrected him. "She'll be all right as long as no complications develop."

"Almost everybody's back from the chase," the man said. "Isn't Eric worried that the 'Bounders will start more fires?"

Renzie shook her head and smelled the smudgy reek of her hair and skin. Even a long soak in the tubs hadn't completely erased the perfume of smoke that clung to her. "No, they'll run to report back to their den. Is that why you asked to meet me, Brad? To ask about the 'Bounders? If you're so curious and concerned, you should talk to one of the fair monitors."

"No, of course not." But he fell silent again.

Renzie pushed herself away from the refreshment stand. "Tomorrow's the last day of the fair. There'll be a lot of work to do and I'm exhausted. Good night."

"Wait, please wait." Brad reached out to halt her. His hand entered the light like a disembodied limb, shockingly three-dimensional in contrast to the flatness of his cookie-cutter outline.

Renzie rocked back out of his grasp, her arms folded tight across her chest, implacable eyes fixed on his dim form.

"I sent you the message to meet me because I wanted to explain about that first day, the fight with Sara," Brad said.

"What's to explain? You've had years to fill Sara's head with all kinds of notions about me."

"I never talk about you at all. That's part of the problem."

Brad's voice startled Renzie with its bitterness, but she ignored it. *"Somebody's* been talking to her," she said. "Imagine my surprise to be informed by a total stranger that I'd deprived you of your Home."

Brad slumped back against the booth's sheet-metal wall. "Ginny told her that. That's what Ginny talked herself into believing after we left."

Renzie snorted. "Even your moronic sister can't believe that a fifteen-year-old drove you away from the Homes. I would have cheered you all on your way if Old George had taken you there when he left the House. You deserve to live in those miserable, depressing dumps. But *he* chose not to. In fact, that's what freed him up so he could end up with Ginny: He'd finally accepted that his family wasn't going to Return. I can't believe that even Ginny's so out of touch with reality that she'd try to make me the scapegoat."

"That's just it," Brad said. "Ginny lives in her own reality. She grew up in a fairy-tale childhood that revolved around the legend of George finding us trapped and starving, rescuing and taking us in as his own. He raised us, protected us, taught us to preserve our Home. Ginny idolized him as the hero with a quest, the shining knight. Still does. She won't believe anything else."

"Oh yeah?" Like a surging ocean swell, Renzie's anger lifted her from exhaustion. "So how does Ginny explain the way Old George treated me and Tuck, his own children? And what about *our* mother? Margaret's the one who really held us together, made sure there was food on the table, kept Old George from plunging off the deep end."

Even in the shadows Brad's discomfort was palpable. "I know

that, but Ginny saw Margaret in a different light. When she was little, I think she thought of Margaret as some sort of caretaker, George's assistant or servant. It's not so surprising . . ." Brad paused as if hunting for tactful words. "After all, George was never affectionate to Margaret in front of us."

Renzie broke through Brad's diplomacy brusquely. "He probably wasn't that affectionate to her in private, either. He was ashamed that he'd shacked up with someone so soon after the Vanishing."

"*I* knew that Margaret always treated us well." Brad swept past the subject. "But when Ginny got old enough to make the connection that George and Margaret were, uh, involved, and understood about sex and where you and Tuck came from, Margaret became the chief villain in her life. Ginny saw Margaret as the evil stepmother who'd lured George away from his sacred charge of caring for the Homes, away from his pure relationship with his original family."

"And me and Tuck?"

Brad matched her bluntness. "Merely bastard children Margaret had foisted onto George to keep him down. The fact that George was always yelling at you and Tuck and not at us didn't weaken her convictions."

"Your sister has a mind like things that crawl under rocks," Renzie said. "I'm glad I didn't know this when we all lived together." She looked at Brad with revulsion. "Do you have any idea how it makes me feel knowing you knew all this back then?"

"I didn't!" Brad protested. "Ginny didn't talk about any of this till after we left. She was always trying to live up to what she thought was George's idea of perfection—I'll bet she muzzled every real, spontaneous reaction she ever had, except how she felt about George. I swear to God, Renzie, I didn't know."

"So what? There were things you *did* know, asshole."

Brad collapsed into silence. After a minute he thrust out his hand again, a white flag in the brightness. "Just give me a moment. Don't leave, please." His voice shook.

Another minute passed. "Okay, we're down to it. Maybe this is the real reason I needed to see you. Yes, I knew about Ginny and George when we were lovers. Before he caught us, I didn't see that there was any connection between the two, no real reason for you to know."

"No connection between the two?" In the ruthless exaggerated light, Renzie's sneer transformed her face into gargoyled sarcasm. "No connection? Must have been just a coincidence that whenever we made love you seemed so sure George would be occupied elsewhere."

"All right, that's true!" Brad said. "I was seventeen years old and I wanted you so badly my whole body ached—when I was working, studying, eating, even when I slept. And it wasn't just the sex. Simple sex is easy, it's everywhere. But with you sex had to do with what you seemed to see in me, with your passion for everything, with your recklessness and anger, with the way you stood up to George. You made me so damned *hungry.*" He was shouting, all shadow-camouflaged discretion and secrecy forgotten. "Yes, I knew when George was tied up with my sister. If I'd told you, would you have turned up your nose and said, 'Oh, we shouldn't make love now'?"

"And when my father accused us of incest, and you knew he was screwing your sister?"

Brad's breath labored in the darkness. "Would you ever betray Tuck, for anything? No matter what he did?" he asked. "You and Tuck always had your secrets. So did Ginny and I. Ginny was so happy when George finally took her to bed. It was all her dreams come true. I couldn't tell anyone, not even you. To be honest, in the back of my mind I figured that if it was all right for them to be together, then it was okay for us, too.

"I went into shock when George walked in on us and blew up. I couldn't believe it. When he started crying I felt like I'd betrayed him. Then I didn't protect you, so I betrayed you too. And I could feel Ginny behind us watching, waiting for me to expose her. So I didn't do anything. God, it was horrible."

He'd slid down, his back against the booth, and sat on the ground slouched in on himself. "I didn't mean to hurt you or George or anyone else. I just wanted something for me in my life, some passion, to let loose. Why shouldn't I get to feel that way, too? What was wrong with that?"

He paused to regather himself.

"When you ran away, I felt guilty," he said. "But worse than that, I was relieved. Especially when a couple of weeks later Ginny told me she was pregnant. I figured you could take care of yourself; you were better off without me, and I would have given anything for you not to find out about George and Ginny.

"Then you came back. You scared me to death, you looked so shattered. I felt like I'd robbed you of all the things I loved most about you. The next couple of weeks passed like one long nightmare. What a perfect punishment for me it was, having to wait and wait for the whole mess to come out.

"By the time we left I was glad. I thought you were well rid of us. I just wanted to put it all behind me. It took me a long time to get involved with someone again."

"Sara?"

"Yes. I wanted her to love me. I was so ashamed of the way I'd treated you I didn't want to even think about it. I told myself that I'd only been seventeen years old and that's why I'd handled everything so badly. I never told Sara about you. I never thought I'd have to see you again.

"Then when the fair came up Ginny started campaigning for the whole family to come along this time. Since it was inevitable that we'd run into you and Tuck, I should have figured that she'd put ideas into Sara's head."

"But you didn't think about it," Renzie said. "You didn't want to, so you just avoided the issue, right? I guess it doesn't make much of a difference if you're seventeen or not. Some things don't change."

"At least this time I came and talked to you," he said.

"Do you think that excuses you? Do you think it makes it all right?"

"No, I guess not," but his tone of voice said that he had thought that it would.

———

Pale and numb, Renzie coasted through the kitchen on the downslope of exhaustion. It was the closest route to her chambers, and at this hour only a skeleton crew rattled about, cleaning up and winding down from the especially long, tense day.

"Renzie, are you all right?" Jorda asked.

Renzie waved a hand in assent. "Yeah, I'll be okay. I went out to the fair for something cold for my throat. The fire really stripped it."

"By any chance did you see Sun today?" Jorda said. "Either at the fire or maybe at the fair? He didn't show up tonight for kitchen duty. No one seems to know where he is."

CHAPTER SIXTEEN

Nesta knew that providing she wasn't careless, no one would question that the Home she'd settled into wasn't really her own. Marauders, raiders, kidnappers, probably even the Heaven Bound wouldn't sleep overnight in, much less settle into, an untenanted Home. After all, if all those billions of people had Vanished once, no matter what your belief system was for explaining that away, there was no guarantee that they might not Reappear just as suddenly and catastrophically as they'd left.

Nesta was immune. She was probably one of the few people on the planet confident that the Vanished were gone for good. She tucked herself into bed each night without fear.

In her childhood this had indeed once been her Home. Her parents had moved the family away when she was still a girl, more than two decades before the Vanishing. Between their departure and the Vanishing the place had been owned by other families.

It had been remodeled at various times, to various degrees. Nesta chose to sleep in what had been the guest room in her youth, since converted into an office/den. Nesta preferred its newer incarnation.

But in the middle of one night when she stumbled half-asleep to the bathroom, she found herself navigating as if from her childhood bedroom further down the hall. She plunged several doors past the bathroom into the master bedroom and felt as embarrassed as if there'd been someone to see her. At the same time she marveled at the terrier-like tenacity of the nervous system to retain decades-old patterns, and at the overwhelming impact one's surroundings could have on one's consciousness, beyond all expectations of logic.

In the bathroom Nesta leaned in the dark against the sink. Her features were kindly dimmed in the mirror—the only reason she could make them out at all was due to the moonlight struggling to breach the bathroom's small, single window.

She thought about the House and the people within. Could it be as simple as that? The House had seemed to her, from the very start, to cast a disproportionate influence over its inhabitants. But perhaps what she'd perceived as an aberrant absorption was in fact a survival mechanism, an adaptation to the constant spatial disorientation they'd chosen to live in.

She returned to her bedroom and wrestled with the idea until she drifted back into sleep. There it continued to haunt her, for she dreamt she walked the corridors of the Hackers' Center at midday. She peered into rooms from sun-brightened hallways in search of Hake or Renzie. Standing in the day's glare, she found empty offices and labs filling with shadows as night pressed in at the windows. The blackness inkily spread. Nesta tried to outrun it down the halls. A shaft of sunlight illuminated a corridor intersection in the distance.

Nesta hurried toward it. The corporate landscape of hallway and identical doors remained unchanged as she passed, but somehow the Hackers' Center was transforming into the House. And she understood, somehow, that when she reached the light she would be fully inside the House. And that she would at last know—Nesta wasn't sure what, except that it was exactly what she needed to know.

She slipped as she ran and skidded without control. Unbalanced, she swayed this way and that, and dreamt that she woke in terror still swaying in her bed, the world rocking and shifting in horrible cadence in the early morning light.

She *was* awake. Nesta feebly clutched the sides of her plunging bed and wondered if she was having a stroke.

A pen rolled off the desk across the room. A box of disks she'd brought with her from Pennsylvania shuffled in place and then fell over on its side. Some pictures hanging over the desk rocked left and right in place. One came loose and crashed down.

Nesta rolled out of bed and scrambled on hands and knees to crouch in the doorway, weakly relieved that she was merely experiencing an earthquake, at the same time wondering if the rickety old Home would come crashing down and kill her.

The temblor subsided. When she'd waited long enough to feel sure that a large aftershock wasn't likely to follow, Nesta crawled back to bed and burrowed into the covers.

Who was she to think of the Housers as being irrationally obsessive? Here she was, an elderly woman living alone in an isolated Home simply out of reaction to her own unacknowledged superstitions.

After she pulled herself together Nesta made her way gingerly around the Home to assure herself there'd been no new structural damage. She arrived at the House late, wondering if she'd find it a shambles. But other than a few food-filled bowls rolling off sideboards and making a mess in the kitchen it was business as usual there. The earthquake had felt larger than it really was in her rickety, aging dwelling.

She'd already missed the school shuttle for the Center. Eric told her there'd be a wagon going up from the Office Building in less than an hour, if she didn't mind traveling in less style. Nesta sat out on the porch and watched the misty rain while she waited. Chloe brought her a big, steaming bowl of milk and coffee, all the more warming and comforting for not being served in a cup.

At the Hackers' Center Jan was Nesta's first stop.

At about the time the rains had started the Hackers' Center Med staff had declared Jan well enough to begin having conferences with Nesta. They were still concerned with the danger of her contracting pneumonia and emphasized that she needed a good deal of rest. Nonetheless, they consented to and even helped Nesta set up a minioffice of a file folder and cassette recorder next to Jan's bed so that Nesta could begin the process of transcribing Jan's records.

"Did you feel the earthquake up here, or are you going to make me feel idiotically oversensitive and say 'What earthquake?' "

Jan smiled wanly. "Oh no, we felt it too. The nursing staff got so flustered they almost forgot to turn me that hour. Imagine—if I'd slept through the quake, I could have gotten two solid hours of uninterrupted sleep."

"It's late this morning anyway. Maybe I should just let you rest."

"Not on your life." Jan patted the recorder on her nightstand. "I filled up a whole new tape for you. Listen through it and see if you've got any questions for me before we start transcribing."

Nesta dutifully put the earphones on. Before she'd gotten fifteen minutes into the tape Jan had fallen sound asleep. Nesta left Jan a note promising to come back later that afternoon. She slid out of the room as quietly as she could.

Hake was in Nesta's office. He'd probably been there since early in the morning, immersed in the long process of setting up the testing, data programs, and experiment models.

"Just in time," Hake said over his shoulder. "I'm stuck here . . . don't know where to put in these columns of figures."

Leaning over him, Nesta tapped in some commands.

"Ah, yes," he said, leaning back. "I should have guessed that." He frowned at the screen, then looked up. "Renzie came by this morning and said you didn't make the bus. I was beginning to wonder if we should send someone over to see if you were all right."

"It wasn't that bad a quake," Nesta said tartly, then felt embarrassed. She'd snapped at him in direct proportion to the fear she'd felt.

Hake just smiled slightly. "Well," he said, "as it was, it got me up early, so I came down and spent most of the morning running backups. And it *was* a bad enough quake that Yorheim popped in to see if everything was okay."

"Want to bet we were the only project he dropped in on?" Nesta said. "His concern is heartwarming."

"Sure was." Hake tapped the computer. "He even offered to help me go through the files to be sure we hadn't lost anything."

"Why doesn't he just give it up?" Nesta said, her crankiness returning. "I told him I'd give him a preliminary report when we began getting results. Hell, we haven't even started yet."

"You haven't asked for any advice, but I think I'll volunteer an opinion anyway," Hake said. "Yorheim likes at least his pinkie in every pie. If you'd capitulate just a little and give him that he might leave you alone."

"I would if I could." Nesta sighed. She didn't want to continue a conversation rapidly disintegrating into Hackers' Center politics— not with her temper sliding downhill. "You said Renzie stopped by.

Where is she? I thought they were going to release her to us by now."

Hake shook his head. "Not yet. As soon as she dropped off the kids she got assigned to help the crew demolishing the Home the 'Bounders fired. What with taking down the fair and everything else, they've had to put it off till now. Don't worry. She'll be here soon enough. She's as irri— as anxious to start work as you are."

Nesta ignored the deliberate slip. "Speaking of work, Jan had a new tape ready for me this morning." Nesta pulled out the cassette player and headphones from her satchel. "She was exhausted, fell asleep as soon as I started listening to it. If I come up with any questions could I run them by you?"

"Sure." Hake didn't seem to take Nesta's or anybody else's bad moods personally. "What's the transcription about?"

"At this point Jan is assembling an overview of all the cults in the area for me." Nesta made little claws with her index fingers in the air around the word "cults" as she spoke. "She's already broken down overall categories of the most 'commonly' reported anomalies." Again Nesta gestured quote marks. "Next she's going to cross-reference similar accounts reported by the different groups."

"Just out of curiosity, what *are* the most commonly reported phenomena?"

Nesta flipped through her papers till she found the list. "Lots of visions in forests—glimpses of 'other places' through the foliage; and day for night, night for day." A frisson of recognition rippled her spine as she remembered her dream of night leaching away a deserted daytime Hackers' Center. She hurried on. "The last two could be put into a general category with other photonic phenomena, like reflection/refraction distortions and color shifts. Then there's various auditory accounts . . . people hearing things, voices, et cetera. Various reports of synesthesia . . . do you really want to listen to all this now? I'll be running a printout for everyone on the team."

Hake held up one hand. "No, that was fine. Just wanted a general idea, see if anything rang a bell."

"Did it?"

"I've heard similar stories. Probably the same stories. When you get it all run off I'll check through it, see if I have anything to add."

He turned his attention back to the programming. Nesta set up the cassette recorder, put the earphones on again, balanced a notebook on her lap, and kicked her feet up on the desk. She settled back to listen.

About half an hour later, out of the corner of her eye Nesta saw Hake shift in his position, interrupting his steady rhythm.

"Ready to take time out to stretch and rest for a moment?" she asked.

"Yes," he said, interlacing his fingers and rotating his intertwined fingers outward till his knuckles cracked. "I'm going to make myself some mint tea. Would you like any?"

"I'd love it."

He brought Nesta a mug. They sat a moment in silence, burying their faces in the astringent steam.

"So, want to run anything by me yet?" Hake asked after a suitable period of reverie. Nesta smiled into her cup, thinking how good he was at pacing her.

"Yes, as a matter of fact, I do." She opened her notebook. "The group referred to as Strieberites—that's pretty self-defining. But Jan alludes to two diametrically opposed factions: the Bens and the Mals. At this point her notes are still quite cursory. Mal . . . *malo,* bad . . . I think I get that. What about the Bens?"

Hake swirled his cup a little to cool it. "You're close on Mal. It stands for 'malevolent.' The Mals believe malevolent aliens kidnapped the Vanished for nefarious purposes. Bens assert that benevolent aliens snatched up humanity to a higher plane; enlightenment, immortality, the whole ball of wax. You can't get the two groups anywhere near each other. As I understand it, the Mals figure if the aliens *do* return that the Bens will go running out to them with open arms and get snatched up and away. And it'll serve them right and good riddance to bad rubbish. As you can imagine, the Bens believe the flip side of the same coin. Next question."

"Not so much a question as that I'd like your opinion. The Koanites. I saw some of them at the fair. The way Jan explains it, they believe the Vanishing represents a Great Koan. Although they're not involved in intellectual or emotional attempts at understanding the Vanishing, Jan says they're interested in and alert to unusual occurrences. I would think that would make them a rich source for our research. Jan, though, seems to think their usefulness limited. Why?"

Hake laughed. "Because they speak in koans about anything involving the Vanishing. That makes it virtually impossible to distinguish between factual account and cryptic lesson."

Nesta sighed and shuffled through the papers. "Look at all of these! Los Milagros, the Three Bears Temporalists, Penitents, Women's

Brigade, Chipheads, Apocalyptics, Neo-Christians, Heaven Bounders, even the Nightwatchers and Homers. This list goes on and on. That's the problem we'll have with all of them. These are anything *but* objective witnesses. Their biases are going to color their perception of any observed phenomenon. Ironic, isn't it? The Vanishing was a purely physical event that initiated a cascade of anomalies. But we can't depend on getting any straightforward accounts because everyone's perceptual abilities are twisted by their reactions to the Vanishing."

"Was it any different back East?" Hake asked.

"Not really, just not so obvious, the groups not so clearly defined, so obviously cults."

"Then just keep on going with the process you've started," he said. "Cross-reference similar anomalies reported by the different groups, see what common denominators arise, then run those through the computer models. And don't forget there are individual accounts as well. Not everyone belongs to a cult."

Nesta shot him a look. "Not everyone? I heard your zoo story at the party, you know. Can you really show me a single person, including yourself, including me, who, since the Vanishing, can't be said to belong to a cult? Even if it's a cult of one?"

CHAPTER SEVENTEEN

Nesta looked out her office window the first morning her team gathered to begin work, noting with satisfaction the spongy, melting skies and soggy foliage of the bushes below the windowsill. A resigned veteran of years of the downpour of East Coast summers, she was amused at her enthusiasm for this wet weather. But she felt her enthusiasm was justified—here the rainfall brought with it a welcome cooling, rather than the hypersteamed, pressure-cooker effect she was used to in Pennsylvania. And even back East people got more work done when rained in.

The weather promised well for the project in other ways—with the risk of fire diminished, her crew wouldn't be so tense and jumpy, ready to be called away at a moment's notice. They'd be more in a frame of mind to concentrate on the work at hand.

Indeed, as they drifted in Nesta noted the cumulative atmosphere: relaxed, yet excited and intent. Except for Jan, the entire team was present: Hake, Renzie, and eleven others from assorted disciplines. Pax Willster had also decided to attend.

Nesta liked Pax and welcomed his input, but hoped that if he'd come to assume the role of devil's advocate that he wouldn't be a constant presence. Further along in the research that would be necessary and useful. At this stage she needed people who'd be willing to suspend their disbelief till results came in.

"We'll be running checks on two separate lines of data," she began, handing out folders. "The first set of papers you'll find in this packet is a summary of Jan's field research. At this stage we're going to treat it as if it were valid, proven, experimental evidence. A more detailed report, to be analyzed and broken down into actual data that can be run through the computers, will be given to the subcommittee assigned to this line of research.

"All of you will need to be familiar with the general material. We'll be bouncing concepts back and forth off each other, correlating ideas.

"And since Jan's going to be out of commission for a while longer, we all need to keep our eyes and ears open for reports of any of the anomalies you'll find listed."

Nesta saw Adrienne Barnett, the chemist, already leafing through the information. Adrienne's eyebrows shot well up into her hairline. Nesta took a deep breath and forged ahead. "And any anomalies you *don't* find listed." Adrienne raised her hand and waved it.

"You have the rest of the morning to scan this information, familiarize yourselves with it," Nesta said, fending her off. "This afternoon we'll dialogue and I'll start you on your setups. I'll take specific questions on the material at that time."

Adrienne lowered her hand, looking put out. She scribbled something down in her notebook—whatever the question might be, Nesta wasn't going to get out of having to deal with it later.

"The next document refers to the type of research most of you are more accustomed to." Papers rustled, followed by a subliminal sigh of relief. At first.

"Wait a minute," one of the physicists said. "Shifts in the Planck's constant, electron shell counts? I'll bite, wild as this stuff sounds, at least as far as researching—but what about your theories on virtual-particle jumps? I thought that's what brought you out here in the first place. That's what got me interested in working with you." He looked around. A few of the others nodded agreement.

"It's a fair question," Nesta agreed. "What was your name again—Steff? I know some of you already, but it'll take me a while to match your names to your faces. I didn't think I'd be going into why I dropped—no, make that shifted—my original line of research in this first session, but maybe it's just as well." She turned her PC monitor at an angle so they could all see if they crowded in together.

"Remember that one of the first hypotheses right after the Vanishing was the matter/antimatter theorem?" Nesta asked. She keyed in a program, then tapped in the beginning of a diagram. "There's no such thing as 'empty space,' but rather a vast 'sea' of negative-energy electrons. If you jump-start one of these 'negative electrons' with enough energy you can pop it out into our reality as an 'electron'—actually, a positron—and it leaves behind a hole in the negative-energy sea."

She typed in another diagram below the first. "The idea was that if you reversed the process, matter could be disappeared off *this* side of reality into the negative-energy sea. Maybe somehow several billion people got melted away off in between the cracks. But before the research went anywhere, like wondering what that really meant as far as whether all those folks were 'dead' or 'alive' or 'retrievable,' the notion got tossed out. Remember why?"

"Energy discharge," Steff said. "The gamma ray bursts would have fried anyone sleeping next to somebody who Vanished, along with most of the rest of the planet. The process would have liberated $E = mc^2$."

"Correct." Nesta typed in the equation, then paged down to a blank screen. "All right, so what attracted me at first to the idea of the virtual-particle jumps is that virtual particles are leaping in and out of reality merrily all the time without that sort of problem. What if *that* was what had happened to the Vanished, on a macro scale? If so, why? And would they leap back into reality, and when, and in what shape?"

She drew a matching set of Feynman diagrams on the screen.

ART TO GO HERE

"Remember these? Electron-positron annihilation looks just like a single electron scattering off a virtual photon. You can read this as the elements moving either forward or backward in time.

"What I found was this . . ." She exited the program, backed up to the directory, and keyed in another file. A long string of equations emerged on the screen. "We're not talking about individual photons moving in straight lines through time and/or space, but an expanding, probably spiral shell—a wave front dilating multidimensionally from the event, scattering and distorting as it goes. If the Vanishing were a macrovirtual jump into the future or anywhere else we'd be dazzled by 'ghosts'—the photons falling backward in time or 'sideways' from other dimensions, in the same way that detritus drifts snowlike down to the ocean floor.

"So in trying to work out the bugs in my own theory I also managed to disprove the original temporal research, which postulated that all the Vanished might have simply jumped forward to some unknown point in the future."

Nesta looked at Pax. "Most of you may be interested in the virtual-particle work, but perhaps you're unaware that it was my closure of that particular line of temporal research that had as much to do as anything with my being invited here."

Pax blushed and the others from the Hackers' Center looked surprised. Nesta guessed that Ernest Yorheim's touchiness related as much to a conflict in agendas as Nesta's thoughtless behavior when she'd first arrived. The oligarchy wanted her to act as a "hit man" to help narrow the lines of inquiry. Instead the powers that be already sensed that she intended to introduce a line of research that extended beyond the wildest fringes of current inquiry.

"What about a jump to the past?" the astronomer asked.

Nesta paged ahead to another set of equations. "There would have been physical evidence—unless it was *way* back, say to the Precambrian, or even the earth's molten, formative period." She nodded at the math on the screen. "And we still would have had photonic 'snow'; up *until* the Vanishing in that case.

"Those aren't the only reasons I finally abandoned the virtual-particle research. I started to hear about the sorts of phenomena I would have expected if my theory had any validity, most of them anomalies involving unusual photonic disturbances. But they generally occurred with accompanying aberrations my theory couldn't account for.

"You'll find all of this in the back of the packets I handed out." Papers rustled as people shuffled through the reports, searching. "I'll answer all of your questions regarding my earlier research, but I don't want to get stuck here. We need to move on to the work itself.

"As I said before, we'll reconvene back here in the afternoon after you've had time to review the material. What I want to do right now is assign you into teams, so that you'll know which information to concentrate on.

"The initial data-processing crew will consist of . . ." She looked at the staff list Pax had compiled. "Haberman, Elise Ngyuen, and Lampwick Jones. The only immediate processing for the three of you will be Jan's research, but I'm also going to have you running models of the lab experiments before we actually set them up.

"Here." She pulled some disks out of the desk drawer. "I want checks run each time you input any data or run any programs. Start with your standard antiviral software." She waved a disk.

"Then go on to these." Nesta slid another disk into her PC, keyed in a folder, then a file. An animated, three-dimensionally rendered simulation appeared: a serendipitous array of objects—brooms, hats, paintbrushes and Bibles tumbled lazily around a simulated kitchen. "You're all familiar with standard Baraff tests for Newtonian physics?"

"Yes," said Elise Ngyuen.

"Good." Nesta popped a window into the test. Floating in the middle of the image it added to the surreal effect nicely. "This is a list of the other tests in the series. See the ones that are asterisked?" She cued in a second window. "Those are the revisions I've made."

Lampwick squinted at the lines of fine type. "Wow! That's different. Did you bring these disks with you all the way from Carnegie-Mellon, or did you alter some of our software?"

"Neither. Hake and I put together this program the last couple of weeks while the rest of you were busy with the trade fair and firefighting."

"From scratch?" Lampwick said incredulously.

Nesta had to grin. "I spent a couple of summers working with Baraff at Cornell."

Someone in the back whistled. Nesta registered the response. Even if it was cheap namedropping, she'd take all the respect she could get. She'd need that and a lot of blind faith to get them over the bumpy parts in the months to come.

"But why do you need tests on Newtonian motion mechanics? The Vanishing puts us in an era beyond *quantum* physics."

"These tests are *not* for verification on the physics. They're to double-check the computers themselves."

Haberman laughed. "What's the matter? Don't you trust the computers?"

When Nesta didn't answer, his laughter faltered, uncertain.

"Once you finish with those," she said, "switch to these." She held up another set of disks. "These are your checks and the basic format for non-Newtonian science. Hake will help you through the initial setup.

"Now, for the rest of you." She turned first to Adrienne Barnett and the biologist, Dodd, a roly-poly man in his mid-forties. "Your initial assignment is to look into an aberration familiar to us all; the hair shimmering effect in the first post-Vanishment generation and the supposed loss of that effect in the succeeding generation. Your fellow researchers can provide you with the physical material for the first-generation and pre-Vanishment control experiments."

Elise Ngyuen ran a hand self-consciously through her radiantly blue-black hair, and some of the other younger researchers also appeared unsettled.

"Look to the mass of kids around here for the resources for the next phase—testing the second-generation post-Vanishment. I'm sure a few of them wouldn't mind donating some hair clippings. What you're looking for is molecular changes in structure resulting in the index of refraction of the protein sheath of the hair, causing it to be more reflective and prismatic. I've already done some preliminary work on this and can tell you that the physical constants have shifted in value and the fine-structure constant is now different."

Adrienne looked incredulous. "You mean it's not 1 over 137 anymore?"

"No," Nesta said. "Look through the folders and you'll find the parameters of what I've already done. Repeat the experiments and then take it from there. When you're finished, run the data past the computer team."

She glanced down at her list for the astronomer's name. "Loren Van Woorden?"

A man so elderly that he made Nesta feel like a young girl raised his hand.

"I want you to run spectroscopic analyses on all angles and times of the night sky. Let's pin down that elusive aurora once and for all—I'd guess in the 'nonvisible' lengths of the spectrum." She had a thought. "Hell, run checks on a twenty-four-hour basis, not just for the night. Let's see what we come up with."

Van Woorden nodded and scribbled down some notes. If he had any questions he kept them to himself.

Nesta sipped some water to clear her throat and took a deep breath.

"We need to keep going on the field research. Renzie, I want you and . . ."—again she checked her list—"Elena, Robert, and Shoebak Morner to make two subteams and go to both the commune at Cosmic Life Acres and Los Milagros' parish. Jan gave me a list of contacts for both places. Elena, Robert, I know this is out of your line of expertise, but it's just temporary till Jan gets back on her feet.

"The expedition to Cosmic Life Acres is for preliminary interviewing. See what they've got in the way of legends and stories of unusual physical occurrences.

"We've already got a lot of information on Los Milagros. What I'm looking for there is more intensive material that we can translate into actual data. And I want backup research into their pantheon of saints, see how closely it correlates with the more traditional Catholics' index of saints, and how this relates to the anomalies associated with them. Let's see . . . Jan especially indicated Saint George, Saint René, Saint Nathan, Saint Charles, Saint Juana, Saint . . . well, you get the idea."

She parceled out the rest of the preliminary assignments. "Okay, that's it for now. You've got several hours to review the material I handed out and to take a nice long lunch. We'll meet back here at one-thirty."

They filed out, all of them immersed in the folders, even Pax. Nesta felt cheered. They'd have tough questions for her in the afternoon, but she could tell she had their interest.

Hake lingered behind. Renzie stood in the doorway waiting for him. "Nesta, let me work on the field research too," he said, surprising her.

"Hake, you're needed here to help with the computer programming."

"Once I get Haberman, Elise, and Lampwick set up I'll just be dead weight until the other data is ready to run. Let me help Renzie's team till then. I'm better suited for it—I'm no physicist, and I've had dealings with all of the groups in the Valley for years."

"Hake, if anything goes wrong with the data runs it would be disastrous. I can't risk that."

"I won't join the field teams till we're both satisfied that the computer crew can run things better than we could ourselves," he soothed her. "And if emergencies come up to pull any of them away I'll jump back in."

He made perfect sense. Nesta couldn't understand why she was so reluctant to let him go. Was she experiencing some sort of intuitive premonition? She scoffed at herself. Since when had she begun to indulge in superstitious nonsense? Perhaps she was rejecting something even harder to admit to herself—that she'd enjoyed his constant company the last few weeks, his willing involvement in the work. That she'd miss him.

"Don't forget that I'm going to have to be gone for a week in the middle of October," Renzie chimed in from the doorway. "I've got to take a pack of kids out for survival training. We'll need someone to back me up here. Hake would be perfect."

"All right, you've got it," Nesta told him.

CHAPTER EIGHTEEN

She found herself staring at the rain from her window at the Hackers' Center a lot those first few weeks, waiting for the initial data to be processed and new findings to trickle in. It was hard not to meddle. But once she'd given her teams their parameters she needed to let them settle in with each other, let them know she had confidence in their abilities. If she left them alone a little they were likely to come up with fresh ideas. After all the time she'd been working in relative isolation she could use new points of view.

The patience and waiting implicit in conducting laboratory experiments was so ingrained that Nesta couldn't be sure it wasn't part of her nature. But waiting for the results of others was another matter.

The rains came down heavier and heavier, soggy blankets casting layer after weighted layer across the sky. Unlike the first day of the project, the weather now oppressed her.

So her mood was not at its best the day that Renzie and Shoebak Morner arrived late to submit a report on their initial interviews at the Cosmic Life Acres commune.

Renzie and Shoebak had volunteered to help the communards with their harvest for a week. In return they stayed overnight to record legends and folk tales that the Cosmicnauts were happy to recount as they relaxed after a day's labor.

Renzie had promised that she and Shoebak would organize their preliminary material and be at the Hackers' Center before lunch. Now it was late afternoon. Night was falling prematurely, thanks to the opaque, slate-colored rain clouds. The ground outside had turned to mush.

As Nesta glared out the window at the darkening drear-on-drear landscape, she heard the door open behind her and two people sidle in. Before she'd even turned Nesta knew what had happened. The smell of smoke still clung to them.

"A fire," she said. "Where? At the commune?"

Renzie nodded. Shoebak, a slight man whose complete baldness made his age indeterminable, added, "Close by, anyway. A bunch of unshepherded Homes on the other side of the Cosmic Life fields. They were due for razing next spring."

Nesta gestured at the deluge outside. "Lightning?"

"No such luck," said Renzie. "Definitely arson."

Nesta thought of the incident that ended the trade fair. She thought of how Jan had almost been lost. "Heaven Bounders. They said they'd be back."

She didn't get the confirmation she expected. Renzie's forehead creased in uncertainty.

"We're not so sure," Renzie said. "If it is, they're trying new tactics. This is like the fire sites in the Milpitas area, only sloppier. There was still some effort to restrain this one. 'Bounders would've wanted it to spread as much as possible. And they would have wanted us to know they were responsible."

"Of course, whoever set this one also risked lives by setting it so close to the commune," Shoebak said soberly. "Just because they might not be 'Bounders doesn't mean they're not dangerous."

"Was anybody hurt?" Nesta asked.

Renzie shook her head. "Some minor smoke inhalation, nothing worse. Thank heavens for the rain." She flipped a pen from the desk through her fingers restlessly.

"I'm glad you're both all right," Nesta told them. "Would rescheduling our meeting for tomorrow afternoon give you enough time to compile your material?"

They nodded. "We're already more than half organized," Renzie said. "In fact, now that I'm up here, I'd like to enter some of the folklore onto the computer so that you can start looking it over in the morning."

Nesta waited about a half hour before meandering by Renzie's PC cubicle.

"How's it going?" she said after watching Renzie punish the keys for a few moments.

"Okay, I guess," the younger woman said, her accompanying shrug manifestly unhappy.

"You're really bothered by the fire—something besides it just being a fire—aren't you?"

Renzie tapped in a save, leaned back in her chair, ran her fingers back along her scalp. "*I* found the other burn sites in the spring. I know better than anyone how weird this is."

Nesta hesitated before speaking again. "Do you think they might be aberrations, or have anything to do with aberrations?"

Renzie looked startled, then laughed. "Not *everything* in the world is a manifestation of your particular obsession."

Nesta flushed but was glad she'd made Renzie laugh. "You said yourself that the situation is bizarre."

Renzie sobered immediately, making Nesta almost sorry she'd persisted, but the physicist couldn't leave a single possible lead uninvestigated.

"I hadn't considered your aberrations because this is weird in a different way," Renzie said. "The fires were set in a standard arson fashion. So why do they limit them? It doesn't make sense. Who would do that? I can't think of any of the cults, including the 'Bounders, who would operate in this way."

"Maybe it's not a cult. Maybe it's an individual. Somebody crazy, or with a grudge." A thought occurred to Nesta. "What about that surly young fellow who disappeared? Didn't he have quite a chip on his shoulder?"

"Sun? He's still missing," Renzie acknowledged. "Normally we'd have figured he'd just up and left, but considering when he disappeared, folks are concerned. In all that ruckus chasing off the 'Bounders, he could have run into them on his own in the underbrush and . . . sst." Renzie drew a finger across her throat. "But we put out search parties and didn't find any bodies. I don't think the 'Bounders would have had time to bury victims while they were running."

"I got the impression Sun wasn't a 'native.' How long has he lived in the House?"

"Seven years," Renzie said. "I'd guess he was in his late teens when he showed up. He's about Tuck's age."

"Is it possible"—Nesta tried to think of a tactful way to ask—"that he might have been a plant, that he might have been raised a 'Bounder and sent here . . . ?" She let the idea dangle.

Renzie looked thoughtful, then shook her head. "He's contrary enough to be a 'Bounder—*too* contrary. I think you could sic brainwashing experts on him for a hundred years and it wouldn't take. And 'Bounders aren't just fanatics. They're *serious* fanatics. If they were going to send us a Trojan horse it would be someone trained to at least try to fit in with us, whereas Sun is always at odds. I don't like Sun, but I wouldn't lay this at his door. Those fires are going to stay a mystery until we find out more about them." Her mood turned grim again. "And no one's safe until we do."

She cocked one eyebrow at Nesta. "So maybe it's finally time for you to move into the House. Besides, the weather is turning cold. I know you don't have any solar hookups at your place. Or I suppose, living all those years back East, that this still feels warm to you."

Her change of subject away from the arson didn't deceive Nesta. Renzie had been frightened by the return of the fires. She's frightened for me, Nesta thought.

Nesta considered the earthquake and how fragile the Home she was living in had seemed. She thought of the House beckoning her from a warm pool of light.

"No, it doesn't feel warm. The chill here penetrates to the bones. And I've got old bones," she said.

"How far are you going to get with your research if you come down with pneumonia?" Renzie nudged Nesta. "We could even do work on the project together in the evenings, if you wanted to."

"What if I take the day off tomorrow and come look the House over, see what's available?" the older woman asked.

Renzie's face relaxed. Her relief was so palpable that Nesta realized that though it was the only accomplishment in an otherwise fruitless day, that was enough.

CHAPTER NINETEEN

The rain slacked off by the next morning. For the first time in days Nesta stayed dry during her stroll to the House. Silver gray clouds raced high overhead, impatient to get away after being tethered to the earth the last week.

Renzie was waiting for her. As Nesta mounted the steps she opened the porch door, looking at the older woman curiously when Nesta lingered on the stairs.

Nesta hesitated because she first wanted to remember what she could of the House from all the childhood tours she'd taken, grasp those images as a discrete, acknowledged part of herself. She feared if she didn't, that once she entered, the House's current reality would sweep them away, taking part of her with them.

That part of Nesta's worry was groundless. Old memories washed over her as soon as she stepped over the threshold. The differences between the House of her childhood overlaid the House of now. The building seemed to swell with new dimensions.

In her youth sightseers had been herded through chutes formed by red velvet ropes strung between brass stanchions. Those artificial passages had channeled visitors through the House in serpentine fashion, so they never visited the same room twice, and allowed the traffic to roll like a river in one direction only.

Now the stands and restricting ropes were gone. The dimensions of the House felt completely different, open to the flux and flow of all possible exits and entrances.

Renzie took Nesta into rooms she didn't remember at first. Then some angle or feature would resonate, the room would reveal its familiarity, and Nesta realized she hadn't recognized it because they'd entered from an unaccustomed direction.

They came across people everywhere. There seemed to be no logic as to who lived where.

The mysterious old séance room, with its single entrance and triple exit doors, was now home to a clutter of electronic equipment and a young man in a wheelchair.

The largest room in the House was the Grand Ballroom; its sole inhabitant a woman with the thick, wavy hair and exquisite profile of an ancient Minoan. She'd filled the Ballroom's numerous display niches with an array of bones, shells, and skulls. Austere and elegant in their bleached whiteness, they lent the near-empty Ballroom the air of a museum lined with Greek sculptures.

Yet only a few rooms away a group of folks were packed together tight as sardines, along with a multitude of plants, into the Southern Conservatory and its system of porches.

And throughout the House, in and out of the hallways, children and cats seemed to conjure themselves up everywhere and then disappear.

Perhaps because of that rhythm—crowding, emptiness, crowding—Nesta felt a sort of compression and decompression as she and Renzie wandered, like swimming head down into ocean depths. Pressure built tangibly on her eardrums and she'd think they were heading toward the center of the House, on their way to discovering its cavernous heart. But that impression would prove to be an illusion. They'd round a corner and emerge onto some airy sun-bright porch. Nesta's ears would clear—it would turn out they'd been worming their way through a series of rooms paralleling the outer walls of the House.

She realized she might be teetering on the edge of discovering an anomaly somewhere in this influx of sensation. Excited and absorbed, Nesta lost track of Renzie's tour guide monologue.

Their arrival at a small room dominated by a single stained-glass window caught her by surprise. She surfaced out of her calculations with a sharp sense of vertigo, followed by equally sharp recognition.

"There are lots of leaded-glass windows throughout the House," Renzie said. "But this one is special because . . ."

Nesta held up her hand. "Stop. I remember this." She moved close to the window, closer than she'd ever been allowed during the old tours of her childhood.

"It's all right. You can touch it." Renzie guessed her desire.

Nesta ran her hands over its surface. The window's colors were muted because no direct sunlight shone through it, had ever shone through it. And lacking that touch of sun, its glass and lead felt as cool and hushed as its colors.

But it was lovely nonetheless. Flourishes of glass ribbon and abstracted floral shapes fanned out across its surface. She fingered the raised, rounded nuggets of rock quartz and crystal that studded the overall pattern.

"It was designed to catch a lot of light, southern light," she said. When she'd been a child and the tour guide had explained this, Nesta had thought she understood. But she hadn't, really. Now she could fully appreciate the intent of the artisan who'd designed the window: How the evenly scattered prismatic forms were meant to first gather the light, then shatter, transform, and fling it out again, spackling the room with a riotous, radiant display, saturating the walls with hues like luminous stains.

Nesta shook her head with regret. "But the owner chose to mount it in a room with only northern exposure."

"And then built other parts of the House up around this section, blocking out even that light," Renzie concurred. She leaned against a doorway, arms folded, watching Nesta's reaction with a sympathetic expression.

"I can't help but think that perhaps just this one time the builder was wrong." Nesta sighed. Somewhere inside of her some final opposition gave way and she recognized the extent to which she'd been resisting the House. Nesta gladly surrendered. She laughed out loud. Renzie looked at her quizzically, but Nesta shook her head. She couldn't have explained.

"Is there some system where I can learn all the routes through the building?" Nesta asked.

"There's several patterns for getting around," Renzie said. "I'll show you the basic ones we teach guests so they can negotiate their way to and from basics like the bathrooms and the dining commons. It takes a long time to learn the whole House, though. Before I completely tire you out, why don't I take you to the addition Eric thought you might like? Once you move in I can show you the rest at your leisure."

That sounded good to Nesta. They followed a stream of children out of the House and across the courtyard to a wing disconnected from the rest of the complex.

"This was the tourist center," Nesta recalled. "It had a kitchen, snack bar, gift shop, game arcade."

"It's been a lot of things since the Vanishing," Renzie said. "When I was real little and the marauders were still about it was the first line of defense for the House. After that it was the lab for a while. The kids have taken it over now. Most of them bunk in here."

The inside looked like a giant clubhouse. Battered display cases had been moved around to define communal spaces. Enormous piled-up cushions and mounds of blankets functioned as slumber-party bedding. Old computer arcade games stood in clusters, a few of them with old bullet holes punched in their backs.

Now youngsters swarmed around them like Hollywood Indians surrounding television wagon trains—over and behind them, too. Some of the consoles' backs were open. Children tinkered in their entrails. Even as they were being repaired, other youngsters seemed to be simultaneously playing on the gaudy monitors in front—or simultaneously manipulating them?

"Wait!" Nesta said as Renzie whisked her by. Nesta caught glimpses of bright tints and flickering shapes on the screens. She thought she saw a figure run across a screen, disappear, reappear on the next monitor, then the next, and the next after that. In its wake the images on the monitors collapsed in sequence into a brief kaleidoscope of colors, then flatlined to an eerie violet glow.

Renzie dismissed the arcade with a wave. "You can come back later, as much as you want to. Right now let's go find Eric." They exited the gift shop through what had once been the main tourist entrance.

The sound of hammering led them to a long, narrow wing jutting out from the House like a slightly crooked, beckoning finger. Nesta didn't recognize the architectural appendage. The shingles furring its sides were fresh and unstained yet, the exposed supports still the light raw color of newly cut wood. They rounded the corner to find Eric, Carpenter, and a woman on Carpenter's crew securing a window frame into place. The new structure bulged out and to the side; a long, skinny, flexed hallway with a swollen room at the end. Now Nesta recognized it.

"The sales kiosk! This is where they sold tickets for the tours!"

Eric leaned out through the window and grinned. "That's right. Renzie pointed out that you seemed to want to live in the House and keep your distance from it at the same time, so this seemed like a good compromise. You can thank Carpenter for the idea."

Carpenter stood on the outside with his back to them as he hammered, too caught up in his work to turn or break rhythm. He mumbled at them through a mouthful of nails. "I always did desire to start bringing Her out on this side. This was the perfect excuse. Someday we'll build more rooms and extensions to come up flush with you and you'll have neighbors."

It occurred to Nesta that if the Hackers' Center resembled rewired circuitry, then the House was a three-dimensional Scrabble board, its smallest angles being filled in with nooks no bigger than two-letter words.

Carpenter looked over his shoulder and misread her silence. "But that won't be for a long, long time," he assured her. "Time enough for you to get comfortable with Her, and Her with you. In the meantime you're sort of like a scout for Her out here. Go ahead, go on in and see if you like it." He waved her in with his hammer.

"It was nice of you to build this for me," Nesta said.

Carpenter ducked his head and smiled shyly in acknowledgment. "Not just me," he said. "I've got my crew, the rest of the folks here too at times, and She helps me a lot Herself; tells me what She wants and who She wants and oftentimes does a lot of the work Herself."

Nesta didn't know what to say to that.

Renzie pulled her around to a doorway. "I hope you enjoyed the discourse. That's more than most people hear out of Carpenter in a year."

Nesta stepped inside to where Eric waited. The room wasn't huge but it was airy enough. A bunk bed with bookcases built in underneath edged out from the near wall. Someone had donated a chair, a stool and a tiny coffee table. Across the room was a narrow door that she assumed concealed a small closet.

"It can't be this big," she protested. "They used to have two people crammed in here, falling over each other if they even had to make change."

"True enough," Eric said. "We took out the back wall and bellied it out in that direction, added some skylights." He pointed to the umbilical passageway connecting the room to the rest of the House.

"The hall is completely open at the far end, but if you want privacy, those are sliding doors you can pull shut." He demonstrated.

Renzie danced from foot to foot. "It's not quite done, but what do you think? Will it do?"

Nesta looked to where a new electrical outlet protruded from the wall. She pointed her chin at it. "Will that accommodate a PC?"

Eric leaned back against a stud, smiling like a cat. "Yep."

"It'll do. When can I move in?"

CHAPTER TWENTY

Renzie shifted her weight to lean more comfortably against the trunk of the chaparral oak she perched in. If she wanted to see the night sky clearly, with its lemon half-wedge of moon and full dusting of aurora, she had to turn back toward the open indentation in the hillside behind her, where the children nested together fast asleep. Her sentry's view of the sky, when she looked away from the clearing, back toward the sloping woods, was obscured by thick foliage.

The survival outing had gone well so far. Four days down, two days to go. The children had taken quickly to making snares and deadfall traps. Hunting and gathering went more successfully than Renzie had hoped for. So far the emergency supplies had gone untapped. Not that they'd be in danger of starving. The site Renzie had chosen, in the rolling terrain beyond Saratoga, was only a day's stiff hike from the House.

The only aggravation so far had come from Chupa, as she'd half expected. The Homer child had bothered and begged Eric, Renzie, and her reluctant parents to be allowed to join the group until they'd given in. But when handed a squirrel carcass to skin and dress, she'd refused, her normally stolid face screwed tight in revulsion. Then she'd burst into tears when faced with killing a possum they'd trapped.

To Renzie's great relief the other children had been remarkably tolerant. Renzie guessed that came more from their determination to enjoy the outing at any cost than any newly acquired regard for Chupa. But no matter what the reason, Renzie was grateful. The trip was proving a great success.

Other than Chupa, the only other mild annoyance so far had been a day of intermittent showers. Renzie chose to view them as more of a benefit than a hindrance. She'd offered this outing to teach survival skills in the wild. The wilds included getting rained on.

The rains had let up yesterday. Residual dampness from the oak branches dripped onto and penetrated Renzie's wool jacket with just the right degree of discomfort to guarantee wakefulness. She'd assigned herself to the middle watch. The two other sentries, Quill and Dinah, one of the Mall girls, could be heard intermittently entertaining themselves with encoded night frog calls.

Renzie had set up the sentry system because, like the rains, the experience was good for the children. And though she didn't seriously think her little band was in danger from 'Bounders or anyone else, since the attack at the fair and the reoccurrence of the fires she thought it wise to be cautious.

For example, that glimmer she'd just caught sight of somewhere across the opposite slope. It was probably the moon's rising light reflecting off a rain-slicked boulder. No, wait, it was too brilliant for that. And its circular glow was too big.

As she strained her eyes, the light brightened further. It had to come from far back behind the trees, since it didn't illuminate them at all, simply threw them into even blacker silhouettes. Someone around the other side of the next hill must have started up a fire.

Renzie slid down her tree and crept back to the camp. She woke Minda and Bite, a tall skinny boy who lived in the House's game arcade.

"Go alert Quill and Dinah," Renzie whispered to Minda. "Then meet me and Bite at my post." Minda disappeared into the woods— small, fast, and silent.

Back at the tree, Renzie and Bite shimmied up its branches together. The light had strengthened but didn't display any of the flickering glare or thick smoke of a forest fire trying to spread through damp foliage.

"See? What do you think?" Renzie asked the boy.

He gave out a low whistle. "Oh yeah, definitely. Megaslip. Downshift skid to the brights."

Renzie sighed. What else should she have expected? A frog peeped at the base of the tree. "Good, Minda's here. Watch us for as far as you can. If you hear any commotion, go wake the others and get the hell out of here. When we can make out what's going on I'll send Minda back to tell you. In the meantime, you, Quill, and Dinah keep coding each other. Got that?"

"If you slip, I slide," Bite agreed.

That almost made sense. Somewhat reassured, Renzie clambered down again.

"We want to move low, real slow, with no noise, watching out for *everything,* not just the light," she told Minda. "If anything surprises us, I'll try to make as much of a racket as possible and you sneak back here. Okay?"

"Okay," Minda said.

They crept toward the brightness. Renzie forced herself to take a breath and relax after each step. She softened her gaze, slid it back and forth across the breadth of the landscape. When they dipped into the dark gully between the adjoining hills she fought a strangling moment of panic. She and Minda would be hidden from Bite's view for several minutes.

The curve of the slope ahead dimmed the mysterious light source. A step, a breath, relax. A step, a breath, relax. They emerged out of the landscape's shadow. In front of them the light had grown stronger. They'd almost reached the turning edge of the far slope.

"Get down," Renzie murmured to Minda. "From here on in we go it on hands and knees." Would they find a band of 'Bounders planning an attack on the Valley? Or merely hunters or trappers camping out for the night? Renzie's heart felt as though it were trying to crash through the wall of her chest as they scuttled the last few feet.

She sat back on her heels abruptly. No camp. No fire. The light striping between the trees before them was sunlight. Bright, blue-skied sunlight. Renzie swiveled her head to look at the pitch-black forest behind her. She looked forward again.

A sunny meadow lay just the other side of the trees. Clouds of gnats hovered, butterflies fluttered about each other above a patchwork bed of spring flowers—neon orange California poppies, low bushes of blooming blackberries and creamy honeysuckle, dandelions, wild iris. Spring flowers in the middle of October. A jay strafed the clearing on iridescent blue wings, beak opening and closing in its hoarse cry.

Except the raucous sound never reached her. Neither did the

subliminal whirring and humming she would have expected from such a tableau. All she heard was the rasp of her own hard-drawn breath, the rustle of Minda squirming beside her. And all she smelled was the chill damp mulch of wet autumnal forest: not the slightest whiff of the warm steamy perfume of new grass and sun-warmed flowers. Here, right in front of them, was one of Nesta's aberrations; a glorious, beautiful miracle.

"Stay put," she whispered to Minda. "If anything happens to me, or I don't come back, run like hell and get the others out. Go tell Tuck and Nesta." Renzie stood slowly, her legs shaking.

"But Renzie . . ." Minda protested.

Renzie waved her back. "It might be spreading. I've got to go see. I've *got* to go."

Renzie advanced one rubbery step at a time toward the vision, almost immobilized by warring emotions of compulsion, fascination and terror.

When I get there, what will I do? Will I just stand in the sunshine like an idiot? I've got to pull myself together and be ready for anything, she thought. Her feet moved as though she were dragging them through glue.

Maybe because of that, the clearing didn't appear to be drawing any closer. In fact, it seemed to be moving farther away. Renzie remembered the Red Queen in *Through the Looking-Glass,* running as fast as she could just to stay in place. I'm moving too slowly, Renzie thought. It's getting away from me.

She pushed herself into a loping run, dodged recklessly through the trees. It seemed to work at first. The clearing stopped retreating. But as she drew nearer its light began to dim. I *can* catch it, Renzie thought. I'm almost there. Lungs aching with effort, legs jarring against the uneven ground, she gathered herself and leapt into the fading meadow.

She landed in darkness, nothing before her but midnight forest. She stood trembling for a moment. It's an optical illusion, she thought. Some sort of light refraction, like a rainbow or mirage. Maybe someone's sending holograms through the ghost fleet of old satellites. Maybe Nesta's anomalies are just someone on the other side of the world playing tricks on us.

So when Renzie turned to look over her shoulder she wasn't surprised to find the meadow there, like a child who'd successfully played hide-and-seek on her. "Ollie, ollie, oxen free-o," she muttered as she started to trudge back.

As she expected, the image slid away from her again, this time in the opposite direction. She didn't pick up her pace, knowing eventually she'd cross through its illusory boundaries. She ignored the small bright movements of the birds and insects.

Then something large shifted at the edge of her range of vision. Some animal that crouched hunched over in the tall grass. Renzie froze automatically, even though she knew that whatever it was would be as ephemeral as the rest of the setting.

The creature dropped lower into the tall pasture, then came erect, showing itself.

Renzie yelped. "Minda!"

Minda stood in a patch of waist-high grasses, curiously bobbing down, then up, then down. Sunlight polished the crown of her hair to a high gloss. A meadow moth lit on her shoulder.

Renzie shut her eyes tight against the sight and tried to think. Just because Minda looked as though she were in the phantom clearing didn't mean she actually was. She was in the night forest, the same as Renzie. The optical illusion must be caused by an angle of reflection in the image.

Renzie ran at full speed toward Minda. Again the meadow dimmed and disappeared before she could reach it. Renzie whirled around to face it again. Minda was still there, but she was wandering out of Renzie's line of sight.

"Minda!" screamed Renzie. "Come back!" The little girl meandered on, deaf to Renzie's cries, until she was lost to sight behind a copse of intervening trees. Renzie dashed back and forth across the elusive vision, again and again. Finally she sank to her knees in exhaustion. Minda hadn't wandered back into view.

Something was changing. She raised her eyes. The meadow had begun to dim. And with it, maybe Minda. Renzie found a last reserve of strength and scrabbled forward.

The light faded slowly, transforming by stages through opaqueness to translucence to transparency. Then, like the Cheshire Cat, it teetered for a moment as a wisp of reality before evaporating into invisibility.

"No," moaned Renzie. "No."

She huddled where she'd collapsed, sobbing for a long, long time. Bite must have heard her yelling. She hoped he'd rounded up the other children and fled. The bright spot could come back—who knew where or when, who it might take next? Renzie shivered uncontrollably. Fear had chilled her to the core. She was so numb that when something gently touched her it took so long for the sensation to penetrate her consciousness that she didn't react. But when the contact came again, she jumped and howled.

"Renzie, what's wrong? Are you hurt? Did you fall?" Minda sounded worried, a little contrite.

"Oh my god." Renzie grabbed Minda and hugged her. The child's body heat contrasted shockingly with her own terrible coldness. She frantically stroked the youngster's soft fine hair, then yanked her hand away. Nothing should feel that toasty on such a cool, clammy night.

"I didn't mean to take so long," Minda said. "I brought you something." She thrust an untidy bundle into Renzie's hand. Renzie almost dropped it in shock. Even when she regained her composure, she could barely force her fingers closed around it. She bent to Minda's gift to verify the evidence of her senses, burying her face in the heady aroma and feathery texture of the flowery bouquet. The warmth of the sun still lingered on silky petals.

<hr>

After she'd force-marched the children back to the House the next day, Renzie knew that her first duty was to go up to the Hackers' Center and report to Nesta.

But she needed something first. The Vanishing shadowed all of her past. The future lay before her as a quicksand marsh of anomalies. There had to be at least one touchstone in her life.

She rested for a moment on the landing above the firearms museum. She couldn't remember when she'd ever been tired climbing any of the House's stairs before. Minda's wilting, dying bunch of flowers were wedged snugly between Renzie's shirt and jacket. She felt as if she'd strapped a bomb to her chest.

She rapped her knuckles once against the door to her brother's room. "Tuck?" she called softly.

He didn't answer, but she heard noises within. Renzie opened the door. "Tuck?"

Two women were bent over a big box overflowing with clothing and household objects. They turned to face her. One was Eileen, who lived alone in the Ballroom. The other woman Renzie hardly knew; one of the communal newcomers who'd moved in last spring.

Tuck's room looked like a half-stripped carcass. The walls were bare. Cartons filled with unfamiliar possessions littered the floor. A few of Tuck's things lay piled in a corner.

"Renzie, do you know Mara?" Eileen introduced the woman. "She decided she was ready for a space of her own, so I said I'd help her move in. She didn't have much stuff of her own so we took up a collection. And Tuck left her some of his stuff."

Renzie felt stupid with disorientation. "Where's Tuck?"

"Oh, that's right. You've been gone. He moved out two days ago. Into the Domes with Le Chell."

CHAPTER TWENTY-ONE

Nesta called a meeting of her team in her office a week later. Besides the PCs, files, and other equipment she'd commandeered since their initial get-together, she'd also set up a screen and slide projector. The team had to wedge themselves in as if they were more of the equipment.

"This is our first approximation of any kind of research results," Nesta began, looking both expectant and tense. "You've all been briefed about Renzie's direct experience of an aberration." As all heads swiveled in her direction, Renzie held herself stiffened against the impulse to tremble.

"Adrienne and Dodd have run tests of the evidence Renzie brought back," Nesta said. "I've asked Dodd to present their findings to the rest of you. Dodd, are you ready?"

"Yes, as soon as someone lowers the blinds," the biologist said. "Lampwick, will you turn on the slide projector? And could somebody turn out the lights?"

The room went black except for the slapping white square of light the projector flung onto the screen. It reminded Renzie of the meadow glimpsed as bright streaks through the night forest.

"The plants Renzie brought back were an assortment of California poppies, wild iris, and honeysuckle," Dodd said. "They appeared to have been picked within twenty-four hours of the time we received them and were in the wilted condition we would have expected. Initial tests revealed nothing unusual about them, until we began to analyze their DNA structure."

The biologist clicked the remote. As a slide glided into place the illusion of the meadow's bright light slid away. Now the screen shone with a luminous expectant black. Two sets of curlicued ribbons like gonfalons cascaded down each side of the projected image.

"This is a slide from research in the late 1900s on drugs being developed from chemically altered DNA," said Dodd. "The intertwined blue spirals on the left represent a normal DNA helix. Notice that the helix on the right looks similar except for the added *portion* of a third strand, called an oligo. The oligo is colored red in this graphic for easier identification. Observe how it's wound into the groove between the two blue strands.

"Oligos originally were specially constructed mirror images of unwanted messenger RNA, of, for example, cancer genes or destructive viruses. By binding to the threatening mRNA the inserted strand inhibited or halted the mRNA's damaging message.

"Within a short time, however, researchers began engineering oligos that acted instead as chemical *catalysts* in the DNA/mRNA couplings, thereby disrupting their normal sequences. That's why these biologicals came to be called 'antisense.' Shortly before the Vanishing, designer-drug oligos peddled under the umbrella term of 'Jabberwockys' began to hit the street trade. The potential of oligos was just beginning to be tapped at that time.

"That's the background for what I'm going to show you next." He clicked in a series of slides in rapid order, each an increasing magnification of some sort of cell.

"These are one of the cross-section sequences we made of the flowers Renzie brought us. This one happens to be a California poppy, but it's representative of all our findings."

As he said this the slide on the screen focused on the interior of a single cell. The next shot was of its nucleus, then the inner nuclear structure, and then the chromosomal strands caught in an instant of tentacular dance around each other. Then another slide, its organic image messily obscure.

"Without an extensive background in biochemical lab work, you probably won't be able to decipher this, so I prepared the next slide as a graphic of the plant's DNA structure so you could see it as a comparison to the oligo pictures."

The slide that followed reverted back to a black velvet background. A single banner composed of two blue strands and a third bright red one twirled down its middle. But this time the red filament wasn't a mere fragment—it curled all the way up and down the spiral.

For a moment nothing could be heard in the room but the warm whirring of the projector; no coughs, no whispers, no muttering.

"All of the samples Renzie brought us, regardless of genus or species, exhibit this genetic structure. It at first appears to be an extended oligo. In fact, it's a natural full third strand of genetic material," Nesta said, breaking the silence.

"What does it mean? Is it some sort of new oligo?" Shoebak Morner asked. "You said that the antisense drugs were biologicals. Could these be mutations that escaped?"

"We don't know," Adrienne said. "The plants seem normal in every other way. One of the speculations we're working on is that the third strand might be some sort of adaptation to allow these plants to continue to develop and function normally in the face of environmental changes. Normal in the face of *what* environmental changes, we don't know. I feel we have to consider the circumstances under which they were found as part of the anomaly of their structure."

In the darkness, Renzie again felt the pivoting of heads toward her.

"Obviously they can't actually be what you call oligos," said Haberman. "With that third strand going all up and down the genetic material, *no* message could get through from the DNA to the mRNA. The very existence of these plants would be an impossibility."

"Yes, with oligos as *blocking* mechanisms," Dodd said. "But don't forget that there were catalytic oligos too. Granted, developed as they were for medical usage, the catalytics also performed a blocking function, but that wasn't their only possible application. *These* strands, whatever they are, could be catalysts for amplifying or adapting. Or something else."

CHAPTER TWENTY-TWO

Renzie went back to her room at the House afterward and sat on her bed, numb, until past nightfall. She'd touched those plants, carried them against herself for almost a day. When she'd told her story at the center and handed over the bouquet, Nesta and Adrienne had donned rubber gloves before picking the flowers up.

She'd thought nothing of it at the time—lab procedure. But now—could contact with those extra strands of genetic material affect her? And what about Minda? The little girl had gathered the flowers. At the meeting no one had raised the issue of Minda's ability to enter the anomaly area when Renzie could not. Why? Did they think Renzie had imagined that? She shook her head angrily. No. In that case they wouldn't have bothered to test the plants in the first place, or been so careful with them.

Renzie had been a hunter too long not to recognize her fright as that of any heavy, clumsy, slow-moving target. She felt everything beginning to turn, to change, and she was standing still. Events were gathering over and around her in an enfolding trap. Renzie needed to talk to someone to gain some perspective. She would have talked to Tuck. But Tuck had chosen to become part of the changes.

Renzie picked at her nagging questions over and over like itching scabs as she walked through the labyrinth of the House, till she reached

the end of the corridor that connected Nesta's archipelago to the rest
of the House.

Nesta and Hake jumped and turned toward her like guilty children
when she opened the door. Hake sat on the bed, Nesta in a chair across
from him, their heads bent closely together, unmistakably intimate.

Renzie felt a surge of all the feelings she'd been suffering the past
week; awkwardness, loneliness, abandonment, and above all, confusion.

She hadn't even thought to knock, hadn't even considered that
Nesta might be having an affair. With, of all people, Hake. Renzie
flushed at her own thoughts. And why not Hake?

"Sorry, didn't mean to interrupt," she said.

Hake had flung his arm over a large box in a counterfeit gesture
of nonchalance. Renzie almost smiled to herself. She'd never seen him
flustered like this before. Nesta and Hake traded a glance. Renzie
cleared her throat in embarrassment and turned to go.

"It's okay, Renzie," Nesta said. "Come on in. You can stop
blushing. It isn't what you think." The older woman looked again at
Hake. "She should know. It's her subteam, too."

It seemed for a moment as if Hake were going to object. Then he
must have realized how that appeared. "I didn't mean to look as
though we don't trust you," he apologized to Renzie. "It's just that
you've been through a lot the last week. I thought maybe you could use
a break from more weirdness for a while."

Renzie's curiosity flared. All the other troubling emotions rapidly
faded. "I don't need a break from the weirdness, just some sort of
reassurance. Tell me—please."

Hake wrestled the box he was leaning on around in front of him.
"This was what we were being so secretive about," he said. Renzie
craned her neck to look, but he kept the top shut.

"Let me explain before I show you," he said. "When Nesta talked
about Los Milagros and their saints at that first conference, something
rang a bell with me. That's why I asked to work with them."

"I took the list of saints she gave me to an old Catholic seminary.
There's still some Catholic Revivalists living in the chapel there.
They've maintained most of the property, including the library. I'd

noticed that some of Los Milagros' saints go by Tagalog names, and others have been so hispanicized I couldn't trace them, but I checked as many as I could against the Catholic lexicon of saints.

"With that background information, I next went to Los Milagros themselves. I've been staying with them the last couple of weeks at their center at the old Santa Clara County library." Hake finally opened the box. "They were incredibly helpful, and even allowed me to borrow these artifacts to show to Nesta."

Inside were brightly painted wooden panels, flat diptych and triptych shrines with hinged doors, small branching icons encrusted with dense narratives of tiny sculpted figures. Hake rummaged around in them, looking for something.

"As you already know, but I've been explaining to Nesta here, Los Milagros are in many ways just another of the cults that tried to find a way to psychically and psychologically survive the trauma of the Vanishing. They're sort of a synthesis of Philippine pantheistic cults, brujaism, and their own particular brand of revivalist Catholicism.

"In some ways I think that, like the Koanites, they're saner than most because they didn't try to find a rationale or justification for the Vanishing, or what happened to the Vanished. They accepted that it happened. The 'reason' they believe it happened is that it ushered in THE AGE OF MIRACLES, in big capital letters. But most of them don't attach any specific dogma to their faith. They keep an open mind, watch for miracles, believing the miracles will show the way." Hake pulled a panel from the gaudy tangle. "This is what I was looking for." He studied it for a moment while he continued his monologue.

"Los Milagros' obsession with saints stems from their belief that there were certain sanctified individuals in the past who experienced miracles—in other words, anomalies—that foretold the Vanishing and the 'Age of Miracles.' By the past, I mean up to centuries ago.

"As I interviewed Los Milagros, took part in their ceremonies, studied their religious artifacts, I did find some matches to saints from traditional Catholicism."

Hake turned the panel around so that Renzie could see. It depicted a pretty young girl in long, flowing Byzantine robes. She carried a silver platter bearing two eyes; evidently hers, for there were only two gaping holes where her own should have been. Her delicate mouth bore a smile, in spite of the painful sightlessness and a long knife thrust through her throat. Her figure was cardboard-cut-out flat against a wild background of vermilion flames and ecstatically golden rays of light.

"Santa Lucia," said Hake. "Or Saint Lucy. According to conventional Catholicism she was born circa A.D. 304, her claim to sainthood simply virgin martyrdom. But folk faith has credited her for centuries with seeing visions.

"That's what I found in general: That all the easily identifiable saints were credited with observation of or participation in supernatural occurrences, rather than other saintly attributes they might possess, like the propensity for good deeds, martyrdom, or proselytization. I don't have retablas or icons for all of them here, but they include"—he ticked them off on his fingers—"Santa Juana, who turned out to be Saint Joan of Arc. Not for her military prowess, but because she heard voices. Saint Teresa, of course. Saint Bridget or Birgitta. Saint Patrick, because he dreamed. Still, these are old-time saints. Their revelations are open to anyone's conjecture, embellishment, or outright invention.

"It was the other saints, the ones that didn't seem to make sense at first because they *weren't* associated with supernatural occurrences; those are where *our* real resources lie." He pulled another panel from the box, and even more obviously and theatrically hid its face. "Let's take San Jorge, aka Saint George, for example. What do we expect? A knight on a stallion slaying a dragon?"

Renzie nodded, playing along with Hake.

"So did I. But look at this." He flipped the board around. Renzie blinked.

It pictured no rambunctious scene of knight and reptile, but instead a static composition like Saint Lucy's. An elderly clean-shaven man dressed in the somber black business suit of the last century stood bearing his eyes on a plate. Mercifully, in this painting his eyelids were closed over presumably empty sockets. Behind him spread a landscape of a European-style hedge maze. Below that appeared a cutaway view of a subterranean maze of a library, peopled with fantastic creatures. The picture was framed inside a border of Celtically sinuous tigers with red amber eyes.

"I don't get it," said Renzie.

"I didn't either, at first," said Hake. "It took me a while to track this fellow down. He really is Saint Jorge, not Saint George; Jorge Luis Borges, an Argentine writer, one of the major influences on the magic realist school." Hake tapped the entwined great cats that bordered the icon as if guarding it. Renzie couldn't remember seeing Hake happy in this way before. Gleeful, almost giddy.

"Los Milagros always depict Borges with tigers because he wrote powerful and beautiful poetry about them, rivaling Blake. The garden and library you see here are among the 'observed miracles' Los Milagros credit him with. They come from his prose fiction." Hake nodded to the table he and Nesta had been bent over when Renzie surprised them. It was piled high with books. Renzie read the title of the top one. *Labyrinths*, by Jorge Luis Borges.

"I brought that for Nesta to read. There are a few stories in there I thought germane to our research." He picked up the book and thumbed through it. "For instance, here's one called 'The Garden of the Forking Paths.' It's not exactly a description of an anomaly, but for Los Milagros, it's one of Borges's most important myths. I thought it might be interesting to run it through the computer model." Hake pitched a glance at Nesta. She declined to catch it. Renzie's interest was piqued.

"Why the eyes?" Renzie shuddered. "Was he martyred, too?"

"No. Borges went blind over a period of years. Los Milagros say 'blind to the light of *this* world so that he could see the other.' Now, if you'd like more direct evidence of anomalies, let's take this fellow, Saint René." He pulled out a triptych from the box and hugged it to his chest.

"According to the saints' lexicon there was only one Saint René. He was a French layman assisting a group of Jesuit missionaries in Canada in the 1600s. Tortured by the Indians he'd been sent to convert, he was eventually killed for making the sign of the cross on an Indian child's forehead. Any bets on what he looks like, what he's wearing?"

"The Canadian version of a coonskin cap?" Nesta guessed somewhat sarcastically.

"Almost close. Ta da!" Hake flipped the icon around.

"I guess looking like an accountant must have some tie to spirituality that I don't understand," Nesta said, after she and Renzie stared blankly at the image for a moment. Again a man in a black business suit, but reproduced here many, many times in a pattern, floating in a white-beclouded cobalt blue sky. Renzie was relieved that he, or they, were painted with their backs turned, sparing her if they too were eyeless. Floating umbrellas were interspersed regularly among the men.

"I can see I'm not in the presence of art lovers," Hake said. "This is, of course, the famous surrealist René Magritte. He actually *was* a devout Catholic. Or rather, his wife was, and he was devoted to her. Almost the same thing."

In spite of feeling mystified, Renzie had to smile at Hake's enjoyment.

"Now, let's take a peek at what really makes Saint René so interesting." With a flourish Hake snapped open the panel doors.

Renzie stopped smiling.

The first door opened onto a somewhat crudely painted forest scene. But the artist's technique was not so rough that Renzie had any trouble making out the image. Shimmering in and out of the trunks of the trees in an impossible manner rode a woman on horseback, the effect horribly similar to the meadow Renzie had pursued that night in the forest.

The second panel insert pictured a house, trees, and a yard at night; the trees darkened to silhouettes, the house cheerfully lit from within, a streetlight shining bright against the dark outside. Yet the sky above shone with the fresh light blue of mid-morning. Renzie felt the blood draining from her face. She observed her fingertips growing cold, as if her body belonged to someone else.

The third panel was a painting of a shattered window that looked out on a snowy mountainscape, focusing on a peak shaped like a pigeon's head. But leftover splinters of glass propped up against the wall also retained the mountain's image.

"These are somewhat crude copies of Magritte's work. This is what his paintings actually looked like." Hake set the triptych on the floor and pulled a thick, glossy book from the pile on the table. A ragged fringe of thin strips of paper poked out of the top. Hake opened the volume at the first place marker.

"The first panel is copied from this painting, *Carte Blanche*. Then there's *The Empire of Lights*. And lastly one of several versions of *The Domain of Arnheim*."

The greater clarity of the images chilled Renzie further.

"Oh my God," Nesta whispered. She took the book from Hake. "How did he know?" Nesta was as pale as Renzie felt.

Hake shook his head. "We can't be sure that he did. It may just be serendipitous. Thumb through the rest of the book: flaming tubas, giant chess pieces and jockeys, images played off against words. But I've tagged other pages where the paintings uncannily resemble or mimic reported aberrations. Or illustrate anomalies we've never heard of but which seem feasible, or at least no more impossible than any of the ones we're already familiar with."

Nesta recovered a little. "Maybe that's it, then. Los Milagros want these images to be real, so they see them. The template for their visions is right here." She patted the book.

Hake shook his head. "That's not what I meant. I just felt we couldn't presume that Magritte experienced anomalies in the way that we do, or that that was the whole of his intent in his work. I didn't expect you, of all people, to play doubting Thomas. I thought you *wanted* reports of anomalies."

Nesta sighed and put the book down. "Not so much doubting Thomas as devil's advocate. Descriptions of aberrations do us no good if they're just hallucinations or folklore. They have to be real. I'm already having to dance the two-step to get around Yorheim. We can follow up fantastic leads—in fact, we have to—but in the end we've got to produce hard data mined through rigorous scientific process."

"All right," said Hake. "I take your point. But Los Milagros only venerate materials which closely match either their own experiences or those reported by people they think they can trust. That's why they're so open to working with us: They want that exchange of information, to know what we come up with. My biggest break with them occurred after the news of Renzie's experience. They became tremendously excited. When I asked, quite tentatively, if I could borrow a couple of pieces of their religious art to show you, they threw this together on a moment's notice, no questions asked." He nodded at the box.

Nesta threw up her hands. "All right, all right. Coordinate your piles of pictures and fiction with phenomena Los Milagros claim to have actually experienced and run them through the software. But not the secondhand reports from other sources. Those are too suspect for our data runs. File those for possible follow-up someday. And you'll have to enter your data during off-hours. I don't want the rest of the team to get wind of this until we get results. This is exactly the kind of unverified weirdness Yorheim is waiting to squash me with. Renzie, do you have any problems with keeping quiet about this for now?"

"No, but if you don't trust other members of the team, why do you keep them on? And if you think they're spying for Yorheim, trying to find reasons to discredit you, why did you hold the meeting today? That was a lot of information to throw to the enemy camp."

Hake and Nesta looked at each other. It made Renzie itch with curiosity, wondering what kind of confidences they'd been sharing.

"I don't consider anyone in the group to actually be a spy," Nesta said. "The Hacker administration picked the individuals on the team for a number of qualifications, such as technical skills. And I'm sure also for a not altogether inappropriate attitude of, shall we say, scientific skepticism? I'd bet they were told that on occasions where I might seem unwilling to listen to reasonable doubts regarding the research that the administration would be glad to lend them an ear.

"Hake used the term earlier: I'd prefer to describe them as doubting Thomases, not spies or enemies. Let's just say that my aim is to convert, not unmask them."

"Which people don't you trust?" Renzie asked, sure that Hake already knew.

Nesta shook her head. "I couldn't really tell you. It's more a matter of whom I *do* trust. Originally just you, Hake, and Jan." The warm pang of pleasure Renzie felt at this eased the sensation of being left out. "Now I'd also add Adrienne and Dodd to the list," Nesta said.

"When we set up the tests for those flowers you brought us, Dodd made it clear he believed that the incident was a fraud or hallucination, and that he'd only go along to prove me wrong. He protested at every test I asked him to do. When we came up with the results of those final DNA tests, they first scared the living bejeezus out of him, then intrigued him, and then finally he caught fire. He's the one who remembered the oligo research, recognized the similarities."

"And you believed him? He could have invented all that—faked the slides and the data to set you up," Renzie protested.

"Like I said, I presume the members of the team to be basically honest, disinterested, and competent. It's fine with me if they're also skeptical." Nesta slid an expression of contrived innocence onto her face. "So I wasn't surprised to find accounts of the oligo research and Jabberwocky drugs in old magazines and newspapers in the research library at the Center: old copies of *Science News,* even annual reports from the *Antisense Research and Development Journal.* And then I took that same material to Dodd to help implement his findings, show my support for his work. Of course, I'd run tests first on scrapings I'd taken off those periodicals. There's no way Dodd could have put together that sophisticated a hoax on such short notice." Nesta grinned at Renzie's openmouthed stare. "It doesn't hurt for me to be skeptical, either."

Renzie burst into laughter. "You're unbelievable."

"Absolutely," Nesta agreed. "I'm glad that put some color back in your cheeks. You were turning pale as milk."

Renzie remembered the fears that had brought her down to Nesta's room, the déjà vu chill she'd felt when Hake revealed the images in the triptych. A shiver started deep within her, like the beginning shudders of an earthquake tremor.

"Renzie, what is it?" Hake asked.

"The oligos, the Jabberwocky drugs, what did they really do to people? How similar are they to those strands in the plants? Could Minda and I have absorbed them through our skins? What's going to happen to us? Why didn't anyone at the meeting bring up the meadow, the daytime at night? Why couldn't I get to it, but Minda could? Does that mean something's wrong with Minda, or with me?" Terror shook Renzie. She couldn't draw enough breath into her tightened chest to get out more questions.

Hake knelt beside her, grabbed her hands in both of his own. "Whoa! Hang on there. Hell, girl, your hands are like ice. Nesta, do something!"

Nesta yanked the blanket off her bed and threw it over Renzie's shoulders. It wrapped the panic down a little. Nesta propelled Renzie back onto the bed. Renzie dropped her head into her hands, embarrassed and still frightened. She had to gulp for air before she could talk again. "Is this part of it? Is this a reaction to those plants? Did they do something to me?"

Nesta put a cool, dry-skinned hand to Renzie's forehead. "You don't have a fever. I'll give you a checkup to set your mind at ease, but it looks to me like a classic panic attack."

"A panic attack?" Renzie said indignantly. "I've never felt like this before." She turned on Hake. "What are you smiling about?"

Hake tugged down the corners of his mouth, but still looked amused. "I didn't mean anything," he apologized and squeezed her hands gently. "It was just that I had a flash that this might be the first good scare in your life where you didn't have a chance to get mad first."

Renzie opened her mouth for an even sharper retort. But before she could think of a good one Hake's words sank in.

Anger was an integral part of her life. Rage that boiled up from the core of her being was her anchor and shield. Hake had hit the mark. She couldn't remember being well and truly frightened before—not like this.

Nesta sat down on the bed next to Renzie.

"If you're feeling better, calmer, I'll try to answer as many of your questions as I can remember," she said. "But I need to ask you something first. Is that all right?"

Renzie nodded.

"Today, when we all met . . . why didn't you ask any of those questions yourself?"

"I guess I was too scared. I hoped they'd come up naturally in the course of the meeting. I thought everybody else would at least be curious."

Nesta leaned back against the headboard, wrapped her arms around herself. "I'm sure they were. I'm also sure of why they didn't ask. They're frightened too. Truly frightened. For the first time some, maybe most of them, are having to deal with the fact that this research might be heading someplace. They're afraid of where that someplace might be . . . as they should be. That's why I only presented the results we've got so far. And that's the way I'm going to continue: no presentations to the whole group until results are solid.

"Now, is there something wrong with Minda, since she could reach the meadow and you couldn't? Probably . . . not wrong, but definitely different. We're *very* surreptitiously keeping an eye on her, and some of the other children too. Now that Dodd and Adrienne have thrown in with us that line of investigation should go more quickly.

"As for you . . . this is a little embarrassing, but I did run some tests on you, rather clandestinely." She raised a hand as she saw Renzie's eyes widen. "It's important to downplay what we're doing. I don't want people to needlessly feel that they're in danger."

"Needlessly?" Hake asked. In the tone of his voice Renzie heard another source of disagreement between the two of them.

Nesta shot a quick glance at Renzie, as if to see if Hake's comment had unsettled her again. Then she turned back to Hake.

"So far there's been no documentation of anyone injured by an anomaly. From panic responses, yes. But not the anomaly itself."

"So far," Hake murmured, half acquiescence and half challenge. "But the destruction from some of those panics . . ."

"Yes. Precisely," said Nesta. She twisted around to Renzie. "That's why I've been so secretive, even in the middle of doing quite public research." It was an explanation, not an apology.

"But how?" Renzie asked. At the blank looks from her elders she added, "How did you run tests on me without my knowing?"

Both of them laughed. The tension between them snapped.

"One doesn't need to be so obvious as sticking people with needles like they were pincushions, or making them sit endlessly on toilets," said Nesta. "Tests can be simple and unobtrusive. Saliva in a half-drunk glass of water, if the glass has been sterilized beforehand and the water's distilled. Fingerprints in a cultured petri dish, if it doesn't happen to look like a petri dish. There are even sneaky ways to pull off EEGs. Lots of things. You already know what a good lab technician Hake is."

Hake smiled at the compliment.

"Still, I ran a bare minimum of tests on you," Nesta admitted. "Just enough to discharge a minimum of scientific responsibility and assure myself that you were all right, at least as far as any kind of contamination. To tell you the truth, I wasn't that worried. That's never happened"—she paused to shoot a warning frown at Hake—"at least not yet. Not even to me."

"Not even to you?" Renzie felt dull and slow.

"This isn't the first time artifacts—anomalies themselves—have been left behind. And who more than myself would be seeking out and investigating them? I'd like to show you something—in a manner of speaking." Nesta chuckled.

She got down on her hands and knees by the bed, rummaging around in some cartons and piles of folders she had stored underneath. At last she pulled out an old shoebox, its lid tied neatly in place with a piece of twine.

"Here." She handed it to Renzie. "Don't open it yet. See if you can guess what's inside first." She squatted where she was on the floor to watch. "I traveled light coming out here from Pennsylvania. I didn't bring too much more than my disks and what's now in that box."

Renzie tipped the container back and forth in her hands. Whatever was inside slid from side to side. "I can't even begin to guess," she admitted. "Can I peek?"

Nesta nodded. Hake peered over Renzie's arm to watch.

Renzie lifted the lid. Inside was an unremarkable stone, riverworn smooth and veined with quartz. The only thing unusual about it was its size. It seemed too small to account for the weight of the box in her hand. She shifted the box again, the rock sliding as she did so.

Hairs pricked upright on the back of Renzie's neck. She began to feel cold again. When she tilted the box to the right, the stone wouldn't slide into the lowest corner. When she shifted the box back to left, something seemed to slide with the stone, blocking it from the lower left-hand corner. Something she couldn't see.

"What the . . ." came Hake's voice at her shoulder. Renzie's hands trembled, but she forced herself to gingerly pick up the rock out of the box, grasping the stone on the side opposite that unnaturally vacant space. Setting the stone in her lap, she tipped the box again. Something slid back and forth in the empty space. When she began trembling again so hard she almost dropped the box, she could feel the thing inside bouncing around.

"Watch out!" yelped Nesta, as both she and Hake grabbed for the box. "If you drop it, it might take us the rest of the night to find it, even in this small a room."

Hake got hold of the carton. Renzie relinquished it gratefully. He repeated her experiments, then hovered his hand over the box, nearer, farther, as if feeling for heat or cold. "May I?" he finally asked Nesta.

"Of course," she said. "It's perfectly safe. That was my point."

Hake reached into the box and picked up the nothingness. He passed it from palm to palm. "Interesting," he mused.

"What do you feel?" Nesta asked with almost childlike glee.

"Completely flat on one side. That's why it slides so easily. The other side is . . . complex. Sort of rounded but faceted at the top. Feels like it might be glass or metal. Then it tapers into a sort of stalk, with a series of turned edges. Do you know what it is?"

Nesta nodded, looking as if she could hardly contain herself. "It's a doorknob," she said, grinning.

Both Renzie and Hake stared at her. "A doorknob?"

"Well, half a doorknob. We sawed it in two and used the other side to run tests on."

"But why . . . and what is . . . ?" Renzie couldn't even begin to frame the questions.

"We don't know any of the answers, except that it isn't dangerous, at least not in any way we can tell, and I've been handling it for over two years now. It's not radioactive. It's not carrying any viruses or bacteria. But we tried looking at cross sections of it under microscopes, tried staining it, binding it to catalysts, irradiating it. If you can think of a test, we tried it, believe me. It's impervious to all of them. Except for the sense of its weight and mass to the touch, it doesn't seem to exist."

"Where did it come from?" Renzie asked.

"A door, of course," said Nesta. "Two and a half years ago a fellow went back to the Home he'd abandoned after the Vanishing—only back East we call it the Disappearance. At first he thought someone had vandalized the place and for some strange reason taken the doorknob. When he tried to push the door open he bumped into it. Scared the daylights out of him. A friend of his had heard I was looking into this sort of thing and put him in touch with me.

"Like I said, it's not dangerous in the least." Her mood shifted, though, and became somber. "But what I do find scary is . . . Look at it—what a miracle it is that it was found at all and made its way to us. And how lucky we were that Renzie happened to be out in the middle of nowhere last week for that brief period of time the other aberration lasted, and that Minda just happened to be with her and was able to get inside and bring the flowers back. Just how often are the anomalies occurring? What's happening all the times we're *not* there?"

CHAPTER TWENTY-THREE

In a dove-colored dusk typical of early November, Renzie finally walked over to the Watchers' Dome to find Tuck. Although the Domes were close—just across the garden clearing—that evening Renzie felt as if she could walk and walk and never reach those giant, overturned bowl shapes, never bridge the distance Tuck had chosen between them.

The deep green leaves of winter vegetables—spinach and chard—brushed against her legs as she passed. A team of gardeners from the Domes and the House hurried to finish mulching over the last of the late-summer beds. Watchers and Housers; in the daytime they inter-meshed well, sharing jointly owned community lots and chores with efficiency and grace. Yet they led such different lives after nightfall.

Like the rest of the Housers, Renzie knew all of the Watchers, had grown up alongside them, saw them almost daily. But in the weeks since he'd left she hadn't caught a single glimpse of Tuck.

Renzie ducked as she always did when she entered a Dome. The doors and ceilings inside were more than tall enough, but it was an instinctive movement. Something about the Domes seemed lowering compared to the House.

Dinner had begun. Just within the doors patient lines of Watchers crowded the lobby, waiting their turn for food. Behind the old snack bar cooks ladled out a simple supper of soup, fresh bread, cheese and wine.

Renzie scanned the line, looking for Tuck and Le Chell. A few Watchers she knew well said hello or nodded, but she sensed their gaze upon her after she'd looked away. She'd felt their growing reticence toward her ever since Tuck had left to join them. It wasn't hostility in any way. More like a kind of watchfulness, a concern held in abeyance. Concern for her, Tuck, or Le Chell—Renzie wasn't sure which.

She followed the line around to its origins in the belly of the Dome. People sat on the ground nearby, eating from filled plates on their laps. At the far end of the great hall several adolescents swept the floors. Following in their wake, a handful of elders laid out the children's sleeping mats in neat rows. Which the children would rearrange to their own liking as soon as they were bedded down for the night. Renzie smiled, remembering her own brief childhood sojourn in the Domes. When supper finished the adults would set their bedding down, too. The floor would look like some giant's vast patchwork quilt.

Up on the theater's stage the designated Watchers for the evening were already getting ready for the night, putting up card tables where they would play interminable games of poker and bridge, talk quietly among themselves as they Watched, perhaps softly strum guitars. Renzie slowly rotated. Her gaze swept the gallery thoroughly, sieving through the faces for Tuck's distinctive features or Le Chell's unmistakable hair.

"He's not here." The quiet voice came so unexpectedly that Renzie jumped. Le Chell stood just behind her.

"Where is he then? In the other Dome?" Night would soon finish falling. After that, a Watcher would not stay alone outdoors, unWatched.

Le Chell nodded. If she hadn't looked so sad, Renzie would have been angered by the pity that was also in her eyes.

Some foundation deep within Renzie suddenly shifted and fell away, like one of the Homes collapsing under the weight of age, neglect, and dry rot. Before she could marshal the familiar shield of anger tears welled up in her eyes.

"Why this way, Le Chell? I was the one that told him he should be with you."

"I know, Renzie. He told me."

"Then why?" Renzie didn't understand how the tears that had started running down her cheeks could feel so hot when her heart felt rimed with frost. "Damn him. He didn't even leave me a note. Even our mother wrote us a note when she left."

Le Chell put her hand on Renzie's arm. "Renzie, I'm so sorry. I didn't want him to move over here like that." She took a deep breath. "Renzie, he didn't plan on leaving the House while you were gone. The timing just happened that way."

"But it made it easier, didn't it?" Renzie said. The words stung.

Le Chell sighed. "No, it made it harder. He almost didn't move because he felt like he was abandoning you."

"Why didn't he at least write me a message?"

"Tuck tried. He stayed up the first two nights he came here, trying to write you something. He couldn't find the words to put down on paper. He said he had to go see you when you returned and explain it to you face to face. Then you came back early and found out before he could tell you. He knew how much that must have hurt. After that he was afraid to go see you. And every day he's put it off has made it worse. It was already hard for him, just moving over here—we knew it would be, but he felt he was ready to deal with it."

"Is he really so ready? I'd think if he were he would have been able to come tell me," Renzie said, knowing the words might hurt Le Chell.

Le Chell came right back, but firmly, without anger. "Renzie, he misses you. And he misses the House. It's part of him. But I'm part of him too. And he's part of me."

Renzie's breath caught.

"Renzie, please don't make it harder for him. Tuck's so confused. He beats himself up inside. He says he's becoming like his father."

Renzie tried to laugh at that. The laughter scraped like tears. "Like Old George? What a fantasy! Tuck's hardly ever been angry a day in his life. And he can't bear to hurt people."

Le Chell shook her head. "Not like his father in that way. He's afraid he doesn't know how to love, that the wiring is crossed somehow. Tuck says Old George was always compulsive. That's what he's afraid he's doing, too. He starts off so happy when we're together. Then that scares him. He's afraid it's just an infatuation, being in love with the idea of being in love. That it's not something real between him and me. That's why he had to move over here—to find out."

They were silent for a while.

"Le Chell, couldn't you . . . would it be possible for you to live in the House?" Renzie asked wistfully.

"I'm not brave enough. Who would Watch over me? Tuck and I couldn't stay up every night Watching for each other. Would you Watch over us, Renzie?"

Renzie bowed her head.

"It's not that I don't like the House," Le Chell continued. "So many of the things I love about Tuck . . . it's part of who he is. But I feel lost over there. I'm afraid at night. That probably sounds stupid to you."

"No," Renzie whispered. "I understand about being afraid."

Renzie looked up in time to catch a look like wishing in Le Chell's eyes.

"Renzie, what about the other way around? Won't you come and join us here? Please?"

"You'd want me?"

"Yes." Le Chell tried to smile. "Then I could stop worrying about you, night after night over there, un-Watched."

Renzie realized that she meant it. "I wish I could, Le Chell. But I have my own fears." She wiped her eyes on her sleeve. "I'm the one being stupid. He just moved across the clearing, not to Timbuktu." She looked around at the Dome's crowded, happy, claustrophobic mayhem. "When Tuck comes back, tell him I'm not mad at him."

Suddenly Renzie wanted to leave before Tuck returned. She didn't want him to feel that she'd come to face him down in his new life.

She hurried out the front door past the line of Watchers still waiting to be served their dinner. She saw Tuck coming around the Dome's far corner with a group of other Watchers. Renzie stared down at her feet and kept walking. That way if he saw her he wouldn't think that she'd seen him.

Keeping her head straight forward and down, Renzie risked a sideways glance under her lashes. She caught Tuck ducking his head away. Such sad silliness, she thought.

She kept walking and waited till she knew they'd passed each other, then turned. She needed one full glimpse of him, even of just his back.

Just as he reached the door Tuck hesitated. Renzie started laughing to herself. She couldn't help it. She knew what he was going to do. Tuck turned, sad and searching, in her direction, expecting to see a last glimpse of *her* retreating back.

Instead she was standing there grinning hugely. He blushed scarlet with embarrassment. Renzie started laughing openly.

The next thing she knew he was next to her, whirling her up off her feet. "You are *such* a pain in the butt," he said fiercely. "No wonder I miss you."

She hugged him back. "We're too much alike. You can't get rid of me so easily. You'll have to go a lot farther than just across the garden."

Tuck let her slide down. "Renzie, I never wanted to get rid of you. And of all the people in the world, I never wanted to hurt you."

"I know," she said. "I know."

CHAPTER TWENTY-FOUR

By November Nesta's crew was feeding in new data from the field research team through the computer models. Nesta herself had organized a series of bubble-chamber experiments that were accruing an impressive set of statistics. Adrienne and Dodd, still tied up running calculations on the imitation oligos, protested that with the influx of fresh biological data they were overwhelmed. They begged Nesta to shift Elise to their team.

As part of the lab's procedure Nesta initiated the delivery of monthly reports to Ernest Yorheim. Hake rolled his eyes when he saw the first one. In point of fact they were not inaccurate or dishonest—at least not technically. Nesta simply made sure they were flooded with math and statistics with very little interpretive text. To be especially safe, she used Yorheim's own graduate research papers as her format.

"You told me to capitulate, let Yorheim have his pinkie in the pie," she reminded Hake.

The rain took off for an extended holiday elsewhere, though the sky remained overcast. The temperature gradually slid lower until they awoke one morning to find the air's scant moisture translated into frost. The entire valley floor was as white and crunchy as if a giant had come along and littered it with sugar-frosted corn flakes.

"This is as chilly as it gets," Shoebak Morner reassured Nesta.

Nesta smiled to herself. To any longtime inhabitant of Pennsylvania winters this display of cold was hardly noticeable.

By December Jan was fully recovered and back in the field. One afternoon she and Hake rushed into the labs in a flurry of excitement. "We did it!" she said as they began rummaging through boxes of AV equipment. "Los Milagros decided to give us access to the recordings from the 'Well of Voices.' "

"The what? And what are you looking for? The tape recorders are in those shelves over there." Nesta pointed.

"We'll need those too," said Hake, "but we especially need the portable dubbing units."

Nesta pulled out a box from beside one of the filing cabinets. "Here. What is this all about?"

"The 'Well of Voices.' It's a spot where noises and voices can occasionally be heard coming out of thin air, or so Los Milagros claim. It's a fascinating place, really." He stopped abruptly. "No, I'm not going to tell you any more. Come with us. This is something you should see for yourself."

"I don't have the time right now," Nesta protested. "Jan, *you* tell me what this is all about."

Jan smiled and shook her head. "Nope. I'm throwing in with Hake on this one. You'll have to join us."

"This is a bloody mutiny," Nesta protested as they trundled her into her coat.

The day was clear, dry and cold. Hake loaded the equipment into the saddlebags of three bicycles. They rode less than a mile due west paralleling the old freeway, then turned north for a couple of miles on the San Tomas Expressway. In the brief distance they traveled they passed only a group of Vietnamese with vegetable-laden goat carts and a truck from the wineries freighting vineahol. A furry, pop-eyed binturong leisurely crossed the road in front of them. Then they zigzagged left again at an angle, heading west and slightly south.

"Here," Hake said as he and Jan dismounted and walked their bikes among a grove of anonymous block buildings. They led Nesta around and through an open grid of steel struts that must have once framed a row of glass doors. They entered a ceramic-tiled lobby. Something about the place tugged at Nesta's memory as if it expected her to remember, though she'd never been there before. It brought to mind coolness, a particular elusive scent, and the color blue, though the walls were painted beige.

Jan and Hake weren't waiting on Nesta's musings. They rolled through another set of doors and parked the bikes against a wall after they unloaded them. This time Nesta stopped to take in the new surroundings.

They'd entered a vast expanse. A vaulted Mylar ceiling stretched up and away from where she stood. In front of her Hake and Jan walked down a shallow set of steps leading to a mad artist's version of a rain forest.

Huge rubber trees and house palms towered overhead. Bamboo and bougainvillea mingled with giant carved and brightly painted versions of the retablas to form dense surreal thickets cut through with trails. Although hidden by this visual cacophony, one of the walls of the habitat must have consisted of banks of windows. The entire space was flooded with light on one side.

Nesta hurried to catch up. "It reminds me of some kind of primitive painting," she said. She felt buffeted by the raucous blues, yellows, purples, reds, deep greens, lime greens, and black.

Hake looked at her approvingly as he set off down a path. "I thought that too, the first time I saw it. A Rousseau, with some Kahlo, Miró and Dubuffet thrown in."

"Where in the hell are we?" Nesta asked, irritated to find herself whispering.

"This whole complex used to be an international swimming center," Jan said. "We're now walking along the bottom of an Olympic-sized pool. It used to be an outdoor pool, but after Los Milagros took it over they put up the ceiling so they could control the internal climate."

Nesta knew then what the scent was she thought she should remember: chlorine. "The sounds are coming from here?"

Jan nodded. "Yes, from a specific spot a little further on, the part Los Milagros refer to as the actual 'Well.' It's cared for by a live-in attendant called the 'Memory of the Word.'"

In spite of its chaotic appearance the shrine had been artfully devised. Paths wound around and doubled back on themselves, making the jungle seem far larger than the length of a swimming pool. Nesta could tell when they neared the far end as the deepening walls of the pool cut the sunshine off.

Then the intertwined foliage and sculptures opened abruptly to form a light well, allowing a godlike stream of rays to illuminate a broad, raised dais. It put Nesta in mind of some sort of savage cathedral or Mayan ruin.

On the far side of the platform stood three red and white striped tents stitched together. In front of them a man bent over several tables strewn with equipment, working. He wore a dolman-sleeved shirt and drawstring pants, both crazy-quilted in a rainbow assortment of colors that blended with the faux wilderness surrounding him. He had a lanky build and pale, plain face. His hair, cut into Roman-senator-style bangs, did not complement his features.

"That's the 'Memory of the Word,'" Jan said. She moved forward to greet him.

"What a grand title. What does he actually do?" Nesta asked.

"His duties consist of maintaining the shrine, receiving any Los Milagros pilgrims who visit, and recording any auditory phenomenon that he happens to hear," Hake said.

"*Happens* to hear?"

"The noises occur infrequently at irregular intervals, often when he's busy with other duties or at night when he's sleeping. So yes, the taped log is spotty. But I think you'll still find it of interest to us."

As Hake explained it, "Memory" recorded one anomaly after another onto a tape with no breaks; with no differentiation made between the different occurrences and no data supplied on the times, dates, or intervals between occurrences. Los Milagros were interested in transcribing a prayer wheel of sound, not in documenting scientific phenomena.

"I know, I know," Hake responded to Nesta's doubtful look. "Not good procedure, therefore not reliable data. But keep an open mind. Wait till you hear the tapes."

Jan gestured them over. She introduced Nesta to "Memory" in what amounted to a formal ceremony. From his curt monosyllabic mutterings she gathered that "Memory" was part religious fanatic and part misanthropic hermit.

"We can listen to the recordings over there," Jan said when the formalities were over. She pointed behind the dais and the tents to a sunken area that resembled a small shallow Greek amphitheater.

"Memory" touched his earlobes ritually. "Drinking at the Well," he intoned.

"Yes," Jan agreed quickly. "We'll go listen at the 'Drinking at the Well.'"

Nesta glanced at Hake, expecting to catch a smile. His face remained rigidly solemn. As Nesta tagged along behind the others she tried to imagine what Hake and Jan must have gone through to win this concession from Los Milagros.

"Memory" adjusted equipment and speakers at the rim of "Drinking" while they seated themselves. When he decided that they were sufficiently respectful he started the tapes.

Hake was right. What sounds the brusque sibyl *had* managed to record proved fascinating: an intriguing collage of noise that consisted of unidentifiable squawks and squeaks, the rumble of machinery, voices too far in the distance to make any sense of.

"Here, we're almost up to it," Jan said. She and Hake tensed and leaned forward. It began: an extended dialogue between at least three people in a language Nesta didn't recognize.

"What is it?" she asked.

"Nobody knows," Hake said. "Not us. And none of Los Milagros. They've had people from every ethnic persuasion left in the Valley listen to it. It doesn't sound even familiar, let alone recognizable, to anybody."

"We thought we'd have one of the data processors—maybe Lampwick—run it through the computers. See if we can get an identification and work up a translation," Jan explained.

When that segment finished they listened a little longer to more of the general clamor. Then Hake and Jan set up their own equipment and began the chore of speed-dubbing the tapes.

Nesta took the opportunity to wander about. "Memory" looked up from fiddling with the machinery on the tables to glare, a warning not to set foot up on the "Well of Voices."

Nesta sat and looked out over its broad flat surface. Most empty stages waited to be animated by the marginal reality of actors and theatrical trappings. This one waited for not even that, but only by ephemeral sound. And she looked beyond the "Well" to where the faux jungle camouflaged the edges of the abandoned swimming pool.

Important as those enigmatic voices might prove to be, Nesta had found several other short segments on the tape to be of equal interest.

To her they'd been reminiscent of the kinds of compressed echoing sounds heard underwater: the muffled, distorted resonances of children's happy cries, the slapping of water against the pool's concrete sides.

CHAPTER TWENTY-FIVE

Between Christmas and New Year's the area rippled with another series of tremors, large enough to generate concern that the area might be building toward a large quake. Nesta's team finished the year obsessively running backups on the computers, just in case.

January passed relatively uneventfully after all of December's excitement. Loren Van Woorden ran test after test on the aurora.

"I don't see it and my instruments don't see it," he told Nesta flatly. "You may still believe it's there just because these kids say so, but I don't." Renzie, standing behind him, made a face.

"Remember that science is as often as much a matter of weeding out untenable hypotheses as proving workable ones," Nesta reminded him, thinking of the invisible doorknob hidden under her bed. The more Van Woorden eliminated the obvious astronomical possibilities, the more her own private theories seemed viable.

At the end of the month the area entered a summerlike spell, beguiling plum trees into a too-early bloom. Then, when cold rains returned with a vengeance in February, their petals were lashed up into the air like a sad pink snowstorm.

By that time Nesta's team had all settled into a regular routine together despite the shocks and surprises inherent in the work. All through February Nesta took note of the steadily rising levels of excitement and satisfaction as each of the subgroups began to make headway with their assigned projects.

Therefore she was caught off guard when on a brisk morning in March Ernest Yorheim stamped into their suite of labs. With one hand he waved a report-filled folder, with the other he dragged along a reluctant and abashed Dodd. Pax Willster followed, his face tight with apprehension.

"For how long did you think I was going to put up with this snow job?" Yorheim spoke loudly. He shook both the folder and poor Dodd at her. He could have meant either one, but Nesta assumed he meant the reports. In which case she had thought she might in fact be able to snow him indefinitely. A thought which she of course did not share with him.

A lifetime of dealing with science bureaucrats had taught Nesta to always speak more logically and calmly than they.

"A snow job?" she inquired politely.

"Yes!" He flapped the report folder about again. "I'm referring to this deliberately obscure, obtuse, indecipherable, and criminal waste of paper."

"Oh dear," she said, even more politely. "I thought that when I chose to send you monthly rather than quarterly updates on the work here that you'd be pleased."

At least she was ready for this. After a moment of rummaging around in her desk looking for a file whose location she knew perfectly well, she drew it out and looked at it with a puzzled expression.

By now all the members of her crew not away on field work crowded in at the door, attracted by the Sturm und Drang.

"Dr. Yorheim, I'm afraid I don't understand your difficulty with these reports." Nesta opened the file and showed him its contents. "As you can see, I chose a format considered classic in the field . . . one developed by yourself." She watched for his reaction behind a mask of innocent surprise. She'd always been curious as to whether he'd been pulling a snow job of his own those many years ago in graduate school.

Yorheim deflated and faltered. At least Nesta had her answer to that. The emperor wore no clothes.

He rallied. "But my work was in context," he said, flustered.

"Look at this, this, and this." His index finger bludgeoned the subtitles of the research she'd handed in. " 'Fine Structure Constants Shifts re: Index of Refraction in Protein Sheaths.' 'Aberrational Correlation with the Register of Apostolic Disciples.' What do they mean?"

"Dr. Yorheim, I'd be happy to explain any questions you might have about our work here. But don't you think that the proper procedure would have been to request a conference with me, rather than rushing in here and disturbing my staff?" Nesta asked with some asperity.

Yorheim looked over his shoulder at the amazed faces of Elise, Hake, Adrienne, Lampwick, Renzie, and even Loren Van Woorden. He paled.

But apparently the issues at stake were greater than his loss of face. "You're right. I apologize. I'd like a conference with you. Now! Please."

Nesta may have scored points, but she hadn't bought herself extra time. She nodded to her group. They reluctantly retreated from the doorway. Dodd tried to join them, but Yorheim hadn't relinquished his grip on the plump biologist. Pax also remained.

"Hake," Nesta called out. "Would you stay and take notes on this meeting for us?" She wanted at least one witness and advocate present. Yorheim glared but knew his lack of protocol had justified her request.

Nesta looked straight back at him and tried to take his measure. She might be able to deflect him with verbal tap dancing, but considering that she had no idea what surprises lay in wait for her from Dodd's unexplained and guilty presence, she doubted it. She decided on a preemptive strike.

"Dr. Yorheim, now that we're relatively alone, would you mind telling me what on earth you're doing mauling my biologist?" She leaned back in her chair.

Yorheim looked at Dodd with some surprise, evidently having forgotten he still clutched the poor man. He let him go with alacrity. Dodd looked relieved, but he still couldn't meet Nesta's eye.

Like some large startled bird that's fluffed itself up and hastily rearranged its plumage, Yorheim gathered himself together. "I approached Mr. Dodd here with questions regarding some of the research that seemed especially pertinent to his domain." Yorheim thumbed through the report folder till he found the papers he sought, then pulled them out.

Nesta's heart sank. It was the analysis of the Rosicrucians' work on medical uses for plants that—like Renzie's midnight meadow—appeared to be anomalies of one form or another.

"I couldn't make heads or tails of this material. The title, 'Collaborative Appraisal of Botanical Anomaly Medical Cross-references,' is so obscure as to be useless. Upon close questioning of Mr. Dodd, I discovered that it in fact refers to a cooperative study with the Rosicrucian cult, a collaboration that you were expressly denied when you requested permission through the proper channels several months ago."

Poor Dodd openly flinched. She'd sensed he was one of Yorheim's informants until the oligo research had brought him solidly into her camp. Now he looked as though Yorheim had used the verbal equivalent of thumbscrews to get this information out of him.

He was right to be flinching, Nesta thought. They'd been safe as long as they had just researched the blatantly religious cults which posed no threat to the elite management of the Hackers' Center. But the Rosies insisted that they too practiced a rigorous though different set of scientific methods. They expected to be treated as equals within the local scientific community. So of course the Hackers' Center considered them anathema.

However, the Rosicrucians' work seemed so promising Nesta had proceeded anyway and tried to mask the results. Internally she cringed as much as Dodd.

Then Yorheim surprised her. "Upset as I was initially by this information, on further consideration I found it a forgivable if undesirable lapse. I can understand how your desire to acquire information led to what I'm sure you considered a mere bending of the rules in the interest of finding the truth."

The look of disbelief on Dodd's face and the way that Pax glanced away told Nesta that in fact this had *not* been Ernest's original reaction to the news she had colluded with the Rosies.

Yorheim's invention of this myth meant she'd successfully outfaced him in front of her staff. He was attempting to make up for his breach in manners by appearing magnanimous now. Having established that to his own satisfaction, he was due to shift tactics any moment. Nesta gazed at him warily.

He didn't disappoint her. "Dodd here defended your actions eloquently." At that Dodd practically collapsed in on himself. "To a great degree he justified them by championing your results in other potentially controversial areas, which I must admit up till then I had insufficiently understood from these reports"—he glared and rattled the papers at her again—"until his helpful explanations clarified everything." Dodd squirmed like a worm skewered on a fishing hook.

Nesta's estimation of Yorheim's intelligence, which had been flagging, rose again. He'd been smart enough to see how he could still use his "defected" spies for information. He knew if he attacked them in just the right fashion they'd be driven to justify the work and their conversion.

" 'Celestial Spectroscopic Analysis,' 'Comparison of Nocturnal Phenomena to 20th Century Oligo Research,' . . ." Yorheim went on to list every single report.

"What do these have to do with *anything*?" he finally said. "When we invited you out here from Carnegie-Mellon I'd hoped your research would, if nothing else, close off fruitless lines of inquiry. Instead you seem to be proliferating more. What does any of this have to do with the Vanishing?" He sounded genuinely bewildered.

Nesta suddenly understood something she should have realized long, long ago. She cursed herself for a fool. Because Yorheim was a politically manipulative animal, she'd thought this was the force that drove him, that defined all his interactions. She had believed his primary motivation had been the same as every other administrator she'd known: to play at master puppeteer, pulling the strings, guiding his marionettes' steps to dance to his tune only.

She'd been wrong. What motivated Yorheim was not a desire to maintain control but rather to find it at last after a search of thirty years. She was not the only one getting old. Time was running out for them all. Yorheim understood that and it scared him. He might—he probably would—die before he really knew anything.

"What does this have to do with the Vanishing?" Nesta echoed, taking the report file from him with deliberately gentle hands. "Perhaps I should restate my hypothesis in less technical terms. By and large the aberrations that we are investigating are phenomena that came into being after, and apparently originated because of, the Vanishing. In spite of a reduced population available for observing these occurrences, it is obvious that they are increasing in frequency of event and type.

"By analyzing them and looking for common factors it should be possible to backtrack to the source of the Vanishing. There's also evidence that some of these anomalies were observed before the Vanishing, which I'm hoping will help indicate the conditions leading up to that catastrophe."

"But what is the actual hypothesis that you're proposing all this research will backtrack to?" Yorheim sounded frayed with frustration. "You've already closed off the macrovirtual-particle and temporal-leap lines of study. What are you currently targeting as the actual cause of the Vanishing? Where did everybody go? What happened to them? When are they . . . are they coming back?"

He resembled a man over his head in deep water, flailing about in a panic. When someone like that gets hold of you they'll take you down drowning with them, Nesta thought. Yorheim was hanging on with a vise grip. He wasn't going to let go till they'd touched bottom together.

"We're focusing on two possibilities. The first is a cosmological phase transition. In that case, the Vanished have been transposed and angled off from us along another wavelength thirty light-years back.

"The second, more likely possibility, is that the Vanished have been 'tunneled' out."

"Tunneled out?" Yorheim looked at Pax for a translation. Pax shook his head.

"Wormholes." Nesta tried to clarify. "Microwormholes."

His face cleared from bafflement to simple incredulousness. "Wormholes as in black holes?"

Nesta nodded.

He looked relieved to find out that she was, after all, just a crazy old lady. "Dr. Easterman, I'm not even going to ask you *how* you think this happened. I'd just like to hear you explain the lack of electromagnetic radiation that always accompanies black holes, and why nothing else in the vicinity of the Vanishing was drawn in with them."

"Precisely because of those origins you don't want to ask about. Whatever the initiating event was, it occurred in a parallel probability, not 'here.' In that continuum the damage from the electromagnetic radiation as billions of entities simultaneously imploded into billions of individual submicroscopic black holes must indeed have been cataclysmic. The effect of the event was catastrophic enough to collapse the fabric of all the conjoined superspacetime continua—including our own—and pull all of those individuals' parallel existences in after them, adding incredible mass to each micro–black hole as they were yanked in."

Well, if nothing else, she'd certainly taken Ernest's breath away. Also Pax's. Only Hake didn't look all that surprised.

"So you think they've been collapsed down black holes, to pop out as white holes somewhere else?"

"Perhaps, but not likely. I'm trying to describe a phase transition even more unique than a shift of particles to waves. This is not a simple singular black hole. I'm talking about an event that crossed the barriers between all the infinite possibilities of the superspacetime continuum. I would guess that where the Vanished have gone, what has happened to them, is that they've been crushed through singularities to emerge in the flashing fraction of an attosecond into several billion separate Big Bangs, becoming entirely new universes."

"Yes, of course," said Ernest Yorheim, his voice shaking. "And in all the universe, all the possible galaxies and solar systems to pick from, this phenomenon chose to happen on this little planet."

Nesta's sympathy for Yorheim fought with her contempt for him. "Of course not. What I just described is what happened *here*. I expect that this was a universe-wide event, though how it expressed itself elsewhere is anybody's guess. If there are instances where the catastrophe caused celestial-sized perturbations, perhaps we'll find out as the light from other stars gradually reaches us." Nesta thought of the "aurora" that Renzie's generation could see and she couldn't. Maybe the evidence was already there, for them at least.

"If this, this . . ." Ernest couldn't think of a word to describe it. "If it originated in another continuum, beyond our control, we'd never know what caused it. We'd never be able to prevent another one. You're insane. If you really believed that, why go to all this trouble? All these preposterous projects you've dreamed up?" Ernest waved his arms at her office, the lab setups.

"I don't think it will happen again. I think that in a sense the Vanishing was a unique event in its own right, and that the changes it wrought have eliminated the factors that would allow a recurrence. But it's exactly those changes that make our research here so important.

"The Vanishing initiated a huge shift of some kind, something as startling as the Vanishing itself. Something that might prove equally disastrous. The Vanishing occurred with no warning whatsoever. But this time we are being warned, if we choose to see it. The anomalies are an indication of this other change and they're increasing in frequency and type. If we want to survive, this research may well be crucial."

Yorheim called an emergency meeting of the Research Tenure Committee and Hackers' Center Board for that noon. In the few hours that gave her Nesta had Hake, Elise, and Renzie pull data out of the computers and reports out of files in a desperate effort to regroup. She prepared a presentation that put all the cards on the table: apologies for her behavior and a detailed explanation of the possibility of a post-Vanishment disaster.

After she spoke the Board made Nesta sit in the hallway outside the conference room for a half hour while they made their decision. When they finally ushered her back in she could see the conclusion in their faces. Nesta didn't need to hear the polite, formal cant that supported it:

They were sure she was following an interesting conjecture, but that she'd misrepresented herself and her research. They were only interested in supporting work that would help humanity survive and find answers to the questions surrounding the Vanishing: How did it happen? How to prevent it happening again? Are the Vanished still alive and is it possible to bring them back? Since these were obviously not her interests, she would have to forgo their sponsorship and leave the premises. They didn't have the resources to fund extraneous research. They wished her luck elsewhere.

"But can't you see that what my research is all about *is* survival?"

They couldn't see it.

Nesta silently ground her teeth. They hadn't absorbed a single thing she'd said. But she also felt the smallest feeling of relief.

Until they'd spoken she thought there might be a chance she'd torpedoed herself simply by being covert. That she should have declared her intentions outright before she'd even come here. Now at least she knew her initial instincts had been correct. They wouldn't have permitted her work in the first place.

So that was it. When Nesta got back to her office Pax was already there directing the team in packing up.

"I'm really sorry, Nesta. I think they're making a big mistake," he said. "I can have all this archived for you until you decide what you're going to do next."

What would she do next? "No, thank you." She wished she could make herself sound less stiff. Pax wasn't an enemy. "I'll get everything out of here in the next couple of days. I can take over from here, thanks."

Pax took the hint gracefully and left. Nesta glanced around at the half-filled boxes, the faces of her team looking for all the world like punished puppies. Dodd was absent, which didn't surprise her. So was Hake, which did.

Nesta walked over to Adrienne and Renzie, running backup disks in tandem off the computer. "Adrienne, when you see Dodd, please tell him not to feel bad. It's not his fault." Adrienne nodded, her face held tightly against tears. Nesta turned to Renzie. "Where's Hake?"

"I don't know. I think he went to maintenance to get more boxes." Renzie's expression was also muffled. Nesta could almost measure Renzie's anger by the extent to which she muted her reply.

"Nesta, it's almost time for me to drive the kids back to the House," Renzie said in careful tones.

Nesta had forgotten about everything but the catastrophe. And she guessed that Renzie must want to escape before she exploded.

Nesta waved Renzie off. "That's right. I forgot. Go on. It's been a long day here." Renzie was right to find a reason to get out of here now.

"A long day for you too." Renzie took Nesta's arm and guided the older woman firmly from the room. To Nesta's surprise, she let her. I must be close to exploding, too, Nesta thought. Or collapsing.

"We'll all come back tomorrow and deal with this after a good night's sleep," Renzie said.

Perhaps Nesta would have felt less bleak if a good night's sleep had been possible. In her kiosk nest back at the House she lay awake for hours thinking of countless ways she could have prevented this disaster. None of them would have worked unless she'd been less self-congratulatory every step of the way, less sure of herself.

The next morning she picked up some coffee and toast in the kitchen, feeling as though it were the last meal for the condemned before she faced the drive back to the Center.

Renzie was already seated in the dining room, picking with little energy at a plate of scrambled eggs. She looked up and tried to smile as Nesta sat down. "Good morning," she said.

Nesta was shocked at the dark rings under Renzie's eyes, at her young face flaccid with exhaustion. She must have gotten even less sleep than Nesta.

Hake joined them a few moments later. Nesta wanted to ask him where he'd disappeared to the day before. But she hesitated when she saw the gray hue underlying his honey-colored skin. He appeared as tired and drawn as Renzie.

The core of the problem Nesta had wrestled with all night hadn't changed. My concern was just for myself, she thought. But here was visual proof that the project had come to mean as much to others, that they were suffering as much as she was. And they were suffering because she'd failed.

"So, are you about finished there?" Renzie interrupted Nesta's reverie. She and Hake had already pushed back their plates.

"Yes. Let's do it and get it over with."

Renzie and Hake marched on either side of Nesta out of the dining room. It's as if they think I might collapse without their support, Nesta realized. She wanted to protest that she didn't need her very own Praetorian guard, but curbed her tongue. They probably needed to do this. Nesta already felt lousy enough—she could at least let them escort her if it made them feel better. It was too late for her research, but not too late to start learning not to be so selfish.

They proceeded down the glassed-in hallway leading to the old coach entrance. But instead of heading straight out the door Nesta found herself, wedged between them as she was, force-marched into an abrupt left-hand turn.

"Did you park the bus out near the front entrance today?" she asked Renzie.

"No, I need to pick up something in my room first."

They passed by the Stairs-to-Nowhere cul-de-sac, climbed one flight of steps to the pressboard storage area, where remnants of the emigrant communal group looked at the little trio curiously as they folded up their bedding. Nesta could hear Carpenter's crew sawing and hammering somewhere nearby.

As they reached the narrow easy risers Renzie and Hake shifted in formation to sandwich her between them Indian file. All the climbing used up Nesta's scant reserves of energy. Renzie's quarters should be somewhere nearby.

Nesta would have been cranky if she hadn't been still coming down off her guilt. The increasing construction noises didn't improve her mood. Yet when she turned back to Hake to protest, the pronounced lack of expression on his face quelled her.

Nesta bumped into Renzie when the younger woman halted abruptly. With her vision obscured by Renzie's back, at first Nesta didn't recognize where they'd stopped—a large unfamiliar room filled with familiar objects and familiar people.

She'd been wrong about Carpenter's crew being responsible for the clamor. Members of her staff—Adrienne, Steff, Lampwick, even Loren Van Woorden, even Pax—unpacked boxes and set up files on shelves being nailed into place one step ahead of them by a work crew of Housers—Eric, Kip, Eileen, Hot Rod. House children were dragging in computers on flattened cardboard box sleds. Even Tuck and Le Chell had come over from the Domes.

Now Nesta recognized the space. It was the barn-eaves storage space adjoining Renzie's sleeping quarters.

Renzie clapped her hands to get their attention. "She's here," Renzie said.

They turned and looked at Nesta, their faces exhausted and expectant.

Hake had come up beside Nesta, deadpan expression gone, grinning like a Cheshire Cat. "Pax told us as soon as you'd left for the Board meeting that the result was a foregone conclusion," he said. "Renzie immediately thought of this space as an alternative research center. I took off and wrangled an impromptu meeting with Eric and the rest of the current House supervisors and they gave us their blessing."

"And you've been here all night moving everything and setting up," Nesta said.

Every one of them nodded. Nesta was overwhelmed. "I was up all night too, worrying—a complete waste of time, as it turns out. The least you could have done was come tell me so I could help too." Her voice began trembling before she could finish her scold.

Hake hugged her, burying her face in his shoulder to save her dignity. "I told you she'd love it," he said over Nesta's head to the others.

CHAPTER TWENTY-SIX

In leaving the Hackers' Center, Adrienne, Steff, and the rest had chosen to become renegades. Eric and Kip found some of them living quarters in various outlying buildings on the property. Lampwick pulled strings with Templeton and fit the rest of them in at the Office Buildings. Pax visited as often as he could. Elise Ngyuen and Shoebak Morner didn't join them.

"Elise liked this project," Adrienne explained to Nesta. "But she's Hackers' Center people. She was born and raised there."

Shoebak at least did come to see Nesta.

"It's not that I don't believe in what you're doing," he said. "The problem is that I do, and it scares me. When all those explanations came out, in the end, I realized that what I really wanted to do was to run. I'm sorry, Nesta."

Nesta was sorry too, that he wouldn't stay.

Even more surprising than Shoebak's defection was the way Loren Van Woorden threw in with the exiles. Nesta questioned him carefully, afraid that Yorheim might still be trying to maintain an informant within the ranks.

"I don't understand much of your research," Loren said. "Can't say I even agree with what little I do comprehend. But after thirty years of dealing with those idiots in the Center, I find you a refreshing, albeit eccentric, breath of fresh air."

Dodd moved over too, though he hid so much at first that he could have been taken for an illusion. Nesta finally sat him down and explained that she understood how Ernest had tricked him, that she felt she was as much to blame as he.

Nesta didn't think he believed her, but he was grateful for what he took to be a grand gesture on her part. After a couple of weeks he began to relax. By then everyone else felt quite settled in.

Before the eviction, Nesta's custom had been to leave early with Renzie for the Center and return with her at the end of the day. Except for meals in the dining room and forays to the bathroom at the other end of the umbilical hallway, most of Nesta's time in the House had been spent in her room, coordinating reports until late into the night.

Now, with research and data facilities jammed into Renzie's extended quarters, Nesta's own room of necessity ceased to function as a sanctuary. It came to serve as both office space and, when necessary, a very cramped conference area. People came and went at all hours of the day and a good part of the night. Nesta took to wandering through the House when she needed time to be by herself and reflect.

What began as a self-protective measure quickly became a pleasure. Nesta found it a soothing challenge to chart her way through new territory and then find the way back to familiar ground.

She could round a corner in a wing she'd thought she had mastered and find herself in completely new territory. People she'd never seen before would peer out of their rooms and ask if she needed directions, which Nesta declined. These occasions added to rather than spoiled her adventure. Not until now did she realize how marginally she'd integrated with the House.

Of course she justified her more extended excursions in terms of keeping her eyes open for possible aberrations. The longer she lived in the House, the more she felt they had to be there; nestled mysteries like puzzles of Japanese boxes hidden within boxes. Nesta liked to think she could sense them lurking nearby, always just one corridor, one chamber away. Like a flavor, she could almost taste their elusive presence.

Certain rooms functioned as touchstones for her. The stained-glass room with its poignantly unlit window drew her like a magnet each time. And she almost always managed to come upon the séance room—invariably by one of the three doors that opened outward.

Hammer quickly learned to recognize her footsteps, or at least the pattern of that moment's pause of nonplussed surprise when Nesta found herself yet again at one of the wrong doors. He'd glide his wheelchair over to open it and catch her before she could sneak off. They'd share a laugh and he'd invite her in for a pot of tea warmed on a hot plate embedded among all his other equipment. Sometimes Nesta lingered to listen while he received messages from what was left of the world.

One mid-morning when Nesta had been crowded out of both her room and the research area and wandered happily exploring new territory, she almost stumbled over a girl sitting morosely alone in one of the conservatories. The child looked lost.

"You're the little girl from the Homes, aren't you?"

The youngster gazed at Nesta glumly, without answering.

"Your name is . . . Chiapa," Nesta guessed.

"Chupa," the girl corrected her.

"Do you need help finding your way out?"

"No! I'm not lost. I just want to be here."

"Shouldn't you be at your Home with your parents?"

Chupa glared at Nesta with undisguised hostility. "Why would you say that? Everyone knows you don't believe the Vanished are coming back. Not my father's family, not anybody's. What would be the point in going Home, helping my father work like a slave?"

"But your parents must wonder where you are," Nesta said, shaken. She should have realized that news of her dismissal from the Center, and why, would circulate throughout the relatively small community of the Valley. She'd never stopped to consider the threat her theories might pose to the Homers.

"They know where I am. I'll go back tonight when I'm ready," Chupa said.

Nesta supposed that by then Chupa would find a way to wander out. Nesta left her sitting there forlornly.

Several turns in the hallway further Nesta ran into Eric. Unlike Chupa, she didn't mind admitting she was lost.

"I'd be happy to be your guide," Eric said.

"Back a little ways there's a girl from the Homes who could use some help too. She might accept it from you."

"You mean Chupa? I run across her all the time. She's pretty stubborn, always insists she knows exactly where she is. I think she finds her way out by smell when dinner starts cooking."

"That's sad."

"What's really sad is how alone she is. The Homers are generally an elderly lot; people who committed to their past lives and didn't start new families. There aren't many other Homer children for Chupa to hang out with. So she comes here. I think she believes if she becomes familiar with the House that the House kids will finally accept her."

"Will they?"

He shrugged. "Who knows?" He changed the subject. "How did you come to be wandering through this part of the House? You're on the opposite end from Renzie's room and the kiosk."

"Part R and R, part meditation, part exploration."

"And maybe more research?"

"That would spoil my ramblings as a vacation," Nesta hedged. "I think the worst I can be accused of is keeping an eye out for landmarks. I still haven't managed to find the second-story passageway to the greenhouse, or the fourth-floor tower."

"If you're not too tired I can show you the tower. It's back up the last set of stairs."

Nesta agreed eagerly. But she was flagging by the time they climbed two more floors straight up. Eric pointed out some built-in benches. "Let's have a seat and just enjoy the view for a few minutes," he said tactfully.

To Nesta's surprise the tower was an open network of porches that curved out of sight around the core of the House. A gentle updraft carried a hint of the perfume of late-blooming freesias and narcissus up from the gardens. "This is wonderful," she said. "And I think I can even find it again."

"The House is like a person. It reveals itself in stages," Eric said. "No one has ever successfully mapped out or drawn blueprint plans for all of it."

"I can believe that. There's so much I haven't managed to stumble upon yet. For example, I've never come across wherever it is that you live, Eric."

He laughed. "You really were holed up in the Hackers' Center all winter, weren't you? I don't live in the House. I'm not allowed to, though I don't mind it. My digs are out in the Foreman's Cottage." He stood up and led Nesta around an angle in the wraparound porch. On this side there was an old-fashioned porch swing instead of benches. "There, that's where I live." He pointed to a narrow, two-story bunga-low set well out beyond the water tower. Then he sat down on the swing and patted the space next to him. Nesta perched on the edge.

"Not allowed to?"

"Not me, not Carpenter, not any of the few of us who have semipermanent duties. It's a system of checks and balances."

"You surprise me," Nesta told him. "I'd never have taken you for a power grabber."

"I'm not," Eric said cheerfully. "Or I'd like to think I wouldn't be even if I had the chance. But there have been others."

Nesta tried to imagine any one person dominating the House. She failed. "Who? Somebody soon after the Vanishing? Someone long gone, I'll bet."

"Not at all." Eric smiled. "Someone still very much present. Carpenter. He developed quite a cult following at one point and tried to take control of the whole House."

Gentle, quiet, hardworking Carpenter as a dangerous cult leader? This Nesta could not picture at all.

"Don't look so surprised. Normally Carpenter is the archetypal introvert. But sometimes a whole other side of him emerges. You know how his duty is to keep up the original tradition of continuously build-ing onto the House, twenty-four hours a day? It's more than just a job to him. He's convinced that the House possesses special powers that can keep future Vanishings at bay.

"A number of years ago, after the marauders had been driven off and things began to settle down, Carpenter made quite a power play. He wanted everyone who lived here to devote *all* their energies to the House—essentially to become part of his crew." Eric shook his head ruefully.

"It didn't work, of course. Wasn't remotely practical even if he could have gotten enough people to go along with him in a full-scale mutiny. Too much energy was needed then just for survival. Carpenter came close to being banished. A big House meeting was held and he was given a warning. He disappeared after that for a few days.

"When he returned he requested another meeting and gave a peculiar apology to the entire House community. You could tell he didn't particularly regret the upheaval he'd caused. It was more like he felt he'd insulted the House itself and was at least sorry for that, and a little afraid, too. He said that the House could pretty much take care of itself, that it needed only a little help from us.

"Hot Rod's take on it at the time was that the House was Carpenter's deity and that Carpenter had insulted his god by not having faith in its omniscience, omnipresence, and omnipotence." Eric smiled to himself as he leaned back in the swing, head tilted up into the sun, eyes shut.

Nesta sat just as fully in the sun, but a rilling shiver played along her spine. A moment's fancy seized her that the House was indeed some kind of demigod, surrounding them, listening in as they made light of it.

She ignored her wayward imagination. "So after making a bid for dictatorship and following it up with an absurd explanation like that, how come Carpenter wasn't evicted?"

"Because of that wild explanation, actually," Eric said. "It was so heartfelt. He really believed that the House didn't want him to help all that much. So he wasn't a danger anymore. You know how he is—a quiet, helpful person that people generally like. We didn't want to lose him if we could avoid it. And banishing him from the House probably would have killed him."

Eric shaded his light blue eyes with one hand as he looked out over the House's landscaping. "Of course, we also made him reduce his crew to the point where he wouldn't have the time and energy to attempt another takeover later, in case he changed his mind." He looked at Nesta and she knew exactly whose idea that had been. They grinned at each other. Nesta wished Eric had been at the Hackers' Center all those months when she thought she'd been handling the politics there so well. Oh well, perhaps it was better that she'd ended up at the House in the end.

"How did Carpenter get to be the way he is?" she asked. "Who did he lose to the Vanishing that would initiate such an overwhelming obsession?"

"No one knows his history, but Hake has a theory. He thinks that Carpenter may not have lost anybody to the Vanishing—that he might not have had anybody to lose in the first place. He could have been just an incredibly isolated and lonely man."

This, at least, Nesta could imagine.

"When the rest of the world joined him in that same predicament he became overwhelmed. He metamorphosed into his own peculiar version of a Don Quixote, with his own unique strategy for saving the world from experiencing that kind of grief again. Hake's theory is as good as any. If it's true, then there's a good deal of irony in the situation."

"How so?" Nesta asked.

"Because it brought Carpenter out of his original isolation. It led him to connect with the world. Quiet as he is, when you see him with his work crew his abilities as a leader are obvious." Eric chuckled. "It wasn't funny at the time, but looking back . . . you should have seen him guiding his revolt!"

Nesta thought of how long it had taken her to acquire even a glimmer of insight into Ernest Yorheim's behavior. "The way the people here let Carpenter stay, Hake's insights, the compassion I hear in your voice . . . the House people are amazing."

"You think we were an enlightened community demonstrating an enlightened tolerance?" Eric's face saddened. "No, it was more like the identification of the crippled with the crippled. The Vanishing damaged everyone, one way or the other."

"You appear to be remarkably unmaimed." Eric seemed whole, stable, pragmatic, incapable of slipping away into madness.

"I've got less to complain about than just about anybody else," he admitted.

"Some people call you a 'Prince of the Valley.' "

"They treat my family like royalty," he agreed. "But nice as my family is, the only reason why is because we *are* still a family, whole and untouched. Me, my parents, my two older sisters all survived the Vanishing. Even both sets of grandparents—one in Iowa and the other in Oregon. And cousins. The Vanishing passed us over. We were Blessed. People gravitated to us for guidance as if we knew something no one else knew, some sort of magic knack for survival and protection.

"And who was I? An average sixteen-year-old kid too busy grieving to know how lucky he was. I hadn't lost my family, but my high school girlfriend and all my buddies were gone. All the dreams and plans I'd had for my life Vanished overnight with most of the human race, and left in its place a scant handful of walking wounded who seemed to think that my parents, my sisters, and I could somehow make everything all right."

He shook his head. "I was a smart enough kid, but not brilliant, and I really didn't know anything about anything, least of all about survival. Christ! When I think about the things the first batch of post-Vanishment children—Kip and Renzie and Chloe and the others—could do by the time they turned sixteen, it makes me embarrassed. And the situation has accelerated. It had to. I don't know a single eight-year-old who can't deliver a baby or hunt and skin enough small game to keep themselves fed and warm. Although . . ." His voice trailed off as he thought of something, evidently considered it, and then decided not to speak.

"Although . . . ?" Nesta pressed him.

"I don't know, maybe it's just because I was so young when It happened that my viewpoint is skewed. But it seems to me that as they've developed into adults, even with all their knowledge and competence and skills, there's something missing in the kids that came after. Something ungrown. Like they've been held back in some way. I just remember adults being more . . . I don't know, more adult." He laughed ruefully. "Of course, that could be just the normal perspective of a passing generation. As I grow older, everyone younger seems too young for their age."

"No, I don't think so," Nesta said. "I think you were right before. The Vanishing didn't leave anybody unscarred. Renzie and Tuck were born here, in the House. You must have known them all their lives. Look at what their father put them through."

Eric knotted his hands together. "In a way I knew them before the House, before they were born." He cocked one sun-bleached eyebrow at the look Nesta gave him. "Truly," he said. "Renzie and Tuck's parents lived across the street from my family before the Vanishing. We were almost the only survivors on our block."

"I had the impression their parents weren't married, that it was a post-Vanishment relationship," Nesta said.

"It was. George lost his wife and first two kids to the Vanishing. Margaret was his next-door neighbor. He took up with her about six months after the Vanishing. He'd been devoted to his first family and was terrified that they wouldn't come back. Then again, he was panicked that they *would* come back and find that he'd started a new family. At the same time, of course, he was petrified that another Vanishing would strike and he'd lose Margaret and the kids to it."

"What about Margaret? What happened to her?" Nesta asked. "Renzie doesn't talk about her much. What was she like?"

Eric got up from the bench and slowly paced along that length of porch, the motion leading his words. "Margaret was unique, a law unto herself. When I was growing up, pretty much everyone on our block was part of a computer industry white-collar family or a comfortably well-off retired couple. Margaret was the last of the blue-collar types that had originally bought into that tract. She worked for one of those air-freight delivery services. My folks said she'd been married and divorced young. Apparently her house was part of the divorce settlement.

"When I was a kid she fascinated me. She was thin, tough, a chain-smoker, quiet but not at all shy. I don't think she'd even finished high school.

"One summer when I was about fourteen I went over to try to talk her into hiring me for yard work. She wasn't interested at first. She said she liked to do it herself. Then she got this thoughtful look and said she'd changed her mind, that I could mow her lawn and trim her hedges.

"I look back on it now and feel funny. My folks made me work for any extra money I needed, though we were pretty well off. And that was good. But I'll bet Margaret didn't have the cash to spare for luxuries like hiring a neighborhood kid.

"Being the age I was, I didn't think of things like that at the time. Instead . . ." He hesitated, and Nesta was surprised to see his ruddy complexion turn even redder, vermilion at the tips of his ears. "Instead, well, I've got to admit that in the beginning I kind of entertained fantasies concerning her.

"There was nothing about Margaret that you would have called beautiful or alluring or feminine. She had shoulder-length dark brown hair, knife-sharp features. Sometimes she'd wear bright lipstick, but never any other makeup that I could tell. And she was only a couple of years younger than my mother. Still, there was something about her that drew you, something kind of sexy. I think it was that she was so utterly and completely herself. No bullshit, no subterfuge, no games. I imagine that later on that had a good deal to do with George ending up with her.

"Anyway, the first few times I worked for her she let me loose on the yard and left me alone. One Saturday, though, she always seemed to be hanging around nearby whenever I looked up. Finally she asked if I'd like to take a break and have a soft drink." Eric laughed and flushed again. "I can't tell you the fantasies I entertained while she was getting me that soda.

"While I drank it she smoked a cigarette and made what I took to be small talk. She asked what classes I was going to take when school started up again, what texts I'd be assigned, if there were any books I'd read lately that I particularly liked.

"After that whenever I did chores for her it was always the same; a Coke, polite questions, then back to work. My hopes that she was working up to a seduction never came to anything.

"School started and between homework, sports, and rainy weather setting in my yardwork dwindled. One weekend in October Margaret came over. She'd bought a cheap bookcase kit—the kind with the shelves made out of particle board. She asked if I'd help her put it together.

"She'd always paid me for my work outside in the yard. I'd never been in her house before. I can't even recall now what I expected. Whatever it was, it certainly didn't match the reality.

"Books, everywhere you looked—books and magazines. And obviously not just for window dressing, to make Margaret look smart. They were piled in stacks everywhere. Some lay facedown with their spines cracking, half-read. Others had battered, turned-down edges, little scraps of yarn and string hanging out from the edges as place-markers.

"As we started assembling the shelves she questioned me the same way she had during the summer. What was I studying? Did I like it? What was I learning? It all began to fall into place. I understood why she'd hired me.

"I've never in my life met someone so hungry for knowledge. Margaret *was* interested in me, but not in the way I'd hoped. I was a contact for her, a possible conduit to all the things she'd never learned in school.

"As if someone had snapped their fingers, the spell I'd woven for myself about her fell apart. I understood her and found myself feeling sorry for her. I know she saw that and I think it . . . amused her."

Eric stopped to lean on the porch railing, more restless in his stillness than he was in pacing. "Afterward I made it a point that whenever I went over to her place I'd have some book or another to lend her, pretending whatever it was that it was 'so good' that she just had to read it. Margaret became my own private charity case.

"What a condescending little horse's ass I was! I look back on it now . . ." He shook his head. "Margaret must have been somewhere around forty at the time. That makes her six years younger than I am now. But she became fixed in my mind as a middle-aged illiterate redneck." He sighed. "My first, sexual response to her was more honest and probably more accurate.

"Nonetheless, she accepted the books gladly, though with an edge of amusement. You know, in my parents' home we never treated books the way Margaret did. We were taught that they were precious objects, to be handled with respect. And again, I believe my folks were right. But the way that Margaret treated books was respectful too, maybe more respectful of what books are really all about." He sighed once more and seemed to be finished.

"But what happened to her?" Nesta asked.

"Margaret had already moved over to the House by the time my parents sent me here during the barricade period against the marauders. She'd brought Brad and Ginny for their safety and George had followed. Margaret was probably pregnant with Renzie by then, but it didn't show.

"We became good friends over the years. In all that time I never had the courage to talk to her about that summer; how I'd felt, and what a fool I'd come to realize I'd been."

"But in the end she left, she deserted Renzie and Tuck, left them with their father." Nesta said. She couldn't keep the disapproval from her voice.

"Yes and no. She did leave." Eric turned to look Nesta fully in the eye. "Margaret was so tough, such a survivor. She made it through the Vanishing, the marauders, Old George, bearing the kids. She was forty-three when she had Renzie. Tuck came along two years later. Both pregnancies were hard on her. But what got her in the end was the smoking.

"She was *always* smoking. She managed to scrounge tobacco years after the Vanishing when all that could be found was ghastly musty salvage.

"When Renzie was about ten Margaret came down ill. Skinny as she was, she lost even more weight. Hake ran tests and found lung cancer. A few weeks later she took off, leaving George and the kids a letter. She told them that she couldn't bear to die slowly in front of them."

"And that was it?"

"Almost. Ten months later another letter and a small packet arrived, hoboed all the way down from the North Bay. Margaret had made it up to Oakland, settled in with a group of folks that had colonized the main library there. She'd asked them to let the House know when she finally died."

Eric hesitated before continuing. "You see, I think what she'd written about not wanting to die in front of her children was true. But I also believe that after eleven years of surviving and taking care of all of them—George, Ginny, Brad, Tuck, and Renzie—I think that at the end she wanted at least a little of her old life back. I like to imagine Margaret spending her last days surrounded by stacks and stacks of books, browsing through them at her leisure."

His eyes were reddening. He looked away. "So that's why Renzie doesn't talk much about her mother. She can let herself feel anger at George. But she doesn't have any safe outlets where Margaret is concerned. Just unassuaged grief."

Nesta thought of what Eric had said about how none of the children really grew up anymore. In this new, new world it was the griefs, rather than the sins of the fathers, that were visited on the sons. And on the daughters. And the griefs of the mothers.

———

"Lampwick, make yourself useful." Nesta handed the gawky young man a stack of equations. "Go upstairs and ask Steff to show you the proper format for these. Enter them in the atomic-substructures directory."

All morning he'd been underfoot in her quarters. Apparently someone had assigned him to do filing to help relieve the clutter down here, but he'd been at loose ends for hours. Nesta had been sequestered in her room for almost a week working on a set of formulas. Having another person's constant presence in those close quarters was adding to her growing claustrophobia.

"I can't," he said.

"Why not?"

"All the computers are tied up."

"What about *your* computer?"

Lampick fidgeted. "Dr. Van Woorden is running figures on it."

"But that's what you're supposed to do for him; run the tests and enter the data."

"I told him that," Lampwick protested. "But all he'd let me do was set up the computer checks. He said he had to do the rest himself to be sure it was done right." Lampwick looked resentful.

"Okay, I apologize—not your fault." Nesta tried to think if there was anyone who could be bumped off a computer. "All right, let's do this. Since he's been on your system all morning, tell him he can stay on till five tonight. You take the rest of the day off and come back and run the figures through tonight."

"Since this morning?" Lampwick laughed. "Dr. Van Woorden took over my computer three days ago. I haven't been able to get close to it, and he won't talk to me or anybody else. Who knows when he'll be done?"

"What?" Nesta marched Lampwick straight upstairs.

Loren Van Woorden was indeed entrenched behind Lampwick's console. With his gray Vandyke beard, glasses pinched up on the bridge of his nose, and the wrinkles in his forehead gathered in a knot of concentration, he looked like a dignified but anciently stubborn schnauzer.

"Loren, what's going on here?" Nesta asked.

"I'm running through the spectroscopic checks on the aurora." He didn't look up as columns of numbers rolled down the screen.

"But you already did that."

"I'm doing it again."

"Lampwick says you've been rerunning them for three days. *Three days,* Loren?"

Van Woorden finally accepted that the stonewalling that had worked on Lampwick wouldn't deter Nesta. He hit a save on the program, called up another file. A spectroscopic graph filled the monitor. He tapped some keys. A window appeared in the middle of the screen. It pictured a quadrant of the night sky.

"I was letting the computer run on this program while I did a final printout. I'd meant to do it before we left the Hackers' Center, but what with the eviction, getting set up here and going on to other assignments, I didn't have the time till now. I came back an hour after initiating the print run and found the visuals onscreen were changing."

"In what way?" Nesta asked. The images on the screen were static and unaltered.

"It took place over a period of time." Van Woorden tapped in another command. "This will speed things up."

At first nothing happened. Nesta rubbed at her eyes as the image blurred. She'd been staring at the monitor too hard.

She looked again. It wasn't her eyes. The pictured stars were changing. They shivered, shifted, danced in sandworm tracks. The black background lightened. The bordering bars of the spectroscopic graph pulsed in a crazy framework; longer and shorter, fatter and thinner as if hopelessly confused, estranged from their former mathematical certainty.

"What in the hell is going on?"

"What indeed?" said Loren dryly. "Apparently many things." He tapped in another command and the view changed to a different celestial quadrant; then another, and another.

"Observe how the sky is getting lighter. That would be a collapse of Olbers's paradox: In other words the heavens are dark—or are supposed to be—because of the expansion of the universe and, more importantly, the age of the galaxies. I've spent the last three days trying to figure out that inconsistency and all the other things that are being manifested here."

Nesta thought of something. When Renzie and Hake had brought her here to surprise her the children had been dragging in computers. The computers had come from the children.

"You didn't get these results at the Hackers' Center?"

Loren shook his head.

"Is it real? Or could it be the computer?"

Loren hesitated. "I've considered that. It appears that the program extrapolated information from the original data and began generating these images. This in spite of the fact that I had Lampwick run appropriate equipment and software tests."

Nesta felt despair settling in her stomach like a stone. This weirdness had to be due to the peculiar modifications she'd seen the children engineering on the computers in the arcade bunkhouse. What about the data being correlated on the other computers? Did this mean all her research was compromised?

"However, I did think of a way to run a sort of backcheck," Loren said. "I know I've always scoffed at the aurora claims. But under the circumstances—" He cleared his throat gruffly. "Last night was the first clear night in a week. I asked two of the second-generation House inhabitants not connected with our research"—he thought, trying to remember names—"Kip and Chloe, if they would help me with an observation. We went out and together looked at the night sky. As I expected, they described an aurora I could not see."

Nesta stared at him. There was nothing surprising in that except Van Woorden's willingness to change his stance.

"I thanked them and dismissed them. I then invited several of the House children outside for a similar viewing. I ascertained beforehand that they had no knowledge of my research."

"And they saw an aurora too."

"Not exactly." Van Woorden tapped the screen with one finger. "They gave a much more detailed description then a mere aurora. What they saw matched what we are seeing here. So it would appear that this phenomenon does not exist solely in the computer. Now, do you suppose that the two of you could leave me alone so that I can do my work?"

CHAPTER TWENTY-SEVEN

Sun hunkered in his rocky post watching the 'Bounders below. His innate stiffness, his normal rigidity, stood him in good stead for his statuelike vigil.

The scurrying down in the gully reminded him of a wasp's nest. People rushed about dismantling tents, pulling supplies from old hillside burrows and pits which were the only remains of a long-abandoned gold mine.

This was the 'Bounders' main camp. And they were on the move. Sun's long sojourn was almost at an end. For the last few weeks small groups of the fanatics had drifted into camp, swelling it like a hive. Now the 'Bounders were ready to swarm down from the Sierra foothills, cross California's Central Valley, and put their plan into effect.

They could not have the House. Sun had sworn that to himself. Nor the people within. Sun knew the House people didn't particularly care for him. But that didn't matter. What mattered was that they didn't change, or disappear, or Vanish. They were like the House, immutable and dependable forever.

Always lean, Sun wasn't noticeably thinner for the hard months of his furtive lookout. He'd been raised knowing how to live off the land. His mountain man of a father had taught him well.

Spying on the 'Bounders—that had been harder. To watch and

listen without being detected. But he had done that well too. The proof was that he was still alive.

And why shouldn't he be? Sun's mouth stretched in a taut, humorless grin. To watch and watch, yet know the instant he was being watched; that had been the best of the lessons his father had taught him.

CHAPTER TWENTY-EIGHT

Dodd announced, "I'm starved and I smell food. It's time for lunch. No one can work properly on an empty stomach," and proceeded to herd the rest of the research team down the switchback of easy-riser stairs to the dining room. Renzie stifled a smile. Freed from the constraints of the Hackers' Center hierarchy the chubby biologist had blossomed into an extroverted nursemaid. He reminded Renzie of the nursemaid Saint Bernard in *Peter Pan*. "You too," Dodd declared as he flushed her out from where she hid in her alcove, surrounded on her bed by piles of books and reports.

"All right," she conceded as she submitted to his shepherding. "I admit that I was wasting away and you've saved me."

Dodd beamed.

Renzie grabbed a sandwich in the kitchen and managed to sneak back up to work, only to find Tuck sitting morosely on her bed. He didn't look as though he'd just dropped by from the Domes for a friendly visit.

"How are things going?" she asked.

He shrugged.

"That good, huh?"

"I've moved out of the Domes."

Renzie sat down heavily next to him. "I," not "we." Not "me and

Le Chell." She considered all the possibilities. Le Chell had fallen out of love with Tuck. Impossible. How could anyone not love Tuck? Tuck had fallen out of love with Le Chell. Sure, right—that's why he looked so morose.

"What happened?"

Tuck leaned back on his elbows. "It's my fault. I moved over to the Domes with this idea in my head that that was going to be it—happily-ever-after time. And at first it was. But after a while . . ."

"After a while?"

Tuck flopped all the way back onto the bed, put his hands over his eyes. "Being in the Domes is like when we all lived together here in the House. It's like living in the middle of your relatives. After a while I realized I was just waiting to be alone with her. But that's not how the Domes work. I began to get anxious and impatient, started taking it out on Le Chell."

"How so?"

"I'd start arguments. Stupid stuff about nothing. It upset Le Chell. I made her miserable. Hell, I made me miserable." Tuck rolled on his side to face Renzie. "I'm not like that." His eyes pleaded with her for confirmation. "But some part of me couldn't accept that it was never going to be just her and me. I was going sour with frustration. And I knew if I kept that up I was going to lose her."

"So you decided to move back."

Tuck nodded. "I wanted to think the whole thing out, figure out a way to make it work for both of us, or a way for me to survive in the Domes and be content with how things are there."

"But?"

"She doesn't understand. Before I was driving her away with the way I was acting. Now I've hurt and confused her. At first she kept asking me what she'd done wrong. Now she's angry. She thinks I'm moving out to punish her. Maybe I've lost her anyway."

Tuck looked at Renzie as if she would have an answer.

Renzie didn't know what to say. She waited a minute, then switched the subject to the only help she could offer him. "Have you found a new place to stay? With Carpenter revamping the earthquake wing people are already doubling up. Normally you could move in next to me but . . . you know." She nodded to the storeroom brimming over with machinery. "Though if worst comes to worst we'll find a way to shoehorn you in."

"Thanks, but I'm okay that way. I'm going to stay with Hammer for a while. We get along and he likes having the help."

Renzie wanted to tell Tuck how bad she felt for him. He must feel as miserable as she had after Brad betrayed her. But Le Chell hadn't betrayed Tuck, and Tuck still loved Le Chell. It seemed to Renzie that there was reason for hope.

After the seesaw spells of winter chill and unseasonable heat the weather finally settled into a gradual spring warming. The year's earlier rains yielded up as lush a mantle of greenery as anyone could remember. Old-timers looked at the bounty of foliage with pleasure mixed with concern; it would be a wealth of dry tinder fuel within weeks. Luckily—and there seemed to be no reason for it but luck—the individual Home arsons, which had continued sporadically throughout the winter, dwindled in frequency and then stopped.

Renzie returned to her old custom of greeting the morning from the fourth-floor tower with pleasure. She told herself she needed the time to clear her mind for the day's work ahead. But usually her thoughts turned to thinking of ways to bring Tuck and Le Chell back together. It seemed to Renzie that after Tuck's efforts it was only fair that Le Chell should try a turn in the House. And if that didn't work out, at least it would help Le Chell understand what Tuck had gone through.

Renzie hated to see Tuck miserable, but the mornings were beautiful and she was optimistic that something, somehow, could be worked out. And she couldn't deny she was happy that he was back in the House. Tuck returned, no fires, no 'Bounders, and the research was going well. She was contented with life.

She scanned the panorama: the House grounds and garden, the peacefully aging Homes beyond, the bulk of the tower hiding the view of the vegetable gardens, baths and the Watchers' Domes. Renzie smiled. She bet that was where Tuck's thoughts were wandering too.

Her eyes came to rest on the Krit's abandoned heap of possessions. The strange old man had been gone for a year now. She should remind Eric that his things should be cleared away.

The bundle shifted. It began to unwind itself.

A scream strangled itself in Renzie's throat.

Two eyes peered out at her from the top of the shifting mound. Then a nose and hint of beard—that was all that could be seen of a face. The head was covered by a knit cap pulled down on the sides, covering the man's ears. A high-collared shirt, bound by a muffler, swathed him from his neck to just below his nose. The rest of him appeared to be swaddled too, in layers and layers of clothing, like a mummy. The Krit was back.

"Now?" said Nesta. She gestured at stacks of disks. The formulas for interpreting Loren's celestial aberration had eluded them for over a month, but now they were close. She was sure. "Hake, you know how important this is." She looked at her watch. "Is this something you could show me when I break for lunch?"

"No, this is just as important. More important." Hake wasn't just adamant—he was grim. "You have to come with me right now. It's Los Milagros."

Outside Hake had leaned two bicycles against the side of the House in readiness. They headed due west, paralleling the freeway, then turned onto the route Nesta had taken only once before. When they turned in at the swim center she was out of breath from trying to query Hake and pedal at the same time.

"Why won't you tell me what this is all about?" By now she was really frightened.

"I can't tell you because I'm not sure," he said as he dismounted. "I want to see what you think. Brace yourself."

His words weren't enough to prepare Nesta. Before, the faux jungle had dominated the space so thoroughly that Nesta had had to be told that it sprang from an Olympic-sized swimming pool.

Now it resembled something a hurricane had left in its wake. Huge rubber trees, bamboo, palms, and sculptures lay heaped in the pool in extravagant piles, as if some giant had been playing a savage game of jackstraws. Only the vaulted Mylar ceiling still stretched serenely overhead, an unconcerned witness to the devastation of the embedded pile of rubble below. With the towering plants felled Nesta could see the structure of the swim center—how the Mylar was attached to a canopy roof that shaded a set of derelict bleachers on the opposite side.

"Oh my lord," Nesta whispered. "When did this happen?"

"A pilgrim came in this morning to visit the shrine and found it like this," Hake said.

The mess was too dense to penetrate. They picked their way along the sides of the pool through litter that spilled over its edges.

The debris thinned out toward the back, near the heart of the shrine. Hake led Nesta through a tentative trail.

The broad raised dais of the "Well" itself was relatively clear. A few stunned people, evidently members of Los Milagros, picked their way around collapsed red and white tents. Several men squatted off to one side of the clearing. As Hake and Nesta approached them Nesta saw that the men were guarding a large bundle covered with a section of canvas from the tents.

"Show her," Hake said.

One of the men drew back the canvas.

The "Memory of the Word" lay beneath it, his body beginning to tinge with the peculiarly nacreous blue hues of death.

Nesta knelt beside him, fascinated in spite of her horror. "Has he been moved at all?" she asked.

Hake looked at the man who had uncovered the shrinekeeper.

"The 'Memory of the Word' was lying on his side," the Los Milagros said. "The woman who found him rolled him over to see if he was still alive, but he hasn't been moved since then."

The shrinekeeper's cantankerous and lonely expression had been bleached by death of all emotion. His hair was swept back a little where the canvas had brushed against him. But other than that, both his clothes and hair had the stiff look of something that had been washed and let dry in place.

Nesta touched his shirt tentatively, then his hair. Dry as stone.

"Would you mind rolling him all the way over?"

They did as she asked. There was no moisture in the back of his clothing or underneath him.

Nesta looked around the clearing, at the devastated jungle. There were no puddles anywhere that she could see. She stood and stepped away from the corpse, gestured to Hake to join her. She walked to the first step of the dais.

"I don't know their religion well enough," she said in a low voice. "We need to do an autopsy. Will they let us?"

"Nesta, is this an aberration?"

She didn't answer right away.

Hake grabbed her arm and raised his voice. "Tell me. Is this an aberration?"

The men had stood up and started to follow them. They were listening.

"Probably," said Nesta nervously. "Yes."

"Then you'll get your autopsy," Hake said.

Now Nesta saw what was in the faces of the men. They were waiting for her to confirm that this was an anomaly. That was why she had been called. For them this had been a terrible miracle, but a miracle nonetheless. What she'd assumed was shock was the anesthetized rapture of the awestruck.

The men drifted back to prepare the body to be taken to the House medic labs.

"Now that you've seen it, do you have any ideas on what happened here?" Hake asked.

Nesta remembered back to the time he'd brought her to this place when they'd dubbed the tapes. She remembered the sounds she'd noticed of the eerie underwater flux of lapping waves. For a moment she distracted herself by trying to calculate the tonnage of water it would take to fill the pool. What would be the impact of that amount of liquid? Not washing or flooding into a space, but instantaneously displacing into that volume of air? How long had it lasted before it just as instantaneously returned to its own continuum? Minutes? Hours? And had there been anything, or anyone, from that other continuum who had displaced along with the water, only to disappear again with it? But what kind of phenomenon would displace only into nonsolid interstices? She would have expected every cell in Memory's body to have been ruptured.

"Yes, I have ideas. But I'll need to do the autopsy to confirm them."

Hake was looking down at her with a strange look in his eyes. "Do you still think the aberrations are harmless?"

"No." Then she rallied. "Which means our research is even more crucial." She looked around at the men and women picking through the rubble. "Get them out of here as soon as possible. It might not happen again for years, or it could be any minute. What occurred here was not the Vanishing. It could, and probably will, happen again."

They rode their bicycles back in silence. Renzie was waiting for them on the front porch. She was very pale. The House was unnaturally still.

"Eric's called a meeting. Everybody's already in the Ballroom."

"You've heard what happened at the 'Well,' " said Nesta.

"Yes, but it isn't that. Hammer and Tuck just got word on the airwaves. The 'Bounders have attacked Orinda."

Over the course of her long explorations throughout the House Nesta had congratulated herself that she was developing a familiarity with the building and its community, a sense of its size. But now, here in the packed Ballroom, she had trouble comprehending the number of people she'd never seen before. Whole clans of unfamiliar and anxious faces wedged together tightly. The smallest children perched themselves up on shelves alongside Eileen's treasures to make more room for the adults packed below. The crowd's muted, troubled murmurs added up to a wavelike sussuration, the muttering of the sea heard in a shell.

Nesta sighed, feeling both rechallenged and a little defeated. Thanks to Carpenter and his crew, the House changed and grew like a vast, slow, wood-and-masonry amoeba. It boasted two large dining rooms, three cooking stations besides the main kitchen, and a population that lived in idiosyncratic shifts. Except for emergencies like this, some people might never come down to the main gathering places. She would never know them all.

Renzie heard her. "What is it?" she asked, her voice edgy.

Nesta laughed ruefully and patted Renzie's arm. She hadn't meant to add to her worry. "Nothing. It's just me." She waved at the packed space. "All these people I don't know. I've been here all this time, and I'm still such a stranger."

"All this time?" Renzie also laughed—a laugh webbed with tension, but a laugh nonetheless. Nesta would have expected her to be irritated. Perhaps Renzie welcomed the diversion.

"Nesta, you didn't move into the House until late last fall. And you didn't actively start living here until the project got kicked out of the Hackers' Center—just months ago. *I* don't know everything about the House, and I was born here."

"So I've got years to go before I get a handle on it?"

Renzie arched an eyebrow in way of an answer.

"Why don't you indulge me then, educate me while we're waiting. Who are they?" Nesta pointed to a group of people running the spectrum of various ages. They looked enough like each other to almost be called a family.

Renzie entered into the distraction willingly. "Those are the Pinellis."

"They're all related to each other?" Nesta was incredulous. If they were, surely she would have heard of them. Eric's family was famous for its survival, yet it was smaller than this group.

Renzie grinned at her tone of voice. "In a way. Not a single one of them is actually named Pinelli—they made that up. They started after the Vanishing with five people who ran into each other and decided that since they looked a little alike, they might as well be a family, since they'd all lost their own. Now, whenever they meet anyone who fills the bill, they invite them to join the clan. And once they started having kids together they really did start a kind of a tribe. You've probably run into a couple of them without knowing it. They're only striking when you get them all together like this."

Nesta smiled to herself. She supposed the ersatz Pinellis were no stranger than the Office Building dwellers' penchant for naming themselves after children's-book characters. Many people had developed a loopy sense of humor to help survive the Vanishing.

"All right then—let's see, who else? What about him?" Nesta nodded toward a sickly, thin, gray-skinned man. His coloring must indicate illness, for in the stifling warmth of the packed ballroom he was dressed in layer upon layer of clothing, as if perpetually chilled. He reminded Nesta of the street people of her youth, down to the oversized knit cap pulled down so far on the sides and in back that it disappeared into the collar of the bulky coat he wore. That must be why he seemed vaguely familiar.

Renzie wrinkled her nose. "That's the Krit. I'm not surprised he's new to you. Supposedly he was a Homer for a long time after the Vanishing. He moved to the House when I was little, but last year he took off. Maybe he returned to his Home. Anyway, he just came back. He lives up in the porches on the fourth-floor tower, so you're not likely to see him much."

Nesta remembered the afternoon she'd spent talking to Eric in that tower. It must have been before the shriveled man had reappeared. "I gather you don't like him."

Renzie shrugged. She looked ashamed. "He's just a sad old guy.

He keeps to himself, like a hermit. He kind of scared me as a kid—gave me the willies. I guess I never got over that enough to feel comfortable around him."

Just then Tuck entered the room, struggling with a huge pad of paper, a sheet of Masonite, and several long pieces of wood attached by strands of chain. Renzie excused herself and went to help him. The two of them began to set up a makeshift easel in the raised dance-band dais.

They'd just perched the pad of paper on a crossbar when Eric and Hammer came in. The crowd somehow shifted enough to form a path for Hammer's wheelchair.

"I'm sorry we took so long. I know you're all anxious to know what's happening. It took us a while to coordinate with all the other communities." At Eric's words the oceanic murmuring of the crowd hushed.

Eric turned to the sketchpad. Tuck handed him a stick of charcoal. Eric drew a large circle in the center of the page. He turned the charcoal on edge to mark four broad, dark arrows leading off from the circle. "This is Orinda," he said, pointing to the circle. "And these are the main roads leading into it." He tapped each in turn. "Old Freeway 24 heading west, 24 heading east, Moraga Way, and San Pablo Dam Road. As you know, the upper, westbound lanes of the old freeway were converted years ago into beds for Orinda's solar panels, their major source of energy and industry. The 'Bounders have taken up positions in the surrounding hills and are shelling the panels."

The murmur in the room began again, this time in an angry chord. "That's why those 'Bounders came last year to the fair," Hot Rod said. "Remember how they were sucking up to the Orindans?"

Eric nodded in agreement. "Now, we have no idea of the size of the 'Bounders' force, but it appears to be considerable compared to skirmishes with them in the past. The Orindan troops that have gone out after them have suffered major losses."

Again the room ebbed to silence.

Eric took a deep breath. "After talking at length with the other community groups, we've reached a consensus. We're sending everyone we can spare who's willing to go. At this moment the Vineyard co-ops are pulling together their fuel reserves of vineahol and the Women's Brigade are reactivating their armory."

He pointed to his crude map. "Pleasant Hill and Concord, which are closer, are also sending help, but we're all going to be limited to coming in from Highway 680 on 24 east. Union City is trying to contact the Oakland gangs' consortium to get permission and guarantee of safe passage so that 24 west would also be available. It may be possible, since the gangs hate the 'Bounders as much as we do."

He paused to let the assembly absorb the full impact of his words, allowed them the time to remember the loss of friends in fighting off the marauders, to think of what the depletion of fuel reserves might mean in a hard year.

"We're going to throw everything we've got at these SOBs, try to get rid of them once and for all. We, the Watchers, Hackers' Center, Viets, Homers, and all the other groups have agreed to send all the heavy vehicles and munitions on hand, and all the manpower that's willing to go."

"I wouldn't do that, if I were you," came a voice from the back of the room.

Everybody turned.

Sun was standing in the doorway.

"It's a trap," he said.

CHAPTER TWENTY-NINE

Sun strode to the makeshift flip pad and took the charcoal from Eric. "Forget about this," he said, scribbling over the 'Bounder positions Eric had marked as surrounding Orinda. "They *were* all there, to scare the bejesus out of the Orindans. The 'Bounders are trying to damage as many of the solar plants as they can with just a couple of rocket launchers. What's left now is just bells and whistles—a small group running a 'magic show' for effect. They want you to think they're still massed there."

"If they aren't there, where are they?" asked Kip. "And how do you know?"

"Why should we believe you?" Renzie chimed in. "You disappear for months and then show up with this wild, bullshit story."

Sun chose to answer Renzie. "You're right, I've been gone for months. Don't you think it's beyond my ability to pull off a hoax by coming back right now and knowing that the 'Bounders are up in Orinda? And why would I? Because of my outstanding reputation as a cheerful, playful practical jokester?" He spun around, looking at all of them. "You don't have to believe me. But if you don't, I'm out of here—again. I'm not going to stick around for what happens next."

Renzie opened her mouth to reply, then closed it, looking thoughtful.

"Calm down," said Eric. "Say your piece."

Sun tore away the sketch and began drawing a new diagram on the fresh page underneath. This time Orinda was a very small circle near the upper edge. He marked a few small x's around the circle. Tapping them he said, "Bells and whistles, dog and pony show." Then he stroked in the same broad arrows that Eric had used to indicate the major routes into Orinda. The longest arrow descended toward the bottom of the page, ending at a bigger circle that Sun labeled "us." Then he went back and drew more tiny x's like embroidery stitches around the thoroughfare arrows at various points.

"This is where the 'Bounders are filtering down to, setting up. Some of these areas are around bridges, others are freeway overpasses, or weak spots in the road. Once those rescue squads you're talking about sending up are well past these points, the 'Bounders will blast the main corridors to oblivion. Anyone who tries to get back after that will have to leave big trucks and weaponry behind and cut cross-country."

"Let me guess," Hake said grimly. "The 'Bounders will have snipers ready and waiting."

"A few, but not that many. Not like you think."

Sun turned again to the diagram. His back blocked the view. The crowd murmured at the sound of the crankily scratching charcoal as he drew more x's—many x's, a frenzy of x's. Then it hushed when he finally stepped aside.

The marks marched as a dark wave across the base of the Fremont hills, where many years ago the marauders had gathered.

"This is where they'll position once the corridor traps are set up. The reason they're pretending to attack Orinda is to draw away our fighting power and strand it up north. The 'Bounders are coming to destroy the Watchers and burn the Homes. They're coming to destroy the Valley."

Hammer had already turned his wheelchair around. "I'll put out a call to the rest of the Valley groups. They have to be warned before they send any of their people up to Orinda."

"No!" said Sun. "Not by radio. Not yet. They've got their own portable radio units. They're already listening in on your responses to the call for help from Orinda. If they know you've been warned they'll just come straight down and start burning."

Eric drummed his fingers on the back of Hammer's wheelchair. "Then that's our advantage. Forewarned is forearmed. We'll have to plan around that.

"The first priority *is* to warn the rest of the Valley. Kip, Whelan, Chloe, and Sue, I want you to dash over to the Domes, Office Buildings, Mall, and Stockyards. I'll need people to bike to the Homers' Council, Los Milagros, the Koanites, Viets, Women's Brigade . . ." As Eric named the rest of the Valley communities hands shot up to volunteer.

"In each group tell whoever is coordinating the Orinda relief effort exactly what Sun just told us, and to drop everything and meet here in three hours. Hake, Jorda, Hot Rod, come with me." He beckoned to Sun. "You have a lot more to tell us. And you never did answer Kip. How did you know? Where have you been?"

No one strayed far from the House the rest of the day. A few people puttered about in the workshops, or in the gardens, talking in low voices with their Watcher neighbors. Only Carpenter and his crew continued with their labors as if nothing had happened. After an hour or so the delegated leaders from the other communities began to arrive. When a group of Los Milagros brought "Memory"'s corpse to the House in mid-afternoon it caught Nesta by surprise. The events of the morning seemed to have taken place in another era.

Yet what had occurred at the "Well of Voices"—whatever it might turn out to be, or something like it—could easily happen here *before* the 'Bounders launched their attack. Nesta sent the body on to the lab and hastily assembled Adrienne and Dodd, wishing fervently that Hake wasn't tied up in the meeting with Eric. She assigned Dodd as chief pathologist, Adrienne to handle getting tissue samples ready for testing, and herself as their assistant. Immersed in the somber task of looking for answers in a dead man's body, Nesta lost track of the time.

"They've called the meeting." Renzie stood at the lab door. Nesta turned to look at her out of a work fog. The younger woman was silhouetted by a darkening sky. "It's going to be held in the main dining room so the Watchers can join us."

The dining room was as jammed as the Ballroom had been earlier. None of the rich smells common to the hour drifted in the air: the cooks had set out big bowls of salads and plates mounded high with sandwiches on the sideboards so that they wouldn't be stranded in the kitchen during the meeting.

Instead of a simple sketchpad an array of blackboards stretched across the front of the room. Jorda and Sun were chalking in maps and diagrams. As soon as they'd finished, Eric wasted no time in starting the meeting.

"Our biggest initial advantage in this situation is the fact that the 'Bounders are monitoring our radio communications," he said. "We'll be giving them a lot to listen to in the next few days. The Valley is going to send up as many of the old military vehicles and big rigs as we can get in shape on such short notice. We've bought ourselves some time by calling Orinda and telling them it'll take us another day to get equipped. The 'Bounders will think the trucks will be crammed with men and munitions."

"Which they won't be, I gather," one of the women from the Watchers' Domes said.

Eric almost smiled. "No. We had something else in mind."

Someone raised a hand far back in the room. "Aren't you asking whoever drives those trucks to volunteer for a suicide mission? Those demolition squads will crucify them as they drive through the ambush points."

"No, that's our second advantage," Eric answered. "The strike at Orinda as a distraction to draw away most of our fighting power was a calculated risk on the 'Bounders' part. They know we'll be on our guard, and that we'll have radios of our own in the trucks. Ambushing us on the way up would be too risky for them. We're approaching from three directions: Moraga Way, 24 east, and we got permission from the Oakland consortium to make our way up to 24 west. The 'Bounders would have to take out all our convoys at exactly the same time or risk warning us in time to get more help from the communities south of the Valley. Which, unbeknownst to them, we're already in the process of—we've got messengers heading south right now."

He pointed to one of the blackboard maps, a refinement of Sun's earlier drawing. "The 'Bounders picked locations on the basis of their effectiveness in blocking our route back, not for timing. They're going to let our trucks pass well out of earshot before blasting the roads. They don't want our convoys to know the return avenues have been eliminated."

"I get it," said Kip. "You're going to have the convoys double back and ambush *them* before they can do that."

"Wrong," said Eric. "We're going to let them destroy the roads. The 'Bounders are limiting their own radio contacts. They don't want to risk giving away their real location. Sun says their main camp expects to receive only a single message—in code—from each of their crews: that our forces are past and well on the way to Orinda and that the roads have been successfully razed. After that there's to be no communication unless they believe something's gone wrong with their plan. Once the main 'Bounder swarm begins its attack on the Valley, the demolition squads' last task is to ambush the trucks when they try to return."

"What's going to stop them?" Renzie asked.

"Not what. Who. You, for one."

Nesta's breath turned to a stone in her throat. Not Renzie.

Eric drew a series of checks around the 'Bounder demolition camps. "Like I said, we have a day's grace. Tonight we're sending teams cross-country to set up in these positions, above and behind the 'Bounder crews. Once the convoys have gotten through, the roads have been obliterated, and the main 'Bounder camp contacted, the 'Bounders aren't going to expect anything. Our teams will wait till the middle of that night, then go in and eliminate them.

"Renzie, if you agree, I want you to head up the main party handling the ambushers at 24 east. You're one of our best backwooders, and that's the stretch of highway you ran the road crew on. We're rounding up some of your roadies from last year. Sun will be going with you too. Highway 24 west will be led by Douc Ng, Moraga Way by Haigha Trent."

Nesta couldn't believe what she was hearing: Eric calmly assigning Renzie to the job of chief assassin. Besides, Renzie detested Sun. Surely Eric wouldn't team them together. But when Nesta glanced over the younger woman was nodding thoughtfully.

Eric went on to the next blackboard. "This illustrates the position of the main swarm of 'Bounders. From there they plan to move south through Milpitas and run a sweep out and down through the Valley.

"While all this action is happening up here on the way to Orinda"—he tapped the first blackboard—"most of the rest of us will be using night's cover to take up places here, in the foothills below the main line of the swarm."

"I'm sure we can knock off a substantial number of 'Bounders in the initial surprise," said one of the men bunking in the Northern Conservatory. "But we won't be able to take out all of them. Any that survive will fall back to the higher hills. God help us when they retaliate. It could be at any time, anywhere."

Eric pointed at the first blackboard again. "Good point, Tom. For that we need to backtrack," he said. "Remember our convoys? They may not be carrying troops as we've led the 'Bounders to believe, but that doesn't mean they'll be empty, either.

"They'll be loaded with off-road vehicles, some weaponry, drivers, shotgun riders, and extra fuel. Since thanks to Sun we know where all the demolition camps are along the routes, the convoys will drive beyond them to areas where they can unload their cargo safely.

"Then the trucks will continue on to Orinda. They'll finish unloading in warehouses there so that the 'Bounders positioned up in the hills won't know they've been scammed."

"Since we can't communicate any of this to the Orindans by radio, they're going to be angry when they find out we've sent them almost nothing," a Houser Nesta didn't recognize said.

"We're not sending them nothing," said Eric. "The most important aid we can give them is information about the nature of the attack against them: that after the initial assault, the 'Bounders' show of force has been mainly illusory. With what Sun's told us of their logistics, it shouldn't be too hard for the Orindans, with the help of our convoy drivers and the folks from Concord, to mop up the remaining ambushers there." Eric looked around the room to see if everyone was following him.

"Good. Now, back to those off-road vehicles. The ones in the convoy heading up Highway 17 to 13 to 24 west and Moraga Way will cut east across country as soon as they unload and rendezvous with the Highway 680 group, which will be camping out till Renzie's group takes out the demolition squad there. Once that's been accomplished, they'll pick up Renzie's team and head south cross-country to take up a line of sniping stations behind the 'Bounders' main force. The rest of us will be located below.

"When the 'Bounders get ready to move, they're going to find themselves sandwiched in by the full force of an army they thought they'd diverted up north. Between the advantages of surprise, numbers, position, and firepower, we should be able to neutralize most of the swarm."

Eric again looked around the room, his face grim. "That doesn't mean we're not going to lose people, but this will be the 'easy' part in that it's straightforward. I'm more worried about what will come afterward."

"What afterward?" a Domesman called out. "You just said they'd be neutralized."

"*Most* of them," Eric corrected. He gestured across the map. "Instead of gathering in a single main camp, the 'Bounders have strung themselves out to get ready to sweep through the Valley. What Tom said earlier was true. Some of them *will* still escape.

"That's when things will get unpredictable and really dangerous. Any 'Bounders that survive are not going to slink off to lick their wounds. They're fanatics and they'll be desperate. What we'll have to deal with afterward is guerrilla warfare. Think of what a single person with matches can do in this dry heat. Everyone who stays behind here in the Valley is going to be put on either support duty or crews to start digging fire breaks and setting traps and deadfalls.

"Jorda is going to be in charge of that for the House. She'll coordinate with Greg from the Domes." He indicated the other blackboards: "Study these so you'll know where the traps will be laid. Hot Rod will organize the fire-break crews. I also recommend that people bury or hide their valuables.

"Now, this is how we've broken down the assignments." He nodded to Hake, who stood ready by a flip pad. "Sniper teams to take out the demolition nests. Convoy drivers. Off-road vehicle crews. The majority of you will be in the frontal forces."

Hake wrote the categories across the top of the page.

"We're expecting reinforcements from Santa Cruz, Morgan Hill, Gilroy, and Los Gatos," Eric continued. "They won't arrive in time for the initial attacks, but we're going to need their help with backup and cleanup operations. Anyone here whom I don't name off now will be assigned later to helping accommodate the reinforcements, working with Jorda's booby-trapping teams, or setting up an infirmary in the smaller Dome." He paused, then said quietly, "You all know that we're going to lose people."

He turned briskly to Hake and the flip pad. "All right, assignments. We'll start with the sniper crews. As I said before, Renzie, you and Sun will be in charge of the Highway 680 team. Some of your group will come from other communities, but from the House and Domes you've got . . ." As Eric called off names Hake wrote them down.

Nesta listened numbly while almost everyone she'd come to know and like in the House was assigned to the battlefront. Most of those Eric left unnamed were very old, very young, or not physically fit. Of her own staff, only Dodd, Van Woorden, and herself remained. Hake was to be in charge of organizing one wing of the off-road vehicles. Nesta looked at him busily listing names. People are going to die again, she thought. Just like right after the Vanishing. What an incredible waste. Nesta felt a sudden rush of hatred for the 'Bounders.

She tried to catch Renzie's eye, but Renzie was looking fixedly elsewhere. Nesta followed her line of sight across the room. Tuck and Le Chell were inching toward each other through the jammed mass. They almost made it—at last only a table ringed tightly with children stood in their way. They stretched across it and clasped hands, so tightly that their knuckles were as white as their faces.

CHAPTER THIRTY

Nesta left the dining room when Eric adjourned to let the various teams meet and begin organizing. She hadn't been assigned to anything yet. She was only in the way. She'd wait to say her goodbyes later upstairs.

She climbed up to the quiet, almost deserted labs. Van Woorden had already returned. The ancient astronomer sat calmly before his console running fresh backups of his work. No doubt they would be the valuables he'd choose to hide.

Dodd came in a few minutes later. All afternoon while they'd dissected "Memory"'s corpse he'd been the calm professional. But now when he saw Nesta he timidly scurried around to his module. Nesta could just imagine what the expression on her face must be. She sighed. What was the use of being so sour and angry?

She couldn't concentrate on her work. Idly she opened one of the books that Hake was always bringing her. This one was of the work of a Dutch engraver named Escher. As she thumbed through it, Nesta first thought that the man must have been a fabric designer—his images fit together in tight patterns.

Then the prints became more pictorial. The intervals of sky between a flock of flying birds took on the shape of carp; the forms of the birds collapsed into waves between the fishes.

In a lithograph called "Cycle" identical dancing men raced down a flight of steps. At the bottom they waltzed themselves into the whirl-igig pattern of the tiling, each man an intertwined template of himself.

In print after print the positive and negative shapes of men and beasts split apart, went their own way, only in the end to meet and blend again.

Nesta froze when she came to a piece titled "Relativity." It pictured an inside stairwell that reminded her uncannily of the House's seven-eleven steps. Except that these stairs interlocked in a preposterous manner, leading to landings set at impossible angles to each other. Yet the landings looked exactly like any landing to be found in the House.

Nesta felt unbearably restless. Where was Renzie? She should have come up by now for at least a change of clothing. Nesta slammed the book shut and left.

The crowd in the dining room had thinned out considerably. Nesta scanned the room. She didn't see either Renzie or Hake. Her other team members—Adrienne, Steff, Lampwick, and the rest—would have returned to their former homes in the Hackers' Center or Office Buildings before leaving on their assignments.

Nesta ducked into the kitchen. A line of workers, mostly children, were assembling packets of dried fruit, loaves of dense breads, hard sausages, and cheeses. The filled parcels were then stacked in one corner of the kitchen.

"Jorda, I don't know what Eric's going to sign me up for, but in the meantime, put me to work. I'm going crazy doing nothing."

"Take Quill's place in line," Jorda said. "That will free him to run in more goods from the storage bins. None of the teams will be able to set up campfires for cooking, so we have to be sure everyone will be able to eat on their feet. Right now we're putting together kits for the convoy groups leaving late tomorrow. The sniper teams have been provisioned and taken off."

Nesta felt a pang. Renzie was gone and Nesta hadn't had a chance to say goodbye to her. Nesta wished now she hadn't let her depression get to her and that she'd stayed in the dining room after the meeting. She took Quill's place, next to Minda. The little girl looked up at her.

"So," said Nesta. "Do you want to show me what to do?"

Minda grinned. "Sure. It's easy."

The hours passed and the pile of provision packets grew high.

"Stop!" Jorda called out. "We're running out of bread. Clear the work surfaces for a baking shift. We don't have time to let yeast rise, so we'll keep it simple with soda bread."

Cheeses and sausages disappeared onto shelves. Bowls, flour, soda, eggs, and shortening materialized as if by sleight of hand. Everything soon became snowy from the flour: the countertops, Nesta's arms, her clothes, Minda's small form next to her. As the first loaves were slid into the ovens the smell of bread enveloped the bakers as cozily as a hearth fire on a cold night. Nesta became lost in rhythms of measuring, mixing, and kneading. The passage of time seemed as insulated and long as winter.

She emerged from her extended trance when a golden brown hand passed through her paled field of vision and gently grasped her powdered forearm. She stared up into Hake's face. He looked calm and alert. She thought, not for the first time, what a handsome man he was. Nesta glanced around at her fellow bakers. Even the children's faces were gaunt and pallid with exhaustion. She wouldn't let herself think what she must look like.

"All considered, you appear remarkably well," she complained.

Hake smiled. "That's because I had a good night's rest."

Nesta glanced back over her shoulder. Light brightened the kitchen's narrow band of windows. It was morning.

"My group had a brief meeting last night," Hake said. "I went up to the lab afterward to say goodbye, but you weren't there. Loren and Dodd didn't know where you'd gone to. You weren't in the kiosk, either. I gave up and went to bed—there's not going to be many opportunities to sleep over the next few days."

The twinge of fear and pain came back. Nesta pushed it away. "How did you finally come to think of looking for me here?"

"I didn't." He gestured to the pile of food packs. "We're due to join with the rest of the community forces this morning to finalize our preparations and strategy. I came to pick up my supplies." He grinned. "I would *never* have thought to look for you here. Brush yourself off so I can hug you goodbye."

Nesta's gaze dropped as she wiped her hands on her pants. "I didn't get to see Renzie before she left."

When he wrapped his arms around her Nesta felt his shared concern. He let her go gently. "Nesta, if anyone will survive, it's Renzie. You heard what Eric said last night. She's superb in the wilds, she's familiar with that area, and she's the best fighter I know. Feel sorry for the 'Bounders instead."

He was still smiling, but his eyes had turned grim. Nesta was suddenly afraid to touch him. She was glad they'd already hugged.

He grabbed up a food satchel from the corner. "I'll be back. So will Renzie."

He hesitated at the door. "Yesterday, with everything that happened, did Los Milagros deliver the shrinekeeper's body?"

"Yes."

"And?"

"We started the autopsy," Nesta told him. "Adrienne took samples for testing but got called away before she could run them. It will have to wait till . . . afterward. From what we could tell from a cursory examination, it would appear as though he drowned, except for the lack of water."

"Drowning victims usually suffocate," Hake said. "It's not uncommon to find little water in the lungs."

"That's not what I meant. There was *no* water in his lungs—or anywhere else. If anything, his tissues were dehydrated."

When the last of the bread was pulled from the ovens Jorda sent the kitchen crew to bed. "Get some sleep," she ordered them. "This afternoon we've still got to throw together supplies for the main force."

As the others filed out Jorda beckoned Nesta aside. "I know you were just volunteering, but would you mind if I asked Eric to assign you to help here? After the main company leaves tomorrow I have to get busy organizing our defenses. That will leave only children available for this detail. Most of them know what to do, but I desperately need a responsible adult to organize them, and you're used to supervising people."

Nesta felt dismay wash across her face.

Jorda raised her hand in a mudra of disavowal. "It won't be that difficult. Just keep it simple—soups and stews, salads and sandwiches. The most complicated thing is making the bread for the sandwiches, and you know how to do that now! Minda will show you where the storage cellars and other supplies are. I know you'll do just fine."

So Nesta was in the kitchen two days later cleaning up after the lunch shift when she heard the commotion. Wiping her hands hastily on the towel tucked into her waistband as a makeshift apron, she peered into the dining room. People were rushing out, turning down the hallway in the direction of the courtyard.

The elderly matriarch of the Pinelli clan hurried by. "What is it?" Nesta asked her.

"I don't know yet," the woman said, worry further creasing her corrugated features. "One of the sentry-post kids came running in and said there was trouble, that someone was coming."

Nesta threw the towel on a table and followed her.

The people who'd rushed from the dining room were clustered at the far end of the courtyard, making their way slowly back to the porch as a mass. As they got closer Nesta could just barely make out a bloody and ragged Pel in the middle, leaning on Hot Rod. One of the bull terriers—Nesta couldn't tell which—limped by its master's side.

Hot Rod tried to wave away the encroaching Housers while he bent his head to listen to Pel, who seemed to be struggling to tell him something.

"Quiet, damn it!" Hot Rod finally shouted at the well-meaning crowd. When they stepped back a little Nesta saw that they were pulling a handcart. On the flat bed of the wagon lay something bulky, swaddled in blood-streaked burlap.

Who *was* wrapped in the canvas? Nesta's breath caught in her throat. Her pulse began to hammer against the inside of her wrists. Renzie, Hake, and the rest would have passed close by the amusement park on their way north. Had the 'Bounders moved to attack sooner than expected?

Evidently other people in the throng were similarly concerned, for Hot Rod yelled again. "No, it was *not* the 'Bounders. Pel says it was a pack of feral dogs that came after his flock. Now, if a couple of you will help me get them to the lab, the rest can clear off." Hot Rod caught sight of Nesta standing on the porch. "Nesta, could you come assist in the lab?"

Nesta caught a glimpse of something white flopping in the back of the cart. "Hot Rod, I've only got the same basic medic training as anyone else," she said. "Just because I'm a scientist doesn't mean I'd be any more help than—"

"I think you'll be useful for this," Hot Rod interrupted. "In fact, if that pet biologist of yours is around, you might want to send one of these folks to fetch him."

"Dodd?"

"That's the one."

Nesta glanced over Hot Rod's shoulder into the wagon. The white she'd glimpsed before was a trembling, white-furred leg.

With some difficulty the wagon was rolled into the lab. Boxes lay scattered about haphazardly—most of the medical supplies had been transferred the night before to the smaller Watcher Dome to help equip it as an infirmary. A low rumbling pervaded the room. Someone must have left some machinery on.

"Is there enough here to work with?" Nesta asked quietly.

"If not, we'll send over for what we need," Hot Rod said. He turned to Pel, patting the examination table. "Sit up here."

"No, I'm okay for now," Pel said. He almost collapsed as he knelt by the wagon. "Take care of Grendel. Please."

The man and woman who'd pulled the cart leaned down to pick up the dog. Hot Rod stopped them. "Wait! Let's check him first before we move him."

He pulled the burlap away, winced, then gently laid it back over the dog. "Tom, run, and I do mean run, to the Department Store and get the best stockyarder left you can find. They're the ones trained for vetting. Shala, you find that biologist."

Grendel's legs had stopped spasming and lay still. His tight black-bead eyes were shut, his jaws closed around what looked to be a scrap of some sort of industrial fabric, its edges raggedly cut. It was rubbery black on one side, a peculiar fuzzy gray synthetic on the other. Nesta would have sworn he was dead, until she realized that the steady low noise wasn't lab machinery after all, but the dog's weak continual growling.

"I'm sorry, Hot Rod, but how can I possibly help?"

Hot Rod glanced up from pulling surgical instruments from drawers. "I don't expect you to help with the dog. I need you for something else. I stretched the truth when I said it was feral dogs. I didn't want to panic anyone." He saw the look on her face. "No, I'm not saying it *was* 'Bounders. Pel, tell her."

Pel looked from where he huddled by the wagon, his face strained and tearful. "This morning, just before dawn, a terrible noise woke me, like I've never heard before—a kind of booming sound. Then the sheep began screaming. It woke the dogs too, which was strange, because they always sense danger coming, long before me. They smell it. But this time they didn't. I grabbed my rifle and cartridge belt and ran out, thinking it was a wild pack.

"I had the sheep penned behind the Octopus ride. I could see something in with them—not clearly at first, because they were stampeding around the fold, trampling each other. I opened the gate and the dogs rushed in. The sounds—the sheep, the dogs barking, the booming noise—were overwhelming. Then I saw them." Pel shook his head, his eyes blind with wonder.

"They weren't wild dogs. I don't know what they were. Like weasels, but huge, the size of Great Danes, with thick bodies and long legs. Three of them, and they'd already killed a number of my sheep, that fast. There was a mound of bodies in the center of the pen. One of the creatures picked up a carcass and looked at me." He shuddered. "Its eyes weren't any color at all. There was a funny feeling, a pressure in the air, and *pop!* it disappeared, right in front of me.

"Grendel and Grendelyn had thrown themselves on another of the creatures. I began firing at the third when *pop!, pop!* two more beasts appeared, in the center of the pen, from nowhere. I was so afraid! How many more were there? Where did they come from? I kept shooting, even when the sheep got in the way. I hit at least one of the monsters. It whirled around and started snapping at its back." Pel put his hands over his ears. "The booming noise it made changed to a sound like machinery grinding together. Horrible, horrible!

"*Pop!* It disappeared. And *pop! pop!* so did the new monsters. Maybe I had hit them too. Only the one that my dogs were fighting was left. I waded through the few sheep that hadn't run out of the pen to get to them.

"Grendel had fastened on to its flank. Grendelyn had it by the throat. But even with her hanging on it was turning and slashing Grendel, over and over again. I couldn't get a good shot because of the way they were all spinning together. I screamed at my dogs, but they wouldn't let go. They never do. I started kicking it in the ribs. It left off Grendel and turned on me."

He looked down at the slashes in his jacket, the wounds underneath, his mangled hands. "I still couldn't shoot it because I might have hit Grendelyn. I jammed my cartridge belt into the beast's mouth, then beat on the top of its head with the rifle butt. It fell over, twitching. At last I could safely shoot it in the chest. Only then would Grendelyn let go."

To Nesta's dismay, Pel put his face in his hands and began weeping. "But Grendel wouldn't," he said through his tears. "I had to go find a knife and cut the creature's skin away where he had hold. I don't think it was quite dead yet, for as soon as I did, *pop,* it was gone."

Nesta looked again at the scrap locked in Grendel's jaws and felt queasy.

"I went to find a cart I could use to bring Grendel here," Pel said. Laughter began to hiccup through his sobs. "When I had loaded him up I heard barking, and there was my good, good girl." He hugged Grendelyn, leaning against his other side. "She had rounded up as many of the sheep as she could find and brought them back to me. I shut them up in the arcade and we began our long walk. That is what happened."

Nesta glanced at the doorway. Dodd was standing there. How much had he heard? His eyes were wide and blinking rapidly. Most of it.

"The kids on the tower just called down that the stockyarders are almost here," he said. "Tom brought three of them."

The stockyarders consisted of two old men and a teenage girl. After looking at Grendel they whispered to Dodd and Tom, who took off at a dead run for the Domes. As the stockyarders lifted the injured dog onto the table Nesta led Pel and Grendelyn out to the stoop and sat down with him there, trying to offer him wordless comfort. She would have done anything to bring back even a spark of his façade as the feckless lothario.

Dodd and Tom returned quickly with a box of medical supplies and disappeared into the lab.

A few minutes later one of the old men joined Nesta and Pel on the lab steps. He was carrying an old-fashioned doctor's bag. "They're prepping your friend in there for surgery," he said, sitting next to Grendelyn. "In the meantime, young lady, let's check you out." He began to look Grendelyn over gently. "Pel, do you want us to send someone up to look after your sheep?"

He prepped a hypodermic. "Just antibiotics," he answered the dread in Pel's eyes. "We'll want to sew some stitches in her later, but she'll be just fine."

"About my sheep," Pel said. "That would be good of you, but don't leave them in the park. I do not want to ever return there. Send someone to bring them back. And whoever goes, I must talk to them first. It is very, very dangerous. These were not just feral dogs."

The stockyarder shot Nesta a questioning glance.

She nodded.

After the man had gone back into the lab Pel turned to Nesta, his eyes fear-haunted.

"It's not just the creatures," he whispered. "The park has been becoming strange for months now. At first it seemed so beautiful to me. I'd wake in the middle of the night and the gridwork of the roller coaster would be singing. I'd lie there and listen. There have been lights too, like the ghosts of fireworks. The old rides have sometimes changed from day to day. Now and then they're unrecognizable and I can't understand what thrills they are meant to offer—they make no sense. And the merry-go-round: the horses transform into fabulous mysterious beasts." That must have reminded him of the animals that had attacked that morning, for he shuddered. "I will never go back. It is no longer my home."

The screen door opened and shut behind them. They looked around and up into Hot Rod's sober face. "I'm sorry, Pel. I'm so, so sorry."

Pel collapsed against Nesta in silence. Feeling his grief, Grendelyn huddled on his other side, trying pathetically to comfort him with her perpetual grin.

Dodd stood behind Hot Rod, his plump features as pasty as marshmallows. He was clutching a cardboard box.

"That's for you, Nesta," Hot Rod said. "To run tests on. We couldn't get it out of his jaws till he died."

Hot Rod helped Pel stand up. "Come back in with me to say goodbye to him."

Nesta still sat alone on the lab steps when across the courtyard a door in the House opened and Loren Van Woorden peered out. He walked across the courtyard to join her.

"I thought you should know," he said. "I've just come from Hammer's rooms. Radio silence has lifted. The fighting has begun."

CHAPTER THIRTY-ONE

Those left in the Valley worked frantically the next few days, but their greatest trial was the waiting. Eric's parents and Abel Howe brought all the Homers in, housing them for safety at the Office Buildings, where they joined in rebuilding the protective maze in the lobby.

Backup forces began arriving from the south. When the contingent from Santa Cruz arrived and crowded into the dining room for supper Nesta recognized a heavyset man who entered differently from the others—not as a bewildered stranger, but as someone grudgingly familiar with the place. It was Renzie and Tuck's father. With him was that other fellow, Brad. They left with the rest of their group as soon as they had eaten.

Wounded started coming in. The infirmary became a center of hectic activity.

Yet for all the frantic preparations taking place throughout all the communities of the Valley, a sense of inertness pervaded; an awareness that compared to the battle raging in the hills to the north, the Valley was the quiet center of the storm. And within the vortex which was the House and its neighbors could be found an even stiller spot, one that they all revolved around, waiting for the least word—Hammer on duty in his radio room.

Nesta, so used to being at the hub of her own world of research

and ideas, chafed at being left behind. She worked long hours in the
kitchen until she could barely crawl to her room and collapse into sleep.
She didn't want to stay awake thinking about the remote events to the
north.

She wasn't the only one to worry. Every day Le Chell stopped by
the kitchen to ask about radio dispatches. Nesta, Jorda, Minda, and all
the rest knew she hoped for news of Tuck, though she wouldn't ask
about him by name.

On the fifth evening after the battle began Hammer wheeled into
the kitchen. "Ring the dinner chimes early," he said. "They've wiped
out the 'Bounders' main force. The first part is over."

People drifted back from the north, bringing more wounded and the
dead with them. Although Eric returned immediately, most of the
Housers came in several days later. One afternoon a convoy drove in.
Tuck clambered out of an old army jeep and helped his sister down.
Renzie lifted up one leg and swung it wide, the crossbow strapped to her
back making her dismount clumsy. Hake and Sun parked a truck
nearby and more Housers hopped down from its tailgate. All of them
were dirty, thin and looked very, very hungry. Nesta wondered how far
their ration packets had lasted.

Renzie took one look at Nesta bedecked in her apron, mixing
bowl in one hand, wire whisk in the other, and leaned against the side
of the jeep, shaking weakly with laughter. "Hake told me," she said,
"but I didn't believe it."

"Why shouldn't I be a good cook?" said Nesta acerbically.
"Cooking is nothing more than chemical interactions. Chemistry is a
science. I'm a scientist." Then, in an aside to Hake, "Is she all right?
Has she been hurt?"

Hake walked over to help Tuck steer Renzie toward the House,
but the siblings waved him away. "She's just exhausted and hungry, like
the rest of us. We've been chasing around in the hills after 'Bounder
stragglers the last three days."

He nodded to Sun. "Sun's information was good, but when we
got up there the 'Bounders had shifted a couple of their contingents—
spring landslides had cut off access to some of their intended positions.
So we missed them in the initial attack. We figure at least fifty 'Bound-

ers got away. And it's not clear whether the Orindans and the convoy drivers got all the 'Bounders harassing Orinda. If not, they could be heading down here. Fifty, sixty people armed with knives, a few guns, and matches—especially matches—can wreak a lot of havoc."

Hake rubbed his temples. "We lost a lot of good folks. Templeton was killed. Whelan and Kip were wounded. After the fighting finished up we found the bodies of some ambushed Koanites. We're going to lose more people before it's over. It's time to dig in, figure out all the contingencies."

"You're asking me a question, aren't you?" Nesta said. "Or at least trying to."

The anguish on Hake's face was plain. "What about surprises we can't plan for? What about your aberrations? Should we be watching our backs for them too?"

Nesta put the whisk into the bowl, freeing up her hand so she could take his arm. "Maybe we should be. Come with me to the kitchen and let me get some food into you. Then I'll tell you and the others what happened to Pel while you were gone."

———

Jorda and her booby-trap crew had taken over anything that qualified as a meeting space in the House and had been working in shifts to educate everyone on where the traps and snares were set. With the smaller Watchers' Dome infirmary also strained past capacity, that night the overflow of Housers, Watchers, neighbors and visitors spilled out to clumps of small campfires in the front garden. Renzie found her team and some of the other Housers gathered around one near the bordering ring of giant old palm trees.

Eric was using the opportunity to query Hake on the last of the cleanup operations up north. "So maybe fifty of them got away," he mused when the older man had finished. "I'd hoped for better, but it could have been worse. Too bad about the 'Bounders that shifted position."

"They were supposed to be on that ridge," Sun protested. "I swear that's where they said they'd be."

"Calm down," Eric said. "No one holds you responsible. How could you have known about the mudslides here?" He grinned. "Seems to me you were kind of busy already this spring, watching the 'Bounders like a hawk. If you hadn't done that, maybe we wouldn't be here to complain about the ones that escaped." There was murmured agreement all around the group.

Sun smiled uncertainly. His new role as a hero bewildered him. Since he no longer encountered resistance to be defensive against, his changed status left him uneasy, at a loss.

"You can smile!" Minda crowed. "It makes you look sunny, Sun. Good day, Sunshine. Good day Sunshine. *Good* day Sunshine." She warbled the lines from an old, old tune. Getting no response to that, she tried another song. "You are my Sunshine, my only Sunshine . . ."

Sun finally decided how to react. "It isn't Sun like that," he said gruffly. "Not sun in the sky sun. It's Son like son of someone. Male child of someone."

Minda has pushed him back over the line into irritation, Renzie thought. Too bad. But he's never told us this much about himself before.

"Like sonny-boy?" Hot Rod's attempt to join the teasing failed. Son looked at him flatly. "No, it stands for Son-of. My name is Son-of-Wolf-Crier."

The older folk looked embarrassed. Hot Rod pulled on his ponytail self-consciously. "Oh, one of those old hippie-style names. Sorry."

"No," Son said again. Something struggled to burst through the emotionally flattened surface of his face. "*I* named him that. I named my father Wolf-Crier. After a story he told me once about a boy who cried wolf. And after I'd named him, that made me the Son-of-Wolf-Crier."

Whatever had strained to break free sank away beneath Son's opaque veneer. He hunched back in on himself and stared into the dying embers.

Renzie felt that Son was like those coals: no longer giving off light, but still capable of heat. Dying down and away, but needing so little to be brought back to life.

"When did you name him Wolf-Crier?" she asked gently.

"I don't know exactly." He shrugged.

Renzie waited a moment for signs of either interest or the usual anger.

"*Why* did you name him Wolf-Crier?" she persisted.

Something flickered in Son, barely. "Because that's what he was," he said in a soft monotone to the fire.

Renzie sensed embers slowly kindling. Son coughed and cleared his throat to speak. The embers had caught.

"When I was little, we lived alone, just the two of us, up in some mountains. I don't even know where, exactly. It was just him and me. I don't know what happened to my mother. I don't know how old I am, when I was born, but it had to be after the Vanishing"—he ran his hands through glowing, mahogany-colored hair—"so she hadn't Vanished. Maybe she took ill and died, or was killed in an accident or by raiders. Maybe she didn't die. Maybe she just left us. I don't know. My father never said.

"But he lost somebody to the Vanishing, if not her, because he was obsessed with it." Son shivered. "He'd get so angry. Angry with me, angry with everything. It wasn't till later when I was on my own that I found that he was just like a lot of other people that way."

Son still spoke to the campfire. His words could have been addressed to Renzie or to any number of the people who sat listening. Or they could have been meant for no one, simply an observation.

"So it turned out that the way he brought me up wasn't all that different from here in some ways, though we lived a lot rougher life. He tried to teach me everything I needed to know to make it on my own if the Vanishing ever came back. He'd go on and on about how I had to be able to survive if he Vanished. It's the earliest thing I remember. It's the thing I *most* remember about being a kid, even more than all the things he taught me—like how to trap deer and skin them, how to leather their hides and dry out their meat. How to carve fishhooks and build a lean-to. How to survive in the snow.

"Then one day when I was littler than Minda is now, it happened. He Vanished."

Nesta coughed, a hesitant sound of dissension. There were no proven cases of Vanishing after the Great Vanishment.

Son looked up at that. "My father *did,*" he said mildly. "He really did Vanish. I woke up early one morning all by myself. It wasn't like he'd gone outside into the woods somewhere. Even his knife and moccasins were still in the hut. The only things missing were him and the shirt he'd slept in.

"That's when I realized that what he'd threatened me with, had warned me about, had come true. He was gone and never coming back. I was going to be alone forever."

Son's gaze dropped again. He picked up a stick of kindling and drew with it aimlessly in the dirt at his feet. "At first I didn't want to believe it. I ran out and looked for him everywhere I could think of. I yelled and screamed for him. Finally I gave up and sat in front of the hut and cried for hours." Son's lip curled in self-derision. "What a helpless, idiotic little baby I was.

"When I got tired of that I just lay down where I sat and slept. When I woke up it was late afternoon. I remember that I didn't feel anything at all, except a kind of hollowness. After a while I realized the hollowness was real; I hadn't eaten all day and I was hungry. I automatically started doing all the things my father had taught me to do. Fetching water from the stream, going out and checking our traps, making sure they hadn't been tripped or raided by bobcats or bear or the big blue cats. One of the traps had caught a possum. I skinned and dressed it, started a fire in the cooking pit to roast it.

"It got to be around dusk. The possum was cooking up nicely. I was almost ready to take it off the spit when I heard a noise. I looked and there he stood—my father.

"He was one hell of a sight. His nightshirt only reached to the middle of his ass. Other than that he was buck naked. Barefoot, too. He walked into the hut, put on a pair of pants, came back out, sat down, and helped himself to some of the possum. I just sat and stared at him. All of a sudden I couldn't eat.

"When he was done feeding he looked at me and said, 'Now you know what it'll be like when it happens. It was the only way I could be sure you'd be ready. I had to know.' He pointed to a nearby ridge. 'I've been watching you from over there all day, boy. I was worried at first. Thought maybe you hadn't learned a damn thing. But in the end you did well.' Then he patted me on the shoulder.

"Do you know how I felt?" The stick snapped in Son's hand. "I was numb and I was crushed. But underneath all that, what snuck up on me was that I was *proud.* I knew I'd just passed a test—the only test that meant anything to him. When that sank in I got hungry again and ate what was left of the possum. I was happy for days afterward." Son's mouth relaxed into a slow, sad smile. Renzie had never seen that expression on his face before. It hurt her heart.

Son's mouth straightened out again into its habitual hatchet line. "Yeah. That was how I felt the first time." He reached down to pick up another stick, but none were in reach. He twitched his hands in his lap instead.

"The *first* time?" Hake whispered. "Dear god."

"The second time," Son continued, "didn't happen till over a year later. What I felt *that* time was . . . well, you see enough time had gone by that I was fooled again. It never occurred to me, since I'd already passed the test, that he'd do it again. So I thought it was real that time, too.

"I felt . . . grateful. I thought how lucky I was that my father had loved me and been wise enough to prepare me, to make me experience what it would be like beforehand, so I'd be ready. And I . . ." Son's voice shook. "I loved him so much for that. I missed him. And I was so, so sad.

"That second time he didn't come back till the next morning. I woke up, and there he was. That's when I understood that the testing wasn't over. It might never be over. That I always had to be on my guard against him."

A long silence held the campsite captive. Renzie hoped that Son's story was finished. No wonder Son had always been on guard against all of them.

But Minda had to know. "So did he do it again?"

Son looked up to smile at her, as if at a joke they shared. "Oh yes. Off and on over the years. The funny thing was, although he said he did it so that the next Vanishing wouldn't be as hard on me as it had been on him, I think that underneath the real reason was different. I think he did it because he wanted to be sure that someone else hurt as much as he did. And that he wanted to make it happen and control it, because *he'd* been so helpless in the first, real Vanishing."

Son had regained his usual rigid composure. "I never knew when it was going to happen. My father had a genius for knowing just when I'd relaxed and stopped expecting it. Somewhere in there I started comparing him to the boy-who-cried-wolf story, started calling him that in my mind.

"He stayed away for different lengths of time; once, a whole month. After the first time he came back wearing crude bush clothes. And though he'd be skinnier, he obviously wasn't starving. I couldn't understand that when I was still little, because he never took a damn thing with him. I finally figured out he must spend a lot of his disappeared time making tools and clothes to stash for the next time."

"But what happened in the end?" Minda persisted. "You ended up here. What happened to your dad? Did he finally Vanish for real?"

"No. I did." Son threw his head back and laughed—laughter overwhelmingly wild, bitter, and real. "When I got to be about Bite's size I thought of a plan. The next time my father Vanished, I started making my own set of tools, some clothes, and an extra pair of moccasins out of little scraps of hide, all in secret. It took me at least a year and a half—he disappeared three times in that period. By the last time I'd built up a nice, survivable cache and hidden it up in some rocks.

"About a month after he came back that last time we had to spend a few days clearing out the nearby spring and putting up a stockade against the big blue cats who came down from the high mountains in the summer. By the end of the second day we still weren't finished. My father was so tired he had trouble staying awake long enough to eat dinner. Around the middle of the night I crept out. I picked up my cache and that was it. I Vanished. End of story."

"But what happened the next day, when he found out you were gone?" asked Minda. "Was he sorry?"

Son looked surprised. "How would I know? I left. I never went back."

"But didn't you want him to know how you felt? Isn't that why you copied him? I bet if you'd stayed he would've said he was sorry."

Son shook his head. "He knew how I felt. That's how he felt once too—except that until I left, he'd only had to go through it that one time with the real Vanishing. But he made me live it over and over again, till it didn't mean anything.

"I didn't want to join in his game of coming and going. I just wanted it to be over. At the end of the story the wolf arrived to fetch the boy who cried wolf, and no one came to rescue him anymore."

Renzie tried to imagine Son as a little boy, betrayed over and over and over again. She thought of her own life. She'd always had Tuck and the House.

There'd never been anyone like Tuck in Son's life. He hadn't had a Hake or Eric or Jorda to turn to. He hadn't grown up in the House. He'd never had a sister to rescue him from his father.

Renzie sat down carefully next to Son, as if she were sitting by an animal tame enough to take food but still too wild to touch.

"Son, why did you follow the 'Bounders? For the House?" she asked.

He nodded. "When that 'Bounder girl cut up Jan and took her hostage, I heard her say they'd be back. The way the 'Bounders talked, and their eyes—they were just like my father when he carried on about the Vanishing. They would have destroyed the House. They would have left nothing and not understood, just like my father."

Son turned suddenly on Renzie. "Do you know what scares me the most?" he said fiercely.

Renzie shook her head, unnerved by his intensity.

"When I catch myself being like him. When I can tell by people's faces that I'm looking and acting just the way he did." Son's eyes were rough and dry as gravel, but he was quivering. "Then I hate myself as much as I hated him. And I think, what right did I have to be so angry with him when I'm the same way?"

Renzie remembered all the times Son's anger had sparked her own. Yes, and what right did I have to be so angry with him when *I'm* the same way, she thought?

Her throat constricted as she understood how those links of anger and fear had bound and chained them all, one to the other: Son and his father, her and Old George, her and Son. But the chains could be broken.

"You're not the same, Son."

He looked at her swiftly.

Renzie's breath caught. For the briefest of moments Son's glance was open and vulnerable. He looked just like Tuck when Tuck had been little.

"You're not the same," she repeated, firmly.

CHAPTER THIRTY-TWO

Renzie fed the guide wires through the pulley slowly. For all her care, they still kept snagging. She yanked the wire in a loop outward, freeing it from a gingerbread cornice. "Shit!" she snarled. Sweat ran down her forehead, stinging into her eyes. The last two days the weather had turned ominously hot, improving neither the situation with the 'Bounders nor Renzie's temper.

She wasn't any worse off than anyone else, though. All about her people were suffering from the heat and struggling with equipment as they tried to set up lines to haul water up to the roof. The 'Bounders were notorious for throwing flaming brands.

"What's taking you so long?" Quill jeered cheerfully at her. He and one of the Office Building boys, Smee, lounged on the third-story porch, fiddling with the other end of Renzie's pulley system, waiting to attach it when she found an angle that would draw buckets up smoothly. Behind the boys and further along the porch Jorda and the Krit were bracing an extension ladder to run more wiring to the back of a cupola on the next floor.

Renzie caught herself before she flung an angry retort up at the boys. She should be glad that so far the children didn't seem to be snared by the fears of the adults. It was a mercy, really. Better to encourage them in their high spirits than to spread her own anger and anxiety.

"I'm just taking my time because I'm having *so much fun* down here," she yelled at the boys as cheerfully as she could.

But she *had* taken too long, because now some of the younger children, led by Minda, popped out onto the porch with the boys and joined in raining catcalls down on her head.

Renzie sighed and mopped her forehead with the back of her hand. The air was so still and stifling that breathing felt like trying to draw glue into her lungs. The stillness was good: The 'Bounders were less likely to set fires with no winds to drive them. But the heat promised disaster when they did.

She looked back up at the children. Easy for them to be in a good mood. She was stuck here on the ground while they were high enough to catch a little breeze. A cooling draft stirred their hair. Renzie felt envious as she watched Minda brush aside a strand that had blown into her eyes. As if shifting with the breeze, a shimmering halo of light like a colorless rainbow played about the little girl's head.

Then Renzie noticed that the curtains in an open window behind the children weren't moving. Neither were Jorda's or the Krit's hair or clothing, although the Krit was perched on the edge of a cornice, much less sheltered from the elements than the children.

Renzie froze in place. Right here, in broad daylight, an anomaly was emerging. Like her midnight meadow. Like the attack on Pel's flock. Like the drowning at the "Well of Voices." Would it become stronger? She had to call out and warn the children. Panic strangled at her throat.

The strange light hinting at unseeable colors intensified. "Quill!" Renzie finally managed to scream. "Watch out!"

As the children turned to look around in confusion the light dimmed to the usual flat brightness of sunlight. The breeze died away, leaving their hair hanging as limp and still as Renzie's.

Quill leaned over the balcony. "What is it?" he called.

Renzie trembled uncontrollably. "Nothing," she managed to stutter up to him. "Just nerves, I guess."

Quill shot her the scathing, patronizing look children reserve for adults who are losing it. "So can we finally finish this up and get on to the next pulley?"

She waved an assent.

Was she losing it? Had she just imagined the aberration? Hadn't anybody else noticed it? She snuck a look at Jorda. Jorda's back was to them, unconcernedly telescoping the extension ladder upward. Renzie sighed.

Then she noticed the Krit. He perched, paralyzed on his cornice like a gargoyle, staring down at the children, his terror-stricken face bleached to the pale hue of fine marble.

Renzie looked up at the guide wires. Their ends disappeared into the bright blue sky.

CHAPTER THIRTY-THREE

The Krit ran to his aerie. He scuttled along the catwalks to its farthest corner and huddled there, his back to the wall.

He'd lived in the House long before he'd become aware of the infection spreading throughout the surrounding Homes. He'd never considered that the House itself might be a source of contagion.

He looked around wildly, the sudden motion tugging at his scars. This space, so spare and inaccessible, that he'd thought so safe, might change at any moment, with him in it.

Sweat soaked through the innermost layer of his cocoon of clothing. He jumped up and ran around to the other side of the fourth-floor tower porches. A covered stairwell there descended along the outside of the House to the second floor. Then it tunneled inward and wound around an elevator shaft to the first floor. The Krit's heart hammered out of sync to the flip-flopping of his feet as he plunged downward.

Out, out and away from the House. The House that had been his refuge when he'd finally abandoned his Home and all hopes for Jennifer's return. And later, the haven he could return to between the seasons of his terrible task.

The Krit crossed Winchester Boulevard and frantically negotiated his way through and beyond the villagelike clutter of the Mall. He didn't stop till he reached its far side.

Even from there he could see the dragon's-teeth roofline of the House. How pervasive was the infection there? How far had it spread? Could he stop it? He thought of all the people living in there, ignorant of the risk. People he'd lived with side by side for years. Could he save them?

The roofline looked like jaws that stretched forever, daunting. The Homes he'd cauterized had been empty. How could he burn the House safely? There were all those people inside. The methods he'd used before—containing the targeted areas, drenching the Homes with flammables—they wouldn't work here. It would be a sloppy, risky job, like the fire he'd watched the 'Bounders set at the end of last summer. And undoubtedly he'd be caught before he could succeed.

Unless . . . The 'Bounders. There was an answer. Everybody knew the 'Bounders set fires. And soon there might be a time when everybody would be out fighting the 'Bounders. The House would be almost deserted then. It would be just him against the House. The Krit pulled his muffler higher on his scarred neck, as if he suddenly felt cold. He gathered his resolve about him like a shield.

He'd have to do it differently this time. He had a lot of research to do. And he'd have to be ready when the right moment came. He prepared himself to return to the belly of the enemy.

CHAPTER THIRTY-FOUR

"On point for hot-spot detail. Small fire and snipers in the Women's Brigade zone. Crews seven and ten meet on the front porch," Quill sang out at the entrance to the bursting dining room. Elsewhere in the House other children on the relay teams from the radio room and sentry posts were shouting the same announcement, gathering firefighters and yeomen together.

Breakfasters scraped back chairs from tables, grabbing last bitefuls of food as they headed for the door. Nesta and some other older folk moved in and began clearing the vacated spaces before the next crush of diners emerged from the kitchen.

Hot spot indeed, thought Nesta. It was a hot spot in here, too. The still, torpid weather intensified the usual heat of the kitchen and dining commons. With the back of her arm she wiped her forehead before sweat trickled down into her eyes. Grunting, she hoisted her first load of dirty dishes and waddled it into the kitchen cleanup area.

She passed Kip perched on a high stool. His crutches leaned against the wall behind him. A bandage wrapped itself around the top of his head and over one eye. His injuries hadn't affected his voice: He boomed out instructions at the cooking crew with jaunty mercilessness. Nesta had to admit that even immobilized he made a more effective kitchen supervisor than she had.

"How are things going out there?" he asked.

"Still packed," she reported. "Announcement of a minor 'Bounder attack in the Women's Brigade area emptied the place out, but it filled right up again."

"It's beginning to slow down some in here," Kip said. "The crowd should trail off soon." The edges of a grin disappeared into his bandages. "Then I start flogging my flunkies to get ready for the next meal."

"Why do I get the feeling they'll be grateful when Chloe comes on duty to take over the next shift from you?" Nesta said dryly.

"Never happen," said Kip. "They love me. Really."

Nesta snorted as she turned and walked back out into the dining room to pick up her next load.

Eric sat with a heavyset stranger alone at a long table cluttered with dirty dishes. Nesta came up from behind and caught his eye. "May I?" She gestured at the mess.

Eric nodded his assent.

The other man ignored her and kept talking. It wasn't till she'd moved around to the other side of the table that she saw that it was Old George. Nesta kept her face passive.

"Haven't they put their lives on the line enough, especially Renzie?" the older man was pleading in a low voice. "Assign them to help with support work." George nodded at Nesta, indicating her task, still without looking at her.

Eric did, though, and locked gazes with her. She dropped her eyes in response, a promise to remain invisible.

Eric returned his focus to Old George. "Tuck is as safe as anyone can be, helping Hammer. That's where we need him most. As for Renzie, she wouldn't accept safer duties even if I assigned her to them. Which I won't. She's too valuable to waste that way. She's too good a fighter. George, of all people, you know that." Eric spoke calmly, but George flushed with anger.

"I didn't risk my life years ago protecting my kids from the marauders just so I could lose them now."

Eric held up a hand to slow him down. "Yes, you did risk your life then. We all did and we survived. Now you have a new batch of children who need protecting."

Old George half rose from his chair, eyes blazing. "You'd throw that up in my face now?"

Eric remained composed. He took his time spearing a wedge of

cantaloupe with his fork. "Sit down, George. You miss my point. The
'Bounders have to be stopped once and for all, for everyone's sake.
Renzie and Tuck are adults now. It's their turn to help."

"There they are now," George said, hunching his head down low
between his shoulders. Nesta looked up from stacking plates. Renzie
and Tuck had just walked in together. Nesta finished clearing the table
and carried her load into the kitchen. Renzie and Tuck were piling food
onto plates and joking with Kip. Tuck was filling up two trays.

"Hungry?" Nesta asked.

"One is for Hammer. He's glued to the airwaves," Tuck explained.

Nesta angled herself so she could see into the dining room. Eric
and George had left. "What are you assigned to today?" she asked
Renzie.

"I don't know yet. I'll check the duty board after I eat. If it's okay
with your slavedriver, why don't you take a load off your feet for a
couple of minutes and sit with me?"

Nesta looked at Kip.

"Go ahead," he said. "The breakfast crowd is slacking off."

Renzie chose to settle in at the same table Eric and George had
been sitting at not five minutes before. She wasn't smiling. Nesta wondered if she'd seen her father.

"Nesta, with all this turmoil going on, what's happening with the
research?"

If it had been any other topic Nesta would have been relieved. She
shrugged, gestured around her at the dining room. "Nothing. This is
what's happening now."

Renzie looked behind her to see if Tuck was coming. "I think I
saw another anomaly. Right here. In the House." She told Nesta about
the uncanny breeze, the illumination that had haloed the children up on
the porch. "I'm scared, Nesta. The anomalies—they can happen anywhere, anytime, can't they?"

Nesta nodded.

"The research we've been doing . . . will it help us predict them?
Is that what we're working toward?"

Nesta took a deep breath. "Maybe. I hope so. But I can't say till
we know more about them. To be honest, that's all we're doing at this
stage: gathering information so we can understand what's happening
someday."

"Someday," Renzie repeated. "But these things are going on all around us *now."* She picked at her scrambled eggs unhappily. "Whether we win and get rid of the 'Bounders or we lose and the 'Bounders burn us to the ground, the aberrations will keep happening."

Nesta nodded again.

"Damn! Damn the bloody 'Bounders." Renzie looked around again restlessly. "What the hell is keeping Tuck?"

As if he'd been conjured up by her pique Tuck appeared in the kitchen doorway, still balancing both trays. He blushed when he caught his sister's glare. The reason why became apparent as Le Chell stepped out next to him. The two lovers made their way over to Renzie and Nesta.

"Yeah, I know, I know," Tuck said defensively. "Hammer's probably starving by now. I'll take the tray up."

Nesta looked at the food. It must be stone-cold.

Renzie just smiled sweetly. "Did I say anything?" she said.

Le Chell reached out for one of the trays. "I'll help you. You don't want to have to carry both of those up all those stairs."

Renzie watched them leave. "Now *that* was a good ploy," she said admiringly. "Tuck will have to walk her back down from the radio room afterward. Le Chell never could find her way out on her own."

Renzie turned back to her own food in better spirits. "At least that's one good thing that's come of all of this. Those two finally understand that they don't have all the time in the world." She beamed. "My guess is that when this is all over Le Chell will at least give living in the House a try."

Renzie finished eating. The two of them walked out onto the back porch. The porch was only marginally cooler than the sweltering kitchen. Renzie shook her head sadly. "Templeton gone—the Office Building parties will never be the same. So many changes."

"But there's good changes, like Tuck and Le Chell," Nesta reminded her.

"True," Renzie agreed. "And other things too, maybe. It was interesting working with Son out there." She gestured to the north. "Either when times are hard he naturally cuts out all the crap, or he's going through some kind of transformation. Damn!"

Renzie's last exclamation startled Nesta.

"The wind's come up," Renzie explained.

Nesta started to smile as she too felt the beginnings of a freshening breeze. But her smile faded when she saw Renzie's scowl.

"Now we're in for it," the younger woman said. "A strong wind heading down-valley. This is what the 'Bounders have been waiting for."

It started two hours later.

"Fire funneling down from Sunnyvale," the runners from the radio room sang out. "Forty 'Bounders spotted. This looks like the big one. Report to the Ballroom for assignments. Line up your weapons at ready in the hallway."

"Why from there?" Nesta asked Kip as they dashed out of the kitchen. In spite of his injuries, with his youth and long legs it was hard to keep up with him. He swung along on his crutches like a racing stork. "I thought the Domes were the most likely target."

"Yes, but the 'Bounders hate the Homes just as much. With a southerly blowing, Sunnyvale is a perfect spot to start a fire that might sweep down the entire Valley."

"Couldn't it be a diversion to draw everyone away from here? With all the fire breaks and deadfalls set up it will take over an hour to get the squads up there."

"That's a possibility," Kip admitted as they rounded the corner into the Ballroom. "But if forty 'Bounders were sighted together, that's a majority of their remaining forces."

They dodged as people dashed out of the ballroom and snatched up weapons. Eric had already started assigning teams.

"Damn it, Hake, aren't you getting too old for this?" Nesta yelled as the black man ran past.

"Apparently not," he called apologetically over his shoulder.

Even Eric was hoisting ammo belts over his shoulder by the time Nesta and Kip pushed their way in. "Hot Rod—you and Renzie organize ground patrols. Son, keep the sentries alert. Forty 'Bounders isn't all of them."

Nesta felt relieved. Of course Eric would have considered all the probabilities.

Kip looked at his crutches with disgust. He gave them a shake before propping himself up on them again. "We might as well get back to the kitchen," he said.

Nesta was amazed that with the injuries he'd suffered he'd be so anxious to get back into the fray. Under her breath she muttered a prayer that he'd live long enough to grow wise.

Then the defenders swept out of the House and were gone. For those who remained there was only the waiting. The minutes paced like caged animals.

"How long has it been?" Kip asked for the twentieth time.

"About forty-five minutes," Nesta answered. "And as you can hear for yourself, no one's called down from the radio room with any news yet."

She walked away. If she had to keep fielding questions from Kip she'd be snapping at him soon. Hot Rod was standing out on the porch, as nervous as Kip, but silently so.

"Is Renzie out on the grounds?" Nesta asked.

"Yes."

"No sight of any 'Bounders?"

"No."

Nesta kept still after that. Right now Hot Rod must be running the same low threshold for questions as she was.

People wandered in and out of the House, restlessly quiet, wanting to hear something, anything—from the sentries, the patrols, the radio room.

And then the silence was abruptly broken by a high-pitched falling sound, a long sleek whistle. Followed by a muffled implosion. The porch rocked under Nesta's feet. She grabbed for the railing. "Earthquake," she gasped.

"No!" said Hot Rod. "Shit, it's . . ."

Another cometlike fall of sound, another ominous impact. Nesta braced for a good shaking. She wasn't disappointed.

" 'Bounders!" Son screamed. He was leaning out from a third-floor balcony, his tanned face pale.

Some of the patrols ran into the yard, including Renzie.

"Can you spot them?" Hot Rod called up to Son.

"No, but those are rocket launchers. They could be up to a quarter mile out. And the only rocket launchers the 'Bounders had were in Orinda. That means—"

"—some of them got away," Hot Rod finished for him. "And we have no idea how many. Are we hit?"

Son shook his head. "No. I think they struck the far side of the Domes. I don't see any flames from here, though."

"The Watchers may be all right for now," Hot Rod said. "Those buildings were reinforced back in the marauder days. Hit the ground! Here comes another one!"

The next strike was closer.

"That one slammed into the garden," one of the children shouted down as the adults below picked themselves up. Hot Rod ran into the House. "I'm going to see how close that was. Anyone else comes out here, tell them to go back in and hunker down on the far side of the House."

"Can you see where they're coming from?" Renzie called to the sentry.

The boy pointed.

"That makes sense," Renzie said. "There's not too many places within a quarter-mile radius on that side where the 'Bounders would have a clearer view of the Domes than the House."

"I know the Domes are supposed to be the preliminary target," said Nesta. "But wouldn't it make more sense for them to attack the House? It's more vulnerable to fire and shelling. We'd make a perfect distraction. If the House went up in flames even the Watchers would have to deal with it."

Hot Rod stepped back out onto the porch. "Unless the 'Bounders want to soften up the harder target first. That garden shot was more on the Dome's side."

Renzie squinted up at the porch. "Come on down, Son. Join us for a little hunting." Son disappeared from his perch. Then Renzie remembered to look at Hot Rod for approval.

He nodded. "I hate to send your team out there, but those rocket launchers have to be eliminated."

Son stepped out onto the porch, two rifles slung across his back.

Renzie and her crew trotted up the steps to join him. "We'll cut through the House to the far side," she told him. "And circle *way* around their position."

As they left Nesta felt the fear for Renzie building again. The 'Bounders would be expecting someone to come out after them. Nesta couldn't stand having to wait and do nothing, once again. "I'll go check on the Domes," she told Hot Rod.

He put out an arm to stop her. "No one's going over there while those maniacs are lobbing shells at us. We'll have to hunker down till Renzie is through."

They ducked again as another missile came plunging to earth. Kip limped out onto the porch. Hot Rod shot him a meaningful glance and nodded to the House, but Kip stood his ground. "Might as well be out here as in there," he said. "How long has it been since Renzie left?"

Nesta groaned inwardly and wondered how many times he'd ask *that* question.

The rockets continued to come down regularly, hammering at the Domes.

"How long has it been now?" Kip asked again. Nesta's patience snapped. She turned on him as quickly as a wolf on a sheep.

"Wait," said Hot Rod. "Listen."

Nesta strained, then heard: There was a battery of popping sounds in the distance, like toy cap guns. Five minutes passed, then ten. No more rockets shrilled through the sky.

"The patrols have caught them," said Hot Rod. "I'm going up-stairs again to see if I can see anything."

Other folks began drifting out of the House, waiting for news. Soon the courtyard was full. Nesta craned her head back to watch Hot Rod. Another five minutes. Her neck began to ache. Then Hot Rod gave a whoop. "There they are. They're coming."

The patrol straggled into the yard, led by Son. They carried two rocket launchers. Son's front was covered with blood.

"Don't worry," he said as people rushed toward him. "It's not mine."

Nesta got to him first. "Where the hell is Renzie?"

"Relax. She's coming. She ran on ahead and detoured by the Domes to tell them it was all over."

Just then Renzie loped into the yard. "The Domes held up amazingly well—the smaller one only took two strikes," she said. "The Watchers have a lot of injuries from falling debris, but no fatalities. They're already getting ready to evacuate."

"Which is exactly what we're going to do," Hot Rod called down. "Hammer just relayed that the big mass of 'Bounders is headed this way. Once they got the fire going they waited for our people to show up, then skirted around the whole mess and headed south. Eric sends word the Viets and the Hackers are handling the blaze while everyone else is backtracking, trying to catch up with the 'Bounders. It's a race to see who gets here first. And we can't be sure it'll be Eric. I figure we've got an hour and a half, tops," he said. "Renzie, make sure Tuck gets Hammer and the portable radio units out and gone *now!*"

Renzie nodded. "I was on my way up there anyway to tell Tuck that Le Chell was okay."

Hot Rod turned to a man from the Southern Conservatory wing. "Josh, I want you to be in charge of loading up all our extra fuel and ammo onto the bus. As soon as you do, take Hammer and Tuck with you and leave immediately for the Hispanics' evac area. It's still safe there. In case the 'Bounders do take the House, let's not leave them any bonuses.

"Jorda, you and whatever Pinellis are around start getting every vehicle we've got—from wagons to bicycles with trailers—lined up and ready to go near the carriage door. Everybody can take one load of anything they can carry. I'm assuming everyone took Eric's advice about burying valuables, so let's think practical here, folks. And think of your housemates who are out fighting, what you can take for them."

Nesta and Renzie looked at each other. Renzie paled. "The research . . ." she began.

Nesta shook her head. "We can't save any of the equipment. All we'll be able to carry out is disks. I started running final backups when this all began, but never got a chance to finish. I'll go upstairs and see how much I can get done now."

Hot Rod was still speaking. "I'll need a couple of volunteers to make sure everybody clears out. Kids, I want you up in the tower sentry posts watching for the 'Bounders, just in case they arrive earlier than expected. But only use the positions that are completely protected."

Renzie turned to Nesta. "I'll come help you as soon as I get Tuck and Hammer sent down-valley."

Nesta opened an empty satchel and slung it between two chairs so she could throw the disks into it, then quickly set up the computer programs. Would there be enough time to run backups on everything left? She looked up. A shabby, raggedy man—the one that Renzie had called the Krit—hovered nervously in the doorway.

"Are you almost done here?" he asked in a shredded voice, his vocal chords as tattered as his clothing.

"Not quite yet. But someone is coming up to help me soon," Nesta reassured him.

His head bobbed about like a toy turtle's; Nesta couldn't tell whether in agreement or general anxiousness. He hesitated as if wanting to say something more, then left.

Renzie arrived several minutes later. "We got Hammer and Tuck off safely," she said as she slid into a seat before a computer and tapped at the keyboard. "Where are you in all of this?"

A few minutes later Bite popped his head in. "You ladies sliding into evac mode?" he asked. He was much less tense than the Krit.

"We're working as fast we can," Renzie said without looking up.

"Your partner was here checking up too, just a few minutes ago," Nesta told him.

Bite looked puzzled.

"The old man." Nesta jogged his memory.

"You mean the Krit?"

Nesta nodded.

Bite frowned. "He's supposed to cover the other side of the House. Like he doesn't think I can slide my own weight?"

"I don't think it was that," Nesta said. "I think he was just nervous, being overhelpful."

"Hyped-up old shifty dude," Bite agreed, and left.

Renzie and Nesta filled the satchel steadily. The whir of computers and the whisking clicks of disks being slid in and out of their ports echoed through the room.

"Listen!" said Renzie suddenly.

Nesta stopped with a disk half inserted. She and Renzie held perfectly still. Then Renzie shook her head. "Nothing, I guess. Just nerves." They bent back to their task.

But a few minutes later Renzie held up her hand. Nesta looked at her. Renzie slid noiselessly to the open doorway at the top of the easy-riser stairs. She stood for a moment, then ducked low and began to creep downward.

Curious, Nesta followed Renzie to the head of the stairway. She still couldn't hear anything.

But she smelled something; the pungent acid of vineahol fumes.

Renzie crouched at the first switchback in the stairs. She put a finger to her lips, listened for a moment, then made a palm-down stay-low motion with her hand and waved Nesta to join her. They made their way down to the stained-glass and pressboard storeroom below in stages.

A halting, unsteady scraping noise came from beyond the far hallway. Someone was dragging something heavy. The stench of vineahol became stronger.

"Stay here," Renzie whispered to Nesta. She slid out into the room and hid behind a tall row of pressboard rolls.

The noise approached the open doorway on the opposite side of the room, then stopped. Nesta flattened herself against the inner edge of the stairwell. The scraping started again. Nesta peered around the edge of the stairway.

A short Koanite with a close-cropped blond crewcut was dragging a canister of fuel backward around the room. The container was tipped at an angle. Vineahol splashed and dribbled out of it with each jerky movement. Nesta saw Renzie tense in her hiding place as the arsonist moved within reach.

Renzie slid behind the Koanite. One arm swept across dark blue in a bear hug. With her other arm Renzie reached in front for a handful of indigo jacket, dragging it across the would-be arsonist's throat in a choke hold. Renzie hauled back and then forward again, slamming the Koanite's head into the canister, which had rocked back with the motion. The arsonist yowled. The container tipped onto the Koanite.

Renzie pulled away to repeat the action, but the Koanite wrenched upward and fell backward onto Renzie, throwing her off balance and down. The Koanite broke free and scrambled up. Nesta saw for the first time that their arsonist was a woman.

Renzie got hold of the arsonist's legs, but couldn't get up herself—her feet were scrabbling for a purchase in the spreading puddle of vineahol. The Koanite tried to kick free, at the same time reaching frantically into her jacket, searching for something.

In seconds she would pull out a knife. Nesta cast around in a panic for something that could be used as a weapon. The closest thing to hand was a tightly rolled short section of pressboard. By the time Nesta grabbed this clumsy staff and turned, the Koanite had found what she was looking for in her jacket: not a knife, but a case of crude, handmade matches. Renzie was trying to crawl up the woman's body and yank her down before she could strike them.

Nesta froze in horror for the briefest moment. Both Renzie and the arsonist were drenched with fuel. They'd go up in a fireball.

Nesta swung the roll of pressboard with all her might at the arsonist's hands. The woman shrieked at the impact. Matches flew to all corners of the room.

Even that didn't completely stop the arsonist. She fell on top of Renzie, kneeing her in the face, finally breaking Renzie's hold.

Nesta swung again. The Koanite dodged the blow and fled up the easy-risers stairway. Renzie got her feet underneath her and was up the stairs after the other woman. She grabbed hold of one of the banister partitions and vaulted up, cutting down the Koanite's lead.

Nesta hurried as fast as she could after them, but she lagged far behind. By the time she'd negotiated all the turns of the switchbacks and reached the lab it was all over. Renzie knelt over the prone arsonist, one knee in her back, binding her with duct tape the way a cowhand might tie up a calf.

"Why on earth would a Koanite want to burn the House down?" Nesta asked.

Renzie turned the captive over. "Don't you recognize her? Maybe you didn't get that close at the time. This is the 'Bounder that knifed Jan, with a new set of clothes and a haircut."

The arsonist spat at Renzie. Renzie's face didn't change in expression. She simply turned the 'Bounder facedown again.

"Speaking of clothing . . ." Renzie bent down, examining the indigo jacket. A long rent ran down the left side under the armpit. The deep blue fabric was stiff and stained almost black there. "Dried blood. Not hard to figure out how she got this camouflage."

Renzie began stripping out of her own fuel-saturated clothing. She disappeared into her sleeping quarters and came back in a moment wearing a fresh change.

"What about her?" Nesta nodded at the still soaked 'Bounder.

"She'll have to take her chances." She looked thoughtful. "Our friend here isn't big enough to have hauled that canister up two flights of stairs. If we follow the track she was laying down, I'll bet it leads to the elevator shafts."

At that the 'Bounder started laughing.

Renzie paled and ran off, hopping into her sandals. She came back a few minutes later. "She'd left two more canisters in the elevator and locked onto this floor. One match and the House would have gone off like a Roman candle."

The 'Bounder squirmed onto her side. "Maybe it still will. God is beside me, helping me," she said. Her voice was calm.

"I sent the elevator down," Renzie assured Nesta. "Someone below will think it's been stuck up here for loading and check it."

"Give up. You can't win. Join me and be saved," the 'Bounder said. "God has cloaked me with His blessing. I've been working side by side with pagans and infidels all day and no one recognized me, just the way I did before."

"And you've been caught both times. Maybe God is trying to tell you something—like give it up," Nesta said dryly.

The 'Bounder's eyes glowed. "Those were only tests, to see if my faith prevails."

At that very moment fire-alarm bells started ringing. Renzie and Nesta jumped.

Then the ear-splitting din was overlaid by three muffled explosions coming from somewhere deep in the opposite side of the House.

Nesta and Renzie whirled on the 'Bounder. She looked as startled as they—at first.

Then the uncertainty in her face cleared. "God is watching over me. My faith has been rewarded," she whispered to herself. Her flashing eyes rolled triumphantly at Nesta and Renzie. "He has sent more Heaven Bound to my aid. Here, I'm here! I'm here!" she began screaming.

Renzie grabbed the duct tape, ripped a piece off and taped it over the 'Bounder's mouth. She slung the disk satchel over her shoulder. Gripping the 'Bounder under the left armpit, near the deadly slash, she hauled the fanatic to her feet.

"Grab the last disks and shove them in your pockets," she told Nesta. "Then give me a hand with this." Renzie shook the 'Bounder. "Let's get the hell out of here."

CHAPTER THIRTY-FIVE

Dragging the 'Bounder between them, it was a long, awkward haul down from Renzie's suite. On the next floor they ran into Quill and Bite hunting for the source of the blasts. First the boys' eyes widened at the sight of the clumsy trio. Next their noses wrinkled as they caught the vineahol-soggy reek of the 'Bounder.

When the boys were told what had happened Bite headed upstairs to evacuate the children standing watch on the upper floors.

"Look out for more 'Bounders," Renzie yelled after him.

Quill relieved the two women of their satchel full of disks and ran downstairs ahead of them to alert the rest of the House and make sure the fuel canisters had been unloaded from the elevator.

By the time Renzie and Nesta wrestled the 'Bounder out onto the kitchen porch children were shimmying down outside pipes from their sentry posts. Watchers and Housers alike hurried in from the gardens and house perimeter, packing the courtyard. Jorda was efficiently organizing the humming throng into fire brigades. She'd already had the bathing tubs drained. The stored water rushed down the garden moat, neatly diverting to the House.

"We're lucky most people are already evacuated," Renzie said. "It looks as though almost everyone not on the lines is out here."

Bite slithered down a pipe next to them. "All the kids are down now. I didn't see any other 'Bounders in there—not even any shifty probablys."

Across the courtyard Nesta saw Le Chell. She nudged Renzie. The red-haired girl was jumping up and down, trying to see over the heads of the crowd. As they watched, her face became taut as a mask, freckles standing out like measles against the unnatural whiteness of her skin. She stopped hopping about and began making her way around to the edges of the throng.

"She's heading toward my kiosk," Nesta said. "It looks like she's trying to get around to the front of the House."

"Oh my God," said Renzie. "She thinks Tuck is still inside."

"Le Chell!" Renzie tried to yell over the clamor of the courtyard. Nesta could hear how the cry strained at her throat. Renzie dumped the 'Bounder at the base of the porch steps. "Watch her," she ordered Son. "Make sure she doesn't go anywhere."

"Don't worry," he said. Renzie turned away and fought through the thickening crowds on the porch. Nesta started to follow, then saw Son draw his hunting knife, heard him say softly, "She's not going anywhere anymore."

"Don't do anything rash. Eric will want to question her," Nesta warned him. "I know how it looks, but she's not the one who started the fire." Son flared his nostrils at the reek of the 'Bounder. Nesta joined him in looking down at the squirming bundle with its hate-filled face and sighed.

"Though it wasn't from want of trying," she conceded. She ran after Renzie, tussling through the evacuating Housers.

Renzie had rounded the corner and was questioning Eileen on the steps at the front door when Nesta caught up with her.

"Le Chell said she had to go find Tuck." Eileen was having a hard time of it, trying to balance two big baskets filled with shells and bones. "That she knew he'd be up in the séance room with Hammer, and that he'd need help bringing Hammer down."

Renzie swore and dashed into the House. Eileen looked at Nesta over the top of her burden. "What is it?" she asked.

"Tuck and Hammer left the House over an hour ago," Nesta told her.

"Oh my lord! Wait," Eileen said, blocking the physicist's way. "Le Chell's not alone. That little Homer girl, Chupa, was helping me carry my things down. She went back in with Le Chell, said she could guide her."

"Eileen, tell somebody—Eric, Jorda, anybody—about this."
Nesta slammed into the House. "Renzie, where are you?" she called.

"Nesta, go back. I can't wait for you," Renzie's muffled yell came
from the left and up a level.

"Don't stop. Just keep hollering as you go. I'll track you." They
shrieked back and forth to each other as they ran; their journey up and
through the House resembled the mating flight of a pair of demented
birds.

Nesta caught up with Renzie again in the séance room. Renzie
had opened all of the doors leading out of it and was dashing from one
to the other, as if her movements were some sort of frantic magic that
would conjure up Le Chell. Nesta leaned against the doorsill, holding
her side against the ache stitched into it.

"Damn, damn, damn!"

Nesta envied Renzie her youth that she still had the breath to yell
after the uphill run.

"She wasn't that far ahead," she said. "Le Chell doesn't know the
House that well—she'd have to go more slowly. She'd have had to come
the way we did. We should have overtaken her."

Nesta panted more slowly, still trying to catch her breath. "Renzie, if she's not that familiar with the House, would she know that
this"—Nesta gestured—"is the only door that opens into the séance
room? That the other doors only act as exits?"

"I thought of that. That's why I opened them all; in case she came
to one of the wrong doors. But if she'd done that we should have heard
her pounding, trying to get Tuck to let her in."

"There may be another reason." Nesta told Renzie about Chupa
volunteering to guide Le Chell.

"Triple damn." Renzie ran both hands through her hair. "Chupa
doesn't know the first thing about the House. I don't know how many
times I've had to lead her out when she was lost. If she's acting as Le
Chell's guide they could be anywhere." Renzie pressed fisted hands
against her temples, clenching all the muscles in her face as she thought.
She released, shook her head. "Come on," she said. "I can think of a
few places where they might have forked off the wrong way."

They stopped at every corridor to call Le Chell's and Chupa's
names, then waited to listen for a reply. And listened also for warnings
of the fire's progress. Which sometimes they heard: a distant riparian
whoosh as a gout of flame conquered and commandeered the channel
of a far corridor, the dimmed cries of firefighters coordinating a coun-

teroffensive. Nesta hadn't smelled the dense bitter odor of smoke—yet. But now and then a whiff of the perfume of overheated wood, like scorched incense, reached her.

"Maybe they've already left," she tried to persuade Renzie. "By now they've got to know they missed the way to the séance room. They'll realize that one way or the other Tuck will have gotten out."

Renzie shook her head. "They're probably lost. We've searched the whole side of the House that still seems safe from the fire. If they'd come out this way they would have heard us yelling. That means they headed into one of the wings that's threatened."

Renzie looked at the older woman with sober eyes. "Nesta, it's one flight down, two turns and a hallway and you're out of here. Please, go. Bring more help."

"No, I already told Eileen to do that. Nobody's come around this way to join us yet." Nesta gestured to the interior of the House. "You can hear folks fighting the fire somewhere on the other side. With almost everyone called away to fend off the 'Bounders, they're short enough as it is of able bodies." Nesta drew herself up, almost as tall as she used to stand when she was younger. She forced an acid tone into her voice. "I'm not all *that* old. In an emergency you might actually find me useful."

"I already have," Renzie said. "Where would I be now, if you hadn't knocked those matches out of the 'Bounder's hands?"

They headed deeper into the House, toward the fire.

Renzie took off down a side corridor. Nesta entered a doorway that opened onto a suite of rooms. The staggered bedding and cupboards indicated that a minicommune lived there together. A guitar lay on one bed, a banjo, harmonica, and dulcimer on another. Undoubtedly this was a busy, lively group. Their absence, the absence throughout the entire House—people, kids, cats—reverberated with all the ominousness of a fortune-teller's flip of the card to the Tower of Destruction.

Something thumped at one of the walls. Nesta rushed over and pounded back. "Le Chell, is that you?"

More knocking, then Renzie's muted voice through the partition. "Nesta, are you in there? Come on over here. I think I hear them, unless it was just you."

Nesta ran out of the suite. The sounds of Renzie's thumps led her into another, single bedroom. Renzie knelt on the bed with the side of her face to the wall, rhythmically rapping.

"Good, it wasn't you. See if you can hear it too."

Nesta pressed her ear against the wall. Dimly, from somewhere beyond came the sound of frantic pounding. But not in the next room. The sounds were too muffled for that.

"Le Chell!" Renzie screamed into the wall.

"Renzie?" They could barely hear her.

"Le Chell, you're in a desk-den suite. Head north and come around out through the bathroom with the spiderweb windows."

"We can't. We tried. It's burning that way." Le Chell's voice was faint.

"Then stay where you are. We'll find a way to get to you."

They pulled away from the wall, neither saying what they'd both felt. The wall had been hot to the touch.

"The fire's between us," Renzie said. "The only way is to go down the seven-eleven staircase and up and around to the other side."

But when they reached the top of the steps Nesta and Renzie looked across the gap of stairwell to a spill of smoke cascading down the opposite stairs like dirty fog.

Renzie looked grim. "It's come around fast."

"We'll pass out in that before we can get to them," Nesta said. "That's even if we're lucky and the fire isn't coming up directly behind that smoke."

"I know. I know," said Renzie. "We've got to find some sort of protection for ourselves." She went back the way they'd come, peering into rooms. She ducked into one. A moment later Nesta heard tearing, then a crashing noise. Renzie returned and thrust a bedspread into Nesta's hands. "Wrap that around your head and face as much as you can," she ordered the older woman. She fashioned a length of curtain into an oversized burnoose and wound herself up in it.

They paused on the edge of the steps, gauging the thickness of the fumes. "Now!" Renzie said. Nesta took a last full breath of clean air. Then they were running down to the landing and up the other side. Hunched over to get under the smoke they scuttled like beetles through several rooms. Nesta found herself counting off seconds, then minutes. Too much time was going by. Too much time had passed since they'd heard Le Chell.

"This has got to be it, the room they were in," Nesta said. Renzie batted at drapery-thick soot billowing out of its doorway.

"They're not here now. They must have gone out the door on the opposite side." Renzie coughed. She dropped to the floor to reach a stratum of fresher air. "Le Chell! Chupa!" she screamed into the room. There was no answer.

She got up and resecured the fabric around her head. Nesta did the same. They plunged into the den. They were lucky. Fire ran along the far wall, but it hadn't eaten into the flooring or swept the underside of the ceiling yet. Still, enough heat fanned them that Nesta felt like a roasting joint of meat as they hurried through. The cloth around her head began to crisp and brown, giving off a burnt-starch stink. She prayed it wouldn't burst into flames before they reached the other side.

They found Le Chell and Chupa two rooms further on. Chupa lay sprawled in the doorway of a side parlor that was puffing out inky vapors like a smudge pot. She'd made it almost back out into the corridor.

Renzie and Nesta dragged her the rest of the way to relative safety. She was a big girl for her age, and all the heavier for her state of collapse. Renzie tilted the youngster's chin back, pinched her nostrils shut and began breathing into her mouth.

Nesta had to crawl past Renzie on hands and knees to clear the lowering ceiling of solid black fumes to look for Le Chell. As in the den, the smoke fanned out and away from its originating fire, allowing her finally to see.

Le Chell huddled below a shattered casement, one of the House's interior windows that looked out over a series of skylight-floored canyonlike breezeways. She lay facing the opening she must have hoped would deliver her from the flames. It was a mistake that had cost her her life. The windows had drawn more of the inferno in from outside.

As Nesta watched, the blazing curtains framing the window disintegrated and dropped in tatters down onto Le Chell's body, igniting her clothes instantly, consuming and replacing her beautiful hair with a blazing mane even redder than her own.

Le Chell's corpse blackened, withered, and curled inward, a charring fetus in death's womb. Nesta wept. She was grateful that Le Chell faced away from her. She crept backward out of the room.

In the hallway Renzie knelt over Chupa, her interlaced hands pumping down rhythmically on the child's chest. Tears tracked greasily down Renzie's soot-stained face. "No pulse," she said. At the end of her count she stopped to breathe into Chupa's mouth again. Nesta could tell from where she stood that the air momentarily ballooning the little girl's chest was Renzie's alone.

Renzie looked up. "Le Chell?" she asked.

"No hope," Nesta said. "Not even that much." She nodded at Chupa.

Renzie pushed past Nesta. "Keep up the CPR for me," she said.

Nesta caught at Renzie's arm. "Renzie, don't go in. She's dead. The fire's spreading in there fast."

Renzie pulled her arm free, gestured at Chupa again. "If we can keep her oxygen and blood moving they might be able to revive her once we get outside." She ducked down and into the room.

Nesta wished she could have stopped her, but she understood that Renzie had to see for herself, had to be able to tell Tuck. No Vanishing, no questions in her mind; just irrevocable, undeniable death.

Renzie returned quickly. Nesta knew she would never forget till the day of her own death the look on her young friend's face. Renzie didn't say a word, just came over to where Nesta labored away on Chupa and clumsily tried to lift the child up. Nesta helped hoist Chupa over Renzie's shoulders in a fireman's carry.

Only then did Renzie speak. "We'll have to stop as much as we can to work on her, if we're going to give the medic team any kind of a chance."

It was Nesta's turn for silence. The fire in the parlor would soon burst into the hallway. They only had two rooms grace back the way they'd come, if that. Somewhere further in the other direction were the flames that had blocked them from Chupa and Le Chell in the first place. And even if they could get back to the other side of the House by some miracle, the 'Bounder's vineahol soaking would have caught by now.

Renzie looked at the smoke pouring toward them from the way they'd come. Then she turned and trudged down the hall in the direction Le Chell and Chupa must have taken in trying to escape. That they'd tried and failed.

Renzie and Nesta made it around only a single turn before they saw ashen clouds coursing from that direction. They stood and stared like drugged animals. Renzie began coughing uncontrollably. Nesta braced Chupa in place when the hacking threatened to dislodge the child from her perch.

"Where in the hell are you going?" A thin angry voice pierced their dumbness. They turned slowly. Minda stood framed in the doorway of a room they'd just passed.

"Come on, *this* way." Minda jerked her head. "And dump that. It's dead." She popped back into the room.

Renzie stared in disbelief. "The only way out of there is another window that lets out onto the breezeway."

Nesta had noticed something else. "Did you see her face? It's hardly smoke-smudged at all. And she's not wearing anything over her head." They gaped at each other.

"Do you *want* to die?" came the high-pitched, imperious voice. "Come *on.*"

Nesta and Renzie followed, maneuvering awkwardly around the chairs and baskets that cluttered the room Minda led them into.

"Let go of that. You can't bring her." Minda insistently tugged at Chupa, making Renzie lose her grip on the Homer child. Nesta pulled up on the potato-sack body from Renzie's other side. The floor tilted as they struggled to balance. They slid en masse to the other end of the room. Only skidding into the wall kept Renzie from dropping Chupa.

"Don't *do* that," Minda said plaintively, at last looking as scared as Nesta and Renzie. "You're making it too hard for me."

Nesta glanced at Renzie.

"The foundation must be going," Renzie said. She clutched Chupa to herself even more tightly.

Minda glared, then turned and threw the window open harder than Nesta thought possible for a girl her size. Nesta climbed out after her, fearfully looking to the left for the flames girdling the room Le Chell had died in.

But there were no flames. The window was unbroken. Much further down the breezeway Nesta saw a faint wisp of smoke seep up from under the eaves, but that was all.

Renzie thrust Chupa's legs out the window. Nesta grabbed them. Renzie clambered out supporting the girl's torso. She teetered on the beams for balance and looked to see how close the danger was. Her face registered the same amazement Nesta felt.

"Don't stop now," Minda called to them. "That was too close a shift. There's fire Here, too." The breezeway's arcade was laced with light crossbeams. Minda tightrope-walked across to the other side and waited on an outcropping porch.

With Chupa slung between them the two women clutched at side struts for support as they crossed the breezeway to join Minda. The beams were light, not meant for heavy load bearing. They creaked dangerously beneath Nesta and Renzie's combined weight. Nesta wondered if they'd been saved from the fire only to be sliced into shreds falling through the skylights below.

By the time they reached Minda they were sweating and panting from the effort. Renzie's earlier chimneysweep appearance had mottled into a sort of monochromatic camouflage. Nesta guessed that she looked the same.

Renzie laid the body down on the floor. As Nesta thought that—"the body"—she knew she'd accepted that Chupa was truly gone.

Renzie felt for a pulse again and resumed CPR. Nesta looked down at her friend in despair. Minda stared too with a look of purest irritation, but she let Renzie continue for a few minutes.

Then she slid open the French doors that entered inward from the porch. "We can't stay here any longer," she commanded. "The fire's not so bad in this Here, but it can cut us off from slipping again." Without further explanation she trotted out into the hallway beyond.

Nesta helped sling Chupa's corpse onto Renzie's back again. They followed slowly behind Minda. Renzie was beginning to stagger.

Minda led them on a tangled circuit through the House. Some of the route Nesta recognized, some she didn't. Minda stopped at the top of a set of stairs. Drifts of inky smoke pooled ankle-deep at the bottom.

By now Renzie was so tired she trembled all over. Chupa's weight against the back of her neck jammed her head down and forward. There was no expression on her face whatsoever; it might as well have been a blank mask, but for the tears coursing down her cheeks.

"I'm sorry." Minda's voice had softened to pity, at least for Renzie, if not for the dead Homer child. "But we've got to go down there so we can slip up again to a Here with no fire, be safe for a while." She took Renzie's hand and led her down, an elf leading a lame hunchback. Nesta followed behind.

And immediately regretted it. What are we doing, obeying this small child unquestioningly? she thought. Minda had marched them straight down and around into a solid wall of smoke. Nesta heard the crackle of flames somewhere nearby.

"Take a deep breath and hang on to Renzie," Minda called back over her shoulder. "We have to get through this part fast." She plunged in. The ashy cloud swallowed her. Renzie, clutching her, was drawn along.

Nesta barely had time to yank the cloth over her nose and grab hold of Renzie's arm before she disappeared too.

Then Nesta was in. She shut her eyes tight against the stinging fumes, slammed blindly against walls and anonymous furniture.

Nesta knocked her shin into something hard, then tripped on something else soft and went down into more softness, losing her hold on Renzie. Nesta flailed about in tractionless puffiness. The smoke thickened. There was no light. She couldn't imagine where they might be, but the space seemed to climb like a stairway.

Renzie seemed to know. Nesta heard her somewhere close by and slightly above her. Renzie had finally roused.

"Minda, what are you doing?" Panic whistled Renzie's voice. "What have you done to us?"

Several heavy thumps told Nesta that Renzie had at last lost her grasp on Chupa. Nesta wondered if the girl's body would come rolling down on top of her.

"You've got to climb," Minda yelled from somewhere higher above Renzie. "You've got to slide up *with* me, or it won't work."

Laughter rose like a shriek in Nesta's throat. How could anyone possibly slide *up*?"

Renzie's response was similar to hers. "You've trapped us!" Renzie screamed, sounding equally angry and terrified.

A scuffle broke out above Nesta. "All right, just sit there." Minda's peevish voice descended. "I'll go get Nesta first." More sounds. A small hand scrabbled against Nesta's face for a moment before reaching around and grabbing the back of her collar, along with a twist of the bedcover and a handful of hair.

"Hey!" Nesta yelled, then choked on a lungful of smoke.

"Sorry." Minda was coughing, too. "Try to keep up with where I'm pulling you."

They scrambled upward through the yielding surface. At last Nesta felt the hardness of stairs underneath her feet, battering her knees. Relieved to at last get some kind of a purchase, she didn't care how badly she bruised herself.

Suddenly Nesta tripped on something again. Her feet flew out backward. Steps slammed into her ribs hard enough to knock the wind out of her.

Minda swore. *"Now* what?"

Nesta started to laugh again and ended in tears. "I think I stepped on Chupa," she sobbed. Now that the weeping had started it didn't want to stop.

"Good. Keep crying. If I can hear you, I can find you again," Minda said. A clunking noise came from below. Renzie must be trying to drag Chupa's body back down the stairs.

Minda grabbed Nesta's arm and pulled her up. Nesta brushed past small, mysterious objects that fell and clattered down after Renzie. Minda braced under Nesta's arm and gave a tremendous heave. The two of them fell up and forward together onto a flat floor and into clean air.

Nesta rolled to a sitting position, braced her elbows on her knees, her head in her hands, and hacked and wheezed, straining to clear her creosote-coated throat and lungs. There was light. She could see again. They were on the parquet floor of a broad landing.

Minda lay beside her, coughing and spitting. Nesta raised her head. The smoke would breach the clean air soon. Fire would follow the smoke. They couldn't linger here. They had to go back in after Renzie and get her out. Nesta turned to Minda. Her small face was now as coal-miner black as Nesta's and Renzie's had been.

"Renzie . . ." Nesta started.

Minda nodded her head up and down wearily. "I know. Give me just another second to breathe."

Nesta glanced nervously at the stairwell, dreading the progress of the column of smoke.

And stared in amazement. It stopped level with the floor, swirling eerily like silver paint marbling through water. Nesta crept forward to study it. It looked as if a pane of glass had been dropped over it. Her heart banged against her bruised ribs. She looked back at Minda again.

Minda misinterpreted Nesta's glance. "I know, I know. If we don't get her out now, she'll be as dead as that Ghost." Minda crawled to the edge of the stairs, her face pinched and drawn. She took a deep breath and lunged through the flat, swirling surface. The portal seemed to absorb her. No sounds of her scrambling downward came back up to Nesta through its glossy surface.

The minutes passed.

Nesta looked about as she waited, concerned that the fire might creep around and catch them from another direction. The landing led to steps angling up to another landing. The second landing opened onto a brightly lit space. Was that light the reflection of the inferno somewhere further along? Nesta glanced briefly over her shoulder for any sight of Minda. If the blaze was outflanking them she'd have to go down after Minda before they became trapped. With a hand bracing her battered side Nesta climbed the shallow steps to the second landing, and across that to the doorway.

And stood there, wondering if she'd lost her mind.

The little room at whose threshold she stood *was* ablaze. But with pure, flaring light, not fire; its source of illumination was a single leaded-glass window.

The abstracted floral shapes and nuggets of quartz and crystal absorbed the clear southern rays pouring through its panes and transformed the streams of light into a majestic, overheated deluge of colors. Blood-vibrant ruby, tiger-eyed gold, absinthe, jonquil, lake-deep lapis blue, the new-leaf green of emeralds, gleaming claret, sapphire, incandescent amethyst—they drenched the walls in glowing, overlapping hues.

Nesta knew at last where she stood in the House. She knew the impossibility of this phosphorescently radiant display. And she knew that the artist who'd crafted this window so long ago had always intended for it to look this way.

Nesta trembled as she walked to the window and peered out through its jigsaw fragments. The sunshine beyond fell through and onto her, transmuted. Nesta felt the light's gentle warmth as it tattooed her face with color. Beyond, she saw what she'd expected. No other parts of the House encroached nearby. The closest was a two-story wing across a courtyard garden she'd never seen before. That she knew did not exist.

That moment, at her back, Minda screamed.

Nesta whirled around, jamming her ribs again, and ran to the doorway. She saw Minda's head float for just a moment above the opalescent gray vapors. Then Minda was yanked back under.

Nesta flew down the two landings and tried to plunge her hands into the smoke. It rebuffed her with trampolinelike resistance. Nesta prayed out loud. "Come back. Come back, Minda. One more time. I'm here. Come back *now.*"

And Minda did, erupting out of that unnatural surface the way a seal stalked by a shark hurls itself out of the sea. Head and shoulders clear, she threw her head back, the cords on her fragile neck straining as she fought for air. It looked as if the smoky floor were trying to suck Minda downward.

"Pull!" she cried. "Put your hands under my armpits and pull as hard as you can." Nesta squatted down, trying to position herself.

"Let go!" Minda suddenly screamed. Nesta yanked her hands away as if scalded. "Not you," Minda groaned. *"Renzie.* She's got hold of the Ghost again."

Nesta reestablished her grip. Minda's frame felt impossibly fine-boned between her hands. "One, two, *three,"* Nesta counted, and straightened her spine with a wrench. She felt something give way as pain lanced through her side. But they fell backward together away from the hole.

Renzie was with them, sprawled between Minda's legs. Minda sprawled between Nesta's. The three of them stacked together like hell's idea of a toboggan team, Nesta thought.

The drapery-mask still wound around Renzie's nose and mouth must have saved her. Nesta reached across Minda to slide it down so that Renzie could breathe clean air. Renzie's eyebrows were scorched off. Her forehead looked red and puffy, soon to be pocked with small blisters.

"I couldn't hold her. I tried. I really did, but I just couldn't," Renzie was muttering to herself. Her tears spilled from milkily red eyes. Even if she hadn't been crying, Nesta doubted if Renzie could see.

"And almost killed us all," Minda said, still angry and frightened as she untangled herself. "You couldn't have brought her through. She was a Ghost—a dead one, too. I don't understand how you did it the first slide, unless it was because it was such a nearby Here, and she was dead there, too."

Minda turned to Nesta. "Can you help me get her up?"

"I think so." Nesta got her feet well planted and lifted, stiffening to keep from crying out against the agony in her ribs.

Renzie took a few steps on her own before crashing into a banister. Tears still flooded her eyes shut.

"She's smoke-blind, I think," said Minda. Then she looked at Nesta with concern. "You're hurt too, aren't you, Nesta?"

Nesta nodded. "Broken ribs, I'd guess. Where's the fire now?" she asked.

"Not in this Here. We're safe for now."

Nesta didn't question Minda's words. "If we could get Renzie cleaned up it might help her eyes. It wouldn't hurt us, either," Nesta suggested.

Minda hesitated. "It wouldn't be a good idea to go outside in this

Here to get to the baths. But we could at least wash up a little in a sink. The nearest bathroom is this way."

They flanked Renzie, who'd been standing silent during their interchange. When Renzie felt Minda's hand on her arm she jerked away from the girl and leaned more heavily on Nesta. "You think I don't know?" she snapped at the youngster. "I know where we were. That was your room. It wasn't possible. What did you do?"

Minda ignored the outburst. "Nesta's hurt. You're making it too hard for her." Renzie allowed Minda to support her on the other side, but Nesta could feel her recoiling from the girl.

Even after Nesta had washed her face clean Renzie was still blinded. Nesta soaked and wrung out a towel, laid it over Renzie's eyes and bound it in place.

Then Minda and Nesta cleaned their hands and faces as well as they could. There wasn't much they could do about their hair or sooty clothes.

"Can you walk okay?" Minda asked Nesta.

Nesta tried to smile. "As long as we don't have to duck any burning timbers."

Leading Renzie, nursing herself, fighting the desire to surrender to exhaustion—these were the concerns that dominated Nesta's awareness for most of the rest of their journey. She and Renzie followed Minda as docilely as shepherded lambs. Renzie stayed swathed in silence.

Although the House still appeared deserted, Nesta heard the sounds of people moving about nearby. At one point she glanced in passing out a window across the gardens to the Domes and saw a red-haired girl who looked very like Le Chell. Beyond her and beyond the Domes Nesta caught a glimpse of a vast verdant wilderness sprawling to the horizon. A sprawl devoid of Homes.

CHAPTER THIRTY-SIX

Even blindfolded, scorched, exhausted, and anesthetized with grief, Renzie could tell they were moving in a westerly direction. And that they'd been traveling that way too long. Huge as the House was, by now they should have exited out somewhere near the farthest reaches of the grounds.

Minda said, "Everybody hold on to each other again." They kept on walking as before, but for a brief moment Renzie experienced a twinge of vertigo. It passed. Soon afterward Minda let go of her to take the lead, guiding them down a set of steep stairs along a hall and then into a room. Renzie ran her spare hand along the surface of the wall, expecting to feel the velvet of linseed-oiled pressboard or the grit of mica-spackled wallpaper. Instead, her fingers met unadorned plaster. They were no longer in the House.

"I'm going to get some help," Minda said. "You wait here."

The place seemed familiar. Renzie thought she could almost recognize its smell, the spring of the floorboards beneath her feet. "Nesta, we can't be in the House," she hissed at the physicist. "We've gone too far. You know that."

"Yes." But Nesta said it calmly. She sounded thoughtful rather than bewildered.

"Do you know where we are? Can you see?"

"The last window we passed before we started down the stairs showed the water tower garden," Nesta said. "This room is a bedroom. Here, come and sit down." Nesta maneuvered Renzie to the edge of a bed.

Renzie pictured the grounds surrounding the House as she fingered the chenille spread. "We're in Eric's place, the Foreman's Cottage. That's impossible."

Nesta sighed. In that simple sound Renzie heard depletion, sadness, peace, and physical pain. At some time during the years-long trip through the House Minda had told her that Nesta's ribs were broken. Renzie remembered Nesta tripping on Chupa's body as they made their way up and out of the Stairs-to-Nowhere—another impossibility.

"Renzie, about Le Chell . . ." Nesta started.

The front door of the cottage opened and shut. "They're in the bedroom," they heard Minda say.

Renzie felt Nesta try to rise from her seat on the bed, then wince and sit down again.

"You two make quite a pair," came Hake's voice from the bedroom door. "The halt and the blind." The sharpness of his jest didn't mask his relief. "Let's check you out."

A chair scraped along the floor, thumped down in front of Renzie. Hands brushed her temples as Hake reached around to untie where the towel was knotted at the back of her head.

"Look at Nesta first," Renzie said, putting a hand out to stop him. "She's hurt worse. Her ribs are broken. She could have internal injuries."

Minda was right, thought Renzie. I could have gotten us all killed. I'm not really blind now. Back in the fire, *that's* when I was blind. In trying to save the already dead I almost destroyed the living. I was ready to sacrifice Minda, Nesta, myself—without even thinking.

"Is that true, Nesta?" Hake said. Renzie flinched. The chair thudded from Renzie to Nesta.

"The part about broken ribs, yes." Nesta sounded a little more like her old, tart self. "I think I could tell if I had internal injuries . . . Minda! You're not going anywhere. You need to get checked out, too." The slight furtive shuffling must have been Minda trying to sidle out the door. "All three of us inhaled a lot of smoke," Nesta continued. "You'll want to do something about that."

"Yes, ma'am!" Hake said. Then, more soberly, "You two ladies had better brace yourselves. When Eileen came around and told us what happened, Jorda had to restrain a few folks from going in after you. They'll be here any minute. All right, Nesta, don't be shy. Hike up your shirt and let's look at those ribs."

Nesta harumphed. "If I'm going to be gawked at, at least it will be by just a few folks. There's one blessing that most everyone evacuated south."

Hake coughed. "Well, not exactly. Hammer had his portable unit going. As soon as they heard the 'Bounders had been routed they headed straight back."

Tuck, Renzie thought, trembling. And Chupa's parents. She heard feet pounding on the stairs leading up to the cottage, taking the steps two at a time. Renzie stiffened, frantically organized her thoughts. How can I tell Tuck? How can I tell him I failed, that Le Chell is gone?

"When did you get back? What about the 'Bounders, the fire up north?" Nesta grilled Hake.

"They're still trying to contain that fire. We started to overtake the 'Bounders headed this way so they split up, went to ground. Trackers are trailing them, trying to find out where their new nest is. The rest of us came right back to help with the blaze here."

People burst into the room, a whiff of soot and smoke drifting in after them. Renzie plucked nervously at the blindfold. She was glad she wouldn't have to see Tuck's face, but she felt terribly vulnerable in her sightlessness.

Hake bumped against Renzie gently now and then, a swath of bandage following his movement, brushing Renzie's arm. He must be taping Nesta's ribs. Minda fidgeted somewhere nearby.

Someone else hurried up the steps, audibly shoving at people blocking the door. "Where's my daughter?" came the voice of Chupa's mother. "Somebody said they saw my daughter going in that place after you."

"No." Nesta finally spoke into the silence that followed. "We went in after her. Her and Le Chell." Another painful pause. "I'm sorry."

"She shouldn't have even been in there," Minda piped up, defensive. "It was her own—" Somebody hushed her.

"They both died of smoke inhalation," Nesta said over the mother's sobbing. "Renzie tried to carry your daughter's body out. But with the smoke and the flames, it was impossible."

The woman shoved her way out of the room, past murmured attempts at consolation. Renzie wondered how she'd find the words to tell her husband. Children were so precious, and they had only had the one.

Moments later more footsteps approached the front door. One more voice in the procession promenading to her in her blindness. But this was the voice she'd been waiting for and dreading all along.

"Renzie, are you in there? Damn it, get out of my way." Tuck's voice was angry with fear.

"Renzie, let me tell him." Nesta's voice was soft at her ear.

"No, I have to tell him," Renzie said. "It has to be me."

CHAPTER THIRTY-SEVEN

That night Eric led Nesta and Renzie outside to eat with all the others in the open air. The declining warmth of the day was nothing compared to the wall of heat rippling from what was left of the House. Nesta flinched away from it as they detoured it in a wide circle.

"It's not out yet?" Renzie asked shakily. After examining her, Hake had said that some of the smoke damage she'd suffered was chemical, from burning plastics and synthetics. Nesta was concerned that they didn't know the extent of the young woman's injuries yet, but perhaps it was a mercy that she couldn't see the House's seared remains.

"Almost," Eric answered. "What you're feeling is the embers. They'll be hot for days. The only part that's still in flames is the greenhouse wing. We almost have that under control." He guided them through the children's video-arcade jumble, untouched by the fire.

"We'll be in good shape providing the rest of the 'Bounders hold off to regroup and the winds don't come up. The 'Bounders suffered a lot of casualties today, but for that reason alone they may choose to attack us now while they have any forces left at all. And where they think we're the weakest," he added.

"Have you been able to find out anything from the 'Bounder we captured?" Nesta asked.

Eric became overly busy as he led them around dispossessed Housers spreading out blankets and bedding in the garden clearing.

"Eric?" Nesta asked again.

"She's dead," he answered at last. "Chupa's parents. Chupa's father started an argument with Son, who was still guarding the 'Bounder; with the bad blood already between them, that wasn't hard. It was a distraction. When everyone else nearby got involved in trying to separate the two of them, Chupa's mother walked behind the commotion and shot the 'Bounder in the back of the head."

Nesta and Renzie stopped, stunned.

"She murdered a Koanite for the clothing, but she wasn't the one who started the fire," Renzie said. "We told Son that."

Eric shrugged. "Not from want of trying. She stank of vineahol. She and at least one other 'Bounder were working as a team. They were going to torch both sides of the House simultaneously. Luckily you two caught her and saved at least that side. Miraculously, the flames never reached there to ignite the fuel."

"Eric, it wasn't quite like that," Nesta said. "When we caught the 'Bounder and the fire broke out, the 'Bounder was as startled as we were. Somebody else burned down the House. And somebody rang the alarm bells *before* the explosions, maybe as a warning . . . or a boast."

It was Eric's turn to pause. "Then we don't know who, or why, or if they'll try again." His voice was grim. "That means more guards. That means everybody will have to be on guard, and not just against stray 'Bounders."

After finding them a comfortable spot to sit among the crowds in the garden and asking a passing Mallite to fetch them some dinner, Eric left to warn the patrols of the new threat.

Friends and neighbors gathered as soon as they'd settled to ask how badly they'd been injured, how long it would take them to recover, to express condolences for Le Chell. Nesta could feel Renzie straining to hear the false note of sympathy, the undercurrent of disharmony that would mark the arsonist. But whoever had betrayed the House was not there; or chose to be silent.

Nesta nudged Renzie to let her know their food had arrived. Jorda was carrying one of the dinners. Minda and Tuck followed behind, carrying glasses and a pitcher. Once he'd poured their drinks Tuck sat down near Renzie, but didn't speak to her or touch her. His face was still gaunt with grief, his eyes red and swollen. Nesta wondered if Renzie knew he was there.

After Nesta and Renzie had had a chance to ease their hunger, the well-wishers' questions began again.

"How in the blue blazes did you get out?" Hot Rod asked. "You disappeared into the House for the longest time, and the next thing we know someone says you're safe in Eric's place. What did you do, teleport?"

"Not exactly," Nesta said. "Minda simply walked us across from the House over to the cottage. Didn't you, Minda?"

Minda squirmed.

"If that's meant to be a joke, it isn't funny," said one of the Mallites. "Everyone was on the lookout for you. With all those people scurrying around diverting water and cutting fire breaks, you would have been seen crossing the grounds."

"I didn't say that we left the House to get to the cottage. Minda took us on a parallel route, through a third-floor passageway directly into the cottage." Nesta smiled into the disbelieving silence.

"The anomalies." Hake had figured it out. "You stumbled onto one of the anomalies and used it to escape."

"We didn't stumble onto it. Minda knew exactly where she was taking us. That's how she reached us in the middle of the fire in the first place. Isn't it, Minda?"

Minda mumbled an assent.

Haberman scoffed. "That's what she told you? After all these months of looking for aberrations like needles in haystacks, she just waltzes you through one in the nick of time?"

"The anomalies aren't rare. In fact, it's looking more and more as if anomalies are all there are, or will be, eventually. I believe that's what it's all moving toward. It's the Vanishing's legacy. And I think the House, or the spot it was built on, has always attracted a concentration of them. It's a place where the walls of reality have always worn thin, even before the Vanishing.

"Consider the possibility of the existence of parallel universes . . ." Nesta stopped to draw a tree in the dirt with her fork. "There's one theory of parallel universes that hypothesizes that immediately after this particular continuum—our reality—was initiated in the fraction of an attosecond in the Big Bang, it split into an infinity of all possibilities. In other words, an infinity of universes exists parallel but separately from each other, with no interaction of any kind between them."

She tapped the ground in front of her. "Another postulated theory is treelike in concept, like this drawing. In this version of parallel universes, each time a 'choice' of any kind is made—an electron zigs left or zags right, Napoleon decides to invade Russia, or not to invade Russia, or to wait another year before invading—the universe branches, multiplies again into an infinity of universes to accommodate all these possibilities.

"Notice that what separates the branches in my drawing is the space between them. Now, we've all seen how saplings planted too closely sometimes grow and merge together.

"What I believe is that the Vanishing initiated a fluctuation that is causing the 'spaces' between the parallel realities—the dimensions that hold them apart—to collapse. The branches are beginning to wind and grow together, eventually forming a laminate of all the parallel universes that share the Vanishment, including our own. I haven't observed or heard of a single anomaly that doesn't fit the theory."

"What about the aurora?" Haberman asked, still willing to play the role of devil's advocate. "We never figured that one out. I don't see how that fits into your theory."

"It fits perfectly. We were just looking through the wrong end of the glass. Instead of searching for the answer out in the stars, we should have been investigating why the post-Vanishment generation could perceive it and we couldn't. I believe that what they're seeing is not truly an aurora borealis. I think it's one of the first indications we have of post-Vanishment adaptation to the changes. They're not seeing just the night sky, but the overlapping auras of closely spaced possibilities of the night sky. Am I close, Minda?"

Son interrupted before Minda could answer. "Why are you asking her? How would she know? She's just a little kid."

"You haven't been paying attention. I'm talking now about a jump in ability from generation to generation. Part and parcel of the laminating process is the change and adaptation of each possible universe's elements. The first post-Vanishment generation unknowingly perceives some of the parallel continuums. The next generation has developed further. They're already beginning to function, to move within the new multiverse continuum. To understand it. Well, Minda?"

The youngster's reluctance was palpable. Nesta felt the withdrawal of all the children in the circle.

"Sort of," Minda said grudgingly. "We don't understand any of that, we just kind of know it, do it. We call it gessying."

"Gessying?"

Minda didn't say anything. She shrugged.

"Subconscious unconscious superconscious meta gestalting," Bite said, for once almost helpful.

"And it's not like we can slip every-Here," Quill pitched in. Minda's peers had decided not to let her field all the questions. "There's lots of Heres or Probablys we can't get to, even if we wanted to. And others that we can't stay in for long. Usually we slide to close-by Heres, with the House and everything else. And sometimes other Heres pop in, well, here."

"Like my meadow and Pel's monsters," said Renzie.

Hake's interest was now fully engaged. "If you, uh, slide to generally 'close by' parallels, which I gather means the ones most similar to ours, are you sliding to ones where you yourselves already exist?"

"Usually." Quill's answer sounded surprised. Nesta would bet he'd never considered the question before.

"Then when you do, are there two of you simultaneously existing?" Hake followed through.

Minda laughed and answered before Quill could gather his thoughts. "Of course not, silly. We just slip into ourselves there. And when the they-we's there slide this way, they-we slip into ourselves Here."

"My head's beginning to hurt," said Hot Rod.

"They're shifting within themselves from dimension to dimension, carrying their various consciousnesses with them intact," Nesta explained. She knew how Hot Rod felt. When they'd been slid through the different versions of the House to safety, had she unknowingly and temporarily merged with another Nesta innocent of the event? Or had Minda picked continuums where she and Renzie didn't exist?

Something like that had occurred to Tuck. Nesta saw him tighten, wind up like a spring. "When something happens to somebody in another parallel, does the same thing happen here? In this Here?" he corrected himself. "If you eat cornbread tomorrow morning, does that mean in all the Heres next door you'll be eating cornbread, too?"

"Of course not," said Minda. "Then there wouldn't be all the different Heres. There'd just be this one. That's where Nesta's not quite right. It won't ever be all one solid Here, like a board, a . . . ."

"A laminate," Nesta prompted her.

"A laminate. Not like a laminate," Minda said. "It's becoming more like a river, or the ocean. The ocean, that's better. One big thing moving in and out with there always being parts of it far away from each other, but those parts could wash into each other someday, and then the other parts would be far away. Much more like an ocean."

Tuck wasn't paying attention to her explanation. He was still following his original line of thought. "So different things happen to people in the different Heres, like eating cornbread here and muffins there."

"Yes," said Minda.

"Could somebody get sick there and not here?"

Nesta could tell where his questions led and recognized his tension as hope. She felt Renzie stiffen beside her.

"Yes." Minda was tiring of the game.

"Could somebody die there and not here? Or here and not there?"

Now Minda understood. "Yes," she said, very low.

"Le Chell? Chupa?"

"Not Chupa. I didn't tell her to go into the House. She decided to do that. It was her own fault. Chupa was one of the Ghosts. She was already dead. She just didn't know it. She's dead everywhere. She's dead in every Here."

Nesta was chilled at Minda's flat statement. "But Le Chell is not, is she?" Nesta said quietly.

"Maybe," Minda muttered. "It wouldn't matter, though. Once you're dead in one of the Probablys, you might be alive in another, but you can't slide back, especially not one of you grown-ups who can't even slide by yourselves in the first place."

"Minda, just before we slid the last time, I looked out a window and saw a young woman with red hair in the gardens," Nesta said. "Could it have been Le Chell, another Le Chell?"

Minda wouldn't answer.

This is something else that hasn't occurred to them, thought Nesta. They're all so young and they've been so protected that none of them have tried to test whether they could beat their own deaths. That's why Minda, at first so self-assured when she'd come to rescue us, became afraid in the burning building.

"So somewhere, someHere, Le Chell might still be alive," Tuck whispered. "*Is* alive, *has* to be alive, with an infinity of possibilities to choose from." He trembled. "Somewhere she's alive and okay."

Nesta glanced at Renzie. The younger woman looked as though she were turning to stone.

"So what about the rest of us, who can't 'slip' around like you kids?" Hot Rod said. "Wasn't the Vanishing enough? How are we supposed to exist in all this madness? How do we deal with all the creatures and places and things that have started dropping in on us? We're not equipped to deal with such an inconceivable reality."

"But it's neither inconceivable or even new," said Nesta. "There have always been places where the dimensions have bled into each other, or been separated as transparently as by glass. The House's site is one of them. Why do you think the woman who started building the House chose this place? Whose were the voices that drew her here? Why do you think she commanded that the House be built onto continuously, so that it was an ever-changing, ever-transforming entity? People have been drawn to it and lived in it for years, ever since the Vanishing. You *have* been living with these changes, all along.

"And it may yet be our salvation." It was her turn to help with the fight. "I think I may have a solution to the leftover 'Bounders. Minda, you and Eric and I need to talk."

CHAPTER THIRTY-EIGHT

Much later Nesta, Eric, and Minda adjourned to the Foreman's Cottage and settled in his sitting room. Minda obviously enjoyed being the center of attention, but kept looking around uneasily as if she wished that the other children were there for backup.

"Eric, where are the 'Bounders now?" Nesta asked. "Do we know?"

"They've been tracked back to the old airport. They're regrouping there." He pulled down a map from a bookshelf and unfolded it. "We've got a team watching them, waiting till they all come home to roost."

Nesta turned to Minda. "When you took us away from the fire, every time we 'slip-slid' we were actually touching you, or at least chained together. Is that the only way for the rest of us to get to other Probablys, other Heres? Through physical contact with one of you kids?"

Minda thought for a moment. "Yes, that's the only way to get to another Probably by leaving from this Here."

Nesta's heart sank. Her plan would be difficult then, too dangerous for the children.

"But it does work the other way 'round too," said Minda. "Instead of going *to* a Probably, sometimes they come to this Here for a while. If they're a close enough Probably to this Here to begin with, then anyone can get into them."

"Like that meadow at night, when you were camping last fall?" Nesta asked.

Minda nodded.

"But Renzie tried to get into that anomaly and couldn't," Eric protested.

"It wasn't quite close enough," Minda said, "but almost."

"Do you know when other Heres will pop in?" Nesta asked.

"Not *know* exactly. And not always. But we gessy them lots of times, yes. Especially in certain places that kind of gather them."

"Focal points," Nesta suggested.

Minda brightened. "Yes. Focal points."

"Especially the House," Nesta said.

"Especially the House," Minda agreed.

"I don't think I like where this is heading," Eric said. "We're not going to put the kids at risk."

"We won't have to," Nesta said. "Certainly no more risk than leaving them as sentries in a House that's being shot at by rocket launchers," she added tartly.

She smoothed out the map. "It shouldn't be too hard to draw the 'Bounders back down here to try to finish us off. We need to evacuate everyone as quickly and quietly as possible. Minda, with the House so badly burned, would it be difficult to maneuver to the first shift or so?"

Minda was studying the map. "Why have to do all that stuff— moving everybody away? There's someplace much closer to where they are and better anyway 'cause it's always been strange. They won't notice they've been shifted and slid till it's too late." The two adults looked to where she was pointing on the map.

"The amusement park," Eric said. "Minda, can Nesta's plan really work? Can the 'Bounders be shifted far enough away that they'll never come back? What about them being a danger wherever they end up? I don't want to leave our garbage on someone else's doorstep."

"There are shift places so different . . ." Minda shook her head, unable to convey the thought in words. "The 'Bounders won't be able to come back. They won't know where they are, or who they are, or what the things are in there with them. If you want to worry, worry for the 'Bounders."

Nesta thought of the creatures that had attacked Pel's flocks and shivered.

"Minda, we're going to bring the other kids here and let you start talking about this, planning. Will you stay here and wait?"

Minda nodded.

Nesta rubbed her eyes as they walked to the cottage's front door. "We'll need to pull this together as soon as possible, before the 'Bounders recover and come up with new plans of their own."

"Agreed," said Eric. "But *we* aren't doing this—*I* am. Nesta, do you realize that you're shaking? You haven't let yourself stop for a moment to think of everything you've been through today. Look at yourself. You've been holding yourself together through sheer nerve."

She was shaking. And her ribs ached with a dull fire. "Eric, this is my idea. You're not going to leave me out."

"I have no such intention—we *need* you if we're going to pull this off. You're the only person who understands all this. But you've got to get some rest, or you'll be no good to us."

"All right. Just let me check in on Renzie first. If you're going to worry about anyone, it should be her."

"I know," said Eric. "That's why she's upstairs here, in the cottage. She's sleeping as though she were in a coma."

Nesta felt uneasy. "Is that wise, leaving her here? What if the 'Bounders sneak back? She's helpless. Shouldn't she be evacuated down-valley?"

Eric sighed. "I wanted to, but she wouldn't have any of it. If I sent her away by force and anything happened to Tuck, I think it would be worse for her. I've assigned a rotating shift of kids to her. If the 'Bounders return, the children will 'shift' her out the way that Minda brought the two of you back. I can't think of anything safer than that. Now get some rest."

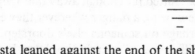

Nesta leaned against the end of the shooting gallery and tried to slow her breathing. She noticed the soreness in her ribs and the way her feet ached with a dry, hot heat from standing. But those sensations only barely registered. They were overwhelmed by her heart hammering in her chest, hard as striking drumsticks. The blond 'Bounder infiltrating the House, the attempt to save Le Chell and Chupa and the fire; that had all been frightening, but it had happened as it happened and she'd been carried along with events like a fish caught in a strong river current.

But this—having so much time to wonder if their thrown-together strategy would work, to know that anything could happen and that the concept "anything" included vistas beyond imagining: This was the overwhelming undiminished terror of anticipation.

Nesta looked at Minda crouching beside her in the narrow fringe of shade, a .22 balanced across small knobby knees. She wished that she too could squat down comfortably on her heels. It had been decades since her joints had had that kind of flexibility. A wave of dizziness seized her briefly. Stop hyperventilating, she snapped at herself mentally. All morning she'd felt that she shouldn't be out there; an elderly woman with a small child, hiding against a derelict shooting gallery, its few remaining rifles broken free from their tethers yesterday to be propped menacingly outward, its rows of targets—the faded die-stamped silhouettes of ducks and deer and rabbits—transfixed in time and space. Ducks, we're like those ducks, thought Nesta. Sitting ducks. A new tide of panic washed through her.

She'd spent hours yesterday trying to explain the physics that made her plan possible. Haberman had tried to help, but the adults had just looked at her blankly and the children were bored. But the adults believed and trusted her, even if they didn't understand, and they didn't trust the children. So here she was. More in the thick of things than she'd planned. She shouldn't have been worried about being left out.

The walkie-talkie buzzed crankily at her belt. Nesta groaned, hoping it wasn't Pel again. She wished he hadn't been crucial to the planning for this site. He'd been out of his mind with fear from the moment they'd snuck into the amusement park the day before.

Nesta extended the antenna and tried not to snap at the caller. "Yes? Nesta here."

Tuck's voice, not Pel's, crackled in her ear. "This is our last walkie-talkie contact in our Here. They've been sighted. They're almost within range. Looks like all of them, even the ones who were reconnoitering the firebreak at 280."

"We're ready," said Nesta, and hoped that was true. Minda scrambled to her feet and handed Nesta the rifle. Then she dusted herself off.

Nesta forced her breath to even out. The tension was turning her to steel. She glanced down the dusty promenade fronting the corridor of arcade stalls. No sign of anyone yet. Then she looked up the walkway to the tangle of roller coasters leading to the far end of the park. From here the top floor of the double-decker carousel could just barely be seen. And the raised dais of the outdoor stage, bare and deserted twenty-four hours ago, now busy with workers directed by Pel, festooned with canisters of fuel, stores of ammo, and the featured stars of the performance, the 'Bounders' captured rocket launchers, ostentatiously mounted and displayed.

The stage was meant to be the first thing the 'Bounders saw as they chased their prey into the park. It was designed to confirm the clues Eric had planted: that the massive firebreak being bulldozed along the horizontal cut of Highway 280 was not merely protection against the 'Bounders' incendiary efforts, but a containment for the backfire the Valley folks meant to set. And that the flurry of activity at the park the 'Bounders had been guided to discover that morning was the installation of a layer of artillery meant to sandwich the 'Bounders into an inferno of poetic justice. And all of it a fiction of misdirection. As soon as the 'Bounders entered the park the crews on 280, led by Hake and Eric, would move up to draw a net around the park, just in case.

Minda stopped fussing at herself. She stood studiously still for a moment, then turned to Nesta. "All the other shift teams have slipped on ahead. Except for us—team number one."

Nesta's gaze flickered up and down the promenade, across to the parallel line of booths across the way. Ball toss, coin toss, bean-bag toss—all of them hiding snipers from the Women's Brigades and the Viets, ready if any 'Bounders strayed from the bait.

Finally Nesta glanced at the back side of the shooting gallery. The view was nothing much to look at: a tangle of overgrown weeds, scattered sheep droppings that showed that Pel's flocks had once kept the foliage cropped short, a mess of discarded machinery butting up against the base of the first of the roller coasters.

The children had told her that there, three feet from where she and Minda waited, was the boundary of a slide spot to a neighboring continuum. That fact contributed to Nesta's unease. There was nothing she could see there; no bleeding through of any kind of anomaly, nothing unusual. Just sheep dung, broken machinery, and the weeds.

"But why should it look any different?" Minda had said when she'd complained. "I told you we'd start with a nearby Here."

Nesta was used to the exoticism of her aberrations. The idea that on her own she could walk five steps and be somewhere else entirely and not even know it, maybe never know, and never be able to get back started her heart sprinting again.

Minda was peering around the front side of the shooting gallery. "Here comes our fox team," she said. Nesta joined her.

Walking swiftly and with purpose, giving no indication that they knew they were followed, a group of about twenty Valley residents entered the lower end of the park. All of them wore packs bristling over with ammo belts and explosives equipment. The fastest children in their early teens, Dinah and Bite, were their shift guides. But for now Son led the way.

The group marched halfway up the arcade throughway, then made an abrupt left turn and cut around to the back of the booths, up toward Nesta and Minda's hiding place. Minda dashed to the other side and waved them on.

Nesta stayed where she was, watching for the following 'Bounders. They came, slowly creeping up, dashing in and out of hiding. Three of them carefully came out into the open where their quarry had cut away from the main avenue. They squatted and studied the roadway, searching for signs of booby traps and land mines. Nesta ducked back as they nervously looked up the gauntlet of booths, searching for signs of snipers.

"Have the hounds started around yet?" Minda hissed at her.

"No, but I think they're about to," Nesta whispered as she joined the girl. Minda was waving wildly as the lure party scuttled noiselessly along the back of the buildings. They slowed as they approached Minda and Nesta.

"Not too fast," Son turned to mutter. "We want to stay out of rifle range but still let them see where we're going."

Nesta backed up. Son was about to walk into her.

And then he was gone.

And all the rest of them: Dinah, Bite, a Pinelli, a Rosie Nesta didn't know, Haberman, the Krit shuffling in the midst of the crowd. They rounded the corner, walked right up to Minda and Nesta and disappeared.

"They're . . . gone." Nesta couldn't make herself say Vanished.

Minda nodded. "To them it will look as though we're the ones that disappeared, right out from in front of them. C'mon. We've got to hurry too. The 'Bounders are coming fast." She grabbed Nesta's hand, pulled her forward to the very corner of the building. Nesta could hear the 'Bounders running now. They'd think the Valley folk had ducked around the shooting gallery and headed up through the roller coaster's underbelly.

Minda doubled the two of them back to exactly where they'd been standing and suddenly they were trotting along behind their friends. Haberman looked over his shoulder and saw them. His eyes widened.

Son had his walkie-talkie out, talking to one of the other shift teams. "Quill says the next slip is just past the Revolution ride. Dinah, do you gessy where that is in this Here?"

Dinah nodded, she and the others already moving off.

"Over here, quick!" Minda ducked behind an Octopus ride. Nesta couldn't remember if it had been there before or not. She and Minda flattened themselves as the 'Bounders boiled around the corner in pursuit.

"We'll shortcut to the next shift." Minda led Nesta off in the opposite direction. When they reached a Wild Mouse she jumped into one of its tiny cars. "Hop in," she said.

"Minda, these rides haven't worked in decades."

"In this Here they do." Minda pulled a lever and the whole chain of cars shot forward. They bumped and whistled around the track, abruptly stopping near the bottom. "However, now in *this* Here they don't. Good thing we don't have to climb far," Minda said as she helped Nesta clamber down.

Nesta opened her mouth, couldn't think of a thing to say, and shut it tightly.

The two of them trotted along until they saw the other shift teams clustered together. Nesta looked about her. They'd returned to the arcade row, although they'd never doubled back. She peered into the shooting gallery. Its targets were now stars, pyramids and globes. She glanced north. The entertainment platform was just where it should be, but the stage was empty.

It finally sank in. They were far, far away. No matter what happened now, the Valley was safe. Then she remembered: *Their* Valley was safe. But not this one that they'd drawn the 'Bounders into.

Tuck was speaking into his walkie-talkie. Quill, his partner, stood beside him. All the shift teams consisted of an armed adult and a child. Nesta looked at her rifle ruefully. Minda could probably shoot it better than she could.

"Have the foxes arrived yet?" she asked Tuck.

"Yes. And the hounds are right behind." He pointed beyond the

Ferris wheel. "That's where they popped in." He nodded at Quill. "All the kids agree that the next open shift is at the carousel."

A sharp report cracked to them through the walkie-talkie. Then another. Then a rapid volley. At the same time they heard the same pattern of noise in the distance as a muted popcorn popping.

"Shit!" came Son's voice through the receiver. "They've figured out that something's going down. They're not tracking and hiding anymore. They're coming right after us."

Nesta grabbed Tuck's walkie-talkie and yelled into it. "Run like hell. And remember, if anyone gets separated from the group, try to get clear of the action so a shift team can get to you and pop you out."

She jammed Tuck's walkie-talkie back into his hands. "Let's hustle. We've got to get to the carousel before them."

The shift teams reached the merry-go-round and hid behind a row of faded wooden horses long before the foxes and hounds arrived. The two groups had slowed down as they stopped to exchange fire.

Tuck swore. "Damn, we have to keep them moving."

The adversarial bands were close enough that Nesta didn't bother with the walkie-talkies. "Come on, Son," she screamed. "This way. Now!"

The children were already scrambling up the steps to the next story of the carousel.

My god, we'll be trapped on the second deck of this thing. The thought seized Nesta before she could censor it. Panic skidded over the other adults' faces. The same idea had occurred to them.

"We have to trust the kids," Nesta said. "They've gotten us this far." Nesta clambered after the youngsters and heard the others following her.

She emerged on the next level in the middle of a huge spiral labyrinth of carved, saddled creatures. They were no longer prancing handsome horses. Don't look at them, Nesta told herself. Just keep going.

She finally burst free to the edge of the merry-go-round and breathed a sigh of relief. In this continuum they were on the bottom level again. The sky was a dark, dull color. She thought she heard a distant calliope.

The shift teams scattered as they broke through. "Get clear!" Nesta shouted. "We don't know how fast they're coming up behind us."

There was the percussion of running feet and the fox team spilled over the edge of the carousel after them. Pinelli and Haberman were supporting the Rosicrucian, who'd taken a bullet in the leg.

"Get her back to our Here *now!"* Nesta ordered. One of the shift teams slung the Rosie lopsidedly between them. The adult, a stockyarder, took most of the weight while his partner, a small boy, frowned in concentration. They shuffled sideways a few steps, and then they were gone.

The other teams were conferring behind a fun house's gaudy façade while Son watched for the 'Bounders. "Where in the blazes are they?" he snarled.

"The kids say there's just one more major slide, then we're almost home free," Tuck told Nesta.

Nesta tried to get her bearings. She looked back at the merry-go-round and gasped. It wasn't two stories tall anymore. The levels went up and up like a pagoda as far as she could see from this close perspective. She gazed about her. There seemed to be three times as many rides, all of them unrecognizable. Roller coasters loomed on the horizon, their twists so rococo they made her dizzy to look at. And was this a fun house after all that they hid behind? It butted up against similar buildings, their doors far too short and wide and shaped like chess pieces, their walls faceted with crazy angles.

Unlike the parks in the other continuums they'd run through, this was the first one that didn't look faded and derelict. It appeared to be just past dawn in this Here. Nesta assumed that explained the lack of people, or whatever lived in this Here.

She turned to the children. "I thought the idea was to work toward less and less habitation, to dump the 'Bounders in an empty continuum."

The children shared a glance.

"We're not done yet," Quill said. "This was the fastest way to get where we're going."

"Unless those bastards come out soon, the only place we're going is back to the last Here to get them," Son said from his post.

"We'll check," said Dinah. She and Bite joined hands and ran off into an edge of oblivion.

"Wait! You can't go by yourselves . . ." Nesta's shout trailed off. Too late. "We've got to go after them."

Several of the other children jumped up.

"Oh no, you don't," Nesta said. "Not you, too."

And then Dinah and Bite were back, grinning. "Yeah, the

'Bounders have hunkered down in There. We slip-shifted right in behind them," Bite said. "They think they gessy that we're all meta-
trapped on the upper level of the carousel. They're getting ready to
burn it."

"And you think that's funny?" The acid in Nesta's voice etched
the smile off Bite's face. "You were supposed to find shifts that
wouldn't endanger indigenous lives or property."

"These two jokers can take us in again behind the 'Bounders,"
Son said quickly. "We'll catch them from the rear. Fox squad!" He
called his group together. "And maybe just two of the shift teams?" he
asked Nesta.

She nodded. She knew what he was trying to tell her. They
weren't returning just to lure the 'Bounders. He intended to inflict
damage. This was a real battle now. The shift teams he'd requested were
a hedge against losing the two fox team shifters in the fighting. Other
than that bare minimum, none of the other children should be there.

"This means all the rest of you will be in front when they come
through. You may have to be the new foxes till we can shift back into
position."

"I know," said Nesta. "I think we can get far enough ahead of
them to be safe." She looked at Minda for confirmation. The little girl
nodded.

Son picked Tuck and Quill and another team. Nesta thought a
prayer for each of them. For Tuck, because of Renzie, she whispered
two.

After they left, the remaining shift teams looked lost, their mo-
mentum gone.

"Don't just stand there," Nesta snapped. "In a few minutes we'll
be knee-deep in trouble."

That motivated them. "This way," Minda said. The route wound
around to what looked like a sculpture park or a miniature golf course
designed by a plumber. The shift site was through a thick arch in the
middle of the course.

"You kids may be fast at sliding, but the 'Bounders can still
outrun you. Take it in relays. When the 'Bounders close in, duck behind
one of those, uh, obstacles and shift out. Don't let them get too close
to you. You can slip back in further down the line."

The adult halves of the teams were tense. Even the children were
nodding soberly, looking less cocksure.

"They're coming," a Mallite boy left on guard called. "They're still way back in there, but they're coming out."

"Positions, everyone." She and Minda sped back around the corner to their positions near the carousel, Nesta holding a hand to her side to brace her ribs.

The 'Bounders could be heard scuttling like rats deep in the belly of the merry-go-round, hiding behind the carved beasts that passed for horses in this Here. They must have been relieved to find that they hadn't been trapped on the second level, but they knew now that something was terribly wrong.

They couldn't hide in there indefinitely. Son and his team, their roles reversed from foxes to hounds now, were driving them out from the continuum at their backs. Nesta could hear the muted reports of rifle fire back near the core of the carousel.

Nesta held her breath. This was the crucial moment. The 'Bounders couldn't be allowed to disperse out into this continuum.

The sun was rising. Its light glazed the sky with a weird, greenish hue. Would caretakers come soon to open the shops, prepare the rides? Would gates open and fairgoers flood in?

The 'Bounders crept out into the street. Those bringing up the rear walked backward, firing sporadically to keep Son's team at bay in the carousel. It looked as though there were ten, maybe fifteen fewer of them. Son's surprise had been effective.

The two closest shift teams moved hesitantly out into the open. The 'Bounders froze, then scattered for cover in the strange angles of the buildings. Now that they were trapped, the 'Bounders responded to the shift team as a threat, not a lure. "Oh Christ," Nesta groaned. "We'll never get them to go around and through the shift now."

Minda tugged at her. "What is it?"

"I put the teams in the wrong place." She'd had to think and act too quickly. "They're more of a barrier than bait where they are. I should have positioned them behind and to the sides to help drive the 'Bounders toward the arch."

But Minda was no longer listening. Minda was no longer there.

She reappeared alongside a building close to the first exposed shift team and gestured to them frantically. They ran back to cover. From her position Nesta could just barely see Minda talking to them excitedly. Then all three of them disappeared. Nesta let out a long-held breath. If Minda could get to all of the teams and get them shifted Out the situation might be salvageable.

The minutes wobbled and teetered like a seesaw. The 'Bounders couldn't go back and wouldn't go forward. Son was holding back from his position in the merry-go-round. Dinah and Bite must have gessied for him what Minda was doing.

Then Minda scurried out into the street halfway to the turn that led around to the arch. Several of the other children joined her, peering nervously toward the carousel area as if wondering what the commotion was.

As if that were a signal, Son's team made their move. They dashed toward the front of the carousel, crouched behind the first line of beasts, and opened fire on the 'Bounders' positions. Something arced through the air in front of one of the 'Bounders' hiding places. It hit the ground and rolled a few feet. Three 'Bounders leapt away, then were flung again into the air as an explosion ripped a hole in the ground. Nesta cheered. She'd forgotten the explosive equipment the fox team carried. She'd thought they were just window dressing.

Another blast exploded. The children—more of them now— screamed, turned, and strafed away up the street and around the corner. The 'Bounders noticed them for the first time. Children fleeing to a safe place. This the 'Bounders understood. They dashed from their hiding places and fled after the kids.

Nesta swore. She couldn't move for a minute as Son's group laid down fire after the 'Bounders, bringing down another three of them. After Son's team passed she grabbed up her rifle and ran to join them. They rounded the corner in a tight pack.

The children had almost made it to the arch, the 'Bounders closing in behind them. Where in the hell were the kids' adult partners? And then she knew. The children had shifted them away, but not back. They'd dumped the grown-ups.

"Minda, no!" Nesta screamed.

A couple of the 'Bounders heard her and spun around, shooting. Someone pulled Nesta down.

"Stay low." It was Bite. "Don't worry. The small fry will be safe as soon they clear the portal."

"You don't know that for sure."

"I gessy best as Minda. You can lay a look too, soon as the 'Bounders overdrive out."

Nesta tried to scramble up, but Bite seemed to know exactly where to throw his arm across her back so that the slightest movement laid a line of fire across her ribs.

Then Bite scrambled up and helped Nesta to her feet. Dinah, Son, and all the others were crowding before the portal, peering into it. Dinah stepped through. Son, with an unsure expression, followed her. The other adults hesitated.

"Get a move on," Bite scolded them. "This kind of slip-chute is minitemporal." He grabbed Nesta's hand and pulled her into the crowd. She caught a glimpse of a funnel of light, and then they were through.

Dinah and Son crouched on the other side, trying to catch their breath after the chase.

A golden glow that shifted every few feet drenched the broad avenue of a giant midway that tunneled away toward an unseeable horizon. Nesta could barely make out the children in the distance. The 'Bounders were closer, still chasing after the youngsters, still spinning around now and then with raised rifles to see if they were being followed yet. Nesta flinched and looked for shelter, backing up into the other adults filing in behind her.

"Relax," Dinah told her. "See where the light changes, like sunbeams overlapping? Those are shift changes. Each one's only a few feet deep. They're lined up in one direction only, like a fish trap. The 'Bounders can't see or shoot back to us." The girl stood and stretched. "The little ones can take them the rest of the way. Time to get out of Here ourselves and go Home. We still have to pick up the grown-ups they dropped off on the way."

"And retrieve the bodies," Son said.

Dinah made a face.

"But what is this?" breathed Nesta.

"A place where all the walls wear thin," said Bite. "A place where Heres fold up tight together and you can surf right through them. For a while, anyway. Maximum instability. And very, very rare. We were lucky today."

"How many times have you done this before?"

"This is the first time." Bite shrugged.

Nesta looked down the funnel. What she'd thought was an extension of the park, row upon row of false façades of gorgeous panoramas, were brief glimpses of whole other universes. It was beautiful, and she was drawn to it strongly.

"Where are they leading them?" she whispered.

Dinah grimaced. "To Pied Piper land. To paradise. 'Bounder paradise. To a place where there's nobody but them. Nobody human, anyway."

CHAPTER THIRTY-NINE

Renzie's lungs healed quickly, her eyes less so. Hake told her the eyebrows would take the longest; that until they grew in she'd wear an expression of continual surprise.

Two days from the fire to the luring of the 'Bounders at the amusement park. Then another day. And another. Renzie counted each one. Each day before the light became too bright Hake changed the dressings on her eyes. She'd glimpse a jellyfish blur of colors which each time became crisper at the edges, attained more depth, promising soon to resolve into recognizable images.

On the fourth morning she stood before the window in Eric's bedroom and saw at last the stark black skeletal icon the House had become. She saw people hauling to it their tribute and prayers of new lumber, salvaged glass for windows, pipes, wiring, tile. She watched Jorda pushing a wheelbarrow, the Krit scuttle painfully along dragging a dolly piled with newly cut shingles like a trove of dragon scales, Tuck and Kip balancing a ladder between them on their shoulders, though Kip's left arm was still in a sling.

Tuck saw her standing at the window and waved to her doubtfully with his free hand, unsure if she could see him. She waved back, her eyesight good enough to see him first hesitate, and then his answering grin.

So later she realized that she shouldn't have been surprised when he came to visit that night. Minda was with him but barely said hello, then went to lurk in the hallway.

The way that Tuck was trying to smile, so weighted and compressed, made Renzie nervous. She could barely force out an equally artificial smile. "I guess Minda and the other kids have gotten sick of baby-sitting me," Renzie said. "She comes to visit but can't stand to stay in the room for more than two seconds."

Tuck glanced after Minda, using the opportunity, Renzie knew, to avoid her eyes. "Minda's not here to visit you," he said. "She's waiting for me." He looked back at Renzie. "You're going to be all right. You can see again. I had to be sure of that."

"Why?" She wanted his answer to be, "Because I worry about you. Because I miss and love you," but she knew it wouldn't be, even if that was true.

"Because I couldn't leave until I knew you were all right."

"Where are you going?" she asked, though she really already knew that, too.

"Minda and I are going back into the House. She's going to lead me to Le Chell."

Le Chell was dead—Here.

"What if you find her alive in another continuum and she doesn't love you, she loves somebody else?"

"I'll keep looking. She has to be somewhere, probably in many, many Heres close by. Someplace she'll have survived the fire, or there won't have been a fire, and she'll still be in love with me."

"I know you only want to find her so you can be with her again," Renzie whispered, "but this is my punishment, isn't it?"

"Renzie, no! Why would you say that?"

"Because I failed. Because I should have been able to bring her out. But I wasn't quick enough, so she died. I failed her, and you. I know that's why you can hardly stand to talk to me. Even not being able to see, I'll bet this morning was the first time you've smiled at me since the fire."

Tuck shook her gently, his face twisted. "Renzie, stop it. If there's anybody who's guilty, it's me. If I'd told Le Chell or sent word to her that I was evacuating the House with Hammer, none of this would have happened. I didn't know the House was going to be torched, but at that point *any* disaster could have happened and she would have needed to know where I was. Everything was so wild and confused that I just didn't think.

"So I lost her and I almost lost you when you went in after her. If I've seemed distant, it's because I've been haunted, wondering if you were going to be blind because of me. It's been almost impossible to live with that and the responsibility for Le Chell's death too. I don't blame you, Renzie. I blame me."

Renzie took his face in her hands. "But I'm going to be okay. I'll be working on the House myself in just a few days. Hake says my eyes are almost healed."

"I know. I couldn't have left if you'd been permanently blinded. That's why I came tonight; to explain, so you wouldn't think I was abandoning you again. Please tell me that you understand, that you'll forgive me?"

"There's nothing to forgive," Renzie said. "Will you . . . do you think you'll ever come back?"

Tuck pulled away and looked at her with more pity than she could bear. "Le Chell died in this continuum. There's no way she can return to it. Renzie, I'm sorry because you don't deserve it, but you are the one who'll suffer most. I'll find Le Chell again, and there'll probably be another Renzie there for me, too. But there will never be a Le Chell and Tuck in this Here again. Can you live with the thought that I'll be somewhere, happy?"

"I'll have to."

"Renzie, I wanted to tell you something before I leave. When you and Nesta escaped from the fire and were being fixed up, Old George and Brad tried to come see you. I asked Eric to keep them away from you."

Renzie shuddered at the thought of having to deal with Brad and her father while blind and helpless. "Thank you," she said.

Tuck shook his head. "I'm not so sure I should have done that. They were scared to death for you.

"Then the morning after the fire, before I joined the crew at the amusement park, the 'Bounders started a fire about a mile from here. It was in the old neighborhood . . . where Eric came from, where his parents live," Tuck said tactfully. "I was assigned out there to cut firebreaks."

Where Margaret's Home was. Where Old George had lived with his original family, Renzie thought.

"Old George and Brad were there, of course, helping with the fire line," Tuck said.

Brad and Ginny's parents' Home was at the end of the block, Renzie remembered. It was beige with a boarded-over front door and kitchen window. Someone—her father—used to trim the bushes in its front yard.

"Old George's Home caught fire. The blaze had crept up from the backyard. We started to work on it and I think we could have saved it. All of a sudden George got this funny look on his face. He ordered us back, told us to work on the break line at the street.

"Eric protested. 'What about your Home, George?' he said.

"George shook his head. 'It's time to let it burn.' "

"And Margaret's place?" Renzie asked.

"It's gone too. That whole side of the block went up."

Renzie thought of her father's garage burning, with the little red and big beautiful purple bicycles stored inside it. How the fire must have curled up and peeled away the paint on their frames before they were crushed beneath the garage's collapsing, blazing roof. She thought of the flash that would have gone up when all the books and magazines in her mother's Home caught fire, how the gaudy feathers on the last of Bartholomew Cubbins's five hundred hats had been translated in the end to magnificent plumes of flame.

"Thank you for telling me." Renzie held Tuck tightly, one very last hug.

She watched him from the window as he went down the Foreman's Cottage front-porch steps, past the water tower, with Minda a slip of shadow beside him. Renzie's eyes weren't healed enough to track them once they started picking their way among the darkness of the burnt timbers. And by then she'd begun to cry. Tears blurred her vision. She ducked her head and the drops fell straight down, clearing her cheeks to streak her chest instead, so she didn't see the odd-gaited figure creeping after them, limping like a crippled spider.

CHAPTER FORTY

The days weren't so bad for Renzie. With all the work on the House to be done, she couldn't take the time to miss Tuck. She moved out of the Foreman's Cottage and joined the rest of the House community in camping outside.

The House was a good third destroyed. When she woke up mornings and rolled over in her makeshift sleeping bag of salvaged blankets, the House's half-charred cadaver greeted her eyes like a reproaching ghost.

If anyone had a right to grieve, it was Carpenter. Yet the wiry builder was thriving.

"You're so brave," Renzie said to him one day. "This place meant . . . *means* everything to you. You must be suffering a world of hurt." As soon as the words were out she regretted them, realizing how they echoed her own pain held at bay.

The corners of Carpenter's eyes crinkled up, though his thick beard and mustache hid his smile. "Nope," he said cheerfully. "She's like a great forest after a forest fire." Renzie remembered what Nesta had said about people shifting within themselves from dimension to dimension, and wondered if this was a slightly different Carpenter than she was used to. Than she was *usually* used to, she corrected herself.

"All the deadwood cleared out and turned into fertilizing ash,"

Carpenter said. "All the seeds way underground germinated by the heat and ready to grow. When you're in there hammering away and setting up drywall, can't you feel how hard She's working away all around you?"

There was more than a little truth to his words. The House seemed to expand faster than they built. Connective corridors appeared that no one could lay claim to building. It had to be Nesta's parallel realities overlapping and filling in, functioning like regenerating tissue.

Renzie wondered if someday she might see Tuck again after all— glimpse him through that dimensional overlay as through a window. With that thought she took comfort.

One evening at the customary time after supper when Eric parceled out the next day's tasks, the foreman offhandedly told Minda she'd be helping with arsonist sentry duty for the House and its parameters. Then he turned to delegate other chores to Quill, Bite, and the other children.

"But I don't have to," Minda complained to his back.

Eric spun on his heel in a double take, his eyebrows arched.

"What I mean is it isn't necessary," Minda said hastily.

Eric sucked in a visible but silent breath to ground his patience. "Minda, we think we got rid of or killed all the 'Bounders, but we can't be sure. Being 'Bounders, the odds are that if there are any left at all, they'll come back and try to finish the job."

"But you don't have to worry about the 'Bounders that way," Minda protested.

"Why not?"

Renzie noticed the other children had become very quiet. Quill motioned at Minda, but she didn't see, or willfully chose to ignore him.

"Because I know they didn't burn the House in the first place. And it's not going to be burned again. I gessy that," she said.

There was a long silence. Something settled behind Eric's eyes. Too late Minda realized she'd said too much.

"Minda, how do you know the 'Bounders didn't fire the House?"

"I just gessy it. I can't explain how, just like slipping-sliding." Minda squirmed and evaded.

"Not good enough. Minda, who did burn the House?"

Minda looked at the dozens of surrounding faces, their implacable attention riveted on her.

"It doesn't matter. He's gone," she muttered. "He can't hurt anybody anymore. He didn't mean to in the first place."

"Tell us."

Minda huffed up her cheeks and plunked herself down on the ground. "All right, I'll tell you, if you're going to make me. It was the Krit. He burned all those Homes too, from before when the 'Bounders came."

Quill's clandestine waving at Minda, though still a small motion, had become frantic. Until he saw Renzie watching him. Then he stopped.

"The Krit?" Hammer's voice expressed the bewilderment they all felt. "That sad old man? Why?"

"He found Homes with things in them that had shifted and slid," Minda said. "He didn't understand. He thought it was like a sickness. That burning would clean them, keep the sickness from spreading."

"Cauterizing," said Son.

Minda nodded. "He didn't know he was being stupid. And it didn't matter that the Homes got burned."

"You knew who was burning the Homes? You and the other kids?" Abel Howe's words were stiff with shock. Quill, Bite, and the other children had begun retreating. "You could have told us!" His voice rose to a shout. "We could have stopped him and saved them!" Kip and Pel were having to hold Chupa's father back from the children.

"We didn't know till just before the 'Bounders came," Quill burst out. The boy looked around at the taut, angry-ugly faces of the Homers. "And he'd stopped burning the Homes by then. We figured out later he'd stopped when he returned to the House. And he never burned any places with people in or near them, till the very end."

Minda stood and faced Abel Howe. "It doesn't matter if the Homes burn," she repeated. "It won't stop the shifting where they are. Soon they'll all be slid over. They'll be gone."

Abel stared at her, his face ashen.

"Wait, there's something more important, if what Minda says is true," said Jorda. "When's the last time anybody's seen the Krit? Where is he now?"

"I saw him a week ago," Hake said from where he sat by Nesta. "I'm not sure just when. We all figured he'd just taken off again, like he did before, especially with his aerie burned down."

Renzie remembered clearly the last time *she'd* seen him. Early in the morning of the same day Tuck had left.

"I *told* you," Minda said. "Nobody listens to me. I told you he can't hurt anybody anymore."

Squatting down brought Eric eye to eye with Minda. "Why not? How can you be so sure? What have you done?"

"Nothing," Minda muttered, scuffing the dirt with her toes. "I just let him follow me when I took Tuck into the House. I let him shift behind us a couple of spaces and left him. He's probably still in the House somewhere, but not in this Here."

Jorda was aghast. "So maybe we're safe here, but what have you set loose on the people in all those other continuums? Even our other selves, if Nesta is right?"

"What about that?" asked Eric, still kneeling beside Minda. "Didn't you realize you were giving him new worlds to burn?"

And Tuck, my Tuck, all the Tucks are out there, too, Renzie thought, chilled.

"No!" Minda stamped her foot, raising little puffs of dust. "He *won't* burn anything anymore. He listened the night Nesta explained everything. We watched him. He thought he understood what she meant. He doesn't think of slippage as a sickness anymore. He thinks it's a set of doors now. He's using them to look for something. He'd never burn anything that might be the door he needs."

"Something, or somebody?" asked Nesta.

"Somebody," Minda admitted.

"Somebody he lost during the Vanishing?" Nesta guessed.

Minda nodded.

"But the people who Vanished are gone for good. If my hypothesis is correct, that's what initiated the mass changes in the first place."

"I know that. You know that," Minda explained as if to a child even younger than herself. "But maybe the Krit didn't think you were right about that."

"Or doesn't want to believe it." Eric sighed as he got back to his feet again, brushed dirt from his knees. "I'll go tell the patrols. Knowing who really burned us out takes a lot of the pressure off."

The spring-tight tension across the campsite began to release. People drifted away. A crew of Housers and some of Nesta's renegade Hackers volunteered to clear the cooking pits. As they scraped and piled the pans and stockpots, Quill and some of the other children hauled the utensils off to the Domes to wash. The youngsters looked anxious to escape more adult scrutiny.

As they finished the work, Jan looked up at the sparkling black sky, unblemished by clouds. "Even with help from down-valley, we've lost too much water with all this," she said. "The rains better start early this year. I wish we had some way of knowing." She shot a sharp glance at Minda, who responded with a secret little smile. Jan looked as if she were trying to decide if that reassured her.

"I saw him," Son said, sitting down next to Renzie by the camp-fire. "I saw the Krit on the day the 'Bounders stabbed you, Jan, way back at the trading fair. They'd just started a fire and run off. I was tracking them and he was standing there, looking scared to death, flinching away from their fire." Son shook his head. "It seems impossible that he was the person running around burning all those Homes."

Renzie remembered when she'd first found the burned-out Homes, when she was working on the road crew a million years ago. Back when she still had a brother named Tuck.

From here on in when people disappear we'll know where they've gone to—the Tucks and the Krits—she thought. We don't know yet what that will mean, not really, but it won't be like the Vanishing. We won't have the same scars as Old George and Son's father. We'll have different ones.

Son sensed her sadness. He shyly put his arm around her, almost the way that Tuck used to. Renzie hesitated a moment, then remembered that of all the people here, Son was the one who knew best what it felt like to have family make the choice to leave you behind. She relaxed against him. It wasn't really the same as Tuck, but it would do.

CHAPTER FORTY-ONE

That night, long after everyone else had drifted off to sleep, Hake and Nesta finished putting the near-somnolent campfire to bed. They raked and banked its coals, causing it to shift, mutter and almost wake from the incandescent visions that make up the dreams of fires.

Then they crept around the garden moat and spread out their bedding together up against the well house, as they had for the last few weeks, protected from the rest of the community's eyes. And ears, for their conversation would continue far into the night. There were so many new details to weave into their ongoing dialogue.

They lay side by side with hands intertwined—Nesta's left hand, Hake's right.

"I don't understand about the Krit," Hake said, his face turned up to the sky. Even without the younger generations' ability to see the aurora, the night's landscape was still splendid with stars.

"About why he went back into the House?" Nesta asked. "Or about how he was able to shift across, as Minda would say?"

"Neither," Hake said. "It's clear that Minda helped him shift away. No, what bothers me is how he was able to get away with torching the House in the first place. Why the kids didn't, or couldn't, or didn't know they should stop him. I'd just begun to get used to the idea that they were omniscient. Now I'm shook up again. They seemed to know—no, make that intuit—everything else."

"Their term for it is to gessy," Nesta reminded him.

"They gessy the Homers as ghosts, entities with no place in the new continuum, rapidly becoming extinct. Minda gessied where you and Renzie were in the House during the fire. It appears as though they gessied much of what the 'Bounders were up to during the attack. Yet they didn't gessy that the Krit was our arsonist."

"Our arsonist in *this* reality," Nesta said. "The House was burning in some of the other continuums that Minda took Renzie and me through and not in others. Perhaps he was the arsonist only here. Maybe it didn't matter—maybe the House was meant to burn here. In that case, they wouldn't have sensed him as a threat."

"But what does that mean? Do they only intervene if an event affects those they favor, or their own long-term survival?" His hushed tone of voice couldn't mask his distress. He'd helped raise the children and now they were alien to him. Nesta knew that he'd never be able to understand their rejection and abandonment of Chupa, their devotion to the House yet their seeming indifference to its burning.

She squeezed his hand. "I can't tell you anything that will comfort you. We're not going to understand them no matter how much we try. And we'll understand their children—if we should live so long—even less.

"Remember the double-slit experiment? An electron at Hole A *knows* whether Hole B is open or closed, as if there's some sort of instantaneous communication. Therefore in principle the electrons might know, or gessy, the quantum state of the entire universe. The children are the metaequivalent of those electrons in this new reality. They gessy all the options and all the blends of all the parallel continuum. We'll never really be able to grasp what they experience. But we can marvel at it."

Hake turned on his side to face Nesta. The softness in his hands as he drew his fingers through her hair was belied by the tension in his voice. "So what do we do now? We're not needed to find out the solution to the Vanishing anymore, but we're left with a whole new world of problems. Is it really any less terrifying not knowing if at any moment we'll be annihilated by monsters like the ones that attacked Pel's flocks, or the flood at Los Milagros' shrine—unless the kids intervene on our behalf? They sure as hell don't need our help to survive." His tone was low, but the words trembled with anger and fear.

"It's true that they'll keep evolving," Nesta said. "But they're still children. They still have to learn, to be taught. Gessying and sliding-slipping in and of themselves aren't conscious acts. They're reflexive and intuitive. The children still need the framework of knowledge and cognizant thought to survive. We can spend the rest of our lives continuing to teach them, and learning what we can from them, and observing and recording the changes."

"Always the scientist. It's bred into your very bones."

Nesta laughed. "Worse than you know. I've already begun running tests in the lab on the towel we bandaged Renzie's eyes with when Minda rescued us. Remember, we brought that back with us from one of the other continuums." She put up a hand to still his stroking, pleasant though it was. "You're afraid, aren't you, Hake?"

Hake sighed, his hand checked where it cupped the back of her head. It rested heavily there. "I think that everyone now, not just me, is beginning to accept your theory of the Vanishing originating with a one-time mega-black hole. With all the years of fear from the Vanishing lifted away I should feel a huge release," he said. "Instead I see all those new dreads waiting in the wings. You talk about observing. We could actually go to Minda or Quill or any of the other kids and ask them to take us shifting and slipping with them, the way you did in the fire, the way they did with the Krit, with the 'Bounders. We could stroll through the 'Garden of the Forking Paths.' " He tried to laugh as if he were proposing a wonderful adventure. His laughter rippled with anxiety.

"I wondered when you showed me that story," Nesta said. "So you figured it out that early?"

"Just guessed," Hake said. "Ha! A garden walk. I didn't think the impact through. Now we can see how it feels to skid in and out of ourselves in other worlds; at least in the worlds we exist in, at any rate." He turned again onto his back, wrapped his arms tightly around himself.

"But that's not what you want to do," Nesta said. She looked back out into the midnight sky.

"No. For the first time in my life I'm not intrigued. I'm too scared." He rocked and shifted a little, as if his back hurt.

"And restless. Hake, what do you want to do?"

"There was something else, something Son said when we first got back from the battle in the Fremont Hills."

"When he talked about his past? Something about his father?"

"Yes, when he told us how he was brought up. But nothing about his father. Just a detail mentioned in passing." Hake's words lagged with reluctance. "Son talked about cats; big blue cats. When he said that, I wondered if they were my cats."

"The snow leopards," Nesta said. "From the zoo." So that story had been true.

"Come next spring, I want to go see if I can find them, see if they're the cats I freed, or their cubs, grown up."

Nesta remembered back to the noisy crowded party. It felt as though it had taken place eons ago. She remembered how mesmerized the children had been by Hake's tale of slaughter; how it had seemed to hold a special meaning for them. She tried to recall what Hake had said about the snow leopards. Something about the first breath of an icy new air that had never existed before. Something about seeds locked deep in the soil, waiting for a fire's great heat to germinate them. And how it was as if their release was all that Hake had ever been meant to do. She understood how now he would need to know if that was true.

"Say something," Hake whispered. "Please. I feel as though I'm deserting you when I've just found you."

Reaching across, Nesta took his hand again. "You are. You will be." She made herself chuckle. "And it's all right."

"But . . . ?"

She had to be honest, too. "Hake, I'm eight years older than you, neither of us are young, and we've lived hard lives for most of the last thirty years. I can't promise I'll still be alive when you get back."

"And I can't promise I'll live to return, but . . ."

"But?"

"It's just coming up the end of summer. We have until next spring. That can be a very, very long time."

EPILOGUE

The Krit wandered through the House, or at least a House. Strange cut-out shapes perforated its wall paneling. Ribbons wound around gingerbread hanging down from the ceiling. Someone—a Carpenter?—had added on to the seven-eleven stairs. It now formed a complete loop: up the stairs, across a landing, down the other side, traverse the lower landing, then up again.

But the loop had a twist in it, so that when the Krit returned to his starting point, he wasn't there at all. He'd been flipped to the suites on the opposite side of that wing. He traversed the stairwell again, trying to make it come out right. This time what had originally appeared to be large windows opening into airshafts revealed themselves to be doors leading down hallways. And what had been doors before, including the one the Krit had entered by, canted off at impossible angles as airshafts.

The Krit succumbed to vertigo for a moment. He sat on the steps and closed his eyes as he clutched a banister shaped like a knight in a chess game. He didn't look over into the stairwell—he knew he wouldn't be able to tell up from down.

The queasiness passed. The Krit stood up. He guessed that if he just kept walking around and around this stairwell that it would eventually fold him neatly into the next House, and then the one after that.

Always going ever further through the House to new Houses, away from what he thought of as First House.

Minda thought she'd tricked him, he knew. But he'd understood she was leading him into exile. That's why he followed her. He thought of it as an agreement, a perfect arrangement; both his punishment and his new quest.

He'd never meant to hurt anyone. He'd always been so careful when he'd burned the Homes. And even when he'd seen the children up on the tower and he'd panicked and burned First House—even then he'd volunteered so that he could be sure that everyone could get out safely, had rung the alarm first before detonating the explosions.

He'd been wrong. Just as he'd been wrong all that time about the changes being part of an infection. He hadn't really understood that until he'd seen the children lead the 'Bounders away through the looping, spiraling portals at the amusement park, when he'd seen the way the very air had slid away as they advanced. As the children passed, the horses on the merry-go-round had mutated into gargoylesque forms. The tracks of the roller coasters flipped and twisted in Möbius configurations not unlike this stairwell. The main promenade transformed into a tunnel of light while the children danced the 'Bounders down its span. Beautiful possibilities glittered like carnival booths along its length to beguile the 'Bounders onward: images of fantasylands of everything they might desire. Candyland, Island of the Lost Boys, Avalon, Atlantis, Shangri-la . . . Heaven.

That was when the Krit had finally understood. All the strangeness he'd thought of as symptoms of infection were something else. All worlds were possible. The aberrations were landmarks, trail indicators to the gateways.

He'd been so wrong. But all the rest of them had been wrong, too. He knew they all believed, back at the First House, that only the children could manipulate and enter the different continuums, shift at will. Yet he'd been able to sense the aberrations, too. He'd just misunderstood their significance. Now that he knew, he could shift, too. As proof, he was far from the version of the House Minda had lured him to.

Yesterday . . . was it only yesterday? . . . yesterday he'd finally seen the color Abelard. Its sheen had reminded him of bronze and port wine, but in a much, much lower spectrum, lingering somewhere below all the hues of black. And he thought he'd seen Strangury and Croze: bright and clear, shimmering at the edge of his eyes' ability to comprehend them.

Today perhaps he'd find the color Magandá, and the entrance to the House where he knew that Jennifer must still live.

THANKS TO:

Jim Hauer for conversations on bicycles and physics. Marianne Leavitt for the use of her extensive library as a resource. Lisa Goldstein for her willingness to be an intrepid fellow explorer during the field research and for her insightful critiques. Alan Bostick for physics feedback and letting me know where "there be dragons." Jeff Fox for ideas on computer madness. Margaret Mathewson for survivalism. Rich Cross of the Kern County fire department for CPR training. Carol Buchanan for being my secret San Jose area liaison officer. Elizabeth Lynn and her writing group for guidance and feedback. Shozo Kagoshima, director of marketing for the Winchester Mystery House, for invaluable help with my research. Merrilee Heifetz, Lucius Shepherd, and C. N. Brown for encouragement and moral support. My husband Richard for support support. Beth Meacham for, thank god, editing, editing, and editing! And last, but not least, Sarah Winchester, the true creator of the House.